# ASHWIN

Kim—
Welcome to Sector Four's favorite neighbor!

KIT ROCHA

ASHWIN



Edited by Sasha Knight
Cover Artwork by Gene Mollica

ISBN-13: 978-1544136899
ISBN-10: 1544136897

*for everyone who's ever felt not human enough*

*or too human*

*you're just right*

# one

The sky was alive with stars.

Before coming to Sector One, Kora had never seen so many stars. The light rising from the city had always drowned them out. But here, behind the Riders' barracks, with nothing but a bonfire lighting the night, they were *resplendent.*

She leaned back, bracing her hands on the wide rock bench, and tipped her face toward the sky. Each glimmer seemed to wink down at her, and the longer she stared, the more rhythmic the twinkle became, until it looked like the whole carpet of stars was throbbing in time with the music.

Kora shut her eyes. She could still feel those stars, pulsing on the other side of her closed lids like a heartbeat, and if she just reached out—

"Kora."

She looked over as Gideon Rios sat down beside her. He was dressed as simply as the rest of his men, in leather pants and boots and a plain white T-shirt. But a closer look showed that the leather was the highest quality, not the stiff, badly tanned cheap stuff, and the shirt had obviously been tailored to fit him.

She slid over to give him more room. "Enjoying the party?"

"Enjoying the chance to celebrate." He sprawled his long legs out and crossed them at the ankle, the perfect picture of a man at ease. But his gaze roved the clearing, marking each of the Riders in turn. "It's been a good week."

If Kora didn't already know better, she never would have guessed that he owned and commanded everything around them. He carried himself like a leader, but not a prince—which he was, of course. The Rios name guaranteed that.

And if his name had comprised the full extent of his power? Well, it might have been easy to dislike him. But his Riders didn't follow him because of his name. They followed him because of his beliefs, his goals. His actions.

Kora liked him very much. "So why aren't you celebrating?"

Gideon slanted a look at her, one dark eyebrow quirked. "Who says I'm not?"

He was teasing her, but he wasn't the only one who could answer a question with a question. "How long have I been here, Gideon?"

"Oh, eight or nine months now?" He went back to surveying the crowd. "Long enough for us to get used to having you as part of the family. I hope you're not thinking about leaving. It would break Maricela's heart."

"Don't change the subject." She gestured toward the space around the fire, where Gideon's baby sister was dancing with one of the Riders, her head thrown back in laughter. "Maricela is having fun. You, on the other hand, are brooding."

His lips quirked. "Maybe brooding *is* fun for me."

"I see." He said it like it was a joke, but Kora had seen people react to what they perceived as Gideon's displeasure. His family didn't rule through force or even popular decision. Sector One's citizens considered the Rios family a manifestation of their God on earth, and no one liked a pissed-off god.

Gideon's smile grew. "Do you know who has the luxury to brood, Kora? Men who aren't fighting wars. After everything we went through last fall, it's nice to have the time to consider all my options before committing to a course of action."

"Even if all you have to decide between is beer or whiskey?"

"Well, I wouldn't go *that* far." He tipped his head toward Deacon, his second-in-command, who was watching them closely. "Has he talked to you about the security precautions for your clinic?"

"At length," Kora answered flatly. "Would it kill you to remind him that I'm actually pretty familiar with the city? You know, seeing as how I used to live there?"

Gideon didn't lose his easy smile. "You lived in Eden before the war. I think you'll find the city you remember no longer exists."

If she thought that was true, she'd have already been back. She wouldn't have let memories and the very real threat of confronting her own ghosts keep her away from people in need. "The walls came down,

Gideon, but there are some things that even war can't change." She matched his expression. "Your favorite lieutenant, for example. Deacon still underestimates me. He treats me like I don't think about all the things that could go wrong. It's...annoying."

"It's his job." Gideon shifted to face her on the bench. The firelight gilded one side of his face and left the rest in shadows, and somehow it made him look stern. Distant. "I put Deacon in charge of the Eden outreach operation. Do you know what that means?"

"That he's the boss?"

"That he speaks in my name. That I trust him to represent my sector and my ideals, to protect my people the way I would." Gideon reached for her wrist and turned it over, revealing the two bar codes tattooed on the inside. Her identification code over her pulse, and the higher one that had granted her special clearance. "Maricela has already declared you family, and that would be all the reason Deacon needs to wrap you in cotton. But you're an invaluable resource, Kora. You're going to have to become accustomed to being protected."

Become accustomed to it? Her whole life had been a never-ending chain of protective custody. Even as a child, her father had rarely let her out of his sight, and she'd spent hours studying at her small desk in the corner of his office. Her medical training had been overseen by the city, and Eden always protected its investments. Then, when she'd gone to work as a doctor on the Base...

Guards. The one constant in her life, whether they were clad in fatigues, military police black, or expensive leather and tattoos.

"Don't worry." She tugged her wrist free of his grasp. "I won't make any trouble for Deacon."

Gideon released her without complaint, but his sudden grin shattered the illusion of the serious, stern leader. "Don't go making any extravagant promises, Kora. Traditionally, my sisters excel at making trouble for Deacon."

"If it happens that often, maybe it's his problem, not theirs." She hesitated, then corrected herself. "Not *ours*."

"That's right." He patted her leg and turned back to the fire. "That's one thing my grandfather got right, even if he didn't always practice what he preached. In a world like ours, everyone needs family."

"Even if it's one we have to make ourselves," she agreed.

Deacon approached them, a drink in each hand, though he offered them neither. "Are you talking about the clinic for the city refugees?"

"It came up." Gideon reached out and snagged the beer from Deacon's left hand. "Are you satisfied with the security detail?"

Deacon grunted. "Am I ever? But we've done all we can. Your assigned guard will just have to handle whatever comes up."

"*If* anything comes up," Kora stressed.

He just stared at her.

Idly, she wondered if Deacon didn't like the situation, or if he didn't like *her*. The likeliest answer was a combination of the two. He undoubtedly had better things for his men to do than babysit her. But he'd do it anyway, because Gideon had asked.

She'd known men like Deacon—soldiers whose dedication ran deeper than their current orders. Whether they pledged themselves to a cause or simply to the mission at hand, they let nothing stand in their way. Not even headstrong doctors.

Kora smiled despite the bolt of pain that shot through her. Yes, she'd known men like Deacon before—and at least one of them had died because of her.

The tense silence shattered when Zeke appeared and threw an arm around Deacon's shoulders. The younger Rider was just as tall as Deacon, but his hair was spiky and blond rather than dark, and he wore a teasing smile instead of a glower. "You guys better not be discussing work."

"What else?" Kora rose and held out her hand. "I hope you've come to save me. I make an excellent damsel in distress."

"Damsels in distress happen to be my specialty." Zeke slapped Deacon on the back and claimed Kora's hand, but he still paused to look at Gideon. "Boss."

"Zeke." Gideon inclined his head. "Go enjoy the celebrations."

Kora followed Zeke closer to the bonfire. "You missed all the fun. I was just irritating Deacon."

"Everything irritates Deacon." Zeke spun her in a dizzy circle before pulling her close enough to dance. "Only mildly, though. Mildly irritated is his default state."

"No, it's not him." Something about Zeke's easy manner invited confessions. "He reminds me of someone I used to know."

"What, like one of the MPs?"

"Sort of. A soldier."

Most of the Riders had been born in Sector One, but Zeke was like her—someone who'd grown up inside Eden's shining walls. The bar code marking him as a city citizen was long gone, but she'd seen his lengthy criminal record—one he'd earned hacking Eden's system to redistribute credits to the citizens who couldn't afford to eat.

So she wasn't *too* surprised when the next thing out of his mouth was a name most people wouldn't have known existed. "Ashwin Malhotra?"

He didn't need her confirmation, so she focused on the ribbed collar of his gray T-shirt instead of answering. There were some things that would always be impossible to confess, because you couldn't even explain them. The feelings refused to solidify into anything as pedestrian as words, so you just had to try and make some sort of silent sense of them.

She'd always known that her patients at the Base didn't process things like human bonds and friendship the way most people did. They'd been engineered to divert their energies to more mission-oriented skills. Most of the time, she'd had no trouble remembering that. But with Ashwin...

She'd let down her guard. She'd forgotten to maintain a professional distance, all because there had been a few moments when Ashwin had looked at her with something approaching interest. And now he was gone.

Tears pricked her eyes, and she closed them against Zeke's pity. "You know too many things you're not supposed to know."

"Yes." He rubbed a soothing circle between her shoulder blades. "I can't regret it, though. Poking my nose where it didn't belong is how I ended up here with Gideon. And this is a good place to be."

He seemed so determined to convince her that she couldn't help smiling. "Since I've practically been adopted by the Rios family, I have to agree."

"Don't forget the Riders." He grinned and spun her around again. "You keep putting us back together. I haven't lost many brothers since you showed up, so I'll give Deacon hell all night long if it'll keep you smiling."

"Deal." Kora would keep smiling—because she

had precious few reasons not to, compared to others who had lived through the war between the city and the sectors. Because she'd found a good life here, with friends and a chance to heal those in greatest need.

Because the only thing she'd lost had never really been hers to begin with.

# two

The Riders were heading into an ambush.

Perched on the roof of a two-story warehouse, Ashwin Malhotra watched through his binoculars as three motorcycles rumbled down the dusty road toward Sector One's central temple. The smooth purr of the engines reached him, joining the idyllic sound of the temple's dozens of wind chimes dancing on the late-afternoon breeze.

All three men were dressed in leather and denim. Helmets obscured their identities. Of course, who they were wasn't as important as *what* they were.

Gideon's Riders.

Holy warriors. Sainted heroes. Outside of Sector One, the Riders were more myth and legend than anything, a band of highly trained, dangerously lethal soldiers whose loyalty was unswerving and absolute. Here, they acted as the voice and hands of the god-king himself, Gideon Rios. Each one was empowered to act as judge, jury, *and* executioner, a position of ultimate trust and considerable power.

To Ashwin, they were a curiosity. He'd synthesized every scrap of data available—every bit of history, every dossier, every mission report or rumor to come out of Sector One. He even fleshed out his analysis with a limited number of personal encounters, but the Riders still made no *sense.*

The whole of One was like that. Its citizens stubbornly subsisted almost completely off the power and network grids that crisscrossed the other seven sectors and the city. Even now, in the wake of a revolution Gideon Rios had helped plan, they remained insular and close-mouthed.

They offered aid to the needy, shelter to refugees. They provided food and clothing and medical care to the hundreds displaced by war. They smiled and preached love and swore by pacifism, leaving any necessary violence in the hands of the Riders. They gave much and asked for little.

In a world that had been broken decades ago, they were an equation that didn't add up, no matter how many times Ashwin shifted the variables around.

Power. Greed. Influence. Faith. They were all difficult concepts that allowed plenty of room for the full range of human folly. Ashwin preferred the reliability of things that could be quantified. Things that could be counted.

Like money.

He swung his binoculars toward the temple. The warehouse he'd chosen as his perch was simple adobe, but the temple's marble face caught the last rays of sunlight and sparkled.

Over the last four decades, the Rios family had preached love and peace. But they'd also trained the people of Sector One to purge their sins from their souls through labor. To give until they had nothing left—and to love doing it. Inside the temple, a month's worth of donations from the faithful sat securely in a basement vault. Credits, cash, valuable possessions—based on Ashwin's best estimates, a small fortune awaited the Riders.

That wasn't the only thing waiting for them.

The motorcycles roared into the courtyard, drowning out the wind chimes. One by one, they pulled to a stop and cut their engines. As they removed their helmets, Ashwin matched their faces to surveillance photos in the dossiers he'd studied.

Fernando Reyes was tall, with brown eyes, golden skin, and black hair that brushed his collar. As the eldest son of Sector One's second most powerful family, he'd been the subject of extensive interest on the Base. Though the analysts had highlighted his family's ambition as a potential entry point to undermining Gideon Rios, Ashwin had seen enough loyalty to recognize a hopeless cause. Reyes would repudiate his family before he betrayed his leader.

The man on the right was also from a powerful family. Hunter West had darker brown skin and hair buzzed close to his skull. His sister had married into the Rios family, and his parents were fanatically devoted to Gideon. The Base's file on them had been brief and to the point—if replacing Gideon became a priority, the entire West family would have to be removed as well.

Unsurprisingly, the third man turned out to be Gabriel Montero, another son of a wealthy family and the third member of what the Sector One faithful referred to as the Royal Trio. Ashwin didn't have to close his eyes to summon the intelligence briefing from memory—a sneering, verbose tirade by an officer disgusted by Sector One's backslide into feudalism. *They've already anointed themselves a king. Soon there will be dukes and knights, all the excesses of aristocracy. And all the vulnerabilities. The maneuvering for power has already begun. With minimal intervention, the families can be reduced to infighting.*

According to the dossier, Gabriel Montero's eldest brother had married into the Rios family, as well. The accompanying prestige had lifted the Monteros—and caused the anticipated friction with the Reyes family.

Whatever their family politics, Reyes, Hunter, and Gabe remained friends—and loyal to Gideon Rios first, though the Base officers doubted that loyalty.

Ashwin did not. He'd been there during the war.

Down below, the three Riders swung their legs over their bikes. Ashwin couldn't hear their words as they started up the temple steps, but the rise and fall of their banter drifted up to him, a comfortable give-and-take punctuated by laughter. They'd made this run a hundred times, secure in the knowledge that they were the dominant predators in their sector.

Unfortunately, war had a way of displacing predators.

The deserters appeared as soon as the temple door closed, flowing from their hiding places with the silent grace that made Base soldiers legendary. With their superior military training and access to whatever equipment they'd stolen, the soldiers fanning out into the courtyard could prey upon the sectors and vanish before anyone could stop them.

Especially when they were smart enough not to underestimate their opponents. Ashwin counted nine men moving into position. The Riders were good, but few people were good enough to survive a surprise ambush by trained killers at three-to-one odds.

Ashwin was.

Moving silently, he slipped back from the edge of the roof and folded his binoculars. They fit easily into his thigh pocket, and he took a moment to check his weapons. Two pistols, six throwing knives, a pair of smoke grenades, a garrote, and a hunting knife strapped to his calf.

He'd taken down nine men with less. But this time he wouldn't have to do it alone.

The drop to the ground was far enough to break bones. Ashwin performed the calculations automatically, redistributing his weight and momentum into a roll that dispersed the force and brought him back to his feet unharmed. He did the same for the angles of visibility, recalling the layout of the buildings and the positions of the soldiers in order to slip through the alley unseen.

By the time he reached the edge of the courtyard, Reyes was stalking toward two of the deserters near the temple doors. "You want to start some shit?" he demanded with a wide grin. "Let's start some shit."

They both pulled guns. Reyes's grin didn't falter. Reckless, even for a man with his reputation, and Ashwin eased a throwing knife free of its sheath and judged the distance to the steps.

His mission would go to hell if he let one of the Riders get killed.

Reyes's confident stalk melted into a run. He slammed into one of the men, knocking him into the other, and the three of them went down in a tangled flurry of limbs. Reyes finally drew his pistol, but only to smash the butt of it across one deserter's face.

The other two Riders were smart enough to maintain distance—and cover. Hunter fired from behind a pillar, taking down two men before a third blasted the pillar, sending shards of marble raking across Hunter's face.

Gabe had chosen knives as his weapons, and he was good with them. As the attacker took aim at Hunter again, Gabe's wrist snapped forward. The bright silver blade embedded itself cleanly in the man's throat. Gabe killed another deserter with a second knife before turning to check on Hunter.

The leader of the group dropped from the roof of the temple, crashing into Gabe and carrying him to the ground. Ashwin surged out of the alley, already calculating the angles and velocity and the chance that any shot he fired might go through the deserter and kill the man he was trying to save.

Low. Acceptable, perhaps, under other circumstances.

Ashwin ran faster.

There were seven steps leading up to the temple. Ashwin vaulted up three of them and landed behind the leader, who had his pistol pointed at the back of Gabe's head, his finger squeezing the trigger.

He was a seasoned soldier, but Ashwin was faster. He grabbed the man's wrist and jerked back. Bone snapped as the gun fired, blowing through the leader's chin to tear off the top of his head.

The body went limp beneath him. Ashwin stripped the pistol from his hand and spun. Six men down, three remaining. One using the bikes for cover, one grappling with Reyes, and one standing out in the open, gaping at Ashwin with naked fear in his eyes.

"Makhai! There's a fucking Mak—"

The bullet silenced him. He toppled backwards,

dead eyes staring up at the clouds.

Reyes reared back and took one last swing, a mighty blow that left the man beneath him still and unmoving. The final deserter, the one hiding behind the bikes, took off, kicking up a trail of dust behind him as he ran.

Letting him get back to rest of the deserters was an unacceptable risk. Ashwin fired, then turned back toward the temple as the man's body pitched to the ground.

Gabe was on his feet, swiping blood from a broken nose. His other hand hovered near his knives, but the wariness in his gaze melted into recognition. "You're the soldier who was helping the O'Kanes during the war."

"I am." Extending his hand in greeting was probably the correct thing to do, but Ashwin had learned early in life not to try and mimic human social gestures. No matter how precisely he thought he'd executed them, people could sense the deliberation behind them. The emptiness.

He'd been genetically engineered to be good at many things. Small talk wasn't one of them.

A shot rang out, followed by another. Reyes was on his feet, his gun still in his hand, standing over the now-dead deserters he'd fought with.

Hunter pinched the bridge of his nose and sighed. "If you were going to fucking shoot them, man, why didn't you just *shoot them*?"

Reyes dragged his arm across his bloodied mouth and shrugged. "Didn't seem fair not to give 'em a fighting chance."

Gabe snorted, then winced, poking gingerly at his nose. "Well, now my face is as busted as yours. It could have been my head."

It likely would have been. "Those weren't ordinary raiders," Ashwin told them. "They're deserters from the Base. In the future, it would be best not to give them any unnecessary opportunities to kill you."

"Deserters, huh?" Blood dripped from Hunter's lacerated cheek. "What are they doing all the way out here?"

Ashwin used his foot to turn the leader's body over. His face was almost unrecognizable, but Ashwin knew who he was. Rick Porter had been one of the elite soldiers. Not as elite as Ashwin—not Makhai—but still trained from birth to excel at strategy and killing. "Looking for the credits and wealth they think they're owed."

Hunter muttered something under his breath and knelt to check another of the bodies as the temple doors swung open. Several acolytes rushed out, their robes flowing as they ran toward Reyes and began fussing over his nonexistent injuries.

Gabe turned to Ashwin. "The priestess will have called for help. Are there more of them out there?"

"A few dozen. Maybe more, if they've been recruiting." Ashwin nudged the leader again. "But I doubt they'll have backup coming. This wasn't a well-planned operation. They were sloppy, overconfident."

"He still might have killed me if you hadn't been here." Gabe extended a hand, and Ashwin had to clasp it. Not doing so would have been awkward. But he disliked the physical contact, and he struggled to judge the appropriate amount of pressure. Too hard would be considered aggressive, too lax would signal weakness.

The intricacies of nonverbal communication had always been tedious, but Ashwin found he had even less patience for them since the war. He gripped Gabe's hand and knew it was too hard when the other man's eyes widened slightly. Irritated with himself, he let his hand drop. "I was doing my job."

"Your job?" Reyes studied Ashwin while one of the acolytes prodded his bruised knuckles. "There's no way the Base sent you to clean out upwards of forty deserters all by yourself."

Hunter scoffed. "Maybe if you hadn't been busy getting your face bashed in, you could have listened."

"To what?"

"The man's Makhai." He straightened and pinned Ashwin with a flat stare. "Forty against one—those odds aren't so bad when you're dealing with a walking science experiment."

If he'd had any feelings to speak of, the mistrust might have stung them. But fear and aversion were the only constants in Ashwin's life. "I was doing recon when they decided to ambush you. A defeat like this may subdue them for a short time, but when the others strike, they'll be better prepared."

"All the more reason to see if these corpses have anything useful to tell us." Hunter moved on to searching the next body.

Reluctantly, Reyes joined him. Gabe crouched and started with the leader.

Ashwin could have told them everything they wanted to know. He could have slipped his scanner from his pocket and used the bar codes on the deserters' wrists to access their service histories. But it was interesting to watch this methodical examination. Instead of tech and gadgets, they used wits and observation.

"Gabriel, mira." Reyes grabbed the toe of Porter's boot and pried a small piece of quartz from the treads. "The gravel pit?"

Gabe took the rock from him and tilted his palm so it caught the light. "They could be camped out there."

“We can—”

The rumble of a truck interrupted them. Ashwin gripped his gun and turned, but at the sight of the open-topped truck that was racing toward the temple, the other men immediately relaxed.

It slid to a stop, and a blonde woman stood up in the passenger seat, her hands locked around the roll bars that formed the top frame of the truck.

*Kora Bellamy.*

Pain sizzled through Ashwin, a teasing shock. The echoes of agony. For the first few seconds, looking at her *hurt*. It hurt enough that a normal man might have turned away from the sight of her.

Ashwin had never been normal.

He catalogued her features like probing a bruise. Her silver-blue eyes, heart-shaped face, and high cheekbones. The narrow bridge of her nose and the elegant arch of her brows. Her lips, full and soft but parted in shock.

There had been a time when the symmetrical arrangement of her features had made his pulse race. When he’d seen her face every time he closed his eyes, a sweet afterimage of the only thing in his life he’d ever wanted.

Now, he couldn’t remember what wanting felt like. Six months of torture had cured him of that particular aberration.

Kora stumbled from the truck. Her lips formed the silent shape of his name, and then she was running, hard and fast. She was still moving when she reached him, and he caught her out of instinct as she slammed into him.

He didn’t care for physical contact, but holding her wasn’t unpleasant. She was made of curves and smooth skin, and tall enough that he could smell her hair. When she'd worked as a doctor on the Base, her scent had been subdued. Mild traces of something floral, nothing he could ever identify. Now she smelled like coconut, and beneath that, spice or incense.

She smelled like she belonged here.

And she was crying. The salty scent of her tears mixed with the sound of her ragged, exhaled sob as she slid her arms around his neck. "I thought you were dead."

It hadn't occurred to him that she'd think any such thing. It hadn't occurred to him she'd *care*. Most people Ashwin had known in his life would feel nothing if he vanished, except perhaps vague relief.

But he should have known. Kora Bellamy wasn't most people.

He didn't know how to soothe her. He wasn't trained for it. Her grip on him tightened, and he moved his hand between her shoulder blades in an awkward circle. "I'm sorry."

"What happened? Where have you *been*?"

"Kora." Deacon Price, the driver of the truck and Gideon's second-in-command, stood nearby, a black bag in one hand. "You need to look at Hunter's face."

"Oh, God. I'm sorry." She pulled back, but it took another few heartbeats before she untangled her fingers from the back of Ashwin's shirt. "Sorry, I'm just... Don't go anywhere."

"I'll be here," he promised, letting his fingers linger on her back until she turned away. Then he lowered his hand, and it didn't hurt to let her go. His bones didn't ache with the need to follow her. When he closed his eyes briefly, he saw only darkness.

The Base had spent close to twenty-one weeks tearing her out of him, one painful memory at a time. They'd practically rebuilt him on a cellular level.

Whatever compulsion had gripped him, whatever obsession had driven him—he was no longer fixated on Kora. He had to believe it. He had a mission to execute, and he couldn't allow her presence to compromise it.

The first stage had gone well. The deserters had taken his bait, including the false schematics he'd planted, hinting that the vault in the basement was beyond their ability to crack. They'd done exactly what Ashwin had anticipated—waited for the Riders to remove the loot for them.

He'd been meticulous. Even if some of the deserters had survived this raid, there was no way for the Riders to trace their intel back to him. And that was the only variable he'd misjudged—the sheer competence of Gideon's men. The three of them had almost taken down the entire squadron before he had a chance to intervene and help.

He wouldn't repeat the mistake of underestimating them.

With a little luck, he'd be in Gideon Rios's house by sunset, one step closer to infiltrating the Riders. Gideon might mouth pieties about compassion and peace, but he was a ruthless enough leader not to squander the chance to have a genetically engineered soldier at his disposal.

Ashwin had planned for everything...except Kora. But he was Makhai. He'd find a way to make it work.

He always did.

# three

Kora had never seen a miracle before.

Even if he hadn't been presumed dead just hours earlier, Ashwin would have looked out of place sitting across from her at Gideon's idyllic table. His brown skin was bronzed by the candlelight, and the shadows softened the usual hardness of his gaze. But not even the romantic lighting could soften the effect of his Base-issue fatigues, and he held the silverware stiffly and precisely, as if he'd studied a manual on proper etiquette but felt uncomfortable with the formality.

She couldn't stop staring at him.

To be fair, it was only pride and arrogance that had led her to the conclusion that Ashwin must have fallen during the final battle with the city. She'd never heard or seen anything that would have confirmed him as a casualty of war. But when it was all over and he never came looking for her, she'd just assumed.

*Silly, silly Kora.* She was a scientist; assumptions were beneath her, especially when there were easier explanations to be found. Ashwin was a soldier. When the battle ended, he did what any soldier would have done—he reported back to his superiors.

She drained her wine, and one of the silent servers standing around the perimeter of the dining room stepped forward immediately to refill it. His task complete, he melted back into the shadows beyond the candlelight that illuminated the small, intimate table.

Gideon lifted his own glass and watched her over the rim. "I assume there are no permanent injuries from today's encounter."

"No," she murmured. "Hunter needed a few stitches and some med-gel. Gabe's nose might be a little more crooked. And I still think Reyes has anger issues."

Maricela snorted, then tried to cover it with a cough. "Excuse me."

Gideon favored his sister with an indulgent smile before turning to Ashwin. "I hear we have you to thank for the lack of casualties."

His answer to Gideon was the same as his posture—stiff and precise. "I intervened in time to assist, but they may have persevered without me."

"Well, I don't like *may*. Not when my men's lives are at stake." Gideon swirled the wine in his glass. "Tell me about these deserters."

"There were thirty-seven of them to start, though I've seen some evidence they may be recruiting other raiders now. Four were from the elite training program, the rest basic soldiers. But even a basic soldier has superior training."

“Superior to what?” Maricela asked.

“To any threats you’re accustomed to facing in this sector.”

“True enough,” Gideon murmured. “We’ve dealt with our share of robbers and raiders, but they’re not much for working together. So why did these men desert?”

Ashwin hesitated, his gaze flicking to Kora and away so quickly she might have imagined it. “There was tension after the war. Some of the soldiers on the Base wanted the generals to declare martial law and occupy Eden.”

“Seize the city?” Kora stared at him. The idea wouldn’t have been so unthinkable back when the Council was running it into the ground. But now that it had been liberated… “Why would they want to do that?”

“You know what the Base is like.” His gaze shifted again, sweeping over the table this time. They were in the smaller family dining room instead of the formal one, but the elegant furniture was still expensive. Candlelight glittered across a feast of fresh produce and perfectly seasoned meat, served on colorful, handmade dishes. “They’re tired of doing without.”

Taking the city would get them nothing. But taking the sectors was a different story—at least on the surface. Surely they remembered that the rebels had burned Sector Six to the ground rather than let the city forces have it.

Kora gripped her knife. “Did the generals disagree on principle or as a matter of practicality?”

“The generals keep their own counsel. I’m not aware of their long-term plans, only my current mission.”

Gideon tilted his head. “And that’s dealing with

the deserters?"

"Yes. Preferably before they cause unnecessary friction between the Base, Eden, and the sectors."

Maricela beamed at him. "Your mutual goals align quite nicely, then."

He stared at her as if he wasn't entirely sure what to do with a young woman beaming at him in happiness—which he probably wasn't. "Our immediate goals, yes."

She leaned toward him. "You knew Kora before the war. I can't imagine her in Eden. What was she like?"

Kora's cheeks heated. "*Maricela.*"

"She was..." Ashwin's gaze was so intense it felt like he was looking *into* her. "Compassionate. Fierce, sometimes. She advocated for patients no one else cared about. She didn't belong in Eden."

Maricela made a soft noise and sat back in her chair, satisfied, as if he'd answered another question entirely. "She belongs here. Right, Gideon?"

"Of course she does." Gideon drained his cup before setting it down. "It was my pleasure to bring Kora into the family. Having a third sister is even more delightful and exasperating than having just two."

Ashwin's expression didn't change, but he seemed almost taken aback by the proclamation, and Kora could sympathize. When Gideon had first referred to her as his sister, Kora had been certain that he meant it in honorary fashion, simply as a way to show his respect for her. It hadn't taken her long to realize he meant it *literally*, that he now considered her as much a part of his family as Maricela or his other sister, Isabela.

In Eden, love had barely existed. Here, it was stronger than blood.

Ashwin spoke, and his words jolted through Kora.

"I'm glad she found family."

Startled, she met his eyes. She was sure—absolutely certain—she'd covered her tracks when she'd pored through the Base files, looking for information on her parents. But Ashwin sounded as if he knew about her desperate search.

And if he knew, did that mean his superiors—her former bosses—did, too?

As if realizing he'd revealed too much, Ashwin reached for his wine. "Your sister is correct. Our immediate goals may be compatible. I have access to resources and tech, but I don't know the area around One as well as your men do."

"I agree. There's definitely opportunity here." Gideon lifted his refilled glass to Kora. "A chance for you two to catch up. And a chance for me to deal with a potential problem before it becomes a serious one."

"I'm not sure how much catching up there is to do." Kora meant for the words to be bland, a casual observation, but they came out with an edge she couldn't suppress.

Six months. She had let herself care about Ashwin, yes, but worse, she'd let herself somehow believe that he cared about her, too. And now, the worst part was not knowing *why* she'd done it. Had she really been so arrogant as to think she could inspire warmth in a Makhai soldier?

Or had she just been that lonely?

Whatever had pushed her over the line, it had led her to make her *assumptions*. To believe that she mattered to him enough that his continued absence—and his lack of contact—meant something dire. But here he was, absolutely fine, looking at her with no more interest than he showed Gideon or Maricela or even the damn table settings.

She was worse than arrogant. She was a fool.

Gideon covered the awkward silence by clearing his throat. "After dessert, I'll take you over to the barracks, Ashwin. We'll give you a place to stay, and you can talk to Deacon. He'll be the one in charge of drawing up any initial plans of attack."

Ashwin nodded, the gesture as stiff and calculated as everything else about him, but then his gaze drifted back to Kora, inscrutable and—

*And what?* She focused on her plate and reminded herself that it didn't matter. She'd gotten over the shock of seeing him after all these months. He was alive, and that was enough. It had to be, because expecting anything more than vaguely courteous concern from the best soldier the Makhai Project had ever turned out was worse than silly, or foolish, or even arrogant.

It was an exercise in futility.

Ashwin knew the basic layout of Gideon's estate. The Base's drone surveillance had yielded high-resolution images, and he'd committed them to memory before embarking on his mission. He couldn't see much in the dark, but he still made note of familiar landmarks on the walk to the barracks.

Gideon's house dominated the front of the property—a palatial building with multiple wings and a massive enclosed courtyard that contained gardens and a pool. The breeze stirred the leaves on the orchards planted on both sides of the house. The Rios orchards produced apples, pears, plums, and cherries, and that bounty alone might have made Gideon a rich man.

But the orchards weren't his only source of income.

The path branched as it reached a clearing filled with a circle of stone benches, wooden tables, and a massive fire pit. Gideon gestured to the path on the left, and Ashwin followed silently. The path to the right, he knew, led to the Prophet's Temple. The building itself was modest compared to the Rios home, but the priestesses who lived there accepted acolytes who showed skill in a trade. The embroidery, pottery, and leatherwork they produced sold for exorbitant prices that further lined Gideon's coffers, while the girls tended to go on to marry into families excited to make use of their skills—and their association with Sector One's royal family.

As far as Ashwin could tell, everything in Sector One lined Gideon's pockets, one way or another.

Ashwin cast a furtive look at the man, but he wore the same easy, relaxed expression he'd maintained during dinner. Objective observation of Gideon Rios revealed little Ashwin didn't already know. The man was nearing forty. He had light brown skin, dark hair with a hint of curl, and brown eyes under severe brows. The lines around his eyes were the ones people called *smile lines*, unsurprising when his lips curved into a half-smile even now.

He wasn't dressed like a leader, but the clothing was a blatant lie. His humble white T-shirt hadn't been mass-manufactured in a factory in Sector Eight but hand-sewn, probably by one of the acolytes in the temple. His leather pants fit too well to be anything but the same. A carefully crafted, tremendously expensive message of humility.

In the sectors, survival generally depended on shows of strength. Only a lethally dangerous man went out of his way to appear harmless.

"Kora seemed unsettled at dinner." The words came out of nowhere, and Gideon's smile didn't falter. But the back of Ashwin's neck prickled, like a sniper had a lock on him.

He debated fabricating a response. Most people were so unnerved by his lack of apparent affect that they couldn't tell when he was lying. But in this instance, the truth might curry sympathy. "I regret any discomfort I caused her. I'm not accustomed to people feeling concern for me, but that was a miscalculation on my part. Kora feels concern for everyone."

"She does," Gideon agreed, still easy and friendly, but Ashwin could sense the trap closing around him. "The way I hear it, that concern went both ways during the war."

The prickle at the back of his neck turned to a warning shock. Heat crawled over his nerves—not quite pain, but certainly not pleasure. A warning not to let the image form in his mind.

Kora, in the middle of a battlefield. Her skin coated with blood, her cheeks smudged with it. Her eyes wide as he dragged his hands over her body, searching for a wound, frantic until he realized the blood wasn't hers—

Light throbbed behind his eyes, and he shut the memory down. Focused on the crunch of gravel beneath his boots. The wind in the trees. The distant sound of a bird singing—most likely a northern mockingbird. If he focused on the volume, he could estimate the distance—

"Ashwin?"

"A stable Makhai soldier isn't capable of concern," he said, choosing his words carefully. "The war was a destabilizing influence on me, but the Base has adjusted my regimen. Kora Bellamy is a good doctor who has always advocated for Makhai soldiers, and many of us feel loyalty to her. I won't betray her location to my superiors, if that's your concern." It was the truth. The Base could ask him for anything they wanted.

Anything but Kora.

"It's not my concern, actually." They reached the barracks, and Gideon turned to face him, his suddenly serious expression barely visible in the scant moonlight.

"If I thought you were a danger to any of my sisters, you wouldn't be on my property. You wouldn't be in my sector. But I am very concerned that you'll hurt her feelings, and that's something I don't want to see."

The thought of Kora in pain was...unpleasant. He disliked it the same way he disliked making physical contact with strangers. It upset the comfortable ordering of his world. "I don't want to see it, either."

"Good." Gideon spun back toward the building and pounded on the door. "Deacon, get your ass out here!"

The door swung open beneath his fist. "Sir."

Gideon's second-in-command had clearly been standing just inside, listening to the conversation. He seemed as unashamed as Gideon seemed unbothered. "Deacon, Ashwin has agreed to stay with us for a few days. I want the two of you to go over everything he knows about this group of deserters. Find out if any of the raids we've had over the last month can be traced back to them."

Deacon stretched his arm across the open doorway, drawing Ashwin's gaze to the tattoo that dominated his shoulder—a tree growing out of a skull with ravens flying from the branches and spiraling down his arm. The symbol of the Riders. "Sure."

"Good." Gideon nodded to Ashwin. "I'll leave you in his very capable hands. If you need anything, let Deacon know. He'll take care of it."

He didn't wait for a reply. Ashwin supposed kings and cult leaders rarely did. He turned and vanished back into the darkness, leaving Ashwin facing the second-in-command.

Deacon had a file at the Base, too—a brief one. No details about family or friends or associates. No relationships that could be exploited, just the observation that he was well-trained and dangerous, and that his loyalty to Gideon Rios was absolute.

Ashwin didn't need a file to understand Deacon. He wore his resume on his arm. All Riders got the skull and tree tattoo, but the ravens were personal. Each time a Rider took a life in the course of his job, he etched a reminder onto his skin, and Deacon's arm was covered with them. They wound down toward his wrist and inside his elbow, crowding each other out in a litany of blood spilled.

He wouldn't be surprised if Deacon's death toll rivaled his own.

Deacon stepped back. "Come inside. We'll get you set up."

The first thing Ashwin noticed when he stepped inside was the electricity. Unlike Gideon's home, which seemed to run mostly on candlelight and rare, strategically placed applications of solar power, the Riders' barracks was brightly illuminated.

In fact, it wasn't so different from a barracks common area on the Base. The main room they stepped into was bigger, perhaps. Less stark. The walls were smooth adobe, patterned in cheerful golds and bronzes. A mural of saints dominated the back wall, painted in vivid, bright colors.

But it *felt* the same. Maybe it was the clatter from the corner where Hunter bench-pressed an impressive amount of weight, or the scent of oil and the whisper of steel over whetstone from the wide table on the opposite side. Maybe it was simply the way everything in the room shifted as he walked in—the subtle *readiness* of trained soldiers who could pivot from relaxation to violence at a moment's notice.

As the Riders turned to stare at him, Ashwin matched faces with names. Gabe was seated at the table, sharpening a sword. Tape across his broken nose was the only sign of the evening's fight. He inclined his head in greeting.

So did the woman next to him, and *that* wasn't like the Base at all. Her leather halter top revealed brown skin over well-formed muscles, and the wary challenge in her eyes told Ashwin she knew exactly how much use the Base had for female warriors.

The tattoo on her shoulder was vivid black. Fresh. No ravens dotted her arm, which explained why she hadn't been part of his research for the mission. She must be new—Gideon's experiment in shattering traditional gender roles. Ashwin imagined she'd earned that wariness a hundred times over.

"Hey, the man of the hour." Hunter racked his weight bar and sat up. He lifted a white towel and dragged it over his face before speaking again. "Thought we'd see you at dinner."

"He had a special invite." Reyes grinned from his perch on the sofa. His expression was friendly on the surface, but with an edge that hinted at imminent bloodshed. "From the royal family."

"Ooooh, fancy." The words came from the blond seated next to Reyes, who had a tablet in one hand, a plate of donuts balanced on his knee, and an eager-puppy grin on his face. Ezekiel James, known as Zeke in Sector One, and for a brief time within Eden as Robin Hood—a nickname he'd earned by hacking into the accounts of rich councilmen and redistributing their money to the poor.

His dossier painted him as a ruthless criminal. The reality was somewhat jarring.

"Don't mind him," Gabe said from the table, where he'd resumed sharpening his blade. "He has a habitually sarcastic mouth. It's why everyone keeps punching him in it."

"Or because you're all jealous of how pretty it is." Zeke waggled his eyebrows at Gabe before turning his attention to Ashwin. "So. A Makhai soldier. Can you tell what number I'm thinking of?"

Ashwin didn't know where the rumor had started, but it seemed most of the people he'd met had heard it. Some Makhai soldiers encouraged the belief. The one he'd been closest to growing up would have analyzed everything he knew about Zeke to provide a guess close enough to unsettle and amaze.

Predicting human thoughts based on their emotional cues wasn't a skill at which Ashwin had ever excelled. "No."

"All right," Deacon rumbled. "Knock it the fuck off. Jaden?"

A man with dark red hair popped up from the floor behind the sofa. "Boss?"

"Malhotra's bunking with you. Show him around."

"Got it." He rose, and Ashwin got his first good look at him—he was *huge*, with a broad chest, wide shoulders, and massive arms, no doubt thanks to his childhood spent working on his family's farm. He jerked his head toward a door at the back of the room, and Ashwin followed him into a narrow hallway.

"Heard you kicked some ass today, soldier."

"I was able to help your friends, yes."

Jaden half-turned, looking back over his shoulder. "Whatever you want to call it, Gideon must have been impressed."

"I think he recognizes the potential in a temporary alliance." And Ashwin had no doubt that once Gideon saw the full extent of his capabilities, he'd be willing to extend the alliance.

Jaden grunted. "Two bathrooms, one at this side of the hall and one at the far end. We share. Kitchen's down there, too, but no one bothers because the cook at the palace temple keeps us fed. You been to the temple yet?" Ashwin shook his head, and Jaden kept talking as he opened the door to his quarters. "You will. Anyway, here we are. Extra bed's over there."

The beds were solidly constructed, wide enough for two or three people to sleep comfortably, with thick mattresses and colorful quilts. Jaden's side of the room was decorated sparsely—a painting of one of the many Rios saints hung on one wall, and he had a shelf full of books and a desk covered with weapons.

The other desk was empty except for the equipment bag Ashwin had brought with him. Gideon had handed it off to a servant when they sat down for dinner, so Ashwin was glad he'd placed nothing incriminating inside. Not that it looked like the zipper had been tampered with, but he'd been watching the sectors for too long to underestimate Gideon Rios.

Ashwin unstrapped the sheath from his thigh and dropped the knife on the desk. "I have some clothes and supplies at a safe house a few miles east of Two. I should probably pick them up tomorrow."

Jaden nodded. "If you need anything else, we can take you around to the market, introduce you to all the vendors. They'll set you up."

"Set me up?"

"Yeah, clothes, personal items. The usual stuff." Jaden dropped to his bunk and stifled a yawn. "Gideon takes care of it."

Ashwin pulled out the chair and sat to unlace his boots. "So Gideon provides everything? Food and clothes?"

"For the Riders." Jaden propped his arm behind his head and grinned. "And our honored guests."

*And for Kora?*

The question wasn't Ashwin's to ask. She clearly had a place here in Sector One. She was as safe as anyone could be in a world crawling back from war. Besides, the men had talked as if his invitation to dine at Gideon's table was a rarity that wouldn't be repeated.

That was optimal. He'd focus on wiping out the deserters and securing his place. And hopefully both would keep him too busy to cross paths with Kora Bellamy.

# four

Kora loved art. It was one of the things that initially made her feel at home in Sector One, the way they splashed life and color in the most conspicuous and unconventional of places. Sculptures, murals, the tattoos that graced their skin.

Even their religious rituals were a thing of beauty. She sat, swathed in diaphanous white robes, as one of the senior priestesses circled her slowly. Delfina was tall and willowy, with a lean, muscled frame that spoke of strength. So did her manner—quiet, not quite stern, but with a seriousness that hinted at near-absolute authority.

Kora focused on the plumes of fragrant smoke that rose from the jeweled censer dangling from Del's hand. "Any ideas?"

"That depends. Maricela?"

Maricela climbed to her feet, took the censer, and continued circling the two of them. Del knelt, so close that her knees brushed Kora's, and clasped her hands. She turned them over and rubbed her thumbs over Kora's palms.

But her gaze was fixed on the bar codes.

Kora had two. The first she'd received at birth—every citizen of Eden did. The second she'd gotten when she'd been granted Special Clearance.

"The marks we carry on our skin make us who we are," Del said softly. She traced the bar codes, one at a time. "The ones given to us mark who we've been, and the ones we take for ourselves shape who we believe we can be. The first day Zeke came to us, he wanted his bar code gone so badly, I think he would have burned it off."

"I like the phoenix you gave him instead," Maricela offered.

"I'm not Zeke." The incense made Kora feel heavy, sleepy—and loosened her tongue. "Besides, I don't want them covered. I want them gone completely. Someday."

"Someday." Del stroked them again with a sigh. "I could cover them or remove them now, but it wouldn't matter. Until you're ready to let them go, they'll always be there. So we'll mark something else today."

Kora understood how this process worked—theoretically. Del was part artist, part psychologist. The people of One didn't request specific tattoos from her so much as they requested her insight. She would read their moods and worries like a book, then mark them with whatever images she chose.

After Ashwin's abrupt reappearance in her life, Kora had considered cancelling this session. But a perceptive person—which Del most certainly was—would have learned even more from that than from her silence.

Instead, she deflected. "Tell me more about Gabe, Maricela."

"Gabe?" The girl wrinkled her nose as she placed the censer on the floor beside the stone bench where Kora sat. "I don't know, he's...Gabe. Why?"

"No reason. He seems nice, that's all."

"Perfectly nice," she confirmed. "And perfectly serious."

Kora liked that about him. He was solid, like a rock, not just physically but mentally, as well. Reliable, easy to read, the kind of man who would never surprise you with the unexpected.

"Too serious." Del's long hair swung as she shook her head. "Sometimes I worry about him and all the *thinking* he does."

Suddenly, Maricela dropped to the floor beside Del and peered up at Kora with suspicion. "You're not trying to set me up with Gabe, are you? Ugh, his family's noble. He'd get all *sorts* of ideas—"

"For *me*, Maricela." Del was still holding both her hands, and Kora pulled them free gently but firmly. "I was asking for myself."

Maricela's suspicion turned to horror. "But—what about Ashwin?"

It hurt. The pain shamed Kora even as she embraced it, used it to center herself. "I hadn't heard from him in six months. Half a year. I didn't know if he was alive or dead, and it probably never even occurred to him to wonder thc same about me. What *about* him?"

Maricela crossed her arms over her chest, her eyes gleaming with stubborn certainty. "He wondered. He must have."

God save her from a Rios who'd already made up her mind. Kora sighed and looked to Del for support.

"Kora's right to be cautious, sweetheart." Del touched Maricela's cheek fondly before flowing to her feet. "I've never met a Makhai soldier, but the record keeper before me did. She said it was the only time she ever looked into a man's eyes and saw nothing staring back at her."

"But..." Maricela tucked her feet beneath her and rested her chin on Kora's knee. "You mourned him when you thought he was dead. Surely that means something."

It did—to her. But that wasn't enough to hang on to a dream, especially for someone who prided herself on being pragmatic. "Enough, Maricela. Please."

"Yes, don't unsettle her, or we'll have to start over." Del circled Kora and trailed her fingers down her back. "Do you know the story of the Two Princesses, Kora?"

"Which two?" She grinned at Maricela to break the tension. "This sector is overrun with them."

"The first two." Del picked up her sketchpad and a charcoal pencil. "Maricela's mother, Juana. And her aunt, Adriana."

"Only what I picked up from the murals at the palace."

Del's hand moved quickly, the soft scratch of her pencil as hypnotic as the way her voice sank into an easy rhythm. "Adriana was a warrior. She fought for her people, killed for them if necessary. She fell in love with her bodyguard and challenged the Prophet himself for the right to marry him. In the paintings, she holds the heart of her people in her hands...but if the occasion called for it, Adriana could tear the heart out of an enemy's chest. Her spine was pure steel."

The scratching paused as Del glanced at Maricela, a smile curving her full lips. "But Juana was different. She married Adriana's brother, the Prophet's only son and heir. She and Adriana became sisters and friends. Juana had no gift for death, but there was nothing she touched that wouldn't grow. No person she touched who wasn't moved." Del nudged Maricela with her foot. "No child she loved who didn't thrive."

Maricela nodded, her eyes bright with unshed tears.

Del went back to sketching. "Adriana's spine was steel, but Juana's was made of roses. And because men can be fools who only recognize one kind of strength, they underestimated her. When the wars came, Juana bent with the wind. She grew stronger and fiercer as she wrapped herself tight around the people she loved. She became a wall of thorns, and no one could touch the people she called hers without bleeding for their trouble."

After a moment of silence, Del turned the sketchpad around. The bold design filled the page in a long vertical line—two sets of vines weaving in and around one another, with blooming flowers and tightly furled buds nestled between sharp thorns.

"I think you're like Juana," Del said, her voice still a husky murmur. "Your gift is life. There's power in that."

Kora's fingers trembled as she reached out and touched the paper. "It's beautiful."

"Thank you." Del tore the paper free and handed it to her before moving to the table that held her tattooing equipment. "I don't give the spine of roses often. Not many have a heart big enough to carry the burden."

"Are you sure that I do?" The question slipped out, unbidden. There were few things in life that Kora had never second-guessed, and her care for others was the biggest. The most important. It had been more than a job, or even her life's work. It had been a calling.

But now, she questioned everything.

"Of course I'm sure." Del returned with a marker in her hand and tilted Kora's chin up. "But that's not enough for you, because you're not a believer."

Kora had tried to study Sector One's concept of God. But he was nebulous, his message and character changing depending on the situation, on interpretation, even on the person writing or speaking about him. As a scientist, Kora couldn't reconcile the wild variances, the seemingly human failings in a being who was supposed to be infallible.

But there were some things she understood without hesitation. "I believe in the Rios family, and in your abilities. If you say I deserve to wear Juana's roses, I'll wear them."

Del didn't release her chin. "You've looked into Ashwin's eyes. Did you see nothingness staring back at you?"

She'd seen confusion, puzzlement. Anger. Terror. And, just once, a need so sharp that she ached to remember it. "No."

"It takes a big heart to see past the death. I've always wondered what Juana would have seen in the eyes of the last Makhai soldier who came to One. Perhaps the same thing you see in Ashwin's." Del crouched down so they were on eye level. "And remember, Kora. There was nothing she touched that didn't grow."

The words played over and over in Kora's mind as she settled into the seat Del indicated. She considered them as Del prepared her skin, as the dull buzz of the tattoo machine filled the room, even through the first angry pricks of the needle.

At one time, she would have believed Del without hesitation. If she was talking about healing, about *work*, then Kora would have had no doubts at all. But emotion was trickier. People were hard to predict.

A Makhai soldier? That was impossible.

No, she had to be more careful this time. She could be polite, courteous, but she couldn't afford to let it go beyond that, because Maricela was right. She *had* mourned Ashwin—longer and harder than she'd thought possible—and only a fool would put herself through that twice.

# five

The trip to the gravel pit had been little more than a formality. No one expected the deserters to be there, but Deacon had brought Ashwin and most of the Riders with him, just in case.

Instead of a fight, they'd found an abandoned camp. A sloppy camp, judging by what they could reconstruct of the way it had been set up, as well as the fact that the deserters had left behind enough information to allow reconstruction.

Ashwin honestly told Deacon that the sloppiness indicated a breakdown in discipline and dissent amongst the self-appointed leaders. There was no reason to lie. Until the Base told him otherwise, the Riders' goals *were* his goals.

So were the Riders' hobbies. Which was how Ashwin

found himself seated at the fire pit next to Deacon, watching an impromptu celebration of a clear spring evening turn into a party. Servants appeared from the direction of the palace carrying heavy metal tubs full of iced beverages, and young women dressed in bright colors trailed down the path from the temple in twos and threes.

Most of them cast looks at him and Deacon before putting their heads close together. Their laughter filled the clearing, rising over the crackle of the fire and the murmur of voices.

"New guy gets all the attention." Reyes tromped around the pit, handed him and Deacon each a cold, open bottle of beer, then settled on the ground in the flickering light. "They don't know you're all work and no play."

Ashwin rubbed his thumb over the cold, uneven glass of the bottle. It wasn't smooth and uniform like the mass-produced bottles that came out of the factories in Sector Eight. Somewhere in Sector One, a family was blowing glass bottles by hand, the same way another cured leather, and a third wove fabric or did any one of a hundred things the rest of the sectors had forgotten—or had never known how to do to begin with.

And yet, they still found time to...play. To celebrate. Ashwin glanced toward the knot of girls and caught them staring at him. They erupted into renewed laughter, and Ashwin looked away, discomfited. "I've rarely had the opportunity to focus on anything but work."

"That's a shame," Reyes observed, though he didn't sound particularly sorry to hear it.

Deacon grunted. "Go be a dick somewhere else, Reyes."

"That hurts." But he was grinning as he rose and headed toward the cluster of acolytes. They parted to let him close and then surrounded him, laughing and flirting and blushing.

At least they weren't looking at Ashwin anymore. He sipped the beer, certain that his metabolism would burn through anything short of the strongest hard liquor before it could compromise his judgment. "Is this something that happens often? These celebrations?"

"When the mood strikes." Deacon swirled the beer in his bottle. "If it's too cold even with a fire, we stick to the barracks. But outside is better. Freer." He pinned Ashwin with a look. "It's good to be reminded what you're fighting for."

Movement along the path from the palace drew Ashwin's attention. Maricela and Kora were drifting toward the clearing, their arms linked together. Maricela's white dress was pristine in the last sunlight, which was as much a statement as her brother's carefully tailored humility. White fabric picked up the grime and dirt of the sectors so easily, almost no one bothered with it.

No one except princesses.

Kora was dressed more casually. She was wearing battered jeans with rips in the legs, little white fringes surrounding tantalizing glimpses of bare skin, and a modest black blouse with sleeves that ended just below her elbows.

She'd worn white once, too, crisp lab coats over subdued shirts and slacks. Sometimes she was the only clean thing he saw for weeks. He would sit in an exam room, his body battered and bruised, and feel distantly, oddly relieved that she lived a life comfortable and safe enough to allow for perfect white coats.

That was how it had started. His...fixation. His obsession. Distant, odd relief. He hadn't recognized the warning signs until the distance had already closed and *odd* became *normal*. When *relief* shifted to *anticipation*.

This time he'd be more careful.

Two of the temple acolytes broke away and met

them on the path. Kora laughed, covered her face with her hands, and turned around.

The black shirt that had seemed so modest from the front was missing its back. The fabric draped from her shoulders and crossed low across her hips, leaving the long line of her spine uncovered.

But not bare. Vivid, fresh ink climbed up her back, an elegant tangle of vines with sharp thorns and bright red roses blooming amidst them. He traced the vines with his gaze, from the small of her back up to her vulnerable nape and back down again, even though it felt like the tattoo needles were jabbing the inside of his skull.

A weak spot in the Base's conditioning and recalibration regimen. Looking at Kora might always hurt, but pain could never be a foolproof deterrent, not for a Makhai soldier.

But he should still stop looking. Because he was being careful.

He forced himself to avert his gaze, and the pain eased. Unfortunately, it was replaced by the sharp taste of displeasure when he noticed Gabe had joined them—and was staring at Kora with entirely too much familiarity.

Gabe whistled softly. "Roses along the spine from Del. That's a statement, all right."

Even Deacon was watching as the acolytes congratulated Kora and admired her ink. "Makes you wonder, doesn't it?"

"Wonder what?" Ashwin asked.

"What she sees for Kora." Gabe settled on the bench next to Ashwin and tilted his head toward the temple. "Del sees into people. I don't know whether it's training or psychology or something more, but she marks the truth of who they are on their skin. Or the truth of who they can become."

"And the roses mean something?"

"They're for people who fight against the darkness by dealing in life instead of death." Gabe glanced at Kora again. "I have a cousin with the roses on her spine. She's spent the last fifteen years raising orphans from other sectors. It's a difficult fight. Giving in to cynicism and revenge is easy. But hope? Hope is *hard*."

Not for Kora. Ashwin would be surprised if the woman knew how to do anything *but* hope. "Then it suits her."

Maricela was laughing as she and Kora reached the brash glow of the fire. "Deacon," she said with mock severity. "You're not dancing."

"No, I'm not." His features softened into a rare smile as he set aside his beer and rose. "Help me rectify that?"

"Gladly."

Kora grinned after them as they left, then slid her hands into the back pockets of her jeans. "Good evening."

Ashwin inclined his head. "Dr. Bellamy."

He regretted the formality when Gabe smiled. "Kora. We were just admiring your ink. Congratulations."

She blushed. "Thank you, but the praise is really Del's."

"You'll have to share it." Gabe rose and gestured to the spot next to Ashwin. "Can I get you a drink?"

"No thanks, I'm good."

Gabe squeezed her shoulder before leaving. Ashwin watched him go and imagined breaking his fingers. Not all of them, just a pinky. They snapped so easily, and no one really needed them for anything vital—

"May I?" Kora asked quietly.

Letting her sit next to him wasn't being careful. But offending her when Gideon considered her a sister ran counter to his mission. "Of course."

The music changed over into another, faster song as she settled beside him. "So. How do you like Sector One?"

Three inches of empty air separated their bodies. Ashwin calculated their respective heights, and then the volume of emptiness between them. Converted to milliliters, it was a soothingly high number. "It's different."

"From the Base, or from the city?"

He let his gaze drift over the crowd. The Riders were dancing and laughing, as if their arms weren't full of ravens marking the deaths they'd dealt. As if the religion they fought for didn't curse them for taking those lives. They were walking dead men, martyrs who had embraced damnation.

And they still laughed. Danced. And talked about *hope*. "From everywhere."

"That's fair." She shifted, and her arm brushed his, setting off a cascade of delicately painful prickles. "I'm always glad I left the city. But on nights like this, the feeling gets a little stronger."

He knew why she'd left the city, perhaps better than she ever could, because he knew where she came from. What she *was*. But he still wanted to ask, because the answer might reveal the one thing Ashwin had never been able to predict—what went on in her quick, agile brain. "Why did you leave?"

"I didn't plan to," she confessed. "When the Council ordered the strike on Sector Two, I packed up some supplies and headed that way. I knew that it didn't matter how many doctors or medics were there, they'd still need help. But when I got to the checkpoint, I covered my bar codes and bribed the guard." She met his eyes. "That's when I realized I'd already decided I wasn't going back. Ever."

He glanced down, where her twin bar codes marred the smooth skin inside her wrist. "You haven't gotten rid of them yet?"

Kora followed his gaze, then covered the dark lines with her other hand. "It seems silly, doesn't it? But I don't think I'm ready to forget."

"Why would it be silly?" He curled his hand around the rough stone seat until the sharp edges dug into his palm. "We all need reminders sometimes. Of where we're from. Of why we left."

"And of why we can never go there again."

She sounded sad but determined. Kora always sounded determined. The Base was a darker place without her, especially for the Makhai soldiers, who had rarely known compassion from their doctors. But her life could be brighter in One. "You're better off here. Gideon won't ever hold you back from helping people."

"I know." Her arm touched his again—firmly this time, purposefully. Like they were sharing a private joke. "I'll never have to fight him on anything the way I did the COs and administrators on Base. There's always that."

The touch triggered pain, and the pain sparked a memory—a mission over the mountains into what remained of California. He'd gotten into a firefight and spent a rainy night on an exposed mountain ledge, digging a bullet out of his thigh so he could suture the wound.

By the time he made it back to the Base, the wound had started to heal, but imperfectly. Since a badly healed wound might lead to degradation in his performance, protocol dictated that his doctor rip out the stitches and undertake full regeneration to preserve mobility.

Protocol did not dictate pain management.

Ashwin had tried to convince Kora to follow protocol. His own temporary pain was far more manageable than the repercussions she might face for angering the COs. But Kora wasn't like the other doctors, who tiptoed warily around the Makhai soldiers and flinched whenever they moved. Kora had fought with him, stubborn and fierce.

*"Protocol would be torture. If that's what you want, you can find another doctor."*

In the end, he'd acquiesced. Forcing her to hurt him would have hurt her, and she couldn't help what she was any more than he could. "We noticed you fighting for us. Not many people bothered."

She fell silent, her lips pressed together in a firm line, tears glittering on her lashes. When the music changed this time, melting into something slow and suggestive with a heavy, throbbing beat, she stood.

And held out her hand. "Dance with me."

Ashwin could think of half a dozen rational reasons to accept. He'd thought of three before her lips formed the final word of her invitation.

He needed to learn how to interact the way the Riders did if he had any hope of becoming one.

He needed to learn more about Gideon Rios, and Kora had spent the last six months or more under the man's roof.

He needed to find out if proximity to Kora was going to be a problem, because it was swiftly becoming clear that *being careful* wasn't a viable option. Better to find out now, when the mission could still be cleanly aborted.

Another reason formed as he stared up into her eyes, blue-gray and bright with tears. If he had to engage in an awkward social ritual with which he had no experience, Kora was the most obvious partner. She'd understand his ineptitude and help him correct it.

Given time, he could probably round the list out to

an even ten. Ten perfectly logical, artfully rationalized reasons why he should dance with her.

When he took her hand, it was for the one irrational reason.

Oddly, distantly, he wanted to.

Kora had dated some very nice men—by Eden's questionable standards as well as her own more exacting ones. Intelligent men who had fascinated her with their expertise. Charming men who had made her laugh.

Those men had kissed her, too. Sometimes it was awkward, like trying to fit together two mismatching puzzle pieces. Other times, it was pleasurable enough to make her body tingle and her head buzz with possibilities.

But none of them had ever made that happen just by touching her hand.

She fought the urge to rub her thumb over Ashwin's hand as she led him toward the small cleared area where the congregated couples were already swaying to the music. "Have you ever danced before?"

"No." His gaze swept over the nearest couples, cataloguing their stances, the position of their hands, how close they stood. When he turned to face her, he settled his free hand low on her back. The very tip of his thumb brushed the skin bared by her shirt, stroking lightly.

"It's not hard to do." She shivered as she wrapped her arms around his neck. Everything about him was warm, a shocking contrast to the gentle night breeze on her back. "Just move with the music."

His other hand settled on her hip, guiding her to move with him as he swayed gently. "Like this?"

Of course he was a natural. All you had to do was watch him to understand that he was in perfect awareness and control of his body. Even his most mundane movements were poetry, so why would this be any different? "Not bad, soldier."

For a moment, she thought he'd smile. She *felt* it, though his lips didn't so much as twitch. "Thank you."

"You're welcome." Her leg brushed his, and she swallowed a gasp. "This is new."

"Is it?" His thumb grazed her lower back again.

She managed not to shiver this time, but she couldn't stop her nipples from tightening. "Not much like most of our previous encounters, I mean. You're wearing clothes, for one."

"And I haven't been shot. Or stabbed. Or pushed off a building." His gaze found hers. Held it. "This isn't much like my normal missions, either."

"What, the dancing? Or the lack of bodily injury?"

"All of it. If I hadn't met up with the Riders, I'd be in a safe house somewhere, analyzing my next step. Trying to make plans. Researching. I've never had time for…this."

"You had time to kidnap me once." She meant to say it lightly. A tease, because she didn't resent it. A man had been dying, and her intervention had saved him. Most of the time, that would be enough. But the moment she breathed the words, she felt the question lurking beneath them, the one that never really left the back of her mind.

*Why me? And why like that?*

Ashwin stiffened. His fingers dug into her hip. "You weren't supposed to know it was me."

"I realize that." She wanted to give him a good reason why she figured it out, some way he'd accidentally given himself away when he'd pulled her out of her bed in the middle of the night. But she just *knew*. "The man you had me save—Ace Santana. Who is he to you?"

"No one." Ashwin's grip eased somewhat, and he began to move with the music again, but more stiffly, almost self-consciously. "But Lorenzo Cruz is in love with him."

"I suspected that might be the reason." She had vaguely remembered Cruz from her internship on the Base, as well as his service in the city's military police force—a huge, quiet mountain of a man who always seemed a little out of step with the other MPs. But it wasn't until she saw him with Ace after the war that she realized *he* must have been the missing link. The only thing that could motivate Ashwin to save a stranger. "Was it a favor for an old friend or a mission?"

"It was a favor for an associate, one that could have proven vital to my mission. Having Cruz owe me might have been important when the war came."

So logical. So well-reasoned. "You could have just asked me."

"That would have implicated you." His jaw tightened, and his lips pressed together—a rare display of emotion. "I regret the distress I caused you. But the choices I made were intended to shield you from potential repercussions."

"Repercussions?" She had to laugh at that, because he had no idea. She'd been high for *weeks* afterward, high on the adrenaline that came from doing something forbidden and getting away with it. On the sheer joy of helping someone because she wanted to, dammit, not because the Base or the city needed to salvage an asset. "I think that night was the first time I realized they don't own me. They never did."

"No," he said finally. "They never did. And you were more than they deserved."

Her humor faded as he stared down at her, his dark eyes swimming with emotions she couldn't pin down, much less name. Spellbound, she tightened her arms around his neck until her chest brushed his. If she could just get closer, close *enough*…

"I wouldn't have endangered you," he said quietly.

"I know." It seemed to worry him, the idea that she would think it possible, and she resisted the urge to smooth the tiny furrow between his brows. "But why not? There are worse things."

"Worse than being endangered?"

"Mmm." Her fingers moved of their own accord, tracing up and down the back of his neck. "There's being alone. Not feeling anything. Living your whole life in some safe little cage."

He inhaled sharply, a tiny, telling gesture. For Ashwin, it might as well have been a groan. "The first two have never bothered me."

She braced herself for the wave of pity—or, worse, rejection. But she was still looking into his eyes, and she saw the lie this time.

Did he even realize it was a lie? She'd spent most of her career arguing with administrators and psychologists who insisted that Makhai soldiers couldn't feel basic human emotions. Some had considered them above such petty concerns, too advanced and focused to waste precious energy and brainpower on inconsequential things. Others seemed to think them *beneath* it all, animals who only understood instinct and survival.

The truth was both simpler and more complicated.

"You were told that it shouldn't bother you," she corrected softly. "Does that necessarily make it true?"

"No," he conceded. "But it makes it practical. You know what happens to a Makhai soldier who lets himself become bothered."

*Elijah.* The name was legend, a whispered cautionary tale. The officers and psychiatrists brought him up every time they needed to defend the necessity of recalibration and pharmaceutical control. The worst-case scenario, a man who had killed himself because of his obsession.

It had happened before her time, but she'd read the file. Fixations and obsessive thoughts weren't unheard of amongst the ranks of the Makhai soldiers, and reading about Elijah seemed like the best way to learn about them. In a sense, he was Patient Zero. Ever since, the Base psychologists had carefully monitored any and all growing preoccupations—and taken special care to prevent them.

It started with his domestic handler. Every Makhai soldier was assigned one, a woman—or man—who, for all intents and purposes, acted as their sole access to normal socialization and human contact. It was an impossible task for a single person to perform, even under the best of circumstances, and Kora had protested the practice more times than she could remember. She even had a few official reprimands in her file because of it.

These days, domestic handlers were reassigned often, but Elijah had the same one for months, a sweet-faced brunette whose name was never recorded, just her number designation. According to the file, Elijah had subverted her loyalties, convinced her to lie for him when administrators asked her to report on his mental status.

According to the gossip whispered by some of the older employees, she and Elijah had fallen in love.

"Maybe Elijah wasn't bothered," she whispered. "Maybe he just understood something none of his doctors could fathom."

Ashwin's eyes were impossibly dark. "What?"

The music ended, and Kora stood still, her cheeks heating. "Sometimes, you just need to feel close to someone."

All around them, dancers were breaking apart and claiming new partners. Ashwin didn't release her. His hands rested heavily on her skin. His body pressed against hers—his hard chest grazing her nipples, his shoulders tight beneath her arms. He was utterly unmoving but *coiled*, as if he could explode into action in the space of a heartbeat.

"Maybe that's true," he said finally.

There it was, at last, burning in those dark eyes. She wanted to stay right where she was, drowning in it, wrapped in his arms under the winking stars.

Instead, she pulled her arms from around his neck, pushed lightly at his shoulders, and stepped back. "Of course it is. I'm a Rios now, remember? We always speak truth."

Ashwin still didn't move. Didn't stop *watching* her, and now that he wasn't holding her, that intense gaze and coiled energy made it seem like he was about to pounce. "No one always speaks truth."

"I've never lied to you, Ashwin." She took another step, anything to stop herself from moving back into the circle of his arms. "I wouldn't start now."

"I know. You're the exception to every rule."

*Not even close.* She usually prided herself on being rational, after all, yet here she was, making eyes at Ashwin. If it had been Maricela interested in a Makhai soldier, Kora would have warned her off. They didn't have to be as unfeeling as the Base painted them to be a bad idea. They were still dangerous men who led even more dangerous lives.

And she and Ashwin had *history*, even if it was mostly in her head. If she was truly as practical as she'd always thought, she'd walk away. She wouldn't risk her heart.

"I'm only human," she murmured. Fragile, fallible—and just as much of a fool for love as anyone else.

# deacon

Deep into the night, with the party still raging under the inky black sky, Deacon watched.

Nothing in particular, not really—the acolytes having a good time, flirting with the Riders. The Riders flirting right back. And Gideon, talking softly with Del while she kept an eye on her acolytes.

Even Ana was enjoying herself. The newest Rider seemed content to chat with Zeke, and equally content when someone dragged him away to dance. She stood there alone, exuding a sense of quiet peace.

And why shouldn't she? This was literally her legacy. Ana might be new among their ranks, but she'd grown up with the Riders, raised by a father more dedicated to service than to his child.

Sad, really. But he doubted she would agree, so he

held his tongue as he approached and offered her his flask.

Ana accepted it and took a long sip. "Not in a dancing mood tonight, boss?"

"I danced." He folded his hands together behind his back. "Twice."

"That many times, huh?" She took another sip before holding out the flask. "I stand corrected."

He accepted it, rubbing his thumb over the warm steel. "First thing tomorrow, we're making a sweep of the sector. Bishop and Lucio aren't back from their trip yet, but I want everyone else. All hands, and we talk to everyone—I don't give a fuck if they herd goats or have a thousand servants painting all their food with gold leaf. Someone has to have seen something, even if they don't realize it yet."

Ana might enjoy teasing him, but when it came to business she didn't fuck around. "Solo, or in pairs?"

"Pairs." It came out more sharply than he'd intended. "I don't want anyone caught alone and off-guard."

She nodded. "Ivan and I will visit the tenements early. And I'll hit up my dad's contacts, ask them to spread the word."

During his time with the Riders, her father had cultivated an impressive network of what could only be termed spies. "As long as they don't know everything. We can't start a panic."

"Got it." She hesitated, then parted her lips like she was going to say something else, but Gideon broke off from Del and strolled toward them, and the moment passed as she turned to smile at him. "Sir."

"Ana." Gideon clasped her hand, returning her smile with genuine fondness. "I need to borrow Deacon. Do me a favor, please, and make sure Kora and Maricela make it back to the house all right?"

"Of course."

She nodded to Deacon and strode off toward the dancing. Gideon watched her go, the smile lingering. "Walk with me, Deacon."

He'd been waiting all evening for a private moment. "I wanted to talk to you about something."

"I know." Gideon turned toward the path back to the house, and Deacon fell into step beside him. The light from the fire receded behind them, leaving the path illuminated by silver moonlight. Once they were far enough away for the music to fade into a soft, thudding beat, Gideon exhaled softly. "Revolution was supposed to make things simpler, but here we are. Things might be better, but they're not simpler."

Not in the slightest. "You know why he's here."

"Lieutenant Malhotra?" Gideon made an amused noise. "No one *knows* why he's here. Not even him, I'd wager."

Only Gideon Rios would get philosophical about a clusterfuck waiting to happen. "He has orders to infiltrate the Riders, that much is clear."

"It seems likely," Gideon agreed. "I know why I have my suspicions. Why do you have yours?"

Because his gut burned with unease every time he looked at Ashwin, for starters. But he had better, more rational reasons, too. "He's making himself at home, and he isn't pushing me hard to move on the deserters. If he was anyone else, I'd say he was being polite—you know, in another man's house, and all. But he's not anyone else. He's Makhai, and he's content for now." Deacon pinned his leader with a look. "Which means his *real* mission is coming along just fine."

"Fair enough." Gideon stopped in the middle of the path and faced Deacon. "What would you do with him, if it were up to you?"

"You're not gonna like it."

"I asked. Tell me, whether I'll like it or not."

"Get rid of him," he said bluntly. "A rabid dog is still a danger, even though it's not his fault."

"What about a whipped one? A dog that's been kicked and starved by its master until the only thing it knows how to do is fight?"

"Depends on the dog, I guess."

"Or on what sort of life you have to offer by comparison." Gideon tilted his head back to stare up at the stars. "You know that if I thought he was a danger to Kora or Maricela, or to any of my Riders, he wouldn't be here."

Oh, he knew. It was why he chose to follow Gideon—not because of the traditions of One, or the mission of the Riders, but because Gideon could look at people like Ashwin and see things like this. How a deeply disciplined soldier possibly sent to kill him had the potential to become a trusted ally, even a beloved brother.

Deacon nodded. "And you know I don't question you. I just needed to make sure."

"No, Deacon." Gideon rested a hand on his shoulder. "I always want you to question me. It's your right. Just like it's your right to know what I'm thinking. And there's one reason I'm confident that the Base miscalculated."

No question what he meant. "Kora."

"Kora." Gideon let his hand fall away and resumed walking. "Either the Base doesn't know she's here, or they don't know the lengths to which Ashwin has gone in the past in order to protect her from them. I think Lieutenant Malhotra is loyal to exactly one person in the world."

Which made the whole goddamn thing even more of a gamble. "It doesn't bother you, that person not being you?"

"No." There was no hesitation. No doubt. "I have faith in Kora's heart."

So did Deacon. But her heart couldn't work fucking miracles, and it couldn't save a man who didn't understand the concept of salvation. Hell, Kora knew that, too, and it still might not stop her from trying. So there was a very good chance that Ashwin would only break her heart.

"But Deacon?"

"Yeah?"

A cold light glinted in Gideon's eyes. "Mercy only goes so far."

"Understood." There were limits even to Gideon's benevolence, lines that could be crossed. And if Ashwin Malhotra so much as inched a toe over one of those lines, Deacon would be there to put a bullet in his skull.

# six

Ashwin hadn't been this close to Eden in nearly six months.

A lot could change in six months.

The first time he'd seen the city had been from the sky. He'd just turned twelve years old and was packed into one of the Base's precious helicopters with seven other Makhai soldiers prepared to embark on their first month of survival training.

From the air, Eden glittered. Sun glinted off the endless glass windows on the tallest buildings. Cars zipped down carefully ordered roads, and people filled the sidewalks, the parks, the open marketplaces and squares. A little slice of the world-that-had-been, a perfect circle of luxury and ease encased in a massive wall that kept out the squalor of the sectors.

As an adult, he'd learned that the graceful perfection was a lie. That the men who ruled Eden were greedy and lazy and oozed hypocrisy. That they preyed upon the people they kept powerless and indulged their every petty urge. That the men and women of the Base lived hard lives of sacrifice and dedication to a common goal, while the politicians they served wasted resources with malicious recklessness.

All from behind the safety of their precious wall.

He remembered the day the wall surrounding the city fell. The memories were still crisp and sharp, but long months of recalibration had stripped them of emotion. He could visualize the chaotic charge, the sector leaders driving for the heart of Eden itself. He could recreate the slow trickle of citizens rising up to join them, until a trickle became a river, and a river became a sea of rage.

He could remember the moment he found Kora in the middle of that madness. The knot of people surrounding her. The Special Tasks soldiers closing in, shooting at them. Shooting at *her*.

He could remember the beautiful simplicity of his rage. The purity of purpose as he charged into the fray, oblivious to the bullets rending his flesh, because every soldier he killed was one who couldn't threaten her anymore.

He could remember the joy he'd felt when he touched her. The devastation when she refused to leave the patient bleeding out at her feet and come with him to safety. The helpless desperation as his hands tightened on her arms until fear filled her eyes.

He could remember feeling. He simply couldn't remember what it had felt like to feel.

Now, staring at the crumbling remains of Eden's walls, he thought there was...a flutter. A tickle across his tongue. Something that tasted like satisfaction.

The people of Sector One had been busy. Where the main checkpoint to Sector One had once stood, now there was a massive stone foundation. Walls rose four feet all the way around, the stones reclaimed from the barrier that had once divided the sector from the city. A temple, according to the Base's intel.

A temple the newly liberated lower class of Eden was rushing to join in droves.

But the temple wasn't the only new construction. A vast array of makeshift shelters spread out from it on either side, some built from the same stone, sound and almost cozy. Others were little more than wood and rope and thin tarps flapping in the breeze.

Ashwin stood next to Deacon and tried to take in the sheer number of refugees—more than could possibly have come from One alone. "I didn't realize there were so many."

"They've been coming from every direction." Deacon indicated the city, then east and west of its former border. "Some out of Seven and Eight, and from Two. And then the homeless from the city."

The bombing of Sector Two had been the catalyst for war—and the final straw that incited a mini-coup on the Base. An airstrike ordered by a petulant, vengeful bureaucrat that had targeted training houses full of would-be courtesans. Not a military threat, not a security risk. Houses full of women and girls.

"Most of the Base regretted what happened in Two." It was privileged information, but Ashwin could see the strategic value in its revelation. Especially when Deacon still didn't trust him. "It fractured the leadership. The general who ordered the strike was permanently relieved from duty."

Deacon laughed, a sound devoid of amusement.

"You'd better tell me that's a euphemism, or I'll kick your ass on principle."

"Yes." Ashwin turned back to the sea of sad little shacks and tents. People milled in front of the closest one, watching Deacon with an awe untouched by fear. "I wasn't there for it, but I've read the reports. Two generals, three colonels, a major, and six captains were killed in the coup. Everyone who was loyal to the corrupt councilmen."

"Good." Deacon's shoulder bumped Ashwin's hard as he brushed past. "Because this isn't even the worst of what they did. These are the survivors. The happy endings."

Ashwin was accustomed to fear. But something far more cutting lurked beneath Deacon's words.

Disdain.

It could be lethal to Ashwin's mission, and that was reason enough for concern. But as he fell into step behind Gideon's second-in-command, he found it harder than usual to compartmentalize the sheer volume of suffering surrounding him. He noticed details this time. The hungry-looking children clinging to their parents' legs as he passed. The men and women with scarred faces and threadbare clothing, smudged with dirt and coughing at the dust. The flimsiness of their shelters every time the wind picked up and threatened to tear them apart.

Did Kora come here? She must. She wouldn't be able to stop herself. The pain would draw her like a moth to the only source of light. She'd take their suffering inside herself and fight it like the highly skilled warrior she was. But it would chip away at her, fracture her psyche bit by bit. Because of the secret Ashwin hadn't let himself think in six months.

Because of who she was. *What* she was.

The only way to protect her from it was to stamp out suffering. To fix the world. The hopeless goal of out-of-touch dreamers.

And Deacon.

He stopped in the center of an open-sided tent clustered with tables, where a man was gathering dishes and silverware into a large plastic tub. "Is Stasa around?"

"In the kitchen." The man grinned widely as he held up an empty bowl. "Hit the line if you're hungry. Beef stew today."

"Thanks. Maybe later." Deacon lowered his voice as they made their way past a serving station loaded with trays. "The families with farms and ranches donate food, and the temple pays the refugees who prepare it. Stasa runs the kitchen. I think she used to cook for one of the brothels in Two."

Stasa turned out to be a short, solid woman with a ready smile and the eyes of someone who could kill a man without that smile faltering. The glasses perched on her nose, the brightly colored apron tied around her waist, and the matching scarf covering her hair gave the appearance of someone pleasantly harmless, but her easy grip on her knife and the way she sized Ashwin up when he stepped into her kitchen told the real story.

"Deacon." She tilted her head so he could kiss her cheek, then waved the knife toward Ashwin. "Who is your friend?"

"This is Ashwin. He's helping us out with a problem."

"Mmm, the raiders." She sniffed with disapproval, then went back to chopping vegetables, her blade flashing. "I have heard a few stories."

If the woman really had worked in one of Sector

Two's training houses, she likely knew more about the darker side of politics than most. "What stories have you heard?"

She muttered something under her breath. "They sound like soldiers, but they act like bandits. Anything these people managed to bring, these men take. Pathetic."

"That explains why no one's come to Gideon yet." Deacon locked his hands behind his head with a groan. "They're targeting refugees."

"I tell them." Stasa dumped the board full of chopped carrots into a bowl and shrugged. "I tell them to go to Rios, but they don't trust leaders. If they were accustomed to fair treatment from them, they would not be refugees."

Robbing refugees would be effortless for men with Base training. It would also be unsatisfying—it was unlikely anyone living in the desperate conditions had much to take. It also explained the reckless haste of their escalation—true, Ashwin had timed his bait about the temple drop carefully, but he'd still been prepared for an organized attack, not the chaotic, disjointed attempt they'd mustered.

The question was whether failure would drive them back to the easy targets, or prompt them to plan their attacks more carefully. "When was the last attack?"

"Yesterday. They robbed a man who's been buying and selling clothes and shoes." The knife hit the small wooden counter with a thump. "Took everything he owned."

"Shit. Thanks, Stasa." Deacon tried to press something into her hand. She waved him away, but he folded her fingers around the money anyway. "I owe you. I mean it."

"You owe me nothing."

"I'll come back later, and we can argue about it some more," Deacon promised. "Take care of yourself."

He ducked out a side exit, leading them into the bright sunlight behind the soup kitchen, near the truck he'd parked at the edge of the small refugee camp. "Money spends no matter what," he growled, "but I can only think of a few reasons why someone would steal clothes."

"Disguises." Ashwin identified the twinge of discomfort, but it took him a moment to recognize it as worry. "Gideon's estate. Is it still secure, even with all of the Riders gone?"

Deacon snorted. "The only thing scarier than a Rider is a Rios family guard." He pinned Ashwin with a sharp look as he yanked open the driver's side door of the truck and reached for the radio inside. "Don't worry, Kora will be fine."

Ashwin stilled, unsure if the words were a test or a warning, but positive they were a message. His concern for Kora had not gone unnoticed. His weakness had been exposed.

Deacon was leaning through the open door, one hand busy with the radio, his back to Ashwin. He could be dead in moments. The first bullet through the radio so he couldn't transmit a call for help, the second through the back of his skull. Quick, painless. His knowledge of Kora's value as leverage would die with him.

So would Ashwin's mission.

His hand crept toward his gun.

The radio crackled with sudden static, then silence as Deacon pressed the button. "Riders, be advised our guests may have ditched their tactical gear in order to keep a low profile. Over."

Ashwin curled his fingers toward his palm. The

instinct to strike fast and hard had been honed by a life in Eden, but here in One, it would do more harm than good. Whatever Gideon Rios's endgame was, the men and women who followed him *believed.* Deacon might needle Ashwin out of personal dislike, but the man wouldn't risk Kora's safety. He wouldn't betray her to the Base.

Ashwin was the only one betraying her right now.

The radio crackled again, and Ana's voice drifted out. "Got it, boss. All clear so far at the tenements. Over."

Gabe came next. "We just finished up at my cousin's estate and are headed out to see Hunter's family. No leads. Over."

"Am I the only one who wants more details?" Zeke asked, his voice scratchy. "Can you be more specific about what we're looking for?"

"Zeke—" Deacon cut off abruptly, rubbing his temple as he blew out an exasperated breath.

"Just a rough idea. We need—"

Gunfire exploded over the radio, followed by screams. Ashwin snapped into action, vaulting over the hood of Deacon's truck and hauling open the door as Zeke's curses spilled out of the speaker. "We need backup. We're at Bradford's silversmith—"

The transmission ended abruptly. Ashwin hauled the door shut as Deacon hit the gas, spinning dirt and gravel as they took off. Deacon steered with one hand, his jaw as set and clenched as his hand around the radio. "Montero," he barked.

"We're on our way," Gabe replied.

"Fuck. *Fuck.*" Deacon slammed the handset against the wheel hard enough to elicit a burst of static from the radio. Then he adjusted it in his grip and spoke more softly. "Ana—you and Ivan head that way, too."

"Got it, boss."

Ashwin braced himself against the door as Deacon took a hard left onto one of the main roads. He watched people scramble out of the way as the truck shot forward, but most of his mind churned over the implications.

He'd miscalculated the stakes and the speed of escalation. *Again.*

Predicting people's actions had never been his specialty, but he should have guessed. He knew all soldiers were given basic training in operating covertly in the various sectors. He should have warned Deacon. The fact that it was tangential to his primary mission was no excuse—before the war, he'd frequently maintained no less than five concurrent objectives without letting the details overwhelm him.

Maybe the six agonizing months of recalibration had damaged him in some way he couldn't properly assess.

Or maybe Kora was already more of a distraction than he realized.

The truck had shot past the edge of the last tenement and out onto the dusty road leading to Gideon's estate when the radio finally crackled. Even through the staticky speaker, Gabe sounded tense. "The remaining threats have been eliminated. No civilian casualties. But Zeke and Jaden are both in bad shape. I don't know if they'll make it to the hospital. Orders?"

Deacon shuddered before lifting the handset again. "Bring them to Gideon's."

"Understood."

After that, silence. Deacon gripped the wheel like he could wrestle events back under his control by will alone, and Ashwin could relate to the responsibility of it, if not the worry. "Kora's there," he said quietly. "I've seen her put men back together when there was barely enough left of them to give her a place to start."

"If they don't—" Deacon bit off the words and turned his head, keeping his eyes on Ashwin instead of the road for dangerously long seconds. "We both know this is on you."

For the space of a heartbeat, Ashwin considered the gun again. Shooting Deacon while they were tearing down a road as fast as the truck could go was reckless, but there was brittle, raw *truth* in the man's eyes.

Deacon wasn't talking about a lapse in Ashwin's judgment or his failure to warn them about the possibilities. Deacon suspected Ashwin's true mission. Perhaps he had from the beginning.

The man was smart. Too smart to trust him.

Perversely, it made Ashwin reluctant to kill him. "Why didn't you put a bullet in my head the first night?"

"Oh, I would have. But Gideon..." Deacon glared at the road ahead. "Gideon believes in miracles."

No leader as clever as Gideon Rios actually depended on miracles. Which meant Gideon was counting on something else. Some*one* else.

Kora.

As plans went, it wasn't even that reckless. Gideon had what few other people alive did—concrete proof that Ashwin had cared enough about Kora to hide her in the dangerous months leading up to the war. But he had no way of knowing that six months of medically prescribed torture had hollowed out Ashwin's weak, vulnerable parts.

Gideon expected Kora to subvert his loyalties. If Ashwin wanted to complete his mission, all he had to do was give Gideon his miracle.

#

Kora wasn't used to people dying under her hands.

Back on the Base, she'd been so far removed from the battles that true emergencies were rare and terrifying. Either the squad medics stabilized a fallen soldier so he could be brought in for regeneration, or they brought him back in a bag.

The war was a different story. But even then, she'd had luck on her side. She could count on one hand the number of patients she'd lost, who had slipped away while she frantically tried to turn the tide.

And she'd never known their names.

Jaden was bleeding out on Gideon's priceless formal dining table. There hadn't been enough time to relocate Kora's equipment to the barracks or the temple, so here they were, silent faces clustered around the opulent room while blood dripped onto the tile floor.

She brushed her hair out of her eyes and reached for another clamp. Jaden should have already been through regeneration treatment. It was the only thing with any hope of restoring his shredded liver, not to mention the bullet hole in his stomach. But Kora had to get ahead of the bleeding first, stabilize him enough to make regeneration therapy possible, and every second that ticked by pushed that goal farther out of reach. As soon as she repaired one severed vessel, she found another bleeder.

And the seconds kept ticking by.

"Kora."

She ignored Gideon's voice and glanced up at the other end of the table, where Ashwin was monitoring Zeke, who was pale and sweaty, hovering somewhere between pained consciousness and oblivion. "How's his pulse?"

"Weaker."

"Dammit, I need more *time*." She'd clamped everything she could clamp, and he was still oozing blood faster than she could replace it.

"Kora." Gideon clasped her shoulder. "Zeke needs you."

"No. I can do this." To hell with the risk. She'd never stabilize Jaden with his liver so damaged. So she turned, replaced her soiled, bloody gloves with new ones, and opened her regeneration kit. "This is his only—"

"It's over," Deacon said quietly. He was standing at the corner of the table closest to Jaden's head, his hand resting on the side of the man's face. Less than an inch from his fingers, Jaden's eyes stared blankly up at the brick-lined vaulted ceiling.

Gabe closed his eyes and whispered a prayer. Next to him, Ivan turned and slammed a fist into the wall, splintering cracks through the plaster.

Gideon laid a hand on Jaden's forehead. "We'll take care of him, Kora. See to Zeke."

She couldn't move. She stood there for what seemed like a hellish eternity, locked in place by shock and shame. She'd failed. All her training, all her years of experience, and she'd come up lacking. Inadequate.

People had called her brilliant all her life, but what did that matter if she couldn't save someone when it counted?

In a fog, she took over Zeke's care, ignoring Ashwin when he fell into position to assist her. She worked in a daze, her hands moving automatically but her mind still focused on Jaden's half-open, staring eyes.

It only made her more ashamed of herself. Zeke deserved one hundred percent of her attention, and she just didn't have it to give. Even when his pulse steadied and his blood pressure normalized, she felt... empty. She started his regeneration therapy, focusing on repairing one thing at a time, like putting one foot in front of the other.

And then there was nothing left to repair, and

Ashwin's hand was on her wrist, guiding her fingers away before she could reassure herself by checking the pulse pounding in the hollow of Zeke's throat. "He's okay, Kora. You did well."

The words pierced through the comforting numbness, and something lurched in her chest, painful and tight. "I need to go."

"Get some rest." The gentle timbre of Gideon's voice couldn't hide his pain, and the sensation in her chest swelled until it threatened to choke her. "I'll arrange for someone to watch over Zeke and let you know if you're needed."

She turned and stumbled into the blessedly dark back hall. Tucked away beyond the kitchens, where she could still smell the cinnamon and vanilla from breakfast, was a narrow staircase leading up to the east wing. Kora made it up three steps before her knees locked, so she leaned her forehead against the cool wall and willed herself—*willed herself*—not to throw up.

"Dr. Bellamy." She hadn't heard his footsteps, but Ashwin's voice came from right next to her ear. His large hand settled between her shoulders, a touch as tentative as the word that came next. "Kora."

"I'm okay." The words scraped out of her throat, strangled and so far from true that she almost wanted to laugh. "No, I'm not."

"No, you're not." He leaned against the wall, so close she could feel him all along her body, but the only point of contact was the gentle touch at her back. "He was gone before he got to you. No one could have saved him."

"I know that." But she'd done plenty of things that *no one* should have been able to do. She'd been trained for that, to step in when other doctors had given up hope. "I know."

"But you still grieve." He stroked her spine. "It's why you're so good. But I wish it didn't hurt you like this."

"Good." The laugh did bubble up then, flat and derisive. "What good is *good* if this still happens?"

He turned her slowly, until her back was against the wall and there was no place to look but *him*. He filled the staircase, a tall shadow clad in black leather and denim. He looked more like a Rider than he did a soldier, especially when he tilted her chin up and forced her to meet his eyes.

No blankness there. His eyes *seethed*. "Zeke was almost gone, too. No one else could have put him back together. Death beats you so rarely, it's all you can see when it happens. But most of the time, you win. You won with Zeke."

She tried to close her eyes, to block out the emotion surging in him before it could make *her* feel things, too. Things she couldn't even think about in a dark stairwell with a dead man's blood on her clothes.

But she couldn't look away.

"Say it, Kora." His thumb smoothed along her jaw, coaxing. "*I saved Zeke.*"

"Ashwin—"

"Just say it."

The pressure in her chest eased, just a little, with her whisper. "I saved Zeke."

"Yes." His thumb trailed down, blazing hot against her skin as he stroked over the pulse fluttering in her throat. "Say it one more time. Believe it."

Her knees weren't locked now. They were weak, and she pressed both hands flat against the wall to steady herself. "I saved him."

"You saved him." Ashwin squeezed her shoulder lightly. "Do you need help getting upstairs?"

"No." Suddenly, she was sure she could make it. That she could do anything. "I'm okay. I mean it this time."

He took a step down the stairs, bringing them almost to the same height. "If you need anything, I'll be in the barracks."

She nodded, turned up the stairs, then stopped. "Thank you, Ashwin."

It took forever for him to answer, as if he wasn't used to being thanked. "You're welcome."

# seven

Throughout his life, even in his moments of most profound psychological fracture, Ashwin had always taken pride in one thing. He might sometimes behave irrationally, but he never lied to himself about it.

Tonight, there was nothing left for him to be proud of.

As he used a microdriver to open the casing on the surveillance drone, he tried to trace back to the start of his mission and identify the first lie he'd told himself.

Was it the night he danced with her, when he'd convinced himself that close contact was necessary for him to adequately assess the risk she posed to his emotional stability? Or was it earlier, when he'd sworn to be careful around her?

Had the lie started the moment he climbed into

Deacon's truck, confident that he could alter his plans to accommodate her presence? Or when she'd flown into his arms, and he'd told himself he'd forgotten what wanting felt like?

Wanting ached. It was less and more and worse than physical desire. Physical desire was chemical, simple. Cause and effect. Visual and tactical stimulus resulting in pleasure, and he understood how it worked within his body.

How it would work in hers.

And there was this wanting. This odd, unprovoked tightening of muscle. The low thrum of arousal. He'd fucked women before. Domestic handlers were easiest to deal with when their loyalties were subverted, and since Ashwin wasn't the type to inspire affection, he'd mostly used pleasure as his weapon. But he'd never felt this... *craving* before. A desire for someone who wasn't already in front of him, who couldn't easily be replaced.

*Lie.*

Was this how easily delusion snuck in for humans? He'd always imagined they lied to themselves desperately, knowingly, battering themselves against the truth until they buried it under their preferred version of reality.

But here he was, lying to himself about when he'd last lied to himself.

He knew this craving. It had built over weeks and months, hollowing him out from the inside, until not having Kora within reach had become physically intolerable. He'd been half-mad with it by the time the war started. Consumed by it.

And then he'd found her during the final battle. Touched her. Tried to take her away, even though a man was bleeding out under her hands. She'd fought him. Of course she'd fought him. And he'd been so frantic that he'd curled his fingers around her arms so tightly she must have had bruises for days.

The bruises weren't the worst part. The fear in her eyes was.

She had always been the one person who never looked at him with terror. The only person who didn't see him as a monster. And he'd *hurt* her.

In that moment, he'd known. He'd *known*. He had to go back to the Base and let them wipe her from his mind, his DNA. His soul. Because if he tried to drag her away, to keep her safe...

She'd break under the fear, and he'd break with her.

Another truth he didn't want to acknowledge hovered as he pulled out the drone's circuit board and started untangling the wires that connected it to its power source. He'd never avoided unpalatable truths before. Doing so now, with the proof of it under his fingers, was evidence of his increasingly irrational emotional state.

If the Base ever discovered that he'd brought a drone into Gideon Rios's grasp, the punishment would be severe. If they found out what he planned to do with it...

Even Makhai soldiers could be court-martialed and executed for treason.

A quiet knock sounded on his door, and he answered without looking up. "Come in."

Kora opened the door and peered inside. "Hi."

*Wanting* exploded through him. He could still feel her skin beneath his fingertips, the racing beat of her pulse under his thumb. Even the pain of looking at her had grown sweeter somehow, a teasing, delicious sting.

For a soldier meant to be free of emotion, he was drowning in impossible feeling.

She hovered uncertainly in the doorway, and the

rationalizations came fast and hard. He should invite her in. Seduce her. Purge all this wanting and bind her to him so tightly that Gideon Rios would have his miracle. Ashwin's place would be secure.

*Lie. Lie, lie, lie.*

Did it make him more or less rational to acknowledge the lies before he gave into them? "Come in."

She slipped into the room, clad in simple cotton pants and a tank top. Clothes meant for sleeping, insufficient protection against the cool night air.

"I didn't come empty-handed." She held up a half-finished bottle of O'Kane whiskey as she closed the door behind her. "I mean, I stole this from Gideon's study."

The label marked it as one of the higher quality liquors produced by the leader of Sector Four. Expensive to come by, but even if Gideon hadn't been rich, his cousin was one of Dallas O'Kane's loyal lieutenants.

Ashwin had never developed a taste for liquor, but he understood the appeal it held for most people—numbness. He couldn't imagine how much alcohol it would take to numb Kora's emotions. Enough to harm her, undoubtedly. "Do you like whiskey?"

"The smooth stuff? The good stuff? Yes." The bottle sloshed as she dropped to the foot of Ashwin's bunk. "But I can't bring myself to drink it. Feels like cheating, you know—like covering the bar codes. Forgetting, when what I deserve is to remember."

The self-flagellation was as much a part of Kora as her brilliance and her compassion. It was baked into her DNA as surely as violence and indifference was coded into his.

The only difference was that he knew it.

He pushed his chair away from the desk and extended a hand. "Come here."

"I'm not feeling sorry for myself," she insisted. "It's just that I can't sleep, and I thought this might help. But then I—I couldn't actually open the bottle and just drink it."

"Kora." He put steel in her name, the edge of command that had left Eden's military police scrambling to fall in line during his brief tenure leading them. "Come here."

She obeyed this time, crossing the room with slow steps before stopping just out of reach to stare down at him with her disheveled hair falling into her face. "You're the only person here who knows me better than you knew Jaden." Judging from the way she clutched her chest, the confession caused her physical pain. "You're the only one who might understand why a man is dead, but I can't stop making it all about me."

He understood better than she did. Better than she ever could. He knew the truth that had been erased from the Base's main files and lingered only in secret archives. That Project Makhai had been one-half of a dual-pronged plan to produce perfect soldiers and perfect healers—and that Project Panacea had been terminated when it became clear that perfect healers were unwilling to respect the chain of command above all else.

Or embrace the idea of acceptable losses.

Kora shouldn't exist. The stress of internalizing so much suffering had driven the first generation of healers mad. The infants of Kora's generation had vanished. Since the Base wasn't above murdering babies who would take up resources and provide nothing in exchange, Ashwin had always assumed they'd all been terminated.

And then he met Kora.

Her eyes were wild. Feverish. Even pressed to her

chest, her hands trembled. The pain of failure and loss had seeped into her like poison. He grasped her hips and pulled her to sit across his lap, tucking her close to him with her head beneath his chin.

Then he wrapped both arms around her and held her. "Tell me."

"I don't know how to stop." Her voice hitched. "I can't get it all straight in my head. I should be mourning Jaden—I want to, I *need* to—but I can't. It isn't that I don't care, I just..." She drifted into silence until a shudder wracked her. "I hit a wall. This place where if I push past it, if I *feel* anything else, then I'll explode."

Ashwin took his time sliding his hand up her back and under the wild tumble of her hair. Brushing her skin with his fingertips sent warning shocks of pain skittering up his spine. Once, during the war, he'd forced a fellow Makhai soldier to inject the torturous drugs meant for aversion therapy into his veins. It had been a last-ditch effort, a desperate attempt to dislodge her from his brain.

It hadn't worked. Oh, he associated Kora with pain. He associated pain with Kora. But the line between pain and pleasure was dangerously thin. As he curled his fingers around the back of her neck, the heat crawling up his spine melted across that line. Obliterated it.

"Close your eyes," he ordered softly.

Her hand clenched in his shirt.

He couldn't tell her it would be okay, and he wouldn't urge her to trust him. There was only one thing he had to offer her. "You need something right now, Kora, and I know how to provide it. But I won't do anything you don't want me to do. It's your choice."

She sat up straight, her brows drawn into a confused frown. But slowly, slowly, she closed her eyes.

He'd never had the luxury of simply studying her

face before. He traced his gaze over the arch of her brows, down the thin bridge of her nose to the place where the tip turned up just a few millimeters. Down farther, to the full curve of her slightly parted lips, and beneath that to the delicate point of her chin.

He'd never noticed her freckles before. There were just a few scattered across her cheeks. He touched one, and she inhaled, sharp and shaky. Then she sank her teeth into her lower lip and tilted her face to his touch.

Such naked need. All the signs of arousal were there—flushed skin, tight nipples. Shortened breath. The openness of it was a soothing change from the way people hid their emotions behind false smiles and frowns.

All he had to do was touch her, and her body spilled her secrets. When he stroked her, she trembled against him. When his knuckle grazed the spot where her throat met her jaw, goose bumps rose on her arms. He took note of her reaction, factoring it in to his overall strategy.

The first time he bit her, it would be there.

Her flimsy top left her shoulders bare. He touched her there next, dragging his fingers down her smooth, unmarked skin. He noted the ticklish spot inside her elbow, and the way her breathing hitched when he brushed a thumb over the inside of her wrist.

There. That was where he'd start.

Without taking his gaze from her face, he lifted her hand and parted his lips. He knew, rationally, that her skin couldn't taste sweet. It had to be his pleasure at the way her eyes flew open, then half-closed with heavy desire when he licked her.

He kissed her palm. The tips of her fingers. Slow, careful. Precise. Her inner arm. Her shoulder. The delicate line of her collarbone. The hollow at her throat.

He lulled her with soft touches until she was clutching at his shoulders, her breath quickening as she pulled him closer. Her hip rubbed against his cock when she squirmed, briefly diverting his attention to his own state of physical arousal.

It would be effortless to indulge himself. She'd go to his bed willingly. Eagerly. With an exhilarating lack of nerves and fear, because she wouldn't be like his domestic handlers—bedding him at first out of duty, and then out of eagerness for the way he could make her body react.

Kora would want *him*.

He could take her to bed and give Gideon Rios the miracle he wanted. A Makhai soldier, infatuated. It would appeal to the man's religious pretensions, his conceit that love was all-powerful. He'd welcome Ashwin with open arms, and there would be no obligation to choose between Kora and his mission.

The bed was right there, but he couldn't do it. She had come to him hurting and wounded, recklessly and foolishly trusting him to make it better. It didn't matter that he'd never asked for her trust, or that he was already violating it in too many ways. By not telling her why he was here. By not telling her who and what she was.

He couldn't do it with this, not with *pleasure*. It was the only thing he could offer her that would be untainted by lies, by their pasts and their uncertain futures, by the impossibility of who they were and the world they lived in.

He would give her this. Release. And as long as he didn't speak, he wouldn't have to lie.

When she squirmed against him again, he tilted her chin up, found that sensitive spot on the edge of her jaw, and closed his teeth on it. Kora sighed, a sound full of sensual anticipation, and grasped his hand. Her eyes locked with his as she tugged his hand from her hip, up under the hem of her thin tank top, to the bare skin of her rib cage.

Had anyone ever touched her like this? He knew she'd dated in Eden, placid, polite dates that ended at her front door. Sometimes he had watched the surveillance videos, barely able to contain the need to find those men and eliminate them before they could hurt her.

And they would have hurt her. Eden's moralistic strictures spurned physical hedonism and tactile affection. Sex was meant to be sterile. Perfunctory. A woman's duty, especially when she'd received dispensation to procreate, but not something she should enjoy.

Kora *felt*. She couldn't hide it. She shivered and flushed and sighed with pleasure, and when he shifted his hand higher to cup the soft weight of her breast, she did all three at once. Her head fell against his shoulder and her lips parted, and he knew—he *knew*. No one had ever touched her like this. If they had, they would have tried to shame these reactions out of her.

He was glad no one had tried. He didn't have time to go back into Eden and kill them.

"Ashwin." Her breath tickled over his ear and then his cheek. She whispered his name again, barely audible in the near-silence of the room, and kissed him.

The pain, which had settled to a low hum, spiked wildly.

*Kora. Agony.*

Hurt was an insufficient word. Acid slid through his veins, the ghost of remembered pain, no less severe for being manufactured by his mind. It boiled higher with the sweet, hesitant brush of her lips over his, like a final, desperate warning.

*Agony. Kora.*

His cock was hard. Extremely, atypically hard. So hard that the next rock of her hip against him drove a hoarse, unintended moan from his throat, and he could no longer separate what felt good from what felt bad. It was all sensation, all heat.

All Kora.

He locked both hands on her hips and hauled her up, breaking their kiss for a miserable, endless moment. Then he settled her on his lap, astride his cock, with only a few layers of cotton and his painfully tight jeans separating them as he dragged her to him.

Her lips parted. Before she could question, before she could say anything that he'd have to answer with a lie, he drove his hands into her hair and kissed her again. It was Kora's turn to moan, and he drank in the sound as she braced her hands on his shoulders and rocked against him.

Eager. *Desperate.* He dropped one hand to her hip and helped her smooth out her rhythm, guiding her to roll her hips in a steady, maddening tempo. When she'd caught on to the motion, he slipped his hand beneath her shirt again, cupping her breast as his thumb found her nipple.

Her teeth sank into his lower lip as she shuddered.

She needed more. A strategic application of sensation, enough to break through the walls holding in her pain. Ignoring the throbbing need in his own body, he watched the color rise in her cheeks, waited for the moment her head fell back and her lips parted on a gasp.

Then he pinched her nipple.

She came with a halting cry of shock and relief. Her nails raked his shoulders as she rode him through the pleasure, and Ashwin focused on each burning line to distract him from pondering how thin the fabric of her pants was. How wet. How little separated her clenching heat from his fingers and tongue.

It wasn't necessary. He'd achieved his goal without adding the complication and temptation of stripping her naked. But as she shuddered and gasped in his lap, Ashwin found himself battling a newly awakened and utterly alien emotion.

Carnal curiosity.

Unlike the wanting, his curiosity was precise and explicit. The list of things he needed to know was well-ordered and action-oriented.

He needed to know how she would react if he stripped off her clothes. If she'd still be shameless when he placed her on the chair and knelt between her spread legs. If the flush rolling down her neck would cover her whole body when he pressed his open mouth to her pussy. If she'd turn shy when he worked his tongue into her. If her thighs would close on his shoulders. If she'd dig her nails into the back of his head, whisper his name when she came. How all of those things would change the second time. If she'd grow more languid with every orgasm, or more tense. How many times she could come before she begged him to stop.

And that was just the first thing on his list.

Kora cupped his face between her hands and kissed him again. Her tongue touched his, retreated, and returned for a more thorough, lingering exploration. The intimacy of it spilled through him, and for a selfish moment he let himself wallow in just...being kissed. Sweetly. Wonderingly.

Like he was a normal man.

But the pain still burning through him was a harsh reminder that he wasn't. So he took her shoulders and gently pulled her back. “How do you feel now?”

“Better.” Her eyes were still glazed, dreamy. “Can I stay?”

“Yes.” The answer came immediately, before he considered the implications. Surely someone as protective as Gideon would be alarmed to find Kora missing from her bed—but it was just as likely that the guards watching over the family knew exactly where she was. Letting her spend the night in his bed could work in his favor.

And if it didn’t...he didn’t care.

“Thank you. For everything.”

Ashwin wrapped his arms around her and rose in silence, unsettled by her gratitude in the face of his deception. When he reached the bed, he let her slide to the floor and turned her toward it. “I still have work to do on this equipment, but you should try to get some sleep.”

She gripped his hand. “Just for a little while?”

She seemed so vulnerable. Undone. The strap of her tank top had slipped down her arm. Her hair fell in a disheveled mess around her shoulders, the strands still tangled where he’d twisted them around his fingers. Tiny, seemingly inconsequential incongruities, but for a woman as efficient and in control as Kora, they were screeching dissonance.

He knew how to take her apart, but not how to put her back together again.

Her fingers clenched around his. Her muscles tensed, as if she was already drawing in tight to brace herself for rejection, and her uncertainty scraped him raw. He’d accepted the imperfect reality that her pain was intolerable to him. But if even her discomfort left him this unsettled...

*Stop lying to yourself.*

Placing his hand between her shoulder blades was dangerous. Guiding her onto the mattress was reckless. Stretching out beside her was foolish. Every spark between them was a lit match in a room full of explosives, but without access to the full truth, she only saw the comforting warmth of the flame.

She cuddled into his side with a soft sigh, and Ashwin wrapped one stiff arm around her, giving her his shoulder for a pillow. The position felt awkward at first. He was acutely aware of the weight of her head, the angle of her neck, the way her breasts pressed against him, the feel of her hip under his hand. He froze when she shifted with a sleepy murmur. Her hand settled on his bare chest, and her toes brushed his ankle.

Then she stilled as her breathing slowed into the steady rhythm of sleep. Her warmth melted through the stiffness in his body until his muscles relaxed and he started to enjoy the pressure of her body against his.

None of his domestic handlers had wanted this. Even the ones who had fancied themselves in love with him had been more interested in fucking. He'd always wondered how they fooled themselves into believing they wanted anything more than the endorphins and pleasure from intense sex when they revealed themselves every time they slipped from between the sheets and crept back to their own beds.

He never blamed them. In all honesty, he'd appreciated being spared the necessity of asking them to leave. Makhai soldiers could get by on a minimal amount of low-quality sleep for periods that would critically damage a normal man, but even he needed rest sometimes. And resting with someone else in his bed? With someone else *touching* him?

Unfathomable.

Not for Kora. She drifted to sleep in his arms as if

it was the only place in the world she wanted to be, and he couldn't process the reaction it produced in him. He had no context for this messy, chaotic clash of emotions. They seethed out of the boxes he'd built to contain anything not necessary to survival—sweet satisfaction at her trust, sour apprehension at knowing he couldn't be trusted...and the dark shiver of foreboding, because the Base would stop at nothing to claim her if they knew what she was.

Lying to himself had been easier. He understood why humans did it, now. If they felt this many conflicting things all the time, it was amazing they weren't crushed under the uncertainty of it.

He needed to get away from her and rebuild those boxes. It was the objective, rational truth. Clearly and unequivocally the safest course of action. For her and for him.

But he was a Makhai soldier. His safety had never mattered more than the mission.

# eight

Kora dreamt of the desert.

She wandered for what seemed like hours, searching for something, but all that stretched before her was nothingness, vast and unforgiving. The sun beat down, and the rock and sand beneath her bare feet had to be scorching, but she couldn't feel it. She couldn't feel anything.

Time stretched, compressed. A revelation danced at the edge of her awareness, but every time she tried to turn and confront it, the knowledge danced away, off into the dreamy distance. Finally, she spotted a flash of color in the middle of the barren expanse, a hint of green. Of life.

It was a rosebush, small and fragile, with one single bud. It was still tightly closed, its blood-red petals just beginning to unfurl. She reached for it, eager to touch the velvet curve, but she pricked her finger on a jagged thorn instead.

It *hurt*, more than it should have, more than anything had ever hurt before. It was pure anguish, a torture sharp enough to cut and deep enough to kill. And it seethed all around her.

Kora drew in the breath to scream, then woke with a start.

Ashwin's room. The blankets clenched in her fists smelled like him, still carried his heat. Early-morning light streamed through the window, gilding his back as he sat at his desk.

She dragged in another deep breath as her father's voice flashed through her mind—*just a dream, wanting to become a nightmare.* Odd words to comfort a frightened child, but psychology was never Dr. Ethan Middleton's strong suit. He'd been a brilliant man, but not a warm one. How he had ever come to adopt and raise an orphaned baby girl on his own was an eternal mystery, one he'd never seen fit to solve for Kora.

She rolled onto her side as Ashwin spoke. "Bad dreams?"

"A little." She slipped her legs over the side of the bed and sat on the edge. "Brains are funny sometimes."

Whatever he was working on beeped softly, and he reached for a tiny screwdriver. "I wouldn't know."

Because Makhai soldiers didn't dream. At least, that's what the Base doctors claimed—that by eliminating unnecessary emotion and preoccupation, they'd also eliminated the subconscious need to process those emotions during sleep.

It was, like everything else they said, a load of complete bullshit.

"You dream. Everyone does." She rose and started

to cross the room, but stopped when she caught sight of the angry red furrows cut across the backs of his shoulders.

Lines left by her fingernails. Her cheeks heated as the memories flooded her in a rush, flashing through her like the stolen moments they were—Ashwin's hands on her bare skin, his lips beneath hers, his low, rough moan vibrating against her mouth.

She'd come to him selfishly, for the comfort she had no right to seek anywhere else, not while the others were mourning the loss of their friend, their brother. But the need for solace had quickly given way to something far more primal—desire.

She wanted him. She'd always wanted him.

And now, here they were. Kora bent and brushed her lips over one of the welts on his shoulder. "I scratched you last night."

His hands stilled, the panel on whatever he was reassembling only halfway fastened. "I don't mind."

"I know." Below the scratches, sweeping lines of ink marked the entire expanse of his back with wings and a skull wearing a black beret, all backed by spikes and a twisting strand of DNA—the emblem of the Makhai Project. Goose bumps rose on her flesh as she traced one line out to his shoulder. "I never understood why you all do this. It's a secret project, and you're supposed to be invisible. But the first thing you do is mark yourself as Makhai."

"There are plenty of ways to be invisible." He tilted his head forward in invitation, and she slid her hand up to the back of his neck. "If I don't want people to know, I don't let them see it."

It was a rationalization, not a reason. An excuse for why it was okay for him to wear this ink, not an explanation. "But why did you get it?"

"Because that's what Makhai soldiers do." He glanced back at her. "We aren't close. Most of us work alone, on extended missions away from the Base. The other soldiers fear us. The COs fear us. People who aren't even sure we exist fear us. But we don't fear each other. And we're not ashamed of what we are."

Her eyes stung, and she had to swallow past a lump in her throat to speak. "It sounds like you're all bound together, in a way. I'm glad." She buried her face in the hollow of his neck and wrapped her arms around him. "You should get to have that."

He stiffened, but only for a moment this time. Then his fingers brushed the back of her hand. "We're loyal to the people who don't treat us like monsters, Kora. If anything ever happens to me—"

"I have people," she cut in. "My family, and the Riders. You don't have to worry about me, Ashwin."

He gripped her hand harder. "They don't know the Base. If anything happens and you need our kind of help, you go to Samson. Promise me."

She knew Samson from the Base, of course, and he and Ashwin had always been friendly, if not friends. But this was more than a suggestion, or even an instruction. Ashwin's voice nearly trembled with a desperation that raked over her, turning her guts to acid.

Something was *wrong*. "Ashwin?"

He released her and picked up the screwdriver again. With quick, precise movements, he finished screwing the casing into place. "Do you know what this is?"

Kora straightened and turned her attention to the machine on the desk in front of him. She'd been so focused on *him*, on all the tiny little things that reminded her of the intimacy they'd shared the night before, that she hadn't really looked. It was sleek, a drab silvery gray that looked like the winter sky before a storm.

Beyond that, it looked like the boxy camera units used for security in the city. "Some kind of drone. Surveillance?"

"Yes." He tipped it up so the pinhole camera pointed at them and reached for a nearby tablet. "Do you know about the isotope trackers?"

"The what?"

His fingers flew as he pulled up a wall of code on the tablet and started typing. "I thought with all the illegal snooping you've done, you'd have run across it. Eden still uses physical trackers on their operatives, but those are easy to cut out. The Base has had a more sophisticated method in place since before the Flares."

The last of her lazy contentment vanished, replaced by a hard knot in her stomach. "You got this from the Base?"

"Technically, it was decommissioned. Incapacitated during a reconnaissance mission."

The knot exploded with tendrils of fear that snaked through her. "So you *took* it?"

"Eighteen months ago." He swiped the screen again. The code disappeared, replaced by an image of the two of them reflected from the camera. "This was a basic reconnaissance drone. After I repaired it, I modified—"

"Turn it off." She covered the camera lens with her hand. "*Now.*"

He tapped the screen, and the image went dark. "It's not broadcasting, Kora. The Base won't see this footage."

Her heart kept pounding. "It's theft of resources—misappropriation, if you're lucky. Ashwin—" He had to know. How could he not understand? "It's treason. If they find out, they'll kill you."

"Not for theft of resources. I'm too valuable an asset." He took her wrist and gently drew her hand away. "But this part? This is treason."

He touched the tablet again. An image reappeared, this time only their outlines, lit up with color. Ashwin's was bright blue, so vivid that it seemed to glow in its intensity. Kora's was dim against the white background of the image, a red so faint it was almost pink.

"Isotope trackers." His words made sense now, and she reached out, her fingers stopping just shy of the tablet's surface. They'd tagged him in a way that couldn't be removed—by injecting him with a radioactive isotope easily traceable with the right technology.

With *this* technology.

She met his eyes. "You're going to use this to find the deserters?"

"Yes. Regular enlisted soldiers show up as green. Elite soldiers as purple."

"And everyone else is red?"

He looked away, a furrow forming between his eyebrows as he studied the screen. With an abrupt nod and a flick of his fingers, he made the image vanish again. "Once I finish recalibrating the settings, it should only take a few hours of sweeps before I can pinpoint their location."

A strange chill settled over her—anger with more than a little fear. "You're right. This is definitely treason."

"So is knowing about it at all." He set the tablet on the desk and pushed his chair back. "The Base doesn't care how many Riders are injured or killed in apprehending the deserters. They'd prefer that I use Gideon's resources over theirs, and you know that's all his men are to them. Resources."

So calm, so logical. Anything to justify his current course of action. "There has to be another way."

"There are plenty of other ways. Slower ones." He grasped her hips and pulled until she was standing between his knees. "This isn't the first time I've committed treason. And I have a good reason to do this. I don't want to see any more of your friends killed."

It *was* a good reason—and she hated it. "It's too dangerous for you."

"Kora." She could feel the heat of his hands through her thin cotton pants, as well as the pressure of every individual finger. "The risk is well within acceptable parameters. Unless you think Gideon Rios intends to betray me to the Base."

"Of course not." But she'd spent months thinking he was dead, and looking down at him now scraped raw all the places inside her that had barely begun to heal. "You may consider the risk acceptable, but I don't. I care about you, Ashwin. I don't—" The words hung in her throat, and she swallowed hard. "I don't want to lose you again."

He stared at her forever. The sunlight slanted over him, gilding his light-brown skin. But his eyes were still dark, his face expressionless. The silence grew heavy, and he started moving his thumbs in slow, soothing circles. "This is the safest way for me, too. If I know where they all are, I can control the variables. An accusation of treason is an unlikely hypothetical. One or more of us getting hurt without this intel is a certainty."

Kora knew it seemed nonsensical on the surface, to be more worried about what the Base might do than the deserters, especially when she'd spent most of the previous evening painstakingly cleaning Jaden's and

Zeke's blood from under her fingernails. The threat from the deserters was present, immediate.

But quantifiable. Terror gripped her when she thought of what the men at the Base were capable of doing—not in the heat of battle, but while sitting behind their polished desks in their crisp, decorated uniforms. Theirs was a fathomless evil, one she'd barely glimpsed, but it still drove her from sleep some nights, wide-eyed and panicked.

"I know what I'm doing, Kora." Ashwin's voice was quiet. Sure. "It's going to be all right."

Terror couldn't be reasoned with or placated. But she locked down her protests and nodded. "I trust you."

His fingers dug into her hips, and the shadows in his eyes deepened. "Kora—"

He cut off abruptly at a knock on the door. A heartbeat later, it swung open, and Deacon stood there in the open doorway. "Good morning."

Ashwin didn't release Kora. "Deacon."

He studied them both with a sardonic expression. "Sleep well?"

"No." Ashwin tilted his head toward the desk where the treasonous drone sat. "I have your miracle."

Kora couldn't suppress a wince, and she opened her eyes to find Deacon watching her with surprising sympathy. "So we're going hunting?" he asked, without looking away.

"Yes." Ashwin stroked her hip one more time before gently pushing her away. "We're going hunting."

"Don't worry." Deacon rubbed her shoulder, the sympathy edged with something almost like calculation. "I'll bring him back, safe and sound. That's a promise, princess."

Ashwin flowed out of his chair so fast, he was standing between her and Deacon before she realized he was moving. The chair tilted backwards, wobbled, and settled back to the floor with a clatter that filled the tense silence.

"I'll find you later, Kora." His voice was no different than usual—even and steady. But the muscles in his back were coiled. Tense.

Neither man looked at her, and the hostility in the room swelled until she could feel it pressing in on her. "Fine. I'll be waiting."

She slipped out and closed the door quietly, carefully. Voices drifted down the hall from the main room, and Kora headed in the other direction, toward the back of the building and the kitchen exit. The last thing she wanted right now was to see the rest of the Riders, not when she might be elbow-deep in their guts soon.

Somehow, she needed to get ready for that.

Deacon was trying to provoke him.

Ashwin was accustomed to being challenged. There were few places left in the post-Flare world where people could afford to be complacent. They'd circle him and test him, poke for weak spots, and retreat when it became apparent he had none. Words couldn't goad Ashwin into an emotional response.

But Deacon hadn't used words. He'd used *Kora*.

He followed her footsteps until they faded at the edge of his auditory range, never breaking eye contact with Deacon. The other man's easy stance and relaxed expression was a lie—he was every bit as ready to fight as Ashwin was.

The only reason Ashwin hadn't already broken the smug bastard's hand was because Kora seemed to like him. "You don't touch her again."

The corner of Deacon's mouth tilted up. "No, you

don't fucking tell me what to do."

He wasn't telling him what to do. It was a simple statement of fact—if Deacon tried to touch her again, Ashwin would stop it from happening. But even he wasn't reckless enough to correct the man on his misunderstanding. Threatening Gideon's second-in-command was counterproductive to his mission.

It should have been easy to choke down the urge. Violence for its own sake had never appealed to him. But the desire to punch the smile right off Deacon's face burned in Ashwin's gut even as he turned away. "I know you don't like me, but what I'm about to show you can't get out. If the Base hears a *whisper* of it, they'll come after me."

"Relax," Deacon snapped. "I don't like you, you're right about that. But I'm not some punk-ass little shit who stabs people in the back."

Ashwin picked up the tablet. "I wasn't implying that you'd do so deliberately. But something could slip in front of a servant or the girls from the temple who party with your men. People talk."

"Riders don't."

It should have sounded naïve. But Ashwin had read all the files. He'd seen one analyst after another categorize the Riders as impossible to subvert. Deacon might be the rare man who could trust in his people's loyalty and not be fooling himself.

He handed the tablet to Deacon and picked up the drone. "I'd rather go out the back exit anyway."

"Suit yourself." Deacon opened the door for him, pitching his voice low so it wouldn't carry down the hall. "How is this thing going to tell anything our people can't? After yesterday, everyone in the goddamn sector is on high alert."

It was easier to show him than try to explain. Once they'd stepped outside, Ashwin set the drone on an empty stretch of gravel and reclaimed the tablet. A Base tablet would have had a slick user interface with preset surveillance routes. Ashwin had done it the hard way, hacking in to override the drone's signal and redirecting it to a single command source.

He entered the code to hover manually, and watched it rise into the air. When it hovered at about a hundred feet, he switched over to the camera view.

The white screen appeared. In the middle, a solitary blue shape marked his presence. Off to the corner, a pale red blur tracked Kora's path back to the mansion.

He hadn't known that she would register at all. The trace was so faint, even now, that it was likely she wouldn't have on a higher altitude scan, which explained why no one else had discovered her. She'd been tagged with the Project Panacea isotope as an infant, but protocol dictated retagging every ten years to retain optimal tracking ability.

Clearly the effects lasted far longer.

Deacon was invisible. So were the rest of the Riders, sitting only a few dozen feet away in the common room. If there had been anyone else in the room when he turned the camera on, Kora would have figured it out. He would have been forced to spin another lie. Or worse, offer her the truth.

He *had* to be more careful.

He waited until she'd cleared the field of view before tilting the tablet to show the screen to Deacon. "Every soldier on the Base is tagged with one of three radioactive isotopes so specialized drones can detect them. Blue indicates a Makhai soldier. Purple is one of the elite soldiers. Green are general troops. It can pick them up inside structures, under cover—even underground, as long as they're not too deep."

Deacon stared at the screen before turning his

incredulous gaze to Ashwin. "Are you fucking insane?"

"By most standard definitions, yes." He killed the display. "You don't want to put any more of your men in unnecessary danger. This ensures you won't have to."

Deacon snorted. "Don't get me wrong, this suits my purposes just fine. But this little toy of yours is dangerous—and not to me."

"I understand the risks." Better than Deacon ever could. Even Kora didn't know how cruel the Base could be, if provoked. "I evaluated them and made a choice."

"Why?"

He had a dozen rationalizations, lies he'd told himself during the night while he held Kora tight against his side. Then he'd picked those lies apart, one by one, until the odd, raw, improbable truth remained. "Do you care?"

Deacon glanced up at the hovering drone, then down the path toward Gideon's mansion. "I wouldn't have asked if I didn't."

"You won't believe me."

"Try me."

Ashwin stared down the path, too. It curved fifteen feet down to disappear into the trees. Kora would be safely back in the mansion by now, snug and protected by guards trained to defend kings and princesses. "Seeing her sad is...unsatisfactory."

"Unsatisfactory, huh?" Deacon laughed, genuine amusement coloring the sound. "Do yourself a favor—find a better fucking way to tell her that."

He didn't have a better way. He was good at this, making plans and taking action. Turning the tablet again, he pulled up the command line and started tapping out the code that would set the drone to scan Sector One and alert him to any positive hits. "This is what I do. I take care of problems."

For thirty-seven seconds—Ashwin counted them automatically—Deacon remained silent. Then he exhaled roughly and nodded. "All right. Then let's take care of this one."

Ashwin tapped in the final command. The drone buzzed higher, until it was almost out of sight, and shot off to the south. "If they're still in Sector One, we'll know by lunchtime."

"So we'd better get ready."

Ashwin followed Deacon back to the barracks, oddly at peace in spite of the line he'd just crossed.

Treason wasn't new to him. He'd been committing it every day since the first time he laid eyes on Kora.

# nine

It took Kora over an hour in the bath to settle down. She would have preferred a shower—warm, rushing water to rinse away her worries along with the stress of the last twenty-four hours. But it was too easy to let the water drown out her thoughts, and she couldn't bring herself to do it. She needed her thoughts in order, her head on straight.

The bath worked. She felt almost normal again as she dried off, dressed, and went in search of Gideon.

Then she found him, and every bit of that roiling emotion came roaring back.

He was in the courtyard. Laid out in front of him on one of the high stone tables was Jaden's corpse, naked except for a strip of white cloth over his hips. She watched as Gideon dipped another cloth into a silver basin, then drew it slowly across Jaden's shoulder.

It had the solemn, sacred air of a ritual, and Kora took an instinctive step back.

"It's all right." Gideon spoke without looking up, his attention fixed on Jaden. "If you want to stay, I'd appreciate the company. But you don't have to."

"I don't want to intrude."

"It's not an intrusion." He dipped the cloth again before starting down Jaden's arm. "Isabela used to help me with this. I can't ask Maricela. She's...close to the Riders in a way Isabela never was."

*Help.* Kora latched on to the word like a lifeline, and she stepped up to the table. "What can I do?"

He nudged the basin toward her. Another scrap of fabric rested over the rim—woven cotton with delicate embroidery around the edges. Kora picked it up and shivered when the warm water sluiced between her fingers, slippery with some sort of oil. It smelled like the incense at the temple, heady and fragrant.

In the city, they employed people to wash the deceased prior to cremation. She'd seen it done, though it involved spray hoses and disinfectant, not perfumed oils. In Sector One, families prepared their dead, relying on guidance from the priestesses as well as older members of their community.

But she'd never seen Gideon do it, not even for the Riders who were killed in action during the war with Eden.

Her confusion must have shown as she stepped around the table to wash Jaden's other arm, because Gideon spoke again. "It's been a while since I did this, almost a year. Josiah. He fell to raiders, but he saved dozens of lives before he did."

"What about the war?"

"Too many died in that final charge." Sorrow

roughened the edge of his voice. "Thirty-one Riders in less than an hour. As many as I'd lost in the decade leading up to it. And once the wall came down, my duty was helping to decide what was going to replace it."

Her first instinct was to wonder why he hadn't asked her for help, but what could she have done? The month after the final battle had passed in a blur of unending work for her, as well, a stream of patients with everything from knife wounds to heart attacks.

It had kept her going, kept her from falling into despair, worrying that her refusal to leave the battle-field with Ashwin had sent him off to his death. Worrying about him in general. In a very real way, her work had saved her.

All Gideon had to show for all his work was *guilt*.

"You can only do so much," she murmured. "Isn't that what you tell me all the time?"

Gideon inclined his head. "True. But you've been here long enough to understand, Kora." He pressed his hand to Jaden's forehead. "If I'd asked him to pull out his gun and shoot himself in the head, what do you think he would have done?"

She stared down at the table. Water dripped off the rough edge and splashed on the stones by her feet. For a moment, she was back in the dining room, standing by another table, and it was blood spilling over the edge, not water.

She knew the answer. And she would never, ever say it out loud.

Gideon resumed his slow, gentle movements. "That's a weight no man should carry lightly. My grandfather did. That's why I stepped in and claimed the Riders. And I'll honor their loyalty with the gravity it deserves."

"I understand." Someone had closed up the bullet

holes and surgical incisions in Jaden's abdomen. Kora dipped her cloth again and washed away the traces of blood that lingered around the wounds. "Reyes said he was originally from Sector Seven. Did he have family here?"

"A sister, Grace." Gideon smiled gently. "She'll be taken care of."

Gideon's guilt alone would have ensured that, even if it wasn't standard procedure for those left behind after a Rider's death. "Do their loved ones ever resent it? The sacrifice, I mean? The Riders are free to make their choices, but it touches their families, too."

"The ones who grew up here? Rarely. They do their grieving the day the Rider joins up—if they have any grief at all. We don't fear death here the same way other sectors do." A sudden tightness around his eyes turned his smile into something wry. Self-deprecating. "Their sacrifice isn't death. It's the blood on their hands when they die. They're giving up their chance to join everyone else in the glory that comes after life. That's why they're revered."

And why they remained alone. The unity of family was a sacred thing to the people in One, a bond that transcended death. For the Riders to separate themselves from that was a profound renunciation of the heavenly rewards that were supposed to await them.

It wasn't just lip service, and the raven tattoos memorializing Jaden's kills weren't just symbols. They were very real reminders of a soul that was now lost forever.

She cleared her throat. "What about you?"

"Me?"

"You," she repeated. "They have different expectations of you, don't they? Their leader, their king. What's your sacrifice—your legacy?"

"I don't know." He squeezed the water from the cloth and watched the droplets fall to form little ripples on the bowl's surface. "I probably shouldn't admit that, so don't tell anyone."

"I'm serious, Gideon."

"So am I. War tore Eden and the sectors apart." He gestured to the water. The ripples had rebounded off the sides of the bowl and were now crashing into each other, creating chaos. "We have the opportunity to put it back together into something better. Maybe that will change my legacy. Maybe it will change theirs. It's too soon to be sure."

Kora had grown up under the kinds of restrictions that you could escape if you ran hard and far enough. But Gideon's responsibilities were part of him, from his name to his blood, and she couldn't imagine the weight of it. "What do you *want*?"

"I came as soon as I heard." The guards bowed their heads as Avery hurried into the courtyard, her red cloak swirling around her legs. She stopped short at the sight of the body on the table, misery shadowing her features. "Oh *no*, not Jaden."

"Avery." Gideon's voice was as gentle as always, but Kora recognized the subtle shift in his demeanor. Her brother vanished, replaced by Gideon Rios, the man who treated every person in his sector like family without letting any of them too close. "I'm sorry. I know you were fond of him."

Stricken, she met his gaze. "Malena was sweet on him. She's one of the refugees from Two—Lotus House. He used to come by and help her with chores or fix leaky faucets—" Her voice broke.

Kora's eyes stung. Her words painted a sweetly domestic scene, the kind that should have been at odds with Jaden's hulking stature and warrior status. But it *fit*, even if playing house was the last thing a Rider like Jaden was supposed to do.

Gideon draped his washcloth over the edge of the bowl. “Thank you for telling me. If she needs anything…” A muscle in his jaw jumped. “Let Maricela know. If she was special to him, then she’s special to us.”

Avery shook her head, and Kora tried not to wince as she read the unspoken words in her dark eyes.

No one could give Malena what she needed, not anymore.

Before Gideon could say anything else, Ivan pushed through the door on the far side of the courtyard. He was dressed in his habitual black, a wraith-like shadow with frozen blue eyes, and his words were coolly efficient. “We have a position on the raiders’ new camp. Deacon’s mobilizing the Riders.”

“And our guest?”

Ivan hesitated for only a heartbeat, but it was long enough to make his distaste apparent. “Ashwin’s gearing up, too.”

Gideon studied the man. “Does that bother you?”

“No, sir.”

It was a lie, and it was the truth. A lie, because Ivan’s disgust was strong enough to show, even through his usual chilly, locked-down demeanor. And the truth, because his personal feelings were nothing in the face of Gideon’s wishes, much less his orders. If Gideon wanted Ashwin back in one piece, every single Rider would fall to make it happen.

Kora didn’t know whether to be relieved or scared to death.

Gideon was neither. He accepted Ivan’s conflict and his obedience without question. “Tell Deacon I’ll be there in a moment to discuss our final plans.”

"Yes, sir." Ivan's nod was almost a bow. He repeated the courtesy to Avery and Kora before spinning on his heel.

When he was gone, Gideon turned back to them. "I hate to impose on you both, but could you stay with him until I get back?"

Avery unfastened her cloak, slid it off her shoulders, and laid it over a bench near the table. "We won't leave him alone."

Kora's fingers had wound so tightly in the cloth she held that she was cutting off her circulation. "Gideon—"

He slid a hand over hers and stroked her knuckles until her grip eased. "He'll come back, Kora. Have faith."

*Faith.* Maybe it really was that simple for him. Whether his prayers were answered or not, he trusted that the outcome was part of a greater plan, his god's will.

Kora didn't have his faith, and she didn't have his assurance. All she had was a glimmer of hope that Ashwin might have feelings for her, after all—a glimmer that would rage into an anguished fire if something happened to him.

Gideon walked away, and Avery touched Kora's shoulder. "Let's get back to work."

It took her a moment to realize what Avery meant—for them to finish the task. "We can't. I don't know what to do."

"I do." Avery picked up the cloth Gideon had set aside. She glanced up at Kora, then shrugged. "I asked one of the senior priestesses at the temple. Not because of Jaden—this was months ago."

Slowly, Kora unwound the cloth from her hands and dipped it into the basin. The water soothed away the pins and needles from the sudden blood flow to her fingers, and she found herself asking, “Why?”

Avery shrugged again. “I was curious about the rituals. Birth, marriage, and death—it says a lot about a society, the way they approach all three, don’t you think?”

An emotion suspiciously like shame scraped at Kora. Gideon had taken her in and provided her with a home—no, with more than a home. With a family. He and his sisters and their whole sector had welcomed her as one of their own, as royalty.

And a refugee fleeing from the destruction of Sector Two had taken more time to get to know their culture than she had.

“Don’t,” Avery murmured.

“Don’t what?”

“Look at me like that. Like I’m such a better person than you.” She paused, then resumed bathing Jaden’s corpse. “Especially since I just lied right to your face.”

Kora stared at her.

“That’s right,” Avery responded, as if the stare was a question, a comment. A condemnation. “What do you know about Sector Two? Before the war?”

Almost nothing that didn’t revolve around its infamous brothel district, but Kora would be damned before she’d open with such a delicate subject. “They focused on trade, mainly. Importing and exporting goods for the city.”

“Don’t shrink away from it. I don’t.” Avery flashed her a knowing look. “Mostly, they traded in whores.”

Kora’s cheeks heated. “Right.”

“They don’t call it the world’s oldest profession for nothing.”

“I guess not.”

Avery went on. "There were different establishments in the Garden, and each House had its own specialty. If you desired a wide-eyed ingénue, you'd get a Dahlia. If pairs were your preference, there was always Ivy House. And if you wanted a truly dangerous woman, as beautiful as she was deadly, then you wanted an Orchid." She swirled her cloth in the basin, then let it drop slowly into the water. "My sister Alexa was an Orchid. You know Lex."

"I do." Kora had first met the queen of Sector Four during the war. "Meeting her was…interesting."

"Yes?"

"Okay, more like awkward. She threatened to shoot me in the face."

Avery huffed out a wry laugh. "Like I said—beautiful and deadly." Her fingers clenched around the edge of the stone table until her knuckles turned white, giving lie to her humor. "I was trained at Rose House. They taught us how to be everything. Hostess, lover, house manager. Pet. That's why I asked about the rites. I had to learn everything I could about Sector One."

As a logical leap, Kora couldn't follow it. "I don't understand."

"My patron died in the bombing." Avery swallowed hard, then looked at Kora, her eyes wide and pleading. "I was taught that I had to be all those things for him. The perfect woman. And I'm still doing it, even though there's no one left for me to be perfect for."

The words punched into Kora, spreading through her chest in a hot ache that traveled up to knot in her throat. For all the questions that had plagued her about her origins, she'd never once wondered who Kora Bellamy was. In her heart, her soul, she knew exactly what she wanted to do with her life, who she wanted to be. It had kept her anchored, even kept her sane at times, and she couldn't imagine feeling lost in her own skin.

Avery was still watching her, silently beseeching, and Kora took her hand. "So do it for yourself. Be perfect for you, or imperfect. Be an absolute mess, if you want. As long as it's what *you* want."

"What I want." Avery considered that, then squeezed Kora's fingers. "Thank you."

"You're welcome."

She pulled away and retrieved her washcloth. She murmured something under her breath, then squeezed a rivulet of the scented water over Jaden's forehead. She paused, then repeated the gesture twice more. For a moment, it was like watching Gideon when she had first come into the courtyard—a sacred ritual, with a meaning she hadn't taken the time to learn.

Finally, Avery spoke. "There's a reason they call it making a home, you know." Her voice was casual, almost purposefully so. "It takes work to build something. It doesn't just happen."

Kora looked down at her hands. She'd twisted the cloth around her fingers again, so she pried them free. "You're right." She couldn't expect to be a part of their community if she still considered herself an outsider.

Avery's next words mirrored the thought. "You don't live in Eden anymore, Kora. And I don't think Gideon—" She faltered, a flush staining her cheeks. "I don't think anyone here would find your questions tiresome. So ask. Find out if you want to make this your home."

Before Ashwin's arrival, it was a question she considered often. Now, he'd completely taken over her thoughts. Until she figured out what was going on between them, everything else had been shuffled aside.

"I'll think about it."

"Please do." Avery returned to her task, satisfied. "This is a good place, Kora. We're both lucky to have found it."

Kora couldn't disagree.

# ana

Deacon was watching her again.

Ana's skin prickled with awareness under his gaze. She ignored it as best she could as she laced her boots, focusing on making them snug, but not too tight. Tying the knot just so, because if she tripped over her laces in her first fight as a Rider—

He moved on, and she exhaled quietly and reached for the knives she kept in her boots. The temptation to look over her shoulder was intense, but she didn't want to draw his attention again for fear he'd find a reason to make her stay behind.

Because Deacon didn't approve of her.

Ana doubted anyone else could tell—maybe not even Gideon. But Ana had always been hyperaware of Deacon. She'd watched him in her teens, idolizing him more than a little. He was the quintessential Rider, everything Ana's father was training her to be. Strong, serious. Quick to help when help was needed. Quick to protect when danger threatened.

Her father had never bothered to warn her that Deacon was also a cranky, autocratic asshole who handed down orders without explanation and expected the Riders to jump if he so much as blinked.

No, that wasn't fair. Her dad had never lied to her about the chain of command, and Ana didn't have a problem with following orders. She just hated the way Deacon snapped them at her, like he was waiting for her to balk or break down. Or change her mind and admit this life wasn't for her, after all.

Being a Rider was the only thing she'd ever wanted. It was in her bones, in her blood. Her legacy from her father, the thing that had brought them back together after her mother's death. He'd wanted this for her as much as she had, and her biggest regret was that he hadn't lived long enough to see her achieve it.

Her biggest relief was that he wasn't here to watch her stew under their commander's quiet, relentless disapproval.

Deacon appeared in front of her, as if she'd drawn him close with only her thoughts. He handed her a bandolier, then waited for her to drape it over her shoulder before stepping around to buckle it. "Make sure you use your stripper clip to load your magazines," he muttered tersely. "They'll be less likely to jam on you, and you won't tear up your thumbs."

Her first instinct was to bristle and snap that she *knew*, but then she realized what the advice meant.

He wasn't going to order her to stay behind. He wasn't keeping her out of the fight. "Okay," she replied, hyperaware of him in a different way now. His fingers brushed her shirt. His breath tickled the back of her neck, which was left bare by the braids winding around the crown of her head—a deliberate choice to deny an enemy a convenient handhold—and she bit back the defensive need to point that out.

She didn't idolize Deacon anymore. Prolonged exposure to his grumpy-as-fuck personality had cured her of that. But he was still...Deacon. The only original Rider left. Not just a legend, but a man with one foot already planted in the realm of sainthood. Wanting to impress him was a hard habit to break.

And she couldn't stop being *aware* of him.

He made sure the bandolier was situated before stepping away to murmur something to Zeke, probably more calm, sage wisdom. By the time Ana finished checking her weapons, he'd moved on to Reyes, and it had become obvious that he intended to make a full circle of the room.

She should have expected it. Deacon was a control freak on a level that made other control freaks take a step back and reexamine their life choices. She wanted to scoff at him for it, but she couldn't. Deacon's methodical obsession to detail kept Riders alive, and she couldn't afford to die. Not this fast, not flaming out in her first battle in brilliant, vivid proof that the first female Rider should be the last one.

The fate of every little girl who wanted to fight for her people rested on Ana's ability to stay alive—or, barring that, to go down in a blaze of glory so fantastic, they sainted her while her body was still warm.

No pressure.

Of the two options, Ana preferred living. She wasn't Ivan, who probably daydreamed about the day he could lunge in front of a bullet meant for Maricela, like his father had for Maricela's aunt. Some Riders joined with fantasies of a different kind of eternal life, one where people got tattoos of you and prayed to you and made your deaths a part of their faith.

It wasn't a bad dream, but it wasn't *her* dream. She wanted to do some damn good before she went down. She wanted the power to fix the broken shit in the world, because God knew there was still plenty of it to go around. Even in Sector One, where life was supposed to be about love and generosity. About taking care of *everyone*, not just the people born already having everything.

High ideals, and Ana believed in them. The problem was, people were messy. They tended to fuck shit up.

Her T-shirt mostly hid the tattoo on her arm, but she slid her fingers under the sleeve to trace the outline of the skull by memory. The ink might be visible proof that she belonged, but that wasn't what made a Rider.

She would kill today. She would end lives, committing the gravest sin that existed in Sector One. And instead of putting aside her life to toil for years until she'd worked away the stain of her transgression, she'd take a little black raven on her arm and accept that her sin might never be forgiven.

Right now, she could still walk away. Her soul was more or less clean. Even earning her first few ravens wouldn't change that. She was young enough to work them off and still have time to enjoy what was left of her mortal life before joining her family in the next world.

She had tried to count the ravens on Deacon's arm once. Impossible. They twined underneath it, down past his elbow and up onto his shoulder. Dozens upon dozens of deaths. Deacon could live to two hundred and not have time to atone for so much killing. When he finally ran into something ornery enough to kill him, he'd be trapped in the stark loneliness of purgatory.

Or so the legend went.

Again, she brushed the empty skin where her first ravens would sit, then dropped her hand and returned to her preparations. Perhaps the possibility of damnation should have bothered her more, but Ana had too much faith.

If an afterlife of punishment was the fate God handed her for trying to protect his people, she'd accept it. But the God *she* believed in, the one whose compassion filled the temple when the priestesses gathered everyone close, the one who urged them to love each other—

He wasn't vengeful. He wasn't cruel. And He was wise enough to know what was in her heart when she was pulling the trigger. If her God turned out to be petty enough to punish those who had given up everything to protect His people?

Well, then Ana would gladly spend eternity in purgatory. Even if she had to spend it with Deacon.

# ten

The deserters had gone to ground at the extreme edge of Sector One. To get there, the Riders had to go north through Hunter's family's lands, then across the river and through the edge of Gideon's sister Isabela's property.

The vineyards stretched to the east in rolling hills, but the road Deacon led them down curled toward foothills that grew into mountains. A smudge of green to the west marked the edge of the closest farming commune. During the long decades leading up to the war, men unlucky enough to end up there had spent their lives in brutal toil, growing the food that people consumed so blithely in Eden. Women in the communes had been given an even more thankless task—producing the next generation of labor.

The communes and illegal farms were undergoing uncomfortable but necessary reforms under the new Council. Normally, Ashwin would find the specifics interesting—assessing the new head councilman's commitment to his vision of a better world was an important task. But it wasn't the mission he'd been given.

His mission—the real one, as well as the one he'd claimed publicly—was at the end of this road. Deacon pulled his vehicle off the road a mile out, and the collection of trucks and motorcycles behind them followed, forming a loose circle around a clear patch of dirt.

Deacon stood in the center, a pair of binoculars raised to his face. After several long minutes, he lowered them. "Bishop, Ivan? Recon."

"Yes, sir," Bishop said. Ivan simply nodded, and they both took off at a jog toward the line of trees.

Reyes drummed his fingers on the side of the truck, then pulled a butterfly knife from his back pocket and began flicking it open and shut, over and over. The handles clicked, and he spun the knife faster, finally rolling it entirely over the top of his thumb only to catch it again.

Hunter ignored him—and the wickedly sharp blade flashing only inches from his arm—choosing instead to squint against the slanting sunlight. "What do you think?"

"Hard to say." Deacon rubbed his chin. "We have to be careful. For Gideon's sake."

He said it regretfully, as if every one of them would eagerly sacrifice their lives—except for the inconvenience it would cause the man who'd sent them to bleed and die. The generals at the Base would give anything for that sort of loyalty.

Zeke hopped into the bed of a truck and pulled out his own binoculars. "Maybe I should scout in the opposite direction—"

"No," Deacon barked. "You'll stay your ass right here."

"Deacon—"

"For *now*," he elaborated.

Gabe leaned back against the truck and elbowed Zeke in the leg. Zeke swallowed whatever he was about to say and resumed staring moodily through the binoculars, as if he could see through the cover of the trees if he just tried hard enough.

Survivor's guilt. He had been with Jaden during the last attack, and no doubt harbored a range of incapacitating emotions. Ashwin had seen men go into battle with the need for vengeance overriding their survival instincts—and he'd seen those men die bloody deaths. Frequently, they took down the men with them.

Silence reigned, until Deacon broke it with a grunt. "Two teams, if we can manage it. No one pairs off, not this time."

The radio at Deacon's belt crackled. "Got eyes on the camp, boss," came Ivan's voice. "Looks like only part of it's above ground. There's some kind of cave—maybe a tunnel."

Reyes swung his knife shut with a loud click. "Lots of old silver mines in this area."

Deacon lifted his radio. "What about the camp?"

"About ten—no, twelve. Mostly drinking and playing cards, but they all have weapons handy. Bishop's checking the perimeter for sentries."

Silence, followed by a second crackle and Bishop's lower voice. "Don't see any. Looks like everyone else is below ground."

"So we're ten," Reyes mused aloud, "up against Christ knows how many. I like those odds."

"Twenty-nine," Ashwin supplied. "According to

my best assessment."

Zeke snorted. "Okay, so Christ and Ashwin know. Just don't go hogging all the kills, Makhai Guy. I saw you during the final battle with the city. You took out, like, a dozen Special Tasks soldiers in under a minute."

More than a dozen, but he'd been considerably motivated. Those Special Tasks soldiers had been firing their weapons in Kora's direction. "I'm sure there will be plenty of risk to go around. These are well-trained Base operatives."

"Like I said, two teams." Deacon pointed at Ashwin. "Malhotra, you take Ana and Zeke and meet up with Ivan and Bishop. You're hitting the mine. Everyone else is with me."

There was a flurry of activity—Reyes snapped his blade shut and shoved it back into his pocket. Gabe checked the hilts of twin knives crisscrossing his back, wicked ones long enough to qualify as short swords, and Ana shouldered a rifle half her own height.

Zeke hopped out of the truck and started toward Ashwin, but Deacon grabbed his shoulders. "Before I send you down there, I need to know you've got your head on straight."

"I'm fine," Zeke promised. "I'll get this shit done."

"You were hurt bad." Deacon pitched his next words low. "No one would blame you for sitting this one out."

"I can't. Deacon—" Zeke's voice turned rough. "You have to let me do this. For Jaden, okay?"

"All right. But you watch your back," he ordered. "No reckless shit."

"Got it."

Deacon released him, and Zeke swept up his rifle and joined Ana. Neither of them questioned being put under the command of a virtual stranger, and they fell in behind Ashwin as he started across the field.

Ivan and Bishop met them at the edge of the woods. "This way," Ivan said, jerking his head to the right before melting silently into the trees. Bishop was equally quiet, and they both moved with the practiced ease of people who'd spent time stalking prey in the wild.

Ana and Zeke followed with the not-so-quiet awkwardness of city folk, wincing at every snapped branch. Ashwin ignored them, concentrating on the sounds growing louder at the very edge of his range—the low rumble of voices punctuated by sharp barks of laughter.

Ivan stopped at the far edge of the trees, behind a large tumble of boulders. Bishop crouched down and eased out far enough to get a visual on the encampment. "Still twelve," he whispered as he shifted back so Ashwin could take his place.

The battlefield spread out before him. He'd already seen the aerial view, but the terrain looked different when viewed from the ground. The deserters had set up their makeshift shelter in a dusty clearing next to an abandoned railroad track. It was about a hundred yards from the edge of the trees to the closest man—enough space that they'd become complacent, sure they'd see anyone coming. Or sure that no one would bother to chase them out here.

They were wrong on both counts.

The first bullet cracked through the afternoon air—a sniper shot that blew out the back of an elite soldier's head. In the clearing, everyone froze for one fatal moment of confusion, barely long enough for the body to hit the ground.

In that time, Deacon's team poured into the camp, already firing.

Zeke tensed, his finger on the trigger, but Ashwin

caught his shoulder. "Wait."

Ivan shot him a wary look. Bishop shifted impatiently. Even Ana was stealing looks at him, and he knew they were wondering if he'd led them out here into some sort of trap. If he was going to hold them back from the fight while their brothers died.

They could mistrust him as much as they wanted, as long as they obeyed.

The chaos in the clearing accelerated. Some of the deserters had reached their weapons and were returning fire. Ashwin ignored them, keeping his attention on the wooden door to the mines. He'd counted to nineteen, and it slammed open. A man with his shirt still unbuttoned spilled out, an assault rifle in his hands.

"I'll take point," Ashwin murmured. "Bishop, cover us. Don't let them shut that door."

"Got it."

A tremor ran through Zeke's body. Ashwin released him. "Go."

They erupted from the tree line, and the adrenaline of battle took over. Time seemed to slow, giving Ashwin ample opportunity to assess and alter course, if necessary. He noted each of the Riders on Deacon's team—all still standing—as well as the positions of their remaining foes. He tracked Bishop as he swung around and kept anyone from shooting them in the back as they raced toward the mine.

But most of his attention was focused on the distance between him and the man at the door. He recalculated the math every few steps until he could lift his gun and squeeze off one precise shot.

It hit the deserter in the neck. He dropped his gun, clutched at his bleeding throat, and staggered back. A second man appeared, his face blanched with shock, and groped for the door.

Ivan shot him three times in the chest.

Ashwin reached the tunnel first and leapt over the bodies, with Ana and Zeke hard on his heels. After a steep drop down, the tunnel took an abrupt turn to the left. Ashwin held up his hand, halting his team, and listened to the chaotic tumble of arguing voices ahead. They were fighting over what to do, but that wasn't what gave him pause.

The voices echoed strangely. He closed his eyes and tried to visualize the kind of space that would make that sort of noise. Something large, with a high ceiling—and plenty of room for them to maneuver.

Plenty of room to barricade themselves, if Ashwin gave them the chance to organize.

"Count to ten," he told them, holstering his side-arm and pulling forward the semiautomatic rifle he'd strapped to his back. "If I don't shout for you to fall back, come in after me."

"What are you going to do?" Ivan asked.

Ashwin gripped his weapon in one hand and tugged open one of the pockets on his cargo pants. The flash grenade fit perfectly in his hand. "I believe the colloquial term is *scare the shit out of them*."

He didn't wait for a reply. He pressed down on the lever and pulled the grenade's pin with his teeth, then swung around the bend in the corridor and lobbed it into the center of the room.

In the five seconds before it went off, three things happened.

First, Ashwin cataloged the open space—a huge cavern with bedrolls around the edge and overturned mine carts serving as makeshift barricades. Fifteen men were scrambling to erect some sort of cover. He marked the location of the elite soldiers in his mind and adjusted his mental tally. Fifteen left.

Then one of the men caught sight of him—a private who'd been one of the laziest, angriest soldiers Ashwin had known on the Base. Ashwin had caught him bullying younger recruits more than once, which meant Private Jones went *very* pale as recognition washed over him. "Holy shit, it's a Makhai—"

Ashwin's bullet cut him off. Precisely timed, because the word *Makhai* performed its usual magic. Men dove for weapons, dove for cover, scrambled in all directions as the elite soldier who'd been trying to organize shouted furiously, "Hold the fucking line, dammit!"

Ashwin closed his eyes. The grenade exploded, painfully bright even through his eyelids, but the sound was worse. It filled the cavern like thunder, vibrating until tiny pieces of rock rained down from the ceiling and dust filled the air.

Terrified and stunned, the enemy floundered. And Ashwin opened fire.

*Fourteen. Thirteen.*

*Twelve.*

At the count of ten, the rest of the Riders spilled around the corner and fanned out on either side of him. Ivan charged straight at the overturned carts, jumping up and over before the men behind them had shrugged off the effects of the stun grenade.

*Eleven men. Ten.*

Zeke was laughing, the sound rough and wild. There was anger in his shots—he took out knees and left people bleeding from gut wounds that thwarted Ashwin's clean count until he finished the job—though Zeke gave him a look of such affronted outrage that he only did it once.

*Nine.*

Ana, by contrast, was silent and laser focused. She ignored the bullets and shouts and chaos around her and quietly lined up precise, deadly shots. The men she targeted fell with perfect headshots that would have made any marksmanship trainer on the Base ranges proud.

*Eight. Seven. Six.*

*Five.*

Three men were clustered behind a thick overturned table, popping up to fire wild shots and disappearing before they could be struck. Ashwin trusted Bishop and Ivan to keep them pinned down while he tried to locate the soldiers missing from his count.

*Five. Five...*

Had he miscounted on arrival? Had he missed a death? Ashwin spun toward the tunnel, retracing the last moments—and heard Ana's shout, "Zeke, *down*."

Ashwin whirled in time to see Zeke hit the ground as a "dead" man lifted his arm and shot at the space where he'd been. Ana swung around and fired, sinking three bullets into the man's chest and two into his head.

Definitely dead now. Actually dead.

*Four.*

Ana dropped the magazine from her rifle to reload. As she did, Ashwin caught a flicker of movement out of the corner of his eye. Instinct kicked in, and he was moving before the crack of the shot sounded. Ashwin shouldered Ana out of the way, knocking her back, and twisted to take the bullet flying at him in the safest spot he could manage.

Pain bloomed in his shoulder, the familiar burn of a bullet wound. He started to lift his other arm to return fire, but Ivan launched himself from the top of the mine cart and crashed into the man's back, driving him to the ground. Two bullets to the head at close range evened out Ashwin's count.

*Three.*

His shoulder hurt. How close Ana had come to getting killed bothered him more. He reached into another pocket and came out with a second grenade—this one not as harmless as the stun grenade. Overkill, perhaps, but getting all of the Riders back in one piece was the only thing that mattered.

He pulled the pin and raised his voice. "Fall back into the tunnel. Bishop—"

He didn't even have to finish. Bishop laid down a spray of covering fire, keeping the three men huddled behind the table as Zeke, Ivan, and Ana retreated into the tunnel. Once they were safely around the bend in the corner, Ashwin jerked his head at Bishop. "Go."

"But—"

"*Now.*"

Bishop bolted, and Ashwin lobbed the grenade and ducked down behind one of the overturned carts. The grenade exploded, sending shrapnel flying through the room at high velocities. The cart shuddered as small, wicked pieces of frag slammed into it, and for a moment he wondered if he'd miscalculated the risk.

But the moment passed. Silence fell. Ashwin rose cautiously and stared at the opposite side of the cart—or what was left of it.

*Zero.*

A few scrapes and bruises among the others, one scary brush for Ana, and a bullet in his shoulder. Not a terrible outcome, considering the odds.

He didn't even mind the bullet wound. It would provide a perfectly rational excuse to let Kora touch him again.

And he wanted her to touch him again.

# eleven

The only thing harder than waiting in Gideon's study to find out how the raid went was trying to do anything else. Kora eventually gave up and resigned herself to pacing in front of the huge fireplace while Gideon sat, still and staring into the flames.

She'd worn a path in the expensive, handwoven carpet by the time Deacon radioed in to say they were on their way back. Her knees went weak, then locked when he mentioned that Ashwin had been injured.

Dimly, she considered the possibilities, running them over and over in her mind, as Maricela and Gideon tried to comfort her with more details. She couldn't stop, even as they led her down the stairs to meet the returning Riders.

She wouldn't be able to breathe until she saw Ashwin.

Then he was there, climbing stiffly out of Deacon's Jeep, and the tension snapped, vibrating painfully through her. She couldn't stop shaking, though the overriding emotion wracking her was pure, sweet *relief*.

He had come back, and he was going to be all right.

Kora's relief lasted until she got Ashwin settled in her makeshift clinic in the palace—and got a good look at the bullet wound beneath his bandage.

He was fortunate. Another inch to the right and the bullet would have shattered his shoulder, making complete repair—even with regeneration—difficult to impossible. He would have been left with permanent damage to the bones and nerves.

Worse, a few inches lower, and the damn thing would have hit his heart.

She drew in a deep breath, but it did nothing to allay the sudden resurgence of dizziness as she dropped the bandage into a surgical tray. "You got lucky."

"No," he replied quietly. "I made a strategic decision."

"Yeah, and what was that?"

"To take a nonlethal shot instead of allowing Ana to suffer a lethal one."

He seemed so *calm*, as if the possibility of dying didn't scare him at all. "And if you'd miscalculated?"

"I rarely miscalculate."

Maybe it was true. Maybe his genetic enhancements and endless training meant that the worry seizing in her gut was not only unnecessary, but counterproductive. He didn't need her falling apart on him right now.

He needed a *doctor*.

For better or worse, she could never be that for him now. Oh, she could patch up his wounds, get him back on his feet. But the thin veneer of professional detachment she'd barely managed to maintain on the Base was gone now.

She supposed that waking up in a man's bed tended to do that.

No, she had to be honest with herself. Her inability to maintain her distance started a long time ago. It had shaken a little more each time he walked into her exam room, and its foundation had cracked the night he kidnapped her and dragged her out to the sectors. This had simply been the last straw.

Kora took another deep breath and started arranging her supplies. Antiseptic. Forceps. Gauze. The small imaging machine that had shown up two days after her offhand comment to Maricela about how she really could use one.

"Kora." His voice was gentle. "I'm fine. You don't need to be concerned."

She turned to face him. "But I can't help it. I never could."

"I know." He reached up, his fingers hovering a few torturous millimeters from her cheek. "You didn't belong on the Base. Or in Eden."

She had to *focus*, and she couldn't do that with him touching her. She ducked away from his hand and cleared her throat. "You got lucky, but regeneration is still going to be tricky. It'll ache for a few days."

"That's acceptable." He let his hand fall back to his leg, but even that was somehow graceful. "Does it bother you so much to deal with my injuries?"

"Treating you? No. Knowing that you were hurt?" She shrugged, suddenly self-conscious. "Yes, it does."

He studied her for a few seconds, then inclined his

head. “Then I’ll avoid it as much as I can.”

It was so absurd she almost laughed. He wouldn’t avoid taking a bullet to save himself the physical pain and injury, but he’d do it because she didn’t like the thought of him being shot.

The only thing that kept her from laughing was knowing that he was dead serious. So she picked up the antiseptic instead and began cleaning his wound. He endured it in stoic silence for so long that she’d almost fallen back into a familiar rhythm when he shattered it again.

“Knock knock.”

She blinked, but the words came automatically. “Who’s there?”

“Control freak.”

“Con—”

“Now you say control freak who,” he interrupted, still stoic and stone-faced, as if he hadn’t just told a joke. But his gaze fixed on her face, full of such sharp anticipation that she felt it like a blow to the midsection.

She’d started telling him knock-knock jokes as a way to loosen him up, something to say just to break the distant silence. It had always confused him more than anything, because silly little jokes and highly trained, lethal warriors didn’t exactly go together.

Somewhere along the way, somehow, he’d made the effort to figure them out.

She wanted to kiss him. Smooth her fingers through his hair and thank him. Cry.

In the end, she smiled and shook her head. “You got me with that one.”

His lips...curved. Not a full smile—she’d seen him attempt that, but it always seemed a little forced. Empty. This barely qualified as movement, but she *felt* it—the tiniest spark of satisfaction and pleasure. “I researched jokes," he told her. "Did you know they used to publish books that were nothing but jokes?"

"I did." She picked up a prefilled injector full of anesthetic. "There were people whose entire jobs involved telling jokes. I used to watch the vids sometimes, but they didn't make much sense. It was a lot of social and political commentary."

"Mid twenty-first century politics were extremely divisive." Ashwin didn't even flinch as she injected him. "The Energy Wars lasted for almost two decades. I imagine the conflict evidenced itself across most of popular culture. You know what the result was."

Eden. A self-sustaining city, beacon of the future, saved from the solar flares that had fried infrastructure across the country simply because they hadn't turned it on yet. "I studied it all, of course. The Flares, the military takeover of the Eden Project. It's just hard to reconcile." That didn't make any sense, so she tried again. "The pop culture, I mean. It was all so focused on things that didn't matter, not when the world was crumbling around them."

"Irrationality is the only human constant I've been able to discern." That almost-smile returned. "Take the O'Kanes in Sector Four. Their world did crumble, but they still threw parties. Maybe the only true human constant is that, as a species, we have no concept of a no-win situation."

"True. And they were right all along, weren't they? We're still here."

"So far." Ashwin rubbed his thumb absently over the twin bar codes imprinted on his wrist. "I don't identify with many of the traits I observe in people, but I understand that one. I've never met a Makhai soldier who could conceive of a no-win situation."

"Human nature," she murmured.

"So does that make us less human, or more?"

"About as human as the rest of us, I'd say." With the potential for all the same strengths and weaknesses, hopes and dreams. Joys and pain. "Are you going to the memorial?"

"Yes. Gideon requested that I attend."

Gideon wasn't exactly subtle when it came to his interest in pushing Ashwin and Kora together, but Jaden's memorial was a solemn event. A sacred one, and matchmaking had to be the last thing on his mind. "Do you think he'll ask you to stay in One?"

Nearly twenty seconds of tense silence passed before Ashwin nodded. "Most sector leaders would. I'm a formidable ally."

What Gideon wanted and what the Base would allow were two different things. "Won't administration want you back now that the deserters are gone?"

"You know them. What do you think they'd say if I told them Gideon Rios wanted me to stay on his estate?"

They wouldn't pass up the opportunity to form an alliance. They couldn't afford to, not when Gideon had access to every other sector leader—and all of their information, sensitive or otherwise. "I think...they'd expect a return on the investment of their resources, and that could get ugly for you."

His slightly quirked eyebrow left him looking almost wry. "If I leave Sector One, they could give me an even more uncomfortable assignment. That's my life, Kora. It's my job."

That was the part that scared her. "It's your job," she agreed flatly. "The question is, how well will you do it?"

"I used stolen drone technology and exposed our isotope tracking system to Gideon Rios's right-hand man." He smiled. "So far, I don't seem to be doing well."

Another forced, empty smile. Kora shuddered, nearly dropping her forceps. "You can't do anything that will hurt them. Promise me, Ashwin."

The smile vanished. This time, when he lifted his hand, he didn't let his fingertips hover. They brushed her cheek, warm and calloused and rough against her skin. "Hurting them would hurt you. You have to believe that I'll do anything within my power to avoid that, including commit treason. Again."

She tilted her face to his hand for a moment, chasing the contact before she caught herself. "Thank you."

"Don't thank me." His thumb traced a small, shivery circle on her cheek. "I'm not a good man, Kora. But you shouldn't have to be grateful that I won't hurt you."

Except what usually held people back from hurting others was morality—simply put, *emotion*—and he'd spent so much time telling her that wasn't a factor. Not for him. "I'm grateful anyway."

"All right." He touched her one last time before dropping his hand again. "I should let you finish. We're both expected at the memorial."

"Right." She still had to fully assess the damage, set up for regen, go through the painstaking process of rebuilding the damaged tissue...

And now her mind was reeling, not only with revelations but with possibilities. If Ashwin was going to be here, if he was going to stay—

*No*. She locked the thoughts away, forcing her attention to the task at hand. She couldn't let herself get distracted by what might be, not until it *was*. More than his health was at stake.

There was also her heart.

Ashwin was accustomed to the discomfort of regeneration tech.

He couldn't remember the first time he'd experienced it. His earliest memories remained difficult to sort into chronological order, but he must have been no more than six or seven. A nasty fall or a fight with another trainee—something had resulted in that first trip to see the regen techs in their white coats.

The forced growth of new cells hurt. Civilians were always offered some sort of anesthetic, but the Base wanted their Makhai soldiers to develop a tolerance for pain early. Over the years, Ashwin had been put back together so many times that a tech had once joked that he didn't have any of his original parts left.

The tech had been new. And Ashwin's blank, unamused stare had cured him of trying to joke with Makhai soldiers.

Kora was always different. His blank, unamused stare had never stopped her from telling jokes, and the Base's protocols had never stopped her from doing what she could to mitigate his pain. Here, in Sector One, she was free of the Base's cold rules and strictures. Under Gideon's protection, and with his encouragement, her skills had flourished.

A gentle ache was the only souvenir he carried of the bullet he'd taken in the shoulder. He'd touched the spot once while getting dressed, unsure why the shiny new skin felt so sensitive. Anticipation, perhaps. He could imagine her touching him there, her brow furrowed in concern. Her fingertips would trace the boundaries of the newly healed skin, as they'd done dozens of times before. Never impersonal and clinical. Always gentle and caring.

And now he knew what she sounded like when she came.

For all his ignorance of social customs, Ashwin knew it was an inappropriate thought. It was also inappropriate to let his gaze slide to the opposite side of the Rios family temple, where Kora stood between Maricela and the head priestess. Her blue eyes were trained on Gideon as he eulogized Jaden, and tears gathered on her lashes.

It was inappropriate to imagine her in the grip of pleasure, but it was preferable to the way his gut churned when he saw her pain. There was no enemy to fight here. No action to take. No bullet he could absorb with his body to keep it from hers.

Her grief was an impossible foe. Against it, Ashwin was helpless.

She glanced at him, her eyes locking with his for a fraction of a second. Then she bent her head, and the gathered tears rolled down her cheeks.

Ashwin looked away. He distracted himself by naming the muscles that had to flex to curl his fingers toward his palm. *Flexor digitorum superficialis. Flexor digitorum profundus. Flexor pollicis—*

A murmur of feminine voices seized his attention. He refocused his gaze in time to watch the string of robed acolytes filing toward where Gideon stood. Beside him, a sketched outline of Jaden decorated the tan stucco wall. One by one, the girls kissed their fingertips and pressed them to the drawing. Gideon's sisters followed, and then Kora, her fingers trembling as they brushed the wall.

The tall priestess—Del—came last. She put her palm on the center of the drawing, eyes closed, fingers spread wide as her lips moved in a silent benediction. When she was done, she turned to touch Gideon's arm. "Tomorrow?"

"Tomorrow," he agreed, then raised his voice. "Thank you all for honoring our fallen brother. Tonight, you'll help us celebrate his life. But for now..."

"We have somewhere else to be," Del finished firmly, waving a hand at her charges. Each dropped a short curtsy to Gideon before heading for the door. Everyone who wasn't a Rider was filing out, in fact, even Gideon's sisters. Ashwin turned to follow Kora, but a hand on his arm stopped him.

"Stay." The gentle kindness in Gideon's voice did nothing to soften its command.

Kora hesitated, and even Maricela stared at Gideon with wide eyes. A moment later, an encouraging smile supplanted her shock, and she tugged Kora toward the exit.

Kora's blue eyes stayed locked on him until the door closed behind her.

All around the room, the stiff, stoic posture of the Riders began to relax. Their line broke apart, and murmured conversation filled the cavernous silence. Some drifted around the room toward other portraits on the walls, while others followed Deacon to a table behind Gideon. A dozen handmade paintbrushes sat next to colorfully glazed stone bowls holding a rainbow's worth of colors.

Gideon gestured for Ashwin to follow him to the center of the temple. From there, they had a view of the long walls and the paintings that adorned them. The figures started on the far wall behind the altar—thirteen men, ten of them painted in vibrant colors with elegant skill, the last three still simple black outlines.

One depicted Deacon. The second was Adrian Maddox, Gideon's cousin who'd fled to Sector Four. The last was Gideon himself.

"The original Riders," Gideon murmured.

"Thirteen of us—a little on the nose, symbolically. Though, unlike my grandfather, I've never claimed to be directly descended from God himself."

Ashwin watched Ana climb the steps to stand in front of one of the original thirteen—a tall, rangy black man exquisitely painted with closely cut hair, a square jaw, and piercing brown eyes.

"Her father," Gideon supplied. "He died during the assault on the City Center inside Eden, and Ana petitioned to take his place. She put all of the men petitioning alongside her into the dirt during the initial tests."

Ashwin remembered the wary, challenging look she'd given him the first night he stepped into the barracks. Women had, from time to time, demanded the right to fight alongside the soldiers on the Base. A very few had been accepted into the infantry in the early days, but the generals had quickly abolished the practice. No matter how the women excelled, the male soldiers seemed incapable of coping with their presence.

It was a foible Ashwin had never understood. Humans came with a limited range of skills. Most were terrible at almost everything. When one exhibited aptitude, wasting it over inconsequential details like gender was a criminal mismanagement of resources. "If she's good at fighting, it's smart to let her fight."

Gideon's lips twitched. "A very logical assessment." He turned to the right and gestured to a spot halfway down the wall. Ana's portrait was at the end of the line, a simple black outline that still managed to capture her tumble of curly black hair, the tilt of her nose, and the challenging set of her lips. "It's the first ritual we experience as Riders. And the last. From the day they join, every Rider knows that death is coming for them. They face it on this wall. The beginnings of their own funerals."

Ashwin let his gaze slide back along the wall. Plenty of people were already painted in, but there were other outlines—Reyes, sleepy-eyed and defiant. Ivan, looking as stern and unfeeling as any Makhai soldier. Zeke, with his clean-cut features and spiky hair. Hunter, tall and broad, his impressive strength captured as much by his commanding expression as the outline of his biceps.

On the opposite wall, Jaden's outline was similarly large. Gabe approached with one of the brushes and carefully painted deep amber onto the hair falling over Jaden's brow. Reyes joined him with a lighter shade of orange, blending the colors together.

"Some of them are quite good at this," Gideon said quietly. "Del will come in later and finish the portrait, but the first brushstrokes are always fellow Riders."

A bonding ritual, then. Ashwin could appreciate the cunning of it. The Base had refined such tactics, elevating the creation of a cohesive team unit to precise and cynical science. Even the Makhai soldiers weren't immune—the ink decorating Ashwin's back proved that. Until Kora questioned it, he'd never considered the rationale. He was too accustomed to mimicking the actions of those around him.

But the tattoo mattered. The bonds between soldiers on the Base—forged by shared experience—*mattered*. When Lorenzo Cruz had reached out to him, desperate to find assistance to save his mortally wounded lover, Ashwin hadn't considered denying him, though he'd had to utilize Kora's skills to do it.

It was a code on the Base. An understanding. A favor asked. A favor owed.

Seven months ago, Ashwin had redeemed that favor. With his mind fragmenting and his thoughts circling more and more frequently back to Kora, he'd asked Cruz to find a safe place to hide her. And he'd asked him not to reveal that location, even if Ashwin demanded it.

A favor owed. A favor redeemed. Cruz had come through. Not in the way Ashwin had anticipated—Ashwin had expected Cruz to find a safe house or get her away entirely, perhaps taking her up into the mountain communities. Not to move her all of half a mile, from the makeshift hospital to the home of the man running it.

But because he hadn't anticipated it, it had worked. He hadn't been able to find Kora, not even when he went looking. And Cruz had kept his favor. Faced with Ashwin's destabilized rage, he'd shot Ashwin in the leg.

And after that, he'd *hurt* him.

*Fear hurts, Ashwin. It can break a person. If you try to take her somewhere right now, you'll terrify her. You'll hurt her. You can't keep her safe, not until you get yourself under control.*

It was the hardest truth anyone had ever given him. Few else would have dared. But Ashwin had felt the muzzle of Cruz's gun at the back of his head, had tasted his own death on the air—and he'd known Cruz was right.

He'd been no use to Kora like that. Breaking down. Wild. Obsessed with the scent of her, the sight of her, the *thought* of her. So he saw the sectors through their war, and then he went back to the Base to submit himself to recalibration.

They stripped Kora out of him. It had taken months of concentrated torture to return him to calm, reasoned logic. To cold numbness. To the peace of stillness.

She undid weeks of work every time she touched him.

"Malhotra."

Ashwin turned to find Deacon standing a pace away, holding out a paintbrush, handle-first. Though the critical part of his brain had no problem recognizing the emotional manipulation Gideon had orchestrated, honest assessment revealed a...twinge. Surprise and something else, sharp and minty, like the herbal tea he'd acquired as a gift in order to subvert the loyalties of one of his domestic handlers.

Makhai soldiers didn't belong. The other soldiers on the Base might be willing to trade favors and follow the code, but social moments were another matter. No one relaxed around a Makhai soldier. Few were willing to overtly shun them, but a thousand tiny comments and gestures carried the message clearly enough for even Ashwin to hear.

He was never wanted. He was not accepted. He was barely human.

Ashwin watched his fingers curl around the brush's wooden handle. Someone had crafted it lovingly, polishing it until it was perfectly smooth. He gripped it between his thumb and fingers and battled the seductive lie it embodied.

Deacon stepped aside, clearing a path to the table and its colorful paints, and Ashwin recognized the precariousness of his situation.

Gideon Rios was fighting the battle for Ashwin's soul on multiple fronts. With Kora, and the promise of affection and passion. With the Riders, and the possibility of brotherhood and belonging. No doubt Gideon would complete the assault by offering absolution for the terrible things Ashwin had done.

He was Makhai, beyond the frailty of human emotion. None of Gideon's attacks should tempt him. It wasn't just his duty to hold strong in the face of such an offensive, it was his *nature*.

Ashwin dipped the brush into the paint, then watched it obscure the tan brick with orange, the color so vibrant and alive it defied the grim sorrow that should have defined a memorial for the dead. Every last painting in the room seethed with life, bright and joyous in the face of loss.

Nothing followed the rules in Sector One.

Maybe he wouldn't, either.

# twelve

The party in the Riders' barracks wasn't like the bonfire. It was smaller, more intimate, tucked away behind the thick adobe walls. There was still music and dancing, liquor and laughter, but the vibe in the air felt different to Kora. Not desperate, not exactly, but focused. Intense.

It was still a celebration, but it was more careful than carefree, and not because the Riders were avoiding their grief. On the contrary, they seemed to be embracing it, folding it into the chaotic swirl of emotion that came with living.

That was Sector One—every moment experienced to the fullest, wide open, because every moment could be your last. It was fact, something to be mourned and revered in equal measure.

"Here." A bottle of cider appeared in front of Kora. Nita Reyes waited until Kora accepted it before dropping to the couch beside her, her legs tucked up beneath her colorful patchwork skirt. "One of my cousins brews this. My parents sent four cases as a memorial gift."

"Thanks." Nita was curvy and self-assured, dressed simply in the patchwork and leather she seemed to prefer over her temple robes. She had the same coloring as her brother, but that was where the similarities ended. Whereas Reyes was irreverent and unpredictable, Nita was more serious, almost reserved.

She sipped her cider and sighed. "Honestly, it's actually really good. Antonio has a gift for this. But my parents frown on anyone starting a business that isn't a natural extension of the ranch. He only gets away with this much because he's Tia Cristina's favorite, and no one argues with my aunt. Not even my father."

"I know how that feels." Kora twisted the cap off the bottle. "My adoptive father was a doctor. He made it pretty clear I would be, too. No arguments."

Nita tilted her head and studied her. "But you're so good at it. I'm trying to imagine you doing something else. Though I suppose that's the problem—of course we're good at the things they make us do from the time we're babies."

Kora couldn't fathom a life without medicine, without the ability to help those in need in an immediate, tangible way. "I would have become a doctor anyway," she admitted. "Sometimes it's more about wanting the choice than wanting something different."

"I understand." Nita leaned closer. "I always assumed that's why my brother did it." She nodded to where Reyes and Zeke were dancing with a pair of acolytes. "He was supposed to marry Maricela, you know. It had been arranged forever, and it was a huge scandal when he joined the Riders instead. But he wasn't rejecting Maricela. He *adores* her. He simply refuses to have his choice taken away."

"Oh, I don't know. He might have been rejecting me a little." Maricela bent over the back of the couch and snagged Kora's bottle of cider. "Something about how I kept giggling every time he tried to kiss me."

Nita groaned and closed her eyes. "I thought we had a rule, Maricela."

"Right—no talking about your brother's mouth and what he does with it." She paused. "Do yourself a favor and don't look across the room, okay?"

The words may as well have been a command. Kora glanced up to where Zeke and Reyes were dancing—or *had been*.

Zeke still was, though it could barely be called dancing. He was holding a blonde acolyte in his arms, her legs around his hips, her hair tangling with his as he nuzzled her neck. There was a slightly manic edge to his laughter that raked over Kora's nerves like metal against metal, and she averted her eyes.

Reyes had backed his dance partner up against the painted wall, one hand spread wide over the blue folds of a saint's robe. He was kissing her, the kind of kiss where no matter which way you turned your head, you couldn't get deep enough.

Nita cracked one eye open and groaned again. "By all the Saints..." She turned her back firmly on the sight and scrunched up her face at Maricela. "You're mean."

Kora rescued her cider and calmly took a sip. "When they're done, we should ask him if she still has her tonsils."

Maricela burst out laughing. "No, *she's* mean."

"I should go dance with Gabe or Ana," Nita

grumbled. "I bet he wouldn't take it half as calmly as I do."

"Too late." Maricela gestured to the hallway, where Reyes and his partner were slipping into the shadows. "Now you'll just have to do it for fun."

"I think I will." She finished her cider—definitely not her first—and rose. She swayed a little before she caught herself, then crossed the room to where Ana stood with Hunter and Gabe, listening to something Ashwin was saying.

Nita didn't settle for one partner. She grabbed Ana and Gabe both and dragged them toward the dancing crowd. A knot of Riders and acolytes broke apart and reformed around them, everyone swaying together, joyous and affectionate and uninhibited.

Ashwin remained, watching Kora. This expression was new, softer, open enough for her to sense what lay behind his dark gaze. Patience, peace—and desire. That part wasn't new, but it made her pulse speed up to see it like this, shared instead of locked away.

"Go," Maricela whispered, already pulling the bottle from her hand again.

Kora stood, the blood singing in her ears. Ashwin met her in the middle of the makeshift dance floor, his strong hands sliding to her hips. He wasn't awkward this time as he pulled her against his chest. "Hello, Kora."

It was even more knee-melting up close, all the *wanting*. "Hi."

He slid his hand to the small of her back, tugging her even closer as they moved with the music. "Is my dancing improving?"

He was teasing her, and she tried to quell her smile. "It wasn't bad to begin with. But you knew that."

"I suspected." He stroked her hair back from her

forehead. "I'm having illogical thoughts about you."

"The best kind." She snuck her fingers under the hem of his shirt, and the muscles in his stomach tensed. "Tell me."

"Are you certain?" He touched her temple, then traced a warm line down to her jaw. "You used to tell me your hypothesis. That Makhai soldiers have feelings."

Kora shivered. "I don't think it's the sort of thing you can take out of a person. Not easily."

"What if you're wrong?" His hand settled on her shoulder, his thumb resting at the base of her throat. "I want you in my bed, Kora. But not until you've considered all the risks. Not unless you know that the possibility is there."

"Which one?"

"That I'm empty," he answered simply. "That I'm broken. That I can promise to protect your body, but I may never have the capacity to make the same promise about your heart. That I might destroy it without meaning to."

She could taste the truth in his words. But they'd already had this conversation, with a different question—and the same answer. "There are worse things, remember?" She swayed closer to the mesmerizing heat of his body. "Being alone. Not feeling anything. I'd rather take the chance."

"I can make you feel." The pressure of his thumb increased slightly. A warning. "I know what your body needs, and I know how to give it to you. Be sure you want it. It will be intense—"

"Ashwin."

"It matters, Kora." His eyes were serious. Intent. "Women come to us willingly because they know we can please them, but they build fantasies about who we are. They lie, because no one who looks us in the eye really wants the monster staring back at them. I need to know you're not lying to yourself."

Guilt. Pain. She let them wash over her, then shook her head. "Would it matter to you if I was?"

She watched his face as he recognized the trap in her words. If he didn't care, they'd already be in his bed. And if he *did* care…

His mouth flattened into a firm line. He gripped her hips for a moment, then cupped her ass and dragged her up his body until she wrapped her legs around him. Her eyes were level with his, and *empty* was the last word to describe their deep-brown depths. "I warned you," he rumbled as he started for the hallway.

"You warned me," she agreed, then slanted her open mouth over his.

His kiss was focused, deep. He kissed her without missing a step, as if he could navigate the barracks with his eyes closed already. All she knew was the pressure of his lips and the tease of his tongue until her back thudded softly against the door to his room.

For two delicious heartbeats, he held her pinned against it, trapped between the door and the hard wall of his chest. Then the door vanished, and he tightened his arm around her waist before the sensation of falling backwards could claim her. Distantly, she heard him kick the door shut and nudge a chair out of the way.

Distantly. Because he was kissing her like he could do it forever.

Panting, she tore her mouth from his. They were next to the bed, and she held her breath as he lowered her to stand beside it.

"Hold up your arms."

She started to obey, but her hands had other ideas. They brushed his chest and lingered, pressing through the fabric. "Do I need to ask *you*?"

His brow furrowed slightly. "Ask me what?"

"If you're sure." She twisted her fingers in his T-shirt. "I'm not the only one who could get hurt."

"I don't mind physical pain." He slid his hands over hers, gently freeing them from the fabric. "And if you hurt me some other way...you'd win, wouldn't you?"

He was serious. Kora tilted her head back and met his gaze. "It's not about being right or proving a hypothesis. It's your *life*, Ashwin. That matters to me."

He lifted one of her hands and kissed the center of her palm. "That's why I'm sure."

She didn't know until he said them exactly how much she needed to hear the words, too. She tried to tell him so, but her breath caught again, and she raised her arms above her head.

He moved slowly. Precisely. It was everything she'd ever known of Ashwin—his seriousness, his meticulous attention to detail—distilled into the gentle glide of his hands as they traced down her arms and over her sides.

He didn't strip off her dress all at once. He took his time, gathering the soft blue fabric in his fists and coaxing it up inch by inch. It tickled over her skin, an unending caress that he dragged out until the breath she was holding escaped on a moan.

"I have a plan," he murmured as the dress cleared her head, sending her tousled hair cascading around her face. Ashwin dropped the dress and smoothed the locks back from her cheeks, his fingertips lingering to caress the shell of her ear. "I formulated it when you came to me last night, but I've been revising and refining it all day."

"All—" Her voice broke, and she swallowed—hard. "All day? Surely it's not complicated enough to warrant that."

"It's not about being complicated." He brushed glancing, maddening touches over her back and the line of her spine on his way to the clasp on her bra. One efficient twist of his fingers and the fabric went loose, one strap slipping from her shoulder. "It's about being thorough. A man who wouldn't be meticulous in devising the best way to give you pleasure is a man who doesn't deserve to touch you."

"Really?" Another moan built in her throat, and she released it on a shaky sigh. "I think figuring it all out should be part of the fun." She touched his face, drawing a line from his cheekbone to the corner of his mouth, and smiled when he sucked in a breath. "See?"

Something dangerous burned in his eyes as he turned his head to nip at her fingers. It almost hurt, and the sensation zipped along her nerve endings like an electric shock.

She was trembling now, so she dropped her hand to his shoulder and pulled at the soft cotton of his shirt in silent demand.

He answered by lifting his arms.

Kora didn't have his patience. She jerked at the fabric, and it caught on his chin and tangled around his arms. He helped her by stripping it away and letting it fall to the floor.

She'd seen him half naked more times than she could count. Most of their interactions had involved his partial nudity. It was different now that she was undressed, too, and that look in his eyes—

Kora slid her arms around him, traced the scratches she'd left on his shoulders the night before, then stepped back until her legs hit the edge of the mattress.

He followed her, looming over her for a dizzying moment before sinking to his knees. He smoothed his thumb over the edge of her simple black panties as his gaze drifted up to hers. "You've touched yourself before, haven't you?"

The question surprised her—and it shouldn't have. The fact that he wasn't sure he could feel emotion had no bearing on his sexual experience. He'd mentioned other women, and he must have had domestic handlers.

He'd had sex before. Probably lots and *lots* of it. She was the inexperienced one here. "I have."

"Show me." He caught one of her hands and pressed it to her abdomen, her fingers spread wide beneath his. But instead of guiding her down, he slid their hands up. When she was cupping her breast, he let his touch fall away.

Her cheeks heated, but she didn't look away as she squeezed her fingers together, pinching her nipple between them. She shivered at the sudden spike of pleasure, more intense because he was watching her so closely.

"You don't mind it either, do you?" The sudden warmth of his breath on her abdomen kept her shivering. He soothed her with an open-mouthed kiss and the gentle brush of his tongue, so sweet she wasn't ready for the sudden shock of his teeth closing on her skin. "A little bit of pain."

Her voice failed her, so she shook her head.

"It's all right." He hooked his fingers under her panties and dragged them lower. His mouth followed, hot against her hip and so, so soft. "Sometimes pain is a warning. But like this, with someone you trust…" She anticipated the jolt this time, but she still swayed when his teeth sank into her skin. "It's a different kind of sensation."

Her knees would barely hold her. "Ashwin..."

"I know." He pulled her underwear down her legs

and lifted her feet from the fabric one by one. When she stood naked before him, he gripped her hips. "Sit."

He was so close that she had to move her knees to one side of his body to keep them together as she obeyed.

"Kora." He stroked one of her thighs, drawing his fingers all the way from her hip to the rounded tip of her knee. He didn't exert any pressure, just rested there as he studied her face. Something shifted behind his eyes—or maybe it was in his touch. She *felt* the swell of protective tenderness before he slipped his free hand into her hair and pulled her into a deep, overwhelming kiss.

*Oh.*

She'd kissed him already, and he'd let her, but that was a whole different thing. An indulgence, really, definitely not this focused, driving need. It cut through her self-consciousness like a hot knife through ice, and she melted.

His mouth left hers only to travel to her jaw. Sweet kisses. Soft. No teeth or sudden jolts this time, simply warmth and tingles as he kissed his way down her neck and back up her throat to claim her mouth again. His fingers brushed her inner thigh, subtly stroking, and she realized that she'd opened her legs—shamelessly, wantonly, like she couldn't wait for him to touch her.

She couldn't wait for him to touch her.

Anything to keep this delicious tension building. Kora rocked forward just as Ashwin leaned closer, and the contrasts made her head swim. The hardness of his body against the softness of hers, his heat enveloping her while she could still feel the cool tile beneath her toes.

The way the world fell away, even as it suddenly made sense.

This. Whenever she'd wondered about the nature of happiness or the significance of pleasure or the meaning of life, it was only because she hadn't found *this.*

"Yes," he murmured against her throat, as if he'd heard the thought. His hands swept up her body, not so gentle anymore as they cupped her breasts, his thumbs unerringly finding her nipples. His sharp, indrawn breath echoed hers, a quiet fracture in his self-control.

Before she could revel in it, he bent his head and sucked her nipple into his mouth. The wet heat alone was enough to arch her back, but then his tongue brushed the painfully tight peak. She sank her teeth into her lower lip, but the sound still tore from her throat—half protest, half plea.

He gave her more. His teeth grazed her sensitized flesh, sparking a shiver of nervous anticipation. His hand tightened at the base of her neck, holding her in place as he licked and teased. When the pain came, it was from his thumb and forefinger pinching tightly together on her other nipple.

She scratched her nails over his chest, anything to distract herself from the desperation in her own voice. "It's not enough."

"Not yet." The world swam around her, and she realized he was leaning her back. Her shoulders touched the soft quilt spread over his bed, and his mouth found hers again for a desperate moment. Then he was gone, moving back down her body, leaving heat and wet kisses behind. To her breasts, then lower, tracing a circle around her belly button.

He settled between her legs again, pressing them wide as he stroked her inner thighs. "You know what you need." The words vibrated against her hipbone as his thumbs circled higher and higher—but not high enough. "Say it."

"I need to come," she whispered. "I need *you*."

His grip on her legs tightened, just for a heartbeat.

Then he put his mouth on her.

The shock of it almost brought her hips off the bed. She knew it was light, careful—the barest hint of his tongue gliding over her flesh—but it didn't feel that way. It felt like the final step down a long, endless path, like she hadn't even realized how much she'd longed for him until this moment.

She had to touch him, so she slid her shaking fingers through his hair and pulled at the short strands. He hummed in low approval, the vibrations adding another layer of bright, intense sensation. She clung to him as his thumbs brushed her next, stroking and then parting. His next lick was firmer, deeper.

Relentless.

No amount of curiosity or study about how this worked theoretically could have prepared her for this intricate dance. Kora had expected him to be attentive, to act based on her reactions, but she hadn't foreseen how having his hands tremble on her thighs would drive her arousal higher. It wasn't physical—he wasn't doing anything *different*—but knowing how her pleasure affected him…

It was electric.

Suddenly, she understood the appeal of spending a day planning an encounter like this, because it wasn't about planning at all. It was about anticipation.

His tongue swept upward, shattering thought as he drew a delicate circle around her clit. When her hips jerked, he caught her, strong fingers holding her in place so he could repeat the gesture.

Over and over. He held her so she couldn't squirm away, and then, when sensation overwhelmed her, so that she couldn't chase his tongue. It should have frustrated her, and it *did*, but not as much as she craved the leashed strength in his hands, holding her together as she fell apart.

The orgasm that swept through her was just like the one the night before, quick and hard, pleasure and relief in equal measure. She muffled her moan with the back of her hand, pressing until her teeth bit into her lips to hold back the sound.

"Don't." An order, whispered against her still-trembling flesh. Ashwin lifted his head, and his thumb replaced his tongue, gliding in effortless, slippery circles. "Don't hide your reactions. I want them."

"The party—"

"They can't hear you." He kissed the inside of her thigh. "Listen, Kora. The density of the adobe walls muffles sound. You can barely hear the music."

She could feel the bass line vibrating through the barracks, but she couldn't hear the music or the noise from the main room. She pushed up on her elbows and arched an eyebrow at Ashwin. "If you can still think about the density of adobe, I think it's your turn to have your brain melted."

He mirrored her gesture, one dark eyebrow swooping up. Without breaking eye contact, he gripped her thighs harder and ducked his head again. This time, when his tongue swept out, the shock of pleasure twisted with the way he was staring at her—intent. Challenging.

Her arms went as weak as the rest of her, and she slipped back to the bed as he ravished her with his mouth. No careful exploration this time. No slow build. He used his thumbs to hold her open and devoured her. His tongue swept up and down, dipped into her body to tease. Before she could catch her breath he returned to her clit—not gentle circles this time but a ravenous assault.

That would have been overwhelming all on its own. But every noise she made, every jerk of her hips, every time she clutched at his hair or dug her nails into his shoulders—

It was subtle at first. A tightening of his fingers. A rumbling groan. But every layer he stripped away from her seemed to fracture his icy façade. She *felt* it, a feverish prickle as he drove her toward a second orgasm.

She opened her mouth to whisper his name, but the whisper turned into a choked cry as he sucked her clit between his lips. Her whole body clenched as she hurtled over the edge again, writhing on the bed, pulsing with something so desperate that she barely recognized it as pleasure.

He *growled.* Low and guttural, the raw need behind it spilling over her like liquid fire. He turned his face to her thigh and bit her there, a sharp nip that brought her hips up again.

He was there to meet her, sliding one impossibly broad finger into her body. "I can feel you coming."

"*Ashwin.*" He had to stop. If he didn't, she'd burn alive from the inside out.

"I warned you." He pushed her thighs wider, leaving her utterly exposed to his gaze. He pumped his finger in and out as she clenched in helpless release. "I'll make you feel. Do you want me to stop?"

*Yes.* The word dissolved on her tongue as her gaze locked with his. There was nothing cool or distant about him now, not like this. He was watching her like he'd never seen anything so entrancing. Like she was the only thing that existed in the world.

He stilled, his finger buried inside her. "You have to tell me, Kora. Tell me to stop. Or tell me to give you more."

She rocked her hips and moaned when the movement pushed his finger deeper. "Ashwin, *please*."

His thumbnail dragged across her sensitive inner thigh. "You always poked where you weren't supposed to go on any network. Did you find the Sin Servers?"

The breath lodged in her lungs. "Would I admit it if I had?"

"You don't need to admit it." His finger rocked just a little, but the friction was unbearable, stroking over nerves she'd never been aware of before. "You're too curious. Too hungry. You know what you want, Kora, so say it. Use the words that you try not to think. The ones that feel too obscene."

It felt like a test...until she met his eyes again. He wasn't just pushing her—the limits of her experience, the boundaries even she had yet to discover—he was pushing himself, as well. Every word would strip a little more of his control, and the thought alone made her clench around his finger.

She needed it, though *need* was too weak a word to describe this craving. It was like oxygen, water. Necessary to her survival.

"I want to fuck you," she whispered. "Hard. I want you to feel it like I do. To know that when it's over, no matter what happens, you'll never be the same."

"Never," he rasped, a single word that carried all the promise of a sworn vow. He flexed his finger again, working it in slick thrusts, and settled his thumb over her clit. Pleasure jolted back, bright and hot, almost enough to distract her as he pushed a second finger into her.

It hurt and it *didn't*. Instinct took over, and Kora clenched her fists around the quilt for leverage and arched toward him. The pain grew and subsided all at once, meshing with the tension and desire until there was nothing left but an excruciating *something*, sweeping down on her with an intensity that threatened to tear her apart.

He rose, his fingers sliding deeper as he leaned over her. One hand closed on the quilt next to her head, catching strands of her hair that tugged deliciously. His face blocked out the ceiling, his dark gaze locked on hers as he met the impatient arc of her hips, matching her rhythm effortlessly. "Just like that. Show me how it feels."

She braced her hands on his chest, shuddering when his muscles flexed and moved under her touch. The contact anchored her, another point of connection in a world that suddenly contained nothing but the two of them. "It feels—" Her voice broke on a helpless cry.

"Tell me." Tension twisted tighter around her, and he wasn't coaxing slowly anymore. His thumb commanded as much as his voice, slipping back and forth in demanding strokes that set her body on fire. "What do you feel?"

Full. Aching. Drawn tight, like the string of a bow. Words tumbled around in her brain, and the ones that escaped her on a sobbing breath were small. Inadequate. "It's so *good*."

He was breathing so fast. Rough, each exhale almost a groan. "Yes. I can make you feel good."

*Don't stop.* She wasn't sure if she thought the words or screamed them as the tension snapped and wave after wave of hot pleasure crashed through her. It wasn't quick and smooth this time. It was choppy, each pulse glancing off another, until she wasn't sure where it had begun—or when it might end.

His fingers withdrew, leaving her empty and lost, only to return wider and fuller—three of them. "You can take more."

She couldn't, and she did. Pain and pleasure didn't exist as discrete emotions anymore. Every bit of sensation from his slow, careful fingers was just heat, feeding a hunger that made no sense. She was shaking, shuddering, exhausted and weak with bliss—

And she still wanted him.

Her hands trembled as they skipped over his skin, searching for something to hold on to as the waves began to build in strength again, picking up right where they'd left off. Her fingers locked around his belt, and she tried to tell him she was coming *again*, but all she could manage was a whimper. Her toes curled, every muscle clenched, and she clung to him helplessly.

She'd never survive this. And it would be worth it.

Ashwin realized he'd gone too far the fourth time she came around three of his fingers.

Once would have been enough. No, once would have still been too many, because there was no practical reason to push an inexperienced woman so far. Her body had been tight enough around one finger to provide adequate friction to get her off. He could rationalize a second finger by acknowledging her predilection for intense sensation.

Three was simply selfish. It was selfish to savor the way she reacted to the gentle pressure against her boundaries, to drink in the way she wallowed in being overwhelmed. To live vicariously through her unchecked ability to feel so much, so recklessly.

She was his mirror, his opposite, except in these moments where she was so high on sensation she didn't care if the next drop came in the form of pleasure or pain, as long as it came.

And when *she* came—

He stilled his fingers inside her, but her muscles gripped him in shuddering clenches. She was wet and hot, two quantifiable, concrete facts. A third fact: his cock had been hard since the first brush of her skin against his had sparked pain along his nerves.

Disjointed, unrelated facts. He kept them carefully separate in his head as he eased his fingers from her body and soothed her whimper with a gentle brush of his hand. Connecting those facts would be dangerous, because he knew how the math of that equation worked out. He'd already fucked her more thoroughly than any virgin required. He did *not* get to imagine the intense relief of sliding into her body and working her from sleepy-eyed disorientation back to frantic need.

Instead, he lifted her to his chest. Her head lolled back against his shoulder, her expression still dazed. He cradled her close as he settled at the head of his bed, his back against the plain wooden headboard.

She...*fit* in his lap. Her head tucked easily beneath his chin, the blonde locks of her hair tickling his throat. She made a soft noise and slid her arms around his neck.

Trusting. Sweet. He was used to the acidic undertone of guilt provoked by her easy faith in him, but it was harder to contain it when she was like this. Naked, figuratively and literally. Utterly vulnerable and exposed.

He wanted to destroy anything that threatened her.

*He* was threatening her.

She shifted in his arms, and he loosened his grip enough to let her turn and straddle his thighs. The look in her eyes wasn't dazed anymore. Her innate sweetness had melted into something far more predatory, and the tingle of pain as he rested his hands on her bare hips was as much warning as lingering conditioning.

*Inexperienced, not innocent.*

No, the woman staring down at him with suddenly intent blue eyes might be inexperienced, but she was far from innocent. She knew exactly what she wanted.

And Ashwin didn't. No one had ever looked at him like this before.

"So severe." Kora smoothed her hands over his shoulders and kissed the corner of his mouth. "Relax."

He barely felt the pain anymore. It was simply there, a charged sensation not unlike static electricity. "I'm not trained to relax."

"Not even here?" Her hands drifted lower, and she kissed him again, for longer this time. "With me?"

Her fingers brushed his belt buckle, and he'd felt more relaxed when he was balanced on the edge of a building in a windstorm. "You're naked. And you're unbuckling my belt."

Metal clicked, and Kora smiled slowly. "Yes, I am."

He had to wrest control of this situation back into his hands. Standing on the edge of a building was safe by comparison. If Kora knocked him off balance...

"We shouldn't," he said softly, catching her hands. "You'll be sore."

She nodded. "Hurting me would hurt you. I understand." A pause. "Can you trust me?"

*Yes.* He was too disciplined to let the word escape without consideration, but he *wanted* to. When she looked at him like this—gentle, knowing, as if she *saw* him, and she'd always been the only one who seemed to see him—he would stand on the edge of the building if she asked him.

He'd fall, too.

Slowly, he lowered his hands to his sides. "Yes. I trust you."

"Good." She touched her forehead to his. "I wouldn't

betray that, Ashwin. Not for anything."

He waited for the guilt to reclaim him, but her nimble surgeon's fingers had already worked his pants open. No subjective emotion could compete with the immediate, blistering sensation of her warm, soft hand curling around his erection.

Intense physical pleasure. Immediate painful feedback. He gritted his teeth and hissed in a breath, shuddering as the conflicting sensory input blazed through him. "Kora—"

Her grip tightened, and the light kisses she was trailing down the center of his chest turned into her tongue tracing the same path.

His blood was boiling again, surging through his veins in a fury, and if he closed his eyes, he'd be back there. Sitting in a sterile exam room, the one where Kora had treated him a dozen times before. He'd tied the memory of every touch and every smile into the drug his fellow Makhai soldier had injected into him. He'd twisted the agony with Kora until the thought of her hurt, until he'd rewritten every memory with the feeling of acid eating him from the inside out.

It hadn't worked. Pain had never been an effective warning system because he was too willing to disregard it. Even now, the slide of her tongue across his abdomen burned sweetly, but every touch hurt less than it should. She was making new memories.

He fixed them in his mind, because he couldn't stop himself. The sight of her peeking up at him as she stroked his cock with eager curiosity was breathtaking. If someone captured it in paint, he might appreciate art for the first time.

But it was nothing compared to the sight of her parted lips lowering toward the head of his cock. Her tongue flicked out, still so curious...

Lightning.

All of the built-up static discharged at once. His body jerked, and he slammed his head back against the headboard, blinded by pain he couldn't manage, couldn't compartmentalize.

She was still there, behind his eyelids. An afterimage of the moment that had overwritten his base conditioning. Tousled golden hair falling around flushed cheeks. Pink lips parted. Blue eyes gazing up at him with power and anticipation and *want*, actual, specific want.

For a Makhai soldier. For a man.

For him.

Her tongue brushed over him, soft and wet and rough, and this time he hissed in pure, unchecked pleasure. He fisted both hands in the quilt to keep from reaching for her as he forced his eyes open. "Do that again."

She stared up at him, eyes like the desert sky before a storm, and licked a slow, leisurely circle around the head of his cock.

It wasn't the first time a woman had touched him like this. His third domestic handler had been fond of this activity, provided Ashwin catered to her fantasies. Sinking his hands into her hair to play the conquering beast had been a simple enough role, even for him. But he'd always puzzled over the apparent contradiction—why a woman with so little power would dream of having him take away even those scraps.

Now he understood. Because the desire to sink his fingers into Kora's hair was so undeniable, his fingers twitched on the blanket. And if she lifted her head right now and told him to fight an entire squadron with his bare hands, he wouldn't blink.

The fantasy was about this overwhelming madness

inside him. About being desired by the monster so completely that you owned him. So he'd fight for you, kill for you. Protect you.

He'd burn down worlds for Kora. And he couldn't hold back from her.

Exhaling shakily, he threaded the fingers of one hand through her hair. He curled his fingers to cup the back of her head—gentle, not pushing—and let the command roll out of him. "More. Deeper. Suck me."

Her eyes flashed, and she licked her lips. Then she closed her mouth around him and squeezed her hand tight around his shaft.

That alone might have been enough. Considering how long it had been since he'd achieved physical release and how tightly wound he was with the taste of her pussy still on his tongue... No, it wouldn't take much to reach orgasm. And that had always been the goal before. But now he was entranced by the sight of her. By the flush in her cheeks, and the way her lips stretched to accommodate him when he pressed gently on the back of her head and she obediently took him deeper.

Was this part of her genetic makeup? Did the need to soothe pain extend to an eagerness to give pleasure? It was easier to comprehend than the possibility that the enthusiastic noise she made as he guided her head lower could be inspired entirely by desire for him.

He twisted his fingers, gripping her hair hard enough to pull her back up until the crown of his cock balanced against her lower lip. "Do you like this?"

She sat up, tugging against his hold on her hair, and slid astride his lap. Close, closer, until her breasts brushed his chest. "I like this," she breathed, low and throaty, as she wrapped her hand around his cock again. "I like *you*."

Simple truth, offered up so willingly—and dangerously seductive. Ashwin gave in to the fantasy—his first, because a *fantasy* was different than a plan. A fantasy meant disregarding inconvenient realities and embracing improbabilities.

So he did. He tightened his grip in her hair and held her there, her lips so close to his he could taste her on the air. He curled his other hand over the base of his shaft. His fingers were still slick from being inside her, and he shuddered as he stroked up to meet her hand. "Tighter," he murmured, sliding his hand over hers. "You can be rough with me."

"I know." She pulled free of his grasp, dragged her nails across the back of his hand, then rubbed her thumb over the sensitive spot just beneath the head of his cock. "But I can be gentle, too."

She was teasing him. The playful spark in her eyes promised retribution for his methodical seduction, and for all the immediacy of his arousal, it was as if the acid in his veins had been replaced with warm honey.

He'd let her torture him all night.

Kora kissed him—soft, slow, her tongue dancing over his. Their first kiss without the sting of pain, and he tilted his head to deepen it, thrilling in how readily she welcomed him. Then she began to move, rocking her hips to nudge their clasped hands. The friction was minimal, just enough to keep his arousal at a simmer…

Until she moaned into his mouth and squeezed him tighter.

Fire shot through him. He released her hair and gripped the curve of her hip instead, splaying his fingers wide across her ass. "Faster," he groaned into her mouth, guiding her to quicken her pace. Her pussy ground against the backs of his fingers, and she threw back her head with another moan, this one lower, almost primal.

She could come again, and it wouldn't take much. Ashwin pulled their joined hands away and hauled her body to his. Her slick, hot flesh cradled his erection, and she cried out as he gripped her hips and moved her, sliding her clit up and down his shaft.

Kora clung to him, muffling her cries against his shoulder. Then the heat of her open mouth turned to delicious pain as she bit him—not a careful rake of her teeth designed to arouse, but *hard*, like she couldn't stop herself.

The pleasure of it tightened every muscle in his body. He wavered on the knife's edge, uncertain for the first time in his life if he retained the self-control not to orgasm. Then she shuddered in his arms, her moans shifting to the ones he'd already committed to memory—

High at first. Breathy. Then low and full. He could hear the relief wash over her as she came apart.

His control unraveled.

He clutched her hips as he came, pleasure at the center of a storm of irrational, illogical emotion. He stopped trying to process it all and simply *felt*—the slick evidence of her desire, the impossible heat of her body. The way her flesh gave under his fingers, soft and forgiving.

His semen, spilling across their skin, and the pang of regret was the only thing logical about this moment. It was rational to wish that he was coming inside her, because survival was the only instinct no one had never tried to rip out of him. Instinct demanded that he tumble Kora to her back and spread her legs wide, fill her with his cock until the stretch of it burned into pleasure and she sobbed for more. To pump deep and come, because that was what procreation was all about.

Survival. Eternal life for your DNA. It didn't matter that he'd undergone the contraceptive procedure the Base mandated in deployed Makhai soldiers—the *instinct* was still there, maybe stronger in him than in most. His DNA was extraordinarily tailored to survival, after all.

All of it would be more rational than gathering her spent body carefully in his arms, utterly content as she panted against his neck and shivered with delicate aftershocks.

He couldn't blame any of this on survival. He'd simply...enjoyed it.

Far too much.

Kora huffed out a breath, followed by another, her shoulders shaking. He tensed, gripped with the certainty that she agreed—that her silent sobs indicated it had been *too much*.

Then he realized she was *laughing*.

Relief was immediate—but so was something else. A foreign sensation he disliked immediately, one that made him feel exposed. "Is something funny?"

"We are." She lifted her head and brushed her tangled hair back from her flushed face. "We're idiots. We could have been doing this already. We could *live* like this, naked in your bed."

The foreign sensation jerked in the other direction so fast, he finally understood what it was—a pricked ego. Smug pride replaced it, and he reached up to help her smooth her hair from her damp forehead. "That wouldn't be practical."

"Oh, I disagree. I think it's my best idea ever."

Her blonde curls tangled around his fingers, and he took his time coaxing them gently apart. "You're also under the influence of a great deal of oxytocin."

"Pillow talk—it's a thing. You can look it up later."

She traced his lower lip with one fingertip. “For now, you could just say that no one else has ever made you feel like that. That’s a solid line. It works.”

“I don’t need a line.” He smoothed the detangled strands of hair back over her shoulder and followed the line of her collarbone to where her pulse beat in her throat—still elevated. Was it lingering exertion or nerves? “No one else has ever made me feel.”

The quick thump of her pulse skipped. She stared down at him, her eyes welling until they glittered with tears. Her mouth opened, then closed, then opened again. “I’m sorry. *And* I’m glad.”

He hated the tears. They felt like recrimination, stirring a restless need to vanquish whatever made her sad. Instead, he tugged her closer and tucked her head beneath his chin. His fingertips found the roses tattooed on her spine, and he traced the edges of each one in turn, hoping it would feel like absent, soothing comfort.

He wasn’t built to make her happy. The unalterable truths of his existence would prick at her heart, even as she stripped those truths away, one by one. And he would end up as fixated and obsessed with her as he had been six months ago.

And then he’d probably hurt her in new ways.

# grace

Grace's brother was dead.

In all fairness, it shouldn't have come as a shock, or even new information. The families of Riders considered them gone the moment they signed up. They *had* to, because they were meant to mourn them then, to get this wrenching pain out of the way long before the promise of death was ever fulfilled.

It was supposed to be a mercy, a way to keep them from the agony of waiting out the inevitable. But no matter how hard she tried, Grace had never been able to make it work in her head, because she always knew Jaden was out there, breathing and laughing and full of *life*.

And now he wasn't.

She clutched her blanket more tightly around her

shoulders—it wasn't cold outside, but she was shivering. The knot of burning ice in the pit of her stomach wouldn't let her stop.

Grace wandered to the open back door, but the idea of walking inside the house made her throat close with near-panic. It was filled not only with memories of her brother, but with the traditional sympathy gifts that followed a death in the family. Because of Jaden's status as one of Gideon's Riders, they were especially extravagant—not just food and other basics, but gold milagros, double shoulders of soft leather, and bolts of handwoven cloth.

She couldn't look at them right now.

She turned her eyes toward the sky instead. The stars here looked the same as they did back home in Sector Seven, clear and bright against the velvet darkness. It only *felt* like she was worlds away from that place, that time.

After their mother died, Jaden worked all the time to support them—laboring by day in the fields that needed extra hands, and by night in the pub tents where the workers drank away their meager pay. He kept Grace away from it all, never letting her take on more than a little extra washing and mending.

He promised to take care of her, and he kept that promise. Here she was, safe and secure in Sector One, and her biggest problem was that she couldn't stand being in her warm, well-stocked house.

"Grace?"

She recognized the voice. She spun around, and there he was—Zeke James, carrying a bottle of liquor in one hand, dressed in jeans and a pre-Flare T-shirt that was older than everything. He wore a serious expression of concern that didn't suit him at all. His was a face made for smiles, not grief.

Too fucking bad, because grief was what they had tonight.

"Sorry." He gestured over his shoulder, toward the front door. "When you didn't answer, I got worried. I can leave, if you want."

"No, it's fine. I was just…" No possible explanation would make sense, so she moved on. "Is that for me?"

"Yes." He held out the bottle, but he wouldn't quite meet her eyes. "It isn't much, just some bourbon from Sector Four. I wasn't sure…" This time his gesture took in the gifts covering her table and spilling onto the floor. "I figured anything I could come up with someone already would have given you."

"Bless you for not bringing food." She walked into the kitchen and shut the back door behind her, blotting out the sky and the stars and the memories. "I ran out of room in the fridge by lunch. I had to start giving it to my neighbors. There's one older lady who doesn't know—about Jaden, I mean—and I couldn't tell her. I made up some bullshit story about perfecting a new recipe, and now she thinks I can cook." Oh God, she was babbling. *Shut up, Grace.*

Sympathy tightened Zeke's eyes, but all he said was, "It's hard. I've been here over ten years, and the way they grieve...or *don't* grieve…" He shrugged. "It's hard, if you didn't grow up here."

"Yes." It helped that he understood, more than she expected it to. She draped the blanket across the back of a kitchen chair and reached for the bottle. "Shall we?"

"Sure." He handed her the bottle and watched as she retrieved two glasses. "Listen, I know they do a lot of things kind of weird, but there are some things Gideon gets really right. Like taking care of his people. And you're one of his people, you know. You have been since Jaden joined up."

She cracked the seal on the bottle and shook her head. The last thing she wanted to think about was being someone else's responsibility now that her brother was gone, an eternal burden for Gideon to inherit. "I'll be okay, Zeke. I'll be just fine."

"I know." He said it almost fervently, but when she glanced at him, his expression was still serious, almost shuttered. "But hear me out. Please."

Grace poured the bourbon, too much in each glass, and passed him one.

She knew whatever it was mattered to him when he fortified himself with half the liquor before speaking again. "There's a seamstress over on the edge of the East Temple district. I think she's Gabe's second or third cousin, or his great aunt or something. She's getting older and wants to retire, so I was thinking...I could buy her out for you."

Her stomach lurched. Gideon was one thing—he was responsible for everyone in the sector, no matter their situation or status—but this was different. If Zeke bought a shop for her, it would connect them in a very real, tangible way. Even if he never expected her to pay him back, even if he swore she owed him nothing, the link would always be there.

She considered it. She hated herself for it, sure, but she *considered* it. Not for the relative comfort he was offering, but for that connection.

He was still talking. "You can take over the shop, and she'll stick around to help you get going. And you could learn from her—"

"*No.*"

Zeke's teeth snapped together. "At least think about it. It wouldn't even cost me that much—she'll probably cut a deal for one of Gabe's friends. And then you wouldn't have to worry."

Oh, his guilt must have been crippling. Unbearable. "I know you were there with him, Zeke."

His handsome, friendly face just...shut down. "This isn't about that."

"Don't." She reached across the small wooden island that separated them and gripped his forearm, tight enough for her fingers to dig into the tense muscle. "You were his family, too, all of you. Maybe more important than me because he *chose* you. He would have been glad that you made it."

Zeke drained his glass and grabbed the bottle. In silence, he poured another double and tossed that one back, too. He didn't *look* drunk, but Grace was starting to wonder. "He would want you to be taken care of. That's all he ever wanted."

"You don't owe him, if that's what you're thinking."

He slammed his hand down so hard the bottle rocked. "Fuck it, Grace. It's not about *owing*. It's about—" His fingers curled into a fist, and he exhaled roughly. "Never mind."

*He's gone.* Even thinking the words made her chest ache. Saying it would make it real, permanently, inescapably *real*. But of course it was. Jaden was dead. If souls existed, then his was gone. Even his body had already been destroyed, burned on the traditional pyres that were customary in One.

Her brother was dead. According to Sector One's other customs, so was Zeke. Unfathomable, with him standing in front of her, blazing with so much life and anger and pain.

"Jaden's gone, Ezekiel." Her voice was surprisingly steady, and she forged ahead. "It hurts like hell, but there's nothing either of us can do about it. It just *is*. We can't fix it. We just have to get through it."

"I know." Zeke ran his fingers through his hair, and the usually spiky blond strands seemed as deflated as he did. His shoulders slumped, and he reached for the bottle again. But instead of pouring another drink, he found the cap and carefully screwed it on. "If you need anything, ask, okay? For him, if you won't do it for yourself."

She wouldn't need anything, not from Gideon or the other Riders, and especially not from Zeke. She couldn't afford to. "He loved it here. When we left Seven, I wasn't sure where we'd end up, but the minute Jaden set foot in the temple, he was home."

After a moment of hesitation, he reached out, and his fingertips brushed the back of her hand. "Even if you don't need anything, you're not alone, okay? Jaden had a dozen brothers, so you have them, too."

Her stomach twisted again. The words cut, but at least Zeke wouldn't notice. He never did. Not her nervousness or her starry eyes or the way she blushed furiously whenever she got within ten feet of him.

Knowing that he had no idea she was madly in love with him was the only way she had any pride left, and even that was slipping away. Part of her wanted to cling to his words, to ask him to stay. They could finish off the bottle and talk until the sun peeked over the eastern horizon to stream through the windows.

But if he stayed, it would be out of pity, because he felt sorry for the lonely girl who'd just lost the last of her family. And that was the only thing worse than knowing he didn't think about her at all.

"Goodbye, Zeke." She forced out the words before she changed her mind. "And thank you for the bourbon."

He took the hint and started for the door. "Take care, Grace."

"You, too." She didn't watch him leave. Instead,

she tucked the bottle of liquor away on the table along with the expensive cloth and milagros and picked up her blanket. She wrapped herself up in it like armor, and began to plan her next move.

Sector One was always Jaden's dream, not hers. Maybe the best thing to do was to go, to find some place she could feel just as certain about. Wasn't that better than living someone else's life, letting the past simply move her along because she was too frightened to make any real changes?

Three months. She'd give herself three months to deal with losing Jaden, and then she'd find out where she belonged.

# thirteen

Ashwin faced down Gideon's office door with apprehension like sand on his tongue.

There should be satisfaction in this moment. Unless he'd drastically misread the current situation, Gideon Rios had summoned him to formally offer membership in the Riders. It should feel like victory. *Taste* like it—sweet and light.

*Like Kora.*

Her taste had vanished too quickly. He wanted it constantly now. He'd thought of a hundred places he wanted to taste her. Bent over the narrow desk in his room. Backed up against the wall. Spread out on the brick around the fire pit, her blonde hair glowing in the sunlight. Pressed to one of the endless trees in the orchard, gripping the bark with her hands to stay upright as he fucked his tongue into her until she made those helpless, needy little sounds that scraped him raw.

In the pool, under the moonlight—he could hold his breath long enough to make her come.

In his bed.

In *her* bed.

In every damn bed this palace had.

That obsessive, helpless *longing* was the reason for the ash on his tongue. For the low-level hum of trepidation. He was playing a game with Gideon. And Ashwin wasn't sure which of them was winning anymore.

He wasn't sure which one of them he *wanted* to win.

Ashwin rapped his knuckles on the polished walnut door and was answered almost immediately by Gideon's muffled voice. "Come in!"

The interior of Gideon's office was as complicated as the man who sat behind the wide, polished desk. Like most of his palatial home, it relied heavily on natural light from huge windows lining two walls. Three massive wrought-iron chandeliers hung from the tall ceiling in a wide triangle, their candlelight diffused by colorful globes of stained glass.

A Base analyst could have written pages about the chandeliers alone, and the layers of messages it conveyed. The rejection of electric lighting betrayed a fear of reliance on technology—common in the men and women who had survived the Flares, but considered increasingly eccentric with each generation. The use of candles and the intricate glass screamed luxury—even for people who didn't trust the power grid, solar batteries cost far less in the long run than precious, hard-to-replace candles.

They were probably tallow wax. One of the cadet

branches of the Reyes family had a very profitable business rendering tallow from the ranch. No doubt a percentage of the product came to Gideon Rios, tithed to him like everything else in the sector.

Gideon Rios was easily the richest man within a hundred miles. His wealth rivaled the corrupt former councilmen in Eden as well as most of the other sector leaders. And he sat behind his simple wooden desk in a simple cotton shirt, sipping water from a glazed earthenware cup, smiling so earnestly that Ashwin could almost believe there was nothing he wanted to do more than sit down and chat with the man who'd been sent to spy on him.

Maybe there wasn't. After all, Gideon might be winning.

As if he sensed the thought, his smile widened. He gestured to one of the carved wooden chairs on the opposite side of his desk. "Have a seat."

Ashwin crossed the room, but hadn't yet sat when Gideon continued, "And decide which conversation you want to have, too. We can have the one where we tell each other barely concealed lies and analyze the subtext of every word, or we can have the one where we tell the truth and make a wager."

In the space of the next two heartbeats, Ashwin considered killing Gideon Rios.

It was hardly the optimal outcome. Any advantage the Base could possibly gain by checking Gideon's rise to power would be more than negated by the holy war of vengeance that would follow. Gideon might have declared his sister the new head of their grandfather's religion, but pacifists or not, Sector One would still rise up to avenge him.

And Kora would be heartbroken. Not only that the man she cared for as a brother was dead, not even that

Ashwin had killed him. She'd be heartbroken to know that Ashwin was standing in front of him, pondering the practicalities of killing him without the slightest hesitation.

She might have sparked feelings in him, but thus far they hadn't proved contagious.

Lowering himself into the chair, Ashwin faced his adversary and considered him for a moment. "I prefer the truth."

"So do I." Gideon sat back and laced his fingers behind his head, his pose one of deliberate ease, but his eyes were sharp. "I have a question, now that we're being honest. Were the deserters part of your ruse to infiltrate the Riders, or just a convenient excuse?"

Judging from the look in Gideon's eyes, the wrong answer could prove fatal. Luckily, the right answer was the truth. "A convenient excuse. Deserters have been a problem on the Base since the break with Eden. This was the largest group, but there have been numerous soldiers unaccounted for since the war."

"Really?" A hint of curiosity replaced the coolness in the other man's eyes. "Why so many?"

There wasn't much danger in the information, so Ashwin offered it as a gesture of good faith. "Disillusionment. Finding out how Eden had squandered the resources that those on the Base had bled and sacrificed for caused significant unrest."

"I can imagine," Gideon murmured. "The sectors are familiar with bleeding and sacrificing for Eden's greed."

Considering that the sectors had expressed their disillusionment by rising up against the city, there wasn't much Ashwin could say to that.

Gideon acknowledged it with a small smile, then changed the subject. "So. The Base is concerned about me, are they? I'd think that after O'Kane led our little revolution so efficiently, I'd be an afterthought."

Dallas O'Kane, the leader of Sector Four, was no doubt a cause for considerable concern to the Base. But in the six months since the war, he'd seemed content to rebuild his empire of liquor, gambling, and sex, settling once and for all into the role of lustful barbarian.

Gideon, on the other hand, was building a temple.

"The generals have studied pre-Flare military history extensively." Ashwin chose his words carefully. "I haven't been briefed on their explicit concerns, but I assume that the number of refugees currently converting to your family's religion give them pause."

"A fair assessment." Gideon lifted his eyebrows. "I could point out that my sister Isabela is now the official head of the religion, if that would help?"

Ashwin had watched covert surveillance of the assembly where the transition of power had taken place. Gideon had stood on the steps of the largest temple in the sector and visibly—literally—passed the mantle of power to his middle sister.

The Base believed Isabela to be a convenient figurehead. Ashwin couldn't say he disagreed.

After another moment of silence, Gideon laughed. "I suppose not. What confuses them more? That I willingly gave away power, or that I gave it to a woman?"

Ashwin had promised the truth, so he gave it. "I think they believe the transfer of power was merely ceremonial, and your sister is a malleable figurehead."

"They haven't met Isabela," Gideon replied, still smiling. "But that's a philosophical question for another time. The crux of the issue is that they sent you to infiltrate the Riders, and I intend to let you."

And there was the truth, stark and blunt. His mission was simultaneously compromised and successful.

He could obtain his objective, a placement inside the heart of Gideon's empire. He'd been given no indication that the offer was anything but earnest—if anything, the people surrounding Gideon had treated him with cautious respect since the day of Jaden's memorial.

But Gideon knew he'd been sent. He knew anything Ashwin observed or discovered might make its way back to the Base. Rationally, this was only an acceptable outcome if Gideon had nothing to hide, if he was reckless, or if he had full confidence that Ashwin's loyalties could be subverted.

The damn miracle.

The ash on his tongue turned to metallic anger. "Is this your wager? You're pitting the destruction I'm capable of bringing to your sector against Kora's influence on me?"

Gideon's smile *still* didn't falter. "Yes."

"You shouldn't." Ashwin curled his fingers into a fist, overwhelmed by the sudden urge to punch the smug expression off the man's face. "It's irrational. And it's dangerous."

"Is it?"

Of course it was, and not just because of the explicit danger Ashwin represented. It was an intolerable cruelty, placing such an impossible burden on Kora, who was unaware of the responsibility and would *still* never forgive herself if she failed.

When Ashwin didn't say anything, Gideon relented. His smile melted into a more serious expression as he leaned forward and rested his elbows on his desk. "I think you give yourself too little credit, Ashwin. I think you care about Kora, and that you can be trusted to see to her best interests."

"And what if I decide her interests would be best served by getting her far away from you and your sector?"

"Now you're giving *us* too little credit." Gideon met his gaze openly. Squarely. Few men seemed willing to look Ashwin in the eye for long. Humans had instincts, after all—even the dullest ones were honed enough to recognize danger.

But Gideon didn't flinch. "You're a man of reason and logic. I know I won't sway you without giving you full, unlimited access. You need to see who we are, warts and all. And if you see something in us that would make Kora unsafe... Well, I want to know. No one else can assess what I'm trying to build as harshly as you will."

It almost, *almost* made sense—but only in a world where Gideon was exactly what he claimed to be. The least likely of all possible worlds. "You're assuming that I'm capable of caring for another human being. How do you know I'm not pretending affection for Kora? It would be the logical way to manipulate your sentimentality."

"Because logic is your specialty. The heart is mine." Gideon extended a hand. "A wager, Ashwin. Join the Riders. Learn everything you can about who we are and the world we want to make real. I'm willing to bet that I can make a believer out of you."

Ashwin didn't move. "And if you don't?"

"Then you'll do what you think is necessary. And so will I."

There was an edge to the man's voice, a hardness that had as many layers as his expensively humble clothes and his lavishly rustic office. Gideon might claim the heart as his area of expertise, but love wasn't the only thing that resided in men's hearts. Ashwin had seen the shadows all too often.

Maybe Gideon had, too.

In the end, there was no real alternative. He could abort his mission and report his failure to the Base. Whatever reprimand they devised would be manageable. The fact that they'd send someone else in his place wouldn't.

Because Kora would still be here. At best—*best*—her discovery would lead to questions from Eden and the Base. Even if the former was under new, supposedly more benevolent rule, Lead Councilman Markovic didn't strike Ashwin as the sort of man to let a resource as precious as Kora slip uncontested through his fingers.

The Base wouldn't bother to contest. They'd simply come for her. And that was *without* knowing what she truly was.

If they found out...

Slowly, Ashwin extended his hand. This time, he didn't bother trying to judge the socially acceptable pressure—he gripped Gideon's palm with enough force to make his challenge and his warning unmistakable. "A wager."

"Excellent." Gideon smiled as if Ashwin wasn't threatening to crush his fingers. "I'll talk to Del and Deacon and arrange your initiation. Welcome to the family, Ashwin."

Family. A peculiar concept. Another weapon in Gideon's arsenal, and perhaps the most dangerous.

Ashwin didn't know how to fight back against acceptance.

Even months after the end of the war between Eden and the sectors, Kora still dealt with its aftermath every day at her clinic near the city border. There always seemed to be people who were injured during the fighting, but had delayed or sought alternative treatment until they had no choice but to come in. Trust was a difficult thing for the poor and the proud in the best of situations, and this was anything but.

Sometimes, she thought the deadliest thing Eden had ever done to its citizens was teach them that no one cared. That no one willing to help them would ever do so without expecting compensation in return, and always at prices too high to be endured.

So Kora accepted the items they offered as payment, because word would get out if she didn't, and then no one would come back. She told them about the refugee camps, and about the jobs the temple priestesses could find for them. She reset once-broken bones that had healed badly. She treated lingering infections, and tried not to weep at the sight of sick children who weren't sick at all, just *starved*—of food, of safety. Of hope.

The man on her table now had injured himself scavenging. He hadn't said so, but there were bits of ground concrete in the jagged, dirty wound, and his hands were raw from handling sharp hunks of rubble.

She irrigated the wound as Ana prepared the med-gel applicator. The first few times the newest Rider had accompanied her, Ana had watched with barely concealed horror. For someone who had grown up in Sector One, where taking care of the helpless was as much a religious calling as it was a savvy way for noble families to cement their good reputations, Eden's disregard for its sick and hungry was simply unfathomable.

Ana had gotten better at hiding her outrage. But she still flinched when the man pressed a battered credit stick into Kora's hand, one emblazoned with the logo of a posh restaurant in the city. She'd been there exactly once, on one of her infrequent dates. The food was decent and overpriced, which had made it hugely popular with privileged society. It wasn't a place to enjoy a meal so much as it was a place to go and be seen.

The door slammed, snapping Kora back to the present. Ana was already cleaning up, but she nodded to Kora's hand. "That doesn't look like a normal cred stick."

"It's not." She tossed it on the table and turned to the

sink. "Businesses in the city were allowed to pay part of their employees' wages with credit. As if a cook or dishwasher is going to be eating entrees that cost more than their rent."

Ana glared at the stick. "That's such bullshit."

Yes, it was. "If it makes you feel any better, I'm pretty sure the place shut down after the war. They couldn't afford to stay in business when they had to pay their staff with real money."

"Then they must have been shitty to begin with," Ana muttered, sorting the recyclables from the biowaste. "At least he gave us something useless, I guess."

If the man even knew the restaurant was gone. Chances were good he did, but Kora didn't care. "Whatever gets them in the door is fine by me."

"Until they start coming on their own." Ana leaned against the counter. "It's about time to wrap things up for the day. Sun's getting low."

Kora bit back her instinctive protest. There was always more work, and she still thought it was silly for Gideon to worry about her being out near the city border after dark. But it wasn't fair to keep Ana tied up when she surely had better things to do than babysit. "You must have plans, too."

Ana grinned. "I was thinking of crashing gossip hour."

"Crashing what?"

"You know, that quasi-slumber party the temple initiates have every night after dinner? They sit around and work on projects and eat snacks and do each other's nails and talk about their families and which Riders they want to make out with." Ana tilted her head. "You've never gone with Maricela before?"

Maricela had probably invited her—there never seemed to be an end to Maricela's invitations to one thing or another—but Kora usually stayed in her room or in the library. Sometimes, she joined Gideon in his study, but even that was rare. Mostly, she kept to herself.

Avery's words echoed in her head—*there's a reason they call it making a home, you know*—along with her admonitions. Eden wasn't home anymore. Even the Base, where she'd grown up, where she'd trained, where she'd worked, was part of her past.

This was her future.

She shut off the water at the sink and dried her hands. "Can I come with you?"

"Of course." Ana pushed off the counter and swept the credit stick off the table. It joined the rest of the payments in the basket by the door, and she shook it gently. "Think there's anything in here we can trade for some donuts? Bringing baked goods is the best way to crash."

"If not, I'll buy some." Gideon's cook always kept something ready in the kitchens, but bringing sweets from the palace might seem ostentatious. Kora didn't want to show up as Gideon's sister, the princess. Somehow, she had to find out who she was here in Sector One outside of that. Maybe, once she had, it would feel *real*.

"Great." Ana hefted Kora's medical bag, too, slinging the strap over her shoulder. "I know the perfect place."

Ana always seemed to know the perfect place, a legacy of the life she'd built here. She knew exactly which routes to take to avoid the dwindling foot traffic in the market, and which shop would have extra pastries they needed to sell quickly.

She was comfortable here, in a way Kora envied desperately.

It wasn't fair, and it didn't make sense. Gideon

had welcomed her into his home, into his *family*, and everyone in the sector treated her like the princess he'd declared her to be. But she'd only ever found contentment and comfort in her work—it was how she'd been raised, what she'd been taught. All she'd ever learned.

How could she help Ashwin discover the joys of Sector One if she didn't embrace them herself?

Ana steered off the main streets, circling around to a dirt road that threaded through the Rios family orchards. The lemon trees were in full bloom, hundreds of bright little blossoms scenting the air that rushed through the Jeep's open top. The fragrance was sweet, sweeter than the tangy orange blossoms that tickled her nose when she got too close.

The road opened up into a grassy clearing behind the family temple. Ana parked between two motorcycles and reached back for the pastries. They stepped through the heavily guarded side door and climbed the stairs to the living quarters.

The noise greeted them halfway up, and Kora wasn't surprised to see most of the acolytes she recognized on sight gathered in the common room, chatting and laughing as they busied themselves with various tasks or even none at all. It didn't seem to matter.

"Kora!" Nita tossed aside the book she was reading and rose. As usual, she'd abandoned her robes and was wearing a colorful skirt, a simple tank, and a wristful of bangles that clinked together as she caught Kora up in a welcoming hug. Ana got the same embrace. "I'm glad you're both here."

She didn't act like they were crashing the party. She made it seem like their attendance was expected and understood—and maybe it was. "It's good to see you, Nita."

"Come on." Nita grabbed Kora's hand. Ana had

already deposited the baked goods on the table, and two younger acolytes whose names Kora couldn't remember squealed in delight and dove for the sweets. Nita just laughed and steered Kora around them, back toward the couch. "You're going to be popular. We all take turns cooking, so anything we didn't have to make ourselves is a treat."

"It was the least we could do." No one else had gotten up to greet her, but Kora could feel the weight of a dozen curious stares as she settled on the sofa. "I've been meaning to ask you something."

"Anything," Nita replied easily.

"You've been working with Maricela, right? On her sculpting?"

"Yes. Well, when she works with clay." Nita tilted her head. "Are you interested in joining us next time? It's an amazing way to relax, you know. And you work so hard..."

The stares had turned into whispers now. "That's what Maricela said. I've been busy, but I think I can make time."

"You should. I have a potter's shed out back, but the weather's been so nice lately, we were thinking about hauling everything out into the courtyard next time." Nita's gaze drifted to the whispering acolytes, and she gave them a quelling glare. Everyone looked hastily away, and Nita rolled her eyes. "Don't mind them. They're dying of curiosity, but they're too polite to blurt out inappropriate questions. Mostly."

They'd all seen her before, plenty of times. "What questions could they possibly have?"

Nita leaned closer and lowered her voice. "About Ashwin."

Kora's cheeks heated. That, at least, made sense. Ashwin was a stranger, mysterious and sexy as hell.

Most of the women—and men, if they were so inclined—in Sector One were just romantic enough to find the combination irresistibly compelling.

Unless what they were *really* curious about was his involvement with her.

She wrinkled her nose at Nita.

The other woman's lips twitched. "Well...there might be a *little* of that."

One of the acolytes approached, smiling shyly, and handed Kora a stoneware cup of punch. Then she bowed and scurried back to her group, where they turned back to their conversations. Slowly, everyone else followed suit.

Kora sipped her punch. It was delicious, sharp and sweet, made from fresh berries with a hint of citrus. "If they want to know," she observed casually, "they'll have to ask Ashwin."

"Don't tempt them," Nita retorted, relaxing onto the couch with her feet tucked up under her. "Most of the girls here come from families only slightly less exalted than Maricela's. Or mine," she added, her voice turning wry. "Del's hardest job is teaching everyone impulse control. Growing up as nobility tends to leave one a bit spoiled."

"What about the rest of them? The ones who aren't from rich families?"

"Sponsorships, mostly. Usually because they've shown a special talent for some craft. We're all supposed to be here to learn skills that will make us a valuable addition to a family, but..." She shrugged. "Some people have more practical skills than others."

Most of the people Kora had met in One were crafters. Even the ones who provided services tended to combine that with at least one skilled trade, like the food vendors in the market square who also sold preserved vegetables or dried meats. If someone possessed a natural talent for a craft, it was easy to see how much families would value an education that helped develop that craft.

"Take Sola, for instance," Nita continued, nodding toward a redhead tucked into the corner with a board balanced on her knees. "She has talent to burn. She designs these unbelievable lace patterns, so Gabe's family sponsored her. They have a whole spinning and weaving empire already, but with designs like hers, they could start an entirely new business. One of Gabe's cousins is courting her now."

It seemed transactional, almost impersonal, as if their investment in Sola's education was meant to be a sort of dowry. "You make it sound like an exchange, but it can't be. Gideon would never stand for it."

"Oh, no. Sola's free to do with her future as she will. But... Well, most people would be thrilled at the chance to join the Montero family. To join any of the noble families, even if it's not the main branch. It means security, no matter what happens."

A security that Kora herself had stumbled into without realizing it. Logically, she knew what her position meant—being accepted into Gideon's family afforded her money and status, but those were two things she'd had all her life. They weren't new, and she couldn't possibly appreciate them like some of these girls could. On the other hand, she'd never had a real family before, a thing they all seemed to take for granted as much as she did security and luxury.

It was amusing, in a twisted sort of way. No wonder the acolytes stared at her like she was some sort of puzzling, alien creature. "Everyone must have so many questions about how I wound up here."

"Some do, but not as many as you might think."

Nita turned over her arm and showed Kora a thin scar marring her light brown skin. "You can put people back together without leaving a mark. That's a lot more valuable than pottery or sewing or even the most beautiful lace in the world."

Kora wasn't sure she agreed. "I can save people's lives," she countered. "If they wind up with scars, that's not a bad thing. It means we won."

"You're right." Nita rubbed her thumb over her scar before turning her arm again to hide it, but not before Kora sensed her prickle of sadness. Nita hid it behind a smile. "Honestly, I never minded the scar. Or the clay beneath my fingernails, or the burns from my kiln. But my parents have *ideas* about what the eldest eligible daughter of the Reyes family should be, and it's *not* muddy."

Fury blazed through Kora, sudden and ferocious, prickling under her skin. "Well, fuck them."

Nita blinked. Then she laughed, startled, but the sadness was gone. "Kora! I've never heard you swear before."

She didn't, not often, but she didn't know what else to do with the anger welling inside of her. "They should be proud of you. Of who you are."

"Maybe." She caught Kora's hand and squeezed it lightly. "It's okay. I have it pretty good here. And I have family that loves me. Like Xiomara..." She nodded to a pretty brunette who was sitting at the card table. "She's my cousin—well, my uncle's cousin's daughter. And the one braiding Ana's hair? Katya? She's a different uncle's granddaughter." Her brow furrowed. "I think she's related to Hunter, too. Through the brother of one of his mothers, maybe? Hell, I can barely unravel it, and I've been learning royal genealogy all my life."

"If it's that difficult for you, I don't stand a chance."

Kora hid a smile behind her cup of punch. "If I can match names with faces, I'll be happy."

"Well, that's all you have to do. *You're* not related to any of them." Nita laughed. "That's probably at least part of the reason why Ashwin's so appealing, you know. He's definitely not going to turn out to be anyone's cousin."

Unlike Nita's parents and their attitudes, *that* was something she could fix. "Do you think it would help ease people's minds if I offered to do DNA testing? It wouldn't be hard to check for common ancestry."

Nita laughed again. "You know what? Maybe you *should* be doing that. I mean, we're only a few generations in here, but at the rate we're going…" She trailed off and shook her head. "But no, I didn't mean literally, so much as… It's the mystery, you know? They're not sure where he came from or what he's done, so they can imagine all sorts of romantic things."

For a moment, Kora tried to imagine how Ashwin would react, and all she could think of was *anger*, the low, simmering kind you could only sense behind his shuttered eyes. Not that they would wonder about his past, or even that they would romanticize it, but that it might not occur to them to be wary of him.

What would he say—what would he *do*—if they found out everything there was to know about him, and it changed nothing? Would it show him that a man's past didn't have to define him, or would he make the connection at all?

"Kora?" Nita touched her arm lightly. "I know it's easy for me to joke because I'm not from the city. If it bothers you—or him—we can stop it. I know you must have grown up differently than I did."

"What? No, I was just...thinking." She swallowed hard. "You're right. We do come from a very different place. I'm not sure Ashwin is accustomed to having people be curious about him, not personally. I know *I* always seemed to confuse him."

"Really?" The word was gentle, almost teasing. "He never seems confused when he's looking at you. Not to me, anyway."

Kora blushed again. "It's more complicated than it seems."

"Most things are. But I heard Ashwin's officially going to be a Rider soon. I guess you'll have plenty of time to see if it gets uncomplicated."

Unless it just twisted things up even more. The Makhai Project was more complex than its description on paper—they weren't simply creating more efficient, effective soldiers through genetic manipulation and physical conditioning. A large part of it, maybe even the largest, was the mental conditioning. All the things the soldiers were taught—and the things they weren't.

"I don't know if I can explain it to you. It took me years to wrap *my* head around it, and I saw it every day." Kora shifted on the couch, turning to face Nita. "The things your parents tell you—even when you know they're wrong, after a while, part of you starts to believe them. You can't help it."

"No," she agreed softly. "You can't."

"The Makhai soldiers are told all their lives that they don't feel emotions, but they do. I've seen it. *Felt* it. The administrators of the project know it, too. They have a special term for it—destabilization. Any time a soldier feels something unrelated to a mission, that's what they call it. Sadness, joy, fear. Love. It all means they've destabilized. It's the only word they have."

Nita's brown eyes widened as understanding turned to horror. "But...*why*? What purpose could it possibly serve?"

"Control," Kora whispered. "They're given context for the emotions that make them more effective at carrying out orders. Anything else isn't just superfluous, it's counterproductive."

"But...what about the rest of their lives? How do they...?" She trailed off, looking suddenly queasy. "Oh Saints, they don't have lives, do they?"

"Like I said, it would be counterproductive." Nita looked so appalled that Kora didn't have the heart to go on, to tell her that the soldiers who destabilized were submitted to regimented torture in the name of conditioning. "There's a very good reason I left. And only one very important reason I stayed as long as I did."

"Because of him." Nita worried at her lower lip. "No wonder he always seems so...confused by the parties. Don't worry about the other acolytes, okay? I'll make sure they give him some space." Her sudden smile held more than a little mischief. "There are some advantages to being the eldest daughter of the Reyes family. If there isn't a Rios around, I outrank just about everyone."

"I'll remember that." Kora returned her smile. "Ignore me, though. I can't help but feel protective."

"Hey." Nita caught her hand again and squeezed it. "Don't ignore that. Embrace it. That's power. If the Base doesn't know how strong our sadness and our joy and our fear and *especially* our love make us, then that's their loss. And their weakness."

"A miracle worthy of the temple." Maricela stood at the end of the couch, a basket hanging from one arm. "How did you get her here, Nita?"

"Ana brought me along." The grin on Maricela's face was so infectious that Kora barely felt the sting of her words.

"Ah, that makes sense. No one can say no to Ana.

Even Deacon is clay in her hands." She shook the basket. "I made food."

"Made, hmm?" Nita shifted over and patted the couch between them. "Now you're just showing off."

"Doing my duty," she corrected as she sank to the cushions with a sigh. "I have to set a good example for the acolytes." Maricela's squint turned into a giggle. "I sound like my mother."

"Better yours than mine." Nita gestured, and Xiomara leapt up and hurried to pour Maricela a mug of punch. She handed it over with a curtsy before retreating, and Nita smiled. "I was trying to explain the tangle of noble families to Kora. We may need to draw her a diagram."

"I can't think of anything less befitting a party," Maricela declared. "Do you know what Gabe did today?"

Nita's eyebrows climbed. "I thought they were all busy getting ready for Ashwin's initiation."

"Hardly. He spent the day over at the refugee houses with a lady from Sector Two. Her name is—"

"Malena," Kora supplied. They both looked at her curiously, so she explained. "She and Jaden… They were fond of each other."

Maricela groaned. "Oh, I'm an *ass*. I thought he had a secret crush. I didn't realize."

Kora took Maricela's hand. "Not many people knew."

Nita nodded to the basket Maricela had brought. "Maybe the acolytes should follow your good example. It's been a while since we made anything for the refugee houses. I could talk to Del."

"And we'll figure out something for Jaden's sister, too," Maricela said decisively. "Something more like what they do when someone dies in Sector Seven."

"I can help with that." It wasn't one of the roles

Kora had envisioned for herself when she'd come to One—death counselor to the royal family—but it was one she would gladly take on. Because Gideon and Maricela didn't expect people to leave behind their history just because they'd settled in a new place. They expected them to bring it with them, to keep it even as they folded in parts of their new home and culture.

That was a respect worth honoring, and it made her proud to be a part of the Rios family.

# fourteen

The tattoo machine hummed, a hypnotic backdrop to the burning pricks as Del inked in the final branch on Ashwin's new tattoo. She had a light touch, far gentler than the man who'd done the Makhai tattoo that covered his back. They were almost soothing, those little stabs of pain. They reminded him of the way it had tingled and sparked the first few times Kora had touched him.

Thinking about Kora was *not* a good idea. His control over his body's physical reactions was more fragile than ever where she was concerned, and the logo on his shoulder was almost finished. Ashwin wasn't sure what humiliation felt like, but he still didn't relish the idea of walking into the Riders' sacred initiation ceremony with an impossible-to-hide erection.

Even he had *some* social survival instincts.

"There we go." The priestess swiped a cloth over his arm and sat back, smiling at her work. "How does it look?"

"Beautiful, as always." Deacon studied the tattoo with an upraised brow. "Leaves, huh?"

He said it as if there was a deeper meaning, and Del's warm laughter confirmed it as she set down her tools. "All things come in seasons, Deacon. You know that better than anyone."

"I bow to your superior insight." And he did, literally. When he straightened, he gestured to Ashwin. "Come on. They're waiting."

Ashwin rose, gathering his jacket in one hand. His sleeveless cotton shirt bared his tattoo, and he was acutely aware of the play of air across his abraded skin. Everything felt like that now—too sensitive, as if Kora had shattered more than his pain associations. The careful walls he'd erected to dissociate himself from being distracted by unimportant physical stimuli had crumbled.

He felt...alive.

He felt *raw*.

Deacon led him through the heart of the temple, a dome-ceilinged circular room with rows of curved wooden benches facing a raised altar. Dozens of candles flickered on a wide offering rack. More burned around the edges of the room, thin columns of wax nestled into the sand-filled urns in front of each brightly colored mural.

Their saints. Ashwin recognized a few by sight now—the dark-eyed brunette who held a heart cradled between her upraised palms was Gideon's aunt, Adriana. The ethereal woman with glowing bronze skin and a floating white dress was Juana, Gideon and

Maricela's mother. Bright red roses grew around her hips and curled up her arms, ending in a crown around her jet-black hair.

He'd seen both portraits repeated in tattoos worn proudly by everyone from crafters in the marketplace to the gardeners who worked in the Rios orchards. The Rios family's history and legacy was public and inescapable, adorning every wall, every shrine, even their bodies.

Maybe that was what drew Kora to them so strongly.

She'd never known her parents, just like Ashwin had never known his. Oh, he'd met the woman who'd given birth to him, but Natalie Olsen hadn't contributed any of his DNA. She'd simply made a strategic choice in the chaotic aftermath of the Flares—to earn a comfortable post overseeing one of the luxuries warehouses in exchange for carrying a child to term and handing him over without question or expectation. The few times he'd interacted with her, she'd given no indication that she knew who he was. Maybe she didn't.

*Family* simply wasn't a concept on the Base. Only shared purpose and commitment to a higher goal—even if most of the people sacrificing never knew exactly what that goal might be.

Deacon cleared his throat, and Ashwin realized he'd been staring at the mural of Gideon's mother. He resumed walking, following Deacon behind the altar and through the doors leading to the Riders' inner sanctum.

More candles burned inside, this time thick pillars that scented the air with spice. One burned in front of each portrait except for the newest, where Gideon stood waiting for him, the Riders gathered in a loose semicircle nearby.

Ashwin took note of each person out of habit, scanning for weapons and fixing their positions in memory. But most of his attention was drawn to the new black outline decorating the wall.

The likeness was precise. Ashwin studied his straight nose, the flat line of his mouth, the familiar curve of his jaw, and the stern arch of his brow. He recognized his own features, the same ones he saw in the mirror. But the sum of those features, when filtered through Del's brush, were more than their parts.

She'd captured something about him, something unfamiliar and new. The tension in him that was coiled too tight. The *rawness*.

"There's not much to this," Gideon said, the very gentleness of the words somehow lending the moment a breathless sort of import. A vocal trick—lowering the voice to force the listeners to focus—but Ashwin couldn't tell if it was deliberate or instinct.

Gideon bent and picked up a candle as he continued. "Just the vows. Are you ready?"

Del had walked him through the three vows before starting his tattoo. He'd committed them to memory the first time and recited them back obediently, earning a wide smile and a jealous murmur about envying his recall. But they were merely words, words he'd told himself he could echo emptily in pursuit of his mission.

*Lie.*

Ashwin had made vows before that he had no intention of keeping. When the Base had sent him to take over the Special Tasks team in Eden, the corrupt councilmen had demanded any number of sworn promises of obedience and allegiance. He'd spoken the oaths knowing that he intended to break them, and had felt no conflict.

He'd sworn allegiance to the generals at the Base,

too. Those oaths weighed heavier on him, but he'd been quick enough to violate them when he realized Kora needed protection. He could wrap the decision up in justifications about how he wasn't *hurting* the Base by hiding her from them, but the naked truth was that he'd choose her even if he was.

The only oaths he'd held inviolate were the ones he'd never actually sworn—the unspoken loyalty he shared with his fellow Makhai and the elite soldiers like Lorenzo Cruz. Men who could ask favors and be trusted to repay them, men who watched each other's backs because the people in power couldn't be trusted to prioritize the soldiers' lives.

Ashwin shifted his weight slightly, bringing the circle of Riders into his peripheral vision. Wary Deacon. Cold Ivan. Serious Gabe. Brilliant Lucio. Irreverent Zeke. Determined Ana. Watchful Hunter. Ferocious Reyes. Merciless Bishop.

Soldiers, even if they weren't of a kind he recognized. People who deserved better than empty vows he never intended to keep.

The weight of that knowledge made Ashwin's voice hoarse. "I'm ready."

Gideon nodded. "Do you promise to forsake family ties and pledge your loyalty to the Riders as your brothers and sisters?"

The easiest of the three vows. Ashwin had no family to forsake, and he respected the Riders as fellow warriors. From what he'd witnessed inside Eden, *respect* was a far sight better than what most brothers and sisters could offer one another. "I do."

"Do you promise to protect the people of Sector One by giving aid where aid is needed and spilling blood to keep their hands clean?"

Still not difficult. The Base might set their eyes

on the people in power, but for the most part they wanted stability and productivity for the people who made Eden and the sectors their home. And blood on his hands had never bothered him. "I do."

Gideon met his gaze squarely. "And do you swear to protect the Rios family?"

Ashwin waited for him to finish the sentence, but Gideon simply watched him, smiling and expectant, as Del's voice echoed through his head.

*Do you swear to protect the Rios family and obey Gideon Rios?*

Gideon had removed himself from the oath.

The silence grew teeth. Ashwin flexed his fingers and turned the words over in his head. Protecting the Rios family might include Gideon by default, but dropping his name from the vow mattered. It was Gideon's next move in their complicated game of chess.

And it was a vow he could make in good faith, because Kora was part of the Rios family. "I do."

Gideon held out his hand. Deacon was ready with a lighter. It clicked softly in the silence as Gideon flipped it open and sparked a tiny flame. He lit the candle and turned to place it at the base of Ashwin's portrait. "Ashwin Malhotra. Welcome to the Riders."

Deacon stepped up first, one hand outstretched. When Ashwin took it, he drew him into an embrace. Ashwin tried not to stiffen, but no one but Kora had ever hugged him. The solid embrace and the slap on the back was over before he could relax.

Zeke caught his hand next, clasping his arm as he grinned widely. "Can you read my mind now?"

The last thing Ashwin could anticipate was what any of them were thinking. "No."

"Dammit, man." Zeke clapped a hand to Ashwin's shoulder. "We're going to work on this. It'll be an awesome party trick. Just focus."

"For fuck's sake, Zeke." Ana elbowed him aside and gave Ashwin a quick, fierce hug. "Knock him upside the head if he annoys you," she told him as she pulled back. "That's what everyone else does."

"Only Reyes," Zeke countered. "I'd like to discourage anyone else from picking up that habit, actually."

"Then stop talking so much." Reyes laid his hands on Ashwin's shoulders and studied him for a moment, then grinned. "Welcome to the ranks of the damned. Fun never stops."

"I've noticed," he answered, and though it wasn't meant to be a joke, Reyes threw back his head with a laugh.

Hunter stood beside him. He didn't touch Ashwin, made no move to embrace him or even shake his hand, but it didn't feel like a personal slight. He recognized his own patient reserve in the younger man as Hunter nodded slowly, one corner of his mouth tilting up in a rare smile.

Ivan was just as silent, clasping Ashwin's hand with bruising pressure that might or might not be a challenge. Ashwin couldn't tell—Ivan's chilly blue eyes were as blank as his own had ever been. Bishop's grip was almost as hard, but the gleam in his dark eyes was sheer anticipation. "I can't wait to get you in the sparring ring."

"I agree," Gabe said, pulling Ashwin into the same sort of back-pounding hug Deacon had given him. "I imagine we all have a lot we can learn from you."

The furrow between Ivan's brow deepened at that, but Ana's expression brightened with an eagerness that pricked something inside Ashwin.

Training was the only part of that relentless job in Eden that he'd actually...no, *enjoyed* was too strong a word. With most of the Special Tasks soldiers, any satisfaction at the transfer of knowledge and skill had been balanced out by his primary mission—assessing their weaknesses for the day he'd have to kill them.

But the process itself appealed to him. Maximizing effectiveness. Carving away vulnerabilities. Honing talent until it gleamed. He could do that here with a clean conscience—certainly none of the Riders were likely to turn their skills toward plundering the sectors and wreaking havoc.

"I can do that," he said. "Maybe tomorrow—"

"*Not* tomorrow," Lucio interrupted, slinging a friendly arm around Ashwin's shoulders. "Nobody's getting up before noon. You've still got to go on your welcome ride."

Ashwin looked questioningly at Gideon, who laughed and shook his head. "My part in this is done. Your brothers—" Gideon winked at Ana, "—and sister will take it from here."

Metal jangled as Deacon held up a set of keys with an amused, expectant expression. "You do know how to ride a motorcycle, don't you?"

"Yes, but—"

Zeke interrupted him with a laugh. "No buts. Come on!"

The Riders contracted into a group around him, hustling him toward the door. He cast one last glance at Gideon, who stood next to the candle illuminating Ashwin's portrait, studying it thoughtfully. Then they were out the door, their laughter and chatter filling the solemn atrium as they hustled him toward the back corridor that led to the parking lot.

All of the Riders' motorcycles were there, lined up in a gleaming row that caught the last rays of sunlight. Most had been painted in the bright, vivid colors so beloved in Sector One, but the bike at the end of the line was simple, pristine black and chrome.

Ana nudged Ashwin toward it. “You can decide if you want it detailed later,” she said. “But Lucio and I have been working on it all week. She runs like a dream.”

Deacon held out the keys. The metal had warmed from his grip, but the sharp edges still scraped Ashwin’s skin as he closed his fist around the unexpected prize. “You’re giving me a motorcycle?”

“What else are you gonna do, patrol the sector on foot?” Deacon pushed him toward the bike. “Try it out.”

Ashwin approached and swung his leg over the seat. As the engine purred to life, he tried to slot the bike into the same category as any equipment requisition. Gideon wanted him to do a job, and this would help him do it more efficiently. Ascribing any deeper meaning to it was needlessly sentimental.

But then the parking lot was full of the rumble of engines, the vibration of it settling in his bones. Deacon pulled out of the parking lot, and Ashwin’s body performed the necessary maneuvers to follow. The bike operated so smoothly he barely had to think about it.

It left too much of his attention free to focus on the rawness. On the vibrations. On the tangy sensation of yearning that mounted as they broke free of the trees and spread out on the main road, riding toward the sunlit Sierra Nevada peaks.

It was the privilege of Makhai soldiers to operate with an autonomy alien to the strict hierarchy of the Base. They were sent on extended undercover missions and trusted to use their best judgment to achieve mission objectives. Ashwin had always valued his independence more than whatever brotherhood the infantry found together, perhaps because he’d known from an early age that it was the only alternative open to him.

For his whole life, men and women had stared into his eyes and found themselves unsettled by what stared back. Even if they didn't know he was Makhai, but especially when they did. He'd been rejected by the other trainees on the Base. He'd been warily obeyed by the Special Tasks soldiers inside Eden.

Only Kora had ever looked into him and kept smiling. And it had been easy to rationalize her away, because Kora was different. As genetically altered in her own way as he was—and incapable of seeing that darkness always won eventually.

His world had made sense when Kora had been a logical exception to a fundamental rule. But Sector One refused to follow the rules, as if Gideon's power ran so deep that he could announce the sky wasn't blue and the people of the sector wouldn't just believe him, they'd look up and see fluffy white clouds in a sea of green.

He could remake their reality on a whim. And by accepting Ashwin—no matter his motivations—Gideon had upended the physical rules of the universe. He'd bent light. Reversed gravity. He'd created something that should not exist—this emptiness in Ashwin's chest, a longing for the bonds of brotherhood. For acceptance.

With Kora, the longing had crept over him in mathematically inconsequential increments. It had taken years for that odd, distant desire to bloom into fierce, obsessive craving.

This wanting stole his breath with its suddenness. He tightened his grip on the handlebars, iron discipline keeping him steady. But as they roared into the courtyard of the central temple, Ashwin's pulse sped with the heady feeling of belonging.

It only intensified as the front doors flew open.

Robed priestesses and acolytes spilled down the steps, surrounding him the moment he climbed off his bike. He still didn't like close physical proximity to strangers, but the way they beamed up at him as they dropped curtsies and thanked him for his sacrifice—

He'd seen that look before. It was the look Dallas O'Kane got from his loyal followers. The look Gideon drew when he walked among his people. Naked respect. Earnest awe.

*Hero.*

It was antithetical to everything he'd ever been. To the darkness of his past, the body count he'd left in his wake. The blood on his hands and the ambiguousness of his loyalties. Wanting it was as reckless and illogical as wanting to belong to this family of misfit holy mercenaries. As impossible as dreaming of a future with Kora.

Gideon could extend his hand and change the natural rules of his sector, but someday Ashwin would have to cross the border into the real world again. Falling into this fantasy would leave him too weak to survive it when that time came.

But maybe it wouldn't hurt to believe it. Just for a night.

*Lie.*

# fifteen

Kora couldn't settle down. She'd helped set up tables and lay out food and drinks in preparation for the bonfire, even though the acolytes flashed her confused looks when they thought she couldn't see them.

Now, without a task to occupy her, she drifted distractedly, wandering from the light of the growing fire off into the encroaching darkness. Toward the road, her gut twisting into knots, and it wasn't until she heard the rumble of motorcycle engines that she understood why.

Protectiveness. Concern for Ashwin's safety and well-being was familiar, but this—this was *consuming*, an anxiety that bordered on anguish. And it was ridiculous, because he wasn't in any danger of being harmed on his welcome ride.

Or was he?

The queasy sensation in her stomach worsened. He was in such a precarious position, on the verge of opening himself to a world he'd always considered closed to him, and a single snub or rebuff could bring it all crashing down. It could injure him in ways that a gunshot or a stab wound never could, because he was used to physical pain.

If anyone hurt him—

The bikes rolled into sight, headlights gleaming in the twilight. Her heart thudded painfully, and she held her breath as they slowed to a stop.

Then she saw Ashwin.

He looked like a stranger. It wasn't just the scuffed denim pants and leather jacket, or the fact that he rattled under the weight of a small fortune's worth of jewelry. Glinting gold caught the light as he swung off his bike, wearing half a dozen leather straps lined with heavy gold coins. Silver chains clinked against them, adorned with rare jewels that sparkled brightly.

He should have looked absurd, like a pre-Flare pirate showing off his pillaged bounty. But the bright, feverish intensity of his gaze as it locked on to her stole her breath.

Not a stranger. She was staring at the man she'd only caught in glimpses, the one who seethed beneath the tiny fractures in his control.

The tension broke, flooding her with giddy relief—and an entirely different kind of tight anticipation. "Congratulations, Ashwin."

He smiled. An actual smile, full and easy, and just looking at it made the ground shift beneath her feet. He was walking toward her, sure and confident, utterly focused, and she opened her arms without thought. Ashwin caught her around the waist and lifted her, crushing her body to his as they spun in a dizzy circle. "Thank you, Kora."

The coins and jewels around his neck were poking her through her shirt, but she clung to him anyway. "I missed you."

He drew in a shuddering breath. "I'm destabilizing. Rapidly."

"Let's call it something else tonight," she urged, her mouth close to his ear. "Let's call it...*free*."

"Free." His lips grazed her jaw, and his hand tightened on her hip.

Neither of them anticipated the sudden impact from the side as Zeke hip-checked them with a laugh. "C'mon, Kora. Let us party with him a *little* bit before he blows out of his own celebration."

Ashwin turned his head to glare at him, so Kora grasped his chin and directed his gaze back to hers. "Everyone worked so hard to set it up."

It wasn't an argument that would have compelled him before. But his grip eased, and he let her slide slowly down his body until her feet touched the packed earth. "All right."

She held on to his hand, unwilling to relinquish that single point of contact. Reyes rolled his eyes as he walked by, but hid the expression as Maricela approached.

He bowed his head. "Miss Rios. If you haven't promised the first dance to anyone, I'd be honored."

"Maybe," she said lightly. "Probably not, but maybe."

His formal mien melted into a wicked grin, and he winked at Kora before heading toward the fire.

Maricela stretched up on her toes to kiss Ashwin's cheek, and he didn't even flinch away from the contact. "What are you drinking tonight, Rider?"

“Whatever Kora’s having.”

“Just punch.” Before, the very thought of liquor had turned her stomach. Now, she couldn’t bear the thought of anything that might dull the crisp edges of her senses. She wanted to soak in everything about this night—the noise, the sharp, woodsy scent of the fire, the chill of the air on her skin.

The heat of Ashwin’s hand around hers.

Maricela bit her lip, but it couldn’t hide her smile. “Coming right up.”

Del was the next to approach, free of her robes for once and wearing jeans under her thick, knitted sweater. She smiled and extended her hands, offering Ashwin an exquisitely tooled leather belt with two sheathed knives hanging from it.

He released Kora’s hand to accept it and pulled out one of the blades, his eyebrows climbing swiftly as he turned it so the firelight caught the shimmering edge. “Folded steel. It’s impeccable.”

“Our blacksmith and her apprentice made it. Mostly they make kitchen knives, because there isn’t much call for anything else in Sector One. But that’s *our* gift to new Riders. They can make swords, too, though Gabe’s usually the only one who takes them up on it.”

He slid the knife back and threaded the belt and the sheaths through his belt loops with graceful efficiency. When the silver buckle was fastened, he reclaimed Kora’s hand, twining their fingers together. “Thank you.”

“No, thank *you*.” Instead of touching Ashwin, Del reached out to squeeze Kora’s shoulder gently. “Enjoy the celebration.”

The insinuation was unmistakable. Kora muffled a laugh against Ashwin’s shoulder.

When she melted back into the shadows, Ashwin pulled her closer. "They're...teasing us."

"Uh-huh. It's pretty clear they expect us to sneak off at the first opportunity."

His thumb traced a slow, suggestive circle across the back of her hand. "I'm good at sneaking."

Goose bumps rose on her skin, not just at the contact, but at the promise simmering in his words. "I'm not, but you could teach me."

He lifted their joined hands, so graceful and easy it was almost like a dance as he looped his arm over her head and stepped behind her. Their entwined fingers settled near her hip as his arm pressed to her stomach, tugging her back against him. "Sneaking is about timing," he murmured, taking a step back and bringing her with him. "And awareness. I could close my eyes and tell you where every person is standing."

His heat surrounded her now, and she leaned into it. "Because you already committed it all to memory, or you just *know*?"

"I always know." Another step took them into the shadows. "Practically speaking, yes, I committed it to memory. But I don't have to think about it. It's training."

With twilight slipping away, the shadows beneath the trees hid them completely. "Does it matter where they are? They'll see us if we try to slip into the barracks, and the path to the palace is on the other side of the bonfire."

"There's another path." The hard bite of the gold and jewels against her back contrasted with the soft brush of his fingers up her arm. "Through the orchard, leading to the family wing. The palace guard might see us, but they won't stop you."

"Another path?" She'd lived here for *months*, and

she'd never seen it.

"Mm-hmm." His lips touched her temple. "We should go, before we get caught. Or distracted. Distraction is bad for sneaking."

She bit her lip to silence a whimper.

Warm breath feathered over her ear. "Focus, Kora."

She was already turning in his arms when he stepped back, pulling her along as he melted deeper into the darkness.

Ashwin didn't hesitate, and he didn't falter as he slipped between the trees. She knew his night vision was excellent, but this seemed more like muscle memory, as if he'd traveled through the woods often enough to know the way.

Then they broke out into the moonlight, and she knew where they were—the cherry orchard. She'd watched the trees bloom from her bedroom window, moved by their size as much as their beauty. The orchard was old, planted under the direction of the Prophet, so the trees were larger, gnarled and weathered.

The petals were falling now. She'd mourned the trees shedding their blossoms from her window, but from down here, it seemed like magic, a constant rain of soft pink and white floating on the breeze.

Ashwin touched her chin, tilting her face to his. He studied her, his brows drawn together, but she sensed an echo of her own awe in him. "It's so easy for you, isn't it?" he murmured. "Feeling."

"Because no one ever told me not to." She caught one of the petals as it drifted past. "It's beautiful, isn't it?"

"I don't know." He traced his knuckle over her cheek. "How do you know if something is beautiful? If you find satisfaction in looking at it?"

"Sometimes." She shivered. "Your heart races, or it's hard to breathe. Or you just have to stop for a minute and marvel at how *perfect* the universe is, to have created something like that."

Another petal drifted toward her shoulder. Ashwin snared it and rubbed it between his fingers, and the heady scent filled the air. "Then I never saw beauty before I saw you."

Her chest ached. *She* ached—to kiss him, to hold him. To pull him down to the petal-strewn earth. Instead, she slipped her hand back into his and smiled. "I know the way from here."

The stone path at the edge of the orchard led past the greenhouse. Kora barely noticed the guards, and the only indication that they saw her and Ashwin was the tracking of their gazes as they walked past.

The kitchen door was closest, but Kora kept walking to the one that connected to the main foyer via a small side hall. She didn't know why, except that she didn't want to lead him up the back stairs to her bedroom. That would make this feel too much like a secret tryst, a clandestine affair. And she needed this to be *real*, the kind of thing no one could deny.

So she pulled him up the wide, curved staircase that faced the front doors, their steps echoing in the empty hall. She didn't look back, and she didn't stop until she reached her door, though her hands had started to tremble.

"Kora." His arms went around her again, strong and solid. "Is this what you want? Me, in your bed?"

It was all she wanted, a desire so vast and overwhelming that she couldn't recall a single thing she'd ever needed this much. "Yes."

He reached past her to open the door. Then he tightened his grip and the world tilted, and her breath escaped in a gasp as he swooped her into his arms and carried her over the threshold.

She forgot about her nervousness, forgot about everything as he kicked the door shut and carried her to the bed. He was gentle as he lowered her to her feet, but when he pulled back and reached for his jacket, his movements weren't so patient.

"Wait—" She untangled one of the coin-laden straps of leather and drew it over his head. She dropped it into the hammered metal basin on her night table, the one where she slipped books and tablet computers when she finally gave in to the need to sleep. "Slow down a little."

He let the jacket slide from his arms, revealing the fresh new ink on his shoulder—the Riders' skull with a tree growing from the top, the usually bare branches decorated by scattered leaf buds. Ashwin curled his fingers toward his palms and took a deep breath. "I feel..." He hesitated, then shook his head. "I *feel*."

She slid two more straps into the basin and cupped his face between her hands. "Tell me."

"They accepted me." He held the final leather cord in his hand, his fingers wrapped brutally tight around the gold coins. "They're not scared of me. It's irrational. It's reckless. They know what I am, and they still..."

"Treated you like a Rider?"

The look in his eyes bordered on wild. "Like a hero."

He said it as if it was unthinkable, and Kora wouldn't cry. She *couldn't*, not here. Not now. "You assisted the rebellion. You fought in the war. And now you're here, with them, ready to fight again if you need to." She loosened his fingers from the coins, stripped away the cord, and tossed it aside. "You *are* a hero."

"You wouldn't say that if you knew—"

"Yes, I would. I am." She gripped his chin, made him look at her. "It doesn't matter what the Base told you, Ashwin. All that matters is what you do. What you choose."

He stared at her, those dark-brown eyes seething, until his silence snapped. He drove his fingers into her hair with a groan and crushed his mouth to hers. The shock of it sent a jolt rushing through her—desperation untempered by control.

It wasn't like before, the times when she'd managed to push him beyond the limits of his self-restraint. This was raw hunger, unleashed and exposed, and she craved it with a ferocity that startled her. The real Ashwin, stripped of the muffling layers of self-discipline that had been forced on him.

She'd take whatever she could get, the glimpses between the bars of his cage, but she wanted everything. All of him.

"Belt," he rasped against her lips, the command clear. Then he licked her lips, dug his teeth into the lower one, and nipped hard enough to send shocks galloping through her.

Blindly, she reached for the buckle, but her fingers brushed the hard ridge of his cock through his jeans instead. He hissed in a breath, his fingers tightening in her hair. "Fuck."

Heat pulsed between her thighs. She yanked at the belt buckle, sighing into his mouth when it finally fell open. He tilted her head and rewarded her with a deeper kiss, his tongue teasing over hers, stroking, coaxing. His grip on her hair relaxed, then sharpened again, the pressure deliberate this time.

Deliberate—and commanding. It slowed her racing thoughts, narrowed her focus to one simple thing: his pleasure. She pulled away, but just far enough to gather his shirt and ease it over his head. His jeans were worn, the denim soft and supple, and she jerked open the buttons one by one.

Then she slid to her knees on the floor at his feet.

His chest heaved. His eyes sparked. But he watched her with a silent anticipation so sharp she could taste it.

Slowly, so slowly, she loosened the laces on one of his boots. "I keep thinking about the night you kidnapped me," she whispered. "I don't like that word—I don't think it fits—but I'm not sure there's a better one."

"Requisitioned," he murmured.

She bowed her head to hide a smile. "Borrowed, maybe?" He stepped out of the boot, and she started on the second. "I think about what would have happened if you had shown up for another reason. For *no* reason, just because you wanted to see me."

"I was embedded with Special Tasks, under regular surveillance. I wouldn't have exposed you to that level of risk for personal gratification." He exhaled roughly. "But I...wanted to see you."

"So tell me." His other boot hit the floor with a thud. She stripped away his socks, then stretched up to brush a kiss just beneath his navel. "If no one was dying that night. No surveillance, no risk. Would you have come to me?"

"No," he said hoarsely. "I actually would have kidnapped you. Gotten you out of there. Taken you someplace safe."

She hesitated, her fingers wrapped around his loosened belt. She'd never been concerned for her safety. She'd lived in a cage in the city, yes, but it had always been a gilded one, no less luxurious in its own way than her home here. "Where would we have gone?"

"A safe house." He stared down at her, a wariness in his eyes that she didn't understand until he continued. "I had one ready before the start of the war. A place where the Base and Eden would never find you."

He made it sound like they would have looked, which was ridiculous. Kora eased his jeans down, rubbing her thumbs over his hipbones as she went. "Is it still there?"

"Probably. I haven't checked in close to seven months, so I can't say for certain."

The idea of him carefully carving out a haven for them was as moving as it was adorable. For a moment, Kora wondered what sort of place he'd set up for them—then she realized she didn't have to wonder. She knew him, the ways his mind worked and the things that were important to him.

"A different question with the same answer. *Again*." His cock sprang free of his pants. She rubbed her cheek against its hard length and looked up at him. "All you had to do was ask."

"Kora—" Her name was almost a groan. His fingers trembled in her hair. Strong, implacable Ashwin was *shaking* as he stared down at her. "*Please*."

She peeled away his jeans first, so that he stood naked in the moonlight filtering through the windows, every glorious inch of him hard and ready. Teasing him was out of the question, a torment she couldn't even consider. So she gripped him with the same firm pressure he'd shown her before and touched her tongue to the head of his cock.

His taste flooded her, along with the sound of his hoarse moan. Spurred on by his wordless encouragement, she kept licking him, soothing her tongue over his rigid flesh until he was wet, glistening.

Ready for her mouth.

"Do it," he ground out. It should have sounded like a command, but the need trembling through him turned it into a plea, and she answered it by closing her lips around him.

She knew what to do—in theory. He was right when he'd accused her of sneaking onto the blacklisted networks, and though she'd gone there for information, her curiosity had also led her to the vast collection of erotic imagery and videos stashed on the servers.

But none of the videos had conveyed how easy it was to let his reactions lead her, how she knew when to suck harder or take him deeper, just from the pressure of his hand at the back of her head. And they'd completely failed to capture the sheer power of this moment. She might be kneeling at his feet, but all of his attention, every single brain cell, was focused entirely on the slightest brush of her tongue. On her fingernails scratching over his hip, and the clasp of her fingers around the base of his shaft.

She took him deeper, and his fingers twisted in her hair. Not the careful, precise application of pressure he'd used before, but reflexive. As uncontrolled as the jerk of his hips. He cursed and stilled, but his ragged breaths filled the silence. "More."

This time, it was unmistakably a command. Her heart raced, and her hand shook as she began to move it, stroking back and forth in time with her mouth. She could give him this, the same sweet oblivion he'd given her, and it felt *good.*

He came apart for her slowly. Little things at first—the pressure of his fingertips on her scalp, guiding her movements. The tightening of his jaw. The simmering need in his gaze, which never wavered from her face. The way he rasped her name when she took him as deep as she could, until her lips met her own fist.

He freed one hand from her hair and slid his thumb across her cheek to where her lips stretched wide around his shaft. "You're so beautiful."

Her eyes locked with his, and her heart pounded painfully as she let her hand drop to her lap.

His breath caught. He cupped her cheek and eased his hips back a few inches. The fingers still twisted in her hair tightened, preventing her from following. "You like sensation," he murmured as he rocked forward again, thrusting between her lips until his cock barely nudged the back of her throat. "Drowning in it. Being overwhelmed. Don't you?"

He didn't move, and the deliciously heavy weight of him on her tongue, filling her mouth, made it impossible to do anything more than nod.

His thrust was faster this time. Not quite as careful, though he stopped short of choking her. The pull of his hand in her hair sharpened until her eyes watered as he thrust again with a low, helpless groan. "So good."

Her stomach quivered as she picked up his rhythm, meeting each rock of his hips until he stiffened and hissed, dragging her head back. "I'm going to come," he rasped, gripping the glistening shaft with his other hand. "If you don't want it to be in your mouth, tell me now."

Her unspoken hunger for him wasn't enough. He needed the words. "Please don't stop."

His eyes blazed. "Give me your hand."

She obeyed, and he curled her fingers around his erection just below the head before folding his own over them. He tugged on her hair, guiding her parted lips back to his crown, and thrust between the circle of their joined fingers and into her mouth.

Then he started to move. Faster now, rough but controlled by the iron grip of their hands. He was watching her so intently, as if nothing in existence could tear his attention away from this moment, and the effect was almost narcotic. A dizzy warmth stole through her as she stared back, spellbound, and flicked her tongue over him.

He shuddered and came with a noise torn between agony and relief.

Kora squirmed as he spilled in her mouth, salty and hot, nearly overwhelming her. She swallowed and stroked him, easing him through the orgasm until his shudders subsided into tremors.

The room was silent except for their ragged breathing. For an instant, they were locked there, a still, perfect moment in the aftermath of pleasure.

Then she reached for him.

Ashwin dragged her up his body, hoisting her off the floor. His mouth found hers, hot and open, kissing her deep as he turned and sank to the edge of the bed with her straddling his lap.

That quickly, the storm surged again. Lust clawed at her, a desire so sharp it almost hurt...but so did something else. A pressure in her chest, a yearning that had everything and nothing to do with his naked skin beneath her hands.

Oh God, she was in love with him.

His hands scattered the thought, driving under her T-shirt to stroke bare skin. He urged the fabric up and over her head, breaking their kiss just long enough to cast it aside before seizing her mouth again. He kissed her breathless, then left her lips, trailing down her throat to her rushing pulse.

She knew it was coming, and she still cried out when he bit her.

The sting of his teeth eased, replaced with his tongue, soft and soothing. He dragged the straps of her bra off her shoulders, then peeled the fabric away from her breasts, baring them to the cool air. But he left the straps tangled around her elbows, trapping her arms in place.

Then he dipped his head and sucked one nipple into the impossible heat of his mouth.

She couldn't move, but he wouldn't let her fall. Kora closed her eyes as pleasure pulsed in her veins, matching every rhythmic draw of his lips. Then the edge of his teeth grazed her again, rough and sharp, and she cursed her clothes, the only thing standing between her and the heat of his body.

He toyed with her until she was panting, then switched to her other breast and started again. Lips. Tongue. Teeth. He sucked until she squirmed on his lap, desperate to get closer. Until she thought she couldn't take another moment.

His fingers found the twisted clasp at her back, freeing her bra and her arms. But before she could move, he upended them both, dropping her to the mattress on her back. He loomed over her, blocking out the moonlight as he skimmed his hands down her body to the button on her shorts. "We should discuss contraceptive concerns."

It was so unexpected that her hands almost fell to the bed at her sides. "Are there any?"

"Likely not," he murmured, popping open the button. "I underwent the usual procedure. But if *you* still have concerns…" Her zipper rasped softly in the darkness. "There are plenty of safe alternatives."

"I have a contraceptive implant," she told him. "I asked Dylan Jordan to take care of it the last time I was in Sector Four. Because—" Because what? She couldn't tell him that she'd finally decided that she needed to move on with her life, whether she wanted to or not.

“It doesn’t matter why.” He tugged at her shorts and underwear, urging her to lift her hips so he could drag the fabric down her legs. “I’m here. I’ll take care of you.”

But it *did* matter—to her. When he dropped the rest of her clothes on the floor, she wrapped her fingers around his wrist and asked the question she’d been swallowing since he showed up in One. “Where were you?”

He froze—and with other people, *freezing* was a figure of speech. But Ashwin had perfect control of every muscle, and they all turned to ice. For three unsteady breaths, he was a shadow-clad statue. Then he exhaled slowly. “You saw me during the final battle of the war, Kora. I wasn’t...stable.”

She knew what the Base doctors did to unstable Makhai soldiers. Most of the disciplinary citations in her personnel file were there because she’d refused to take part in the recalibration procedures, and because she’d called it what it really was—torture. “How long?”

“I returned to the Base that night. They sent me back out a few weeks ago.”

It was her turn to freeze. Her heart seized, surrounded by a knot of pain that tightened until only a scream could release it, but she couldn’t make a sound.

Months. He’d spent week after week locked in a cell, only to be taken out and delivered into the hands of his tormenters. They used drugs that caused unspeakable pain, and when those didn’t work, they resorted to even more brutal methods. All to break him down completely.

The bed dipped. Ashwin stretched out beside her and pulled her close. “It’s all right, Kora. I’m all right.”

The protectiveness she’d felt at the bonfire roared back, but this time, *consuming* wasn’t a strong enough word. It blazed through her, hot enough to scorch through an entire sector if she unleashed it.

She touched his face instead, her hand trembling on his cheek. "Never again," she whispered. "No one else will ever hurt you like that."

He turned into her hand, his lips brushing her fingers. "It didn't work," he told her quietly. "I thought they'd pulled everything out. I thought they'd pulled *you* out." He caught her wrist and pressed the next kiss to the sensitive skin there. "The recalibration started to fail the first time you touched me."

"Because you're still you, and I'm still me. And this..." She stroked her other hand over his back, scratching lightly with her nails when his muscles tensed beneath her touch. "This is *right*."

"It's right," he echoed, rolling her onto her back. His hand skated down her side and over her hip to rest on her knee.

At the slight pressure, she parted her legs, but she couldn't stop herself from shielding her flushed face against his shoulder.

"Kora." His voice was warm and firm. Steady, even as his fingers traced up her inner thigh. "Don't hide from this."

"I'm not, it's—" She met his gaze, and the hunger burning there made her want to press her legs together again, just to relieve the ache. "It's still new for me."

He splayed his fingers across the top of her thigh, his thumb only inches from her pussy. "Put your hand on my chest. Over my heart."

She obeyed without looking away, sliding her hand over his sternum until she felt the strong thump beneath her palm.

"Do you feel it racing?" His thumb swooped back and forth against her skin. "You make it hard to breathe, Kora. You make me wonder what *beautiful* means. It's new for me, too."

Tenderness swelled through her, driving back the nervousness. "So we'll figure it out together."

He leaned down to kiss her—slowly, deliberately. The first stroke of his tongue across her lower lip coincided with his thumb grazing her pussy, mirrored caresses that coaxed her open bit by bit, until she couldn't remember why she was supposed to be nervous at all.

He pulled back to watch her face as he sank his first finger into her. "Show me the rhythm you like." His thumb settled on her clit. "Move for me."

She had to. It was part instinct, part desperate need for the pleasure she already knew he could give her. She rocked her hips, chasing his hand as the delicious friction curled her toes.

He rewarded her with the firmer touch she needed. His thumb pressed harder as a second finger joined the first, heightening the delicious pressure. His gaze roamed her face, intent. Transfixed. "Tell me how it feels."

"Like you're a part of me. You always are, but—" A shudder wracked her, stealing her words and her breath. "This makes it real."

He edged his knee over hers, tangling their legs together. His fingers sank deeper, meeting the roll of her hips and driving a choked cry from her throat. "Show me. Come."

He said it like he *needed* it, and now she understood. The purest truth of this moment wasn't in his demands or her submission. It was in taking and giving, in the fact that here, like this, they trusted one another enough to be both powerful and vulnerable. Naked and open.

Kora dragged him close and nipped at his lower lip, biting down until he growled. His hand moved faster, and she met every driving thrust of his fingers with a snap of her hips until the tension exploded. The orgasm tore through her, white-hot and mindless, shredding her awareness of everything but *him*.

She felt the loss of his fingers, but only for a second. His body covered hers, warm and hard, forcing her thighs wider as he settled between them. His cock ground against her clit, sparking new shudders through her.

"Hold on to me," he commanded as he rocked his hips, working his shaft against her until it was slick, gliding easily. She grasped his shoulders, but the next flex of his hips left her digging her nails into his skin as the head of his cock pressed against her.

His fingers had felt big, but this was so much bigger. He stopped, retreated just a bit, and then he was back, deeper than before. Logically, she knew it should have hurt, but she was so wet and relaxed, and she'd been waiting so long—

One final thrust, and their bodies collided. Kora stared up at him, her entire body throbbing in time with his heartbeat. "Oh."

He braced his elbows on either side of her body, holding himself carefully still except for his fingers, which crept into her hair, and his thumbs, which stroked her temples. "Okay?"

It would be hellishly rude to laugh, but the question was so absurd that she had to bite her lip. "I don't think that covers it."

That won her another of his precious smiles, along with a gentle flex of his hips. She gasped and arched off the bed as the friction shot fire through her.

"Kora—" He groaned, his fingers tightening in her

hair.

And then he began to move.

He took her with slow, firm thrusts. Each one shattered her conceptions about pleasure, replacing it with a newer, grander ideal. Over and over, until she was rising to meet him, instinct taking over where thought failed her.

His skin grew slick with sweat under her hands, and she clutched him more tightly. Her lungs burned, and soon she was dragging in desperate, hitching breaths, only to release them on sobbing moans. He filled her, *overwhelmed* her, and she was drowning in him.

"Come on, Kora." He gripped her thigh, pulling her leg up his body. His next thrust sank deeper, sharper, the friction unbearable. "Let go."

She came with a shuddering scream. Release surged through her in quick, hot pulses that made her clench around his cock, and every clench sparked another chain reaction of pleasure.

Kora rode the orgasm until every muscle quivered and she was hoarse from crying out, but it didn't end until he stopped moving inside her, still hot, still *hard*, and stroked the hair from her cheeks with a soothing whisper. "Breathe, Kora. Look at me."

"Ashwin." Her voice was rough, like she'd been screaming for days.

He kissed her. Her lips. Her cheeks. The corner of her mouth. The inexplicably sensitive spot on her jaw. Even with the evidence of his unsatisfied arousal buried inside her, he dropped gentle, soothing kisses to her face and throat, as if he had nothing more pressing to want.

She gripped his head, but she couldn't bring herself to pull his mouth from her skin. "Why did you stop?"

"Because I want you to stay with me." He nipped the point of her chin and lifted his head to meet her eyes as he flexed his hips again. "I can do this for as long as you can take it. For as long as you want it."

He spoke of iron will, but she could sense the storm raging beneath the placid surface of his perfect control. She moved without thinking, pushing at his shoulders until he rolled to his back with her on top of him.

She ended up straddling his thighs, his hands resting lightly on her hips. He watched her, patiently indulgent as she surveyed him. He really was beautiful, especially like this—naked and unashamed. Aroused and waiting. If you didn't look closely, you'd miss the tensed muscles, the way his chest rose and fell steadily but a bit too fast. The way his hands shook slightly on her hips.

Not so patient, after all.

That thin veneer dissolved when she wrapped her fingers around his cock. He hissed when she stroked up and down his slick, hot length, and groaned when she moved, guiding him back inside her.

She had to take him slowly, but it was easier this time—one long, languorous motion, and he was completely buried in her, deeper than before. Kora shifted her hips, and had to brace both hands on his stomach to keep from tipping over as he rose to meet her.

"Sorry," he murmured, settling back to the bed. His hands stayed on her hips, steadying, but his grip eased.

"Why?" She lifted her wet fingers to his mouth and traced them over his lower lip. "You need this, just like I do."

He caught her fingers with his teeth and watched her as he swirled his tongue around one. "I need you," he said after he released her. "Any way that gives you pleasure."

"I'm still finding out." She moved her hips again, this time tilting them as she rocked against him. A bolt of sensation splintered through her, reigniting the banked flames of her desire. It didn't matter anymore that he'd just made her come so hard she could barely breathe. Right now, the only thing in her world was Ashwin.

He gritted his teeth as she began to move, the muscles of his chest bunching and trembling under her outspread fingers. It was difficult to recapture the rhythm at first, but Ashwin's fingers pressed harder against her hips, guiding until she found a rolling glide that dragged across all her sensitive spots as she lifted up and then drove low, growling noises from him every time she slammed back down.

He shattered her rhythm by moving his thumb to brush her clit. She jerked and gripped his wrist, but she couldn't deny him. She ground against him, riding his touch as well as his cock, as the tension built again.

"Yes, just like that. Find your pleasure." He held rigidly still, his hand barely grazing her hip now. Only his gaze held her—his eyes dark and delighted as he watched her drive herself higher. "Come around my cock. Let me feel it again."

She couldn't imagine a substance more addictive than the way he was looking at her, anticipation clashing with frenzied desire. The first quaking pulses began deep inside her, tumbling outward until they gripped her entire body. Her heart pounding, every muscle quivering, she tried to maintain her rhythm, but all she could do was slam down against him, harder and harder, until everything exploded.

"*Fuck.*" The rare curse dragged free of him, the only warning before he grasped her hips and dragged her up. A rough thrust followed, his cock driving up into her at an angle so sharp that it tore a shocked cry from her throat. He did it again, and again, each advance punctuated by a grunt so naked, so uncontrolled, she thought she must be imagining the sounds. Hearing what she wanted to hear, what she *craved*.

He pounded up into her one last time and froze, buried deep. Her inner muscles gripped his pulsing cock as he came, gasping her name. They seemed frozen there, her body still thrumming, his rigid in release. When his hips finally sank back to the bed, he pulled her forward to sprawl on his chest, his heart pounding beneath her ear as his unsteady breaths lifted her body.

His skin was damp, and when she pressed her lips to the hollow of his throat, she tasted salt. He had scratches on his chest, ones she didn't remember at all—a testament to just how far over the edge she'd gone.

Her limbs were heavy as she reached up to touch one red welt. "My turn to apologize," she rasped.

He covered her hand with his own. "No. Still mine. I meant to be...gentler. You're going to be sore tomorrow."

She smiled. "I know I say this to you a lot, but... there are worse things."

"I know." His other hand found her spine, tracing her tattoo as if he had the exact shape and placement memorized. "I just feel more comfortable when I know you're all right. More stable. I don't want to hurt or scare you ever again."

He'd frightened her exactly once in all the years she'd known him—in the heart of the city, during the final battle of the war with the sectors. Dallas O'Kane had been mortally wounded, and Kora had been desperately trying to keep him from slipping away.

Then Ashwin had shown up, wild-eyed and determined to drag her out of harm's way, no matter the consequences.

Kora leaned up on one arm and propped her chin on her hand. "Do you know why I was scared that day, Ashwin?"

He studied her expression. "I was extremely irrational. And—and violent. Your fear was logical."

"No, it was because you wouldn't let me do my job. You would have pulled me out of there, and Dallas would have *died*, and it would have been my fault." She drew in a deep, bracing breath. "But if you had been willing—or able—to wait, then I would have come with you. I didn't want to be in danger, it's terrifying. But I couldn't let someone who was injured die just to save myself."

His fingers traced up and down her spine as he turned the words over, and a tiny furrow appeared between his brows. "I don't know how to promise that. Nothing short of another round of recalibration can stop me from prioritizing your safety. You wanted me to feel, and this is what I feel. That it's intolerable to see you in danger."

Her throat hurt, and she had to swallow past a lump in it just to speak. "It always is. But sometimes danger is unavoidable, so we accept the risks and hope for the best."

"Kora..." He broke eye contact with a sigh and closed his eyes. His hand came to rest at the small of her back, his fingers splayed possessively wide. "I can't promise, and I won't lie to you. I can try...but if it comes down to you or anyone else in the world? Or *everyone* else in the world? I can't promise."

"Even if sacrificing others like that would kill me

anyway, in all the ways that matter?"

His eyes popped open, and his hand tensed at her back. "Ouch."

She soothed him with a string of kisses to his jaw. "If it were simple, life would be easy, and love would always make sense."

He turned his mouth toward her ear. "I'm not good at things that aren't logically consistent. You'll have to teach me."

A shiver rushed down her spine, raising goose bumps on her skin. "It might take a while."

"Good. You need to be thorough."

Warmth surged through her again as she grazed his lips with hers. "You can count on me, Lieutenant."

# sixteen

When she was tired, Ashwin suspected Kora could sleep through a siege.

She barely stirred when he slipped from bed to get dressed just after dawn, and only murmured sleepily when he returned to wrap one of the silver chains around her wrist. When the sun spilled through the windows in another hour, the sapphires strung on the chain would catch and refract the light—bright blue, just like her eyes.

A sentimental thought. He recognized it. Examined it from several angles and couldn't find any rationalization that reordered it into something recognizable and manageable. That left only one conclusion.

At some point last night, his psyche had fractured beyond repair.

For a broken man facing catastrophic destabilization, he felt perplexingly…

*Normal?*

Not a word he was accustomed to using. It was imprecise and subjective, useful only within a social construct where norms were clearly defined. Nothing about Ashwin's current situation could be defined as standard. And last night…

Last night, he'd felt the cracks in the wall. Uncertainty, familiar and metallic. The sickening pressure of unexpected vulnerability. He'd been taught to recognize, process, and disregard emotions as chemical stimulus—but no one had ever taught him what to do when they were alien and unidentifiable. When they came too fast to process. Too strongly to disregard.

Last night, he'd felt unstable.

Then Kora had framed his face with her hands and whispered for him to slow down. She'd undressed him with the reverent solemnity of a ritual, unafraid in the face of his shredding control. She'd done what she'd been born to do, drawn the pain and uncertainty from him like the poison it was, until all that was left was wanting her.

Taking her. *Having* her.

The Base spent months stabilizing him with pain. Kora had done it in one night with pleasure. Except that was too simplistic. If simple physical pleasure was enough, his domestic handlers would have sufficed over the years. They'd served as a necessary outlet for tension, but none of them would have been able to handle him in the state he'd been in last night.

None of them would have wanted to. They would have been too terrified.

And that was the heart of everything, wasn't it? No one here seemed *scared* of him. Not even the royal guards, though they watched him attentively as he slipped out the back door into the cool dawn air. Finding a way past them unnoticed would have been possible, but there was no reason to hide.

Gideon was winning. And Ashwin's concern over this fact felt distant and muted. Their game could be tomorrow's problem, or the next day's.

Today he had a different problem, and she was waiting for him in the training room on the second floor of the Riders' barracks, already dressed to spar. Ana had twisted her long braids up on top of her head and kicked off her shoes, and she wasn't alone. While she went through her warm-up stretches, Hunter had wrapped his hands and was standing by a heavy bag hanging from a metal frame in the corner.

"Morning," Ana greeted him, bouncing slightly on the balls of her feet as she stretched her arms. "Thanks for agreeing to this."

Ashwin acknowledged her with a nod and bent to unlace his boots. "Are you participating as well, Hunter?"

"I came up to hit the bag." He smacked the back of his fist against the canvas with a dull thud. "But if you're offering your jaw instead, I'm up for it."

"No jumping the line." Ana watched Ashwin, her brown eyes lit with familiar challenge. "I'm trusting you to be more practical than the rest of these fuckers. They still don't like swinging at *my* jaw."

From a historical standpoint, he understood the cultural prohibition against hitting women. It was an erroneous conclusion springing from good intentions—the idea that the powerful shouldn't perpetuate violence against the weak. The flaw was insisting that physical power followed arbitrary gender lines inherently, instead of being the result of systemic lack of access to training, opportunity, and encouragement.

He'd seen Ana fight. She had the skill, and she'd clearly been given the training and opportunity. Now she needed encouragement.

"I don't have a problem hitting you," he remarked, tucking his socks into his boots before rising. "However, I also expect you to be practical. Having something to prove leads to sloppy decision-making and unnecessary risks."

"Fair enough." She grinned at him. "I can keep my ego under control. Not speaking for anyone else in the room."

Hunter made a show of turning to look over each shoulder, even though he was standing too close to the wall for anyone to be lurking behind him. "Oh, you mean *me*. I see how it is."

She flipped him a middle finger without looking. "Don't worry. I'll let him kick your ass when he's done with mine."

The odds that either of them could defeat him in hand-to-hand combat without an improbable stroke of luck seemed unlikely—though Ashwin might give Ana the higher chance. Even he was susceptible to underestimating a smaller opponent, and Ana *was* small. Lean, well-muscled, and excessively fast, but the top of her braids would barely brush Ashwin's chin. Next to Hunter, who was wider than Ashwin as well as a few inches taller, she looked tiny.

Her unthreatening stature could be one of her biggest assets. Men would underestimate her, and a split second was all it took to press that advantage. Their ignorance could prove fatal.

"All right. Come here." Ashwin pointed to a spot in front of him and waited for Ana to approach. He extended his arm and stopped her when he could reach the top of her head. "Do you know what this is?"

Her eyebrows rose as she rolled her eyes upward, as if she could see his hand where it rested against her hairline. "A good way to get your hand bitten off?"

If she thought he'd frown on biting, she'd be surprised. But that wasn't the current point. He let his hand fall away and gestured to the space between them. "This is your danger zone. My arms are significantly longer than yours. When you're in this area, I can hit you, but you can't hit me back. A smart fighter will try to keep you here."

In retrospect, he should have seen it coming. He *knew* she was fast. But she didn't give herself away with so much as a flexed muscle, and his first clue was the blur of foot flying toward his groin. He wrenched himself to the side just in time to take the blow on the hip instead of in the balls.

He snatched for her ankle, but she was gone just as fast, dancing out of reach with a barely contained smile that radiated false innocence. "My legs are longer than my arms."

Hunter burst out laughing, and he didn't even try to hide it. "Kora would've been so mad at you for landing that shot."

"I wasn't gonna really do it," Ana retorted.

Ashwin allowed the misconception to stand because she certainly wasn't going to come that close to landing it *again*. And hopefully no one would damage *his* ego by telling Kora how close it had come. "No, but you would have on nearly anyone else. You're fast and you're smart, so let's see what else you can do."

Ana squared off with him, and Ashwin fell into the familiar comfort of physical exertion. He kept part of his attention focused on analyzing the strengths and weak spots in her fighting style, and he found himself mentally building a training plan for her. More upper-body work. Practice with locks and grappling. Something to hone her speed and focus her power—

It spread out effortlessly before him in weeks and months, the perfect expression of his methodical quest for efficiency. The desire was back, stronger than it had been on the night of his initiation. The drive to draw out the best in each of them. To customize his training for each Rider. To shore up their vulnerabilities and play on their talents. Maximize their chances of survival.

He would find satisfaction in it. He might even grow to enjoy it. The camaraderie, the companionship. The brotherhood, every relationship forged serving as another thin stabilizer. None of them as powerful and soothing as Kora, but put together…

For the first time, Ashwin could see the hazy outline of something so forbidden, he'd never bothered to imagine it.

A life.

Maybe this was the answer the Base had known all along, the one Kora had sensed because she understood the way not just bodies, but *hearts* worked. The Makhai soldiers didn't have to be cold and isolated and precariously stable, their conditioning maintained through pain. They were simply more efficient that way.

More controllable.

He could feel it already—the slow realignment of his priorities. Whatever the Base doctors had done to his DNA had sharpened and deepened his survival instincts. His capacity for protective rage transcended anything that occurred naturally in the human species. The Base had to make it impossible to subvert a Makhai soldier's loyalty, because if you could…

The line between monster and hero was so, so thin. And it pivoted around loyalty.

Ana was sweating, her limbs shaking by the time Ashwin called a halt to their practice. But she'd broken through his guard twice—once to deliver another sharp kick to his hip and then with an unexpected punch that had split his lip and left him reassessing how much work she really needed on her upper-body strength, after all.

She was good. He could make her great. He could make them all great. And as Hunter strolled forward to take Ana's place, Ashwin crossed that invisible line in the sand and decided he *would*.

If he couldn't stop Kora from running into danger, he could make damn sure she had a superbly trained army ready to follow her.

It was disheartening, really, to learn that loving art didn't necessarily mean you were any damn good at *making* it.

"That's much better," Maricela said brightly as she surveyed the misshapen lump in front of Kora.

"No, it isn't," Kora shot back, stifling a laugh. "And you're a terrible liar."

"It doesn't have to be perfect to be better." Nita winked. She'd stripped down to her tank top, tied up her hair, and hiked up her skirt to make it easier to work the pedal on her potter's wheel. The lump of clay in front of *her* had been misshapen only moments ago. Now it was a smooth pillar that she coaxed taller with absent ease. "It takes practice. You didn't start your career performing surgery, I'd wager."

"Well, you would lose that bet." The memory rose, unbidden. "The first time my father put a scalpel in my hand, I was twelve years old."

"*What?*"

"It's not like it sounds. By that age, I'd been through

more training and simulations than most fourth-year students." Kora wet her hands and squashed her clay back into a round ball. It actually looked better that way. "But it's a lot to expect a kid to handle, literally having someone's life in their hands."

"It is." Nita dipped her sponge into the bucket next to her and dripped water over her clay, her gaze unfocused. "I mean, I grew up with responsibilities. We all did. But the only life-or-death power I had in my teens was over my horse."

It had been difficult. Kora had spent more than one sleepless night sequestered in her bedroom, crying into her pillow to muffle already silent sobs. Slowly, she learned to compartmentalize the pain, and then to control it. Now, it only overwhelmed her on rare occasions—like the day that Jaden died.

"This was your—what did you call him? Your adoptive father?" Maricela asked.

"Yes." Kora abandoned her clay in favor of watching Nita ply hers. It rippled smoothly beneath her skillful hands, responding to her slight, guiding touches. "He was doing what he felt was best for me, and he wasn't entirely wrong. I enjoy my work, and I had a life in the city that most people would envy."

Maricela snorted indelicately.

"*However.*" Kora pinned her sister with a pointed look. "I can't say I was sorry to leave. I'm happy to be right where I am."

Maricela's consternation melted into fondness, and just as quickly into mischief. "Especially now that Ashwin is here."

Nita dripped more water onto her clay, which was slowly taking the shape of a wide bowl. "When I asked Zeke and Bishop to help move my potter's wheel into the courtyard, Zeke mentioned that Ashwin didn't make it back to the barracks until dawn."

"Really?" Maricela threw down her tools, the milagro she was sculpting forgotten. "Well, I wonder where he could have been."

The surest way to disappoint her would be to refuse to talk about it, but Kora saw no reason to hide the truth. She wasn't ashamed of anything. "He stayed with me last night."

Nita laughed and flicked water at Maricela. "That's it then, isn't it? You're going to be high on the power of love to conquer all for *weeks*. Months, maybe."

Maricela put on her best affronted expression, though her twinkling eyes ruined the effect. "Excuse me, but I happen to consider that a universal truth, not a platitude."

"Hopeless, deathless romantic," Nita shot back, and shook her head at Kora. "You've ruined her forever already, so you might as well tell us all the magical details. So we can live vicariously."

Okay, maybe she *did* have something to be ashamed of. "I don't know what that means. I've never discussed my sex life with anyone before."

"Hey, that's okay." Nita smiled at her encouragingly. "Want me to go first and show you how?"

"By all means."

"So, about...oh, two years ago? We had a drifter show up on the ranch looking for seasonal work." Nita dipped her hands into the water and resumed smoothing the edges of her bowl. "He was tall and blond and had this smile that made my stomach do flip-flops because you just *knew* he was trouble. And after about three weeks of flirting whenever we crossed paths, I just *happened* to come back late from riding along the river, and he just *happened* to be in the stables and offered to help me with my horse."

Nita's smile turned into a wicked grin. "So the next thing I knew, he had his head under my skirt and I was biting through my wrist trying not to scream loud enough to bring half the family running. Because the things that man knew how to do with his tongue? I'm pretty sure they were illegal."

Kora's cheeks grew hot. Maricela gasped, but the sound quickly turned into a giggle. "Oh, I remember him. I didn't know you two were lovers."

"Well I don't know if I'd go *that* far. I mean, does it count as lovers when the only conversation you have is when he's tracing the alphabet against your—"

Maricela gasped again and muttered something in Spanish.

But Kora's thoughts were on a different path. "What happened to him?"

Nita shrugged. "He made enough to move on, so he did. I think he was headed up into the mountains, to one of those survivalist communities. We both knew it was never going to be anything more than what it was."

It was a vastly different view of sexuality than what Kora had seen growing up—not that anyone on the Base had ever discussed it with her. But you couldn't exist in a society, in a culture, without absorbing its beliefs, even if you disagreed with them.

In Eden, sex was a necessary evil to be used only for procreation, and even that was severely restricted. In reality, people in the city enjoyed sex as much as anyone else, but that enjoyment was often hindered or twisted by the lessons handed down by the former city leaders.

The *hypocritical* city leaders. Many of Eden's former councilmen had maintained second homes in Sector Two, near the brothel district, where they could avail themselves of the prostitutes' services at their convenience. While they were making speeches about virtue, they were having all the sex they wanted—sometimes with people who weren't at liberty to refuse them.

It was disgusting.

Here, in Sector One, people had sex for lots of reasons—companionship, fondness, love, even just for fun—but no one used others for their own satisfaction without providing it in return. Or, more importantly, without their consent. They were free to do as they pleased, and the only caveat was that they should treat others as they themselves would want to be treated.

Kora still wasn't sure she knew how to exist in a culture that freely celebrated sex, but she was familiar with the rest of it—empathy and consideration and compassion. And she couldn't give Nita and Maricela a scandalous story, but she could offer her own truth, in her own way.

So she did. "I've been in love with Ashwin for almost three years."

Maricela rested her chin on her hands, heedless of the wet clay still caking them. "A forbidden romance."

"Hardly." He had been her patient. She'd known her objectivity had been compromised—it *always* seemed to be compromised, especially compared to the other doctors on the Base—but she hadn't realized how much until she was long gone. Until she was here, crying into her pillow at night again because she thought he was dead.

Nita was watching her with a different sort of fascination. "So you weren't even involved with him back then?"

"I was his doctor. And he was..." Makhai. Untouchable. "He came in once with a laceration he'd sutured himself. The standard of care would have been to remove the sutures and repair it myself. I refused, because it had been a few days, so the wound had already begun to heal. Reopening it would have been unbearably painful for him."

They watched, silent and still, waiting for her to go on.

"He wanted me to do it anyway, and it wasn't because he was a stickler for adhering to protocol. I got the feeling that he didn't want me to get in trouble because of him, and that was...new." New and confusing and *exhilarating*. "I knew that I thought about him way too much. But that was the first time I ever considered that he might think about me, too."

"Did you know then?" Nita asked softly. "That you loved him?"

"No, I'm slow." Kora swallowed a laugh. "I finally figured it out last night."

"By the Saints." Maricela patted her on the shoulder. "I was going to deny it, but I guess you *are* slow."

The laughter bubbled out, and Nita joined in as she returned her attention to the bowl forming in front of her. "You'd think we'd have love figured out by now. But even here in Sector One, where it's the heart of everything, most of us can't put our fingers on where it starts or what it means."

They quieted as footsteps echoed on the tile. A moment later, Ashwin and Ivan walked around the edge of a wall and into the courtyard, and Kora's heart flipped into her throat.

It didn't make any sense. She'd seen him hundreds of times, *thousands*, and now in far more intimate situations than this. But it was like seeing him for the first time.

His hair had grown longer. A bit more and it would

spill down over his forehead, and her fingers already itched with anticipation at the thought of brushing it back. He seemed...easier than usual. Just as casually dressed, but more relaxed.

Then she saw his busted lip.

She forgot all about the clay covering her hands as she stalked toward him. "What happened?"

He blinked, then lifted a hand to his mouth as if he'd forgotten. "Oh. Ana. I was teaching her how to get close to a taller opponent, and she surprised me."

"Oh." The sudden knot in her stomach eased. "You were sparring."

"Yes." He caught her wrist and studied her clay-caked fingers. "You're...sculpting?"

"Badly." She tried not to blush, but when did that ever work? "I think my artistic sensibilities begin *and* end with enjoying other people's creations."

He brushed his thumb over the dried clay clinging to her palm, seemingly oblivious to their audience. She cleared her throat, broke away, and plunged her hands into the bucket of cool water waiting at her workstation.

Ashwin watched for a moment before dipping his fingers into the water. His thumb grazed the back of her hand, rubbing in a slow circle to work the dried clay from her skin. The contact was electric, her response immediate, and she forgot all about Ivan's dubious stare, Maricela's unabashedly fascinated one, even Nita's slightly wistful gaze.

She sucked in a sharp breath, trying to get enough air into her lungs, and shivered. Ashwin's fingers slid over hers, slick under the water. It was innocent and erotic, all at once, and the dichotomy made her head swim.

He didn't say anything, just stroked her hands until the clay was gone, then kept stroking them.

Gentle. Precise. Not quite as innocent, not when his thumb trailed along her index and middle fingers, coaxing them apart in what had to be a deliberate echo of more intimate contact.

Her shiver turned into a shudder. Her skin heated, her nipples tightened, and her fingers trembled under the water. It would have made her feel vulnerable, exposed—if she'd been the only one. But Ashwin stared at her, his pupils dilated, his breathing fast and shallow, and a temptation too great to ignore gripped her. She looked down, her gaze drawn inexorably to the front of his jeans—

Maricela cleared her throat.

Kora jerked her hands out of the water and dried them hastily on her shirt.

"I was just—" Nita's cough sounded suspiciously like a laugh as she used a wire to cut her bowl free of the wheel and transferred it to a wooden board. "Ivan, come make yourself useful. I need to bring this to my kiln."

Ivan's gaze flicked to Maricela.

"Yes," Nita groaned, rising. "She's coming too. Aren't you, Maricela? And Ivan will protect you if anyone jumps out of the trees and tries to murder us."

Maricela scoffed. "That part's easy. It's the smiling that's hard, right, Ivan?"

His lips didn't even twitch as he lifted the board from Nita's hands. "I've heard that smiles can kill, Miss Rios."

"Only the *really* good ones."

Nita rolled her eyes and waved her hands, urging them forward. But on her way past, she winked at Kora.

She stifled a sigh. "I guess we'll have to get used to that."

"Hmm?" He reached for her cheek, swiping his

thumb in a gentle circle. "How did you get clay on your cheek?"

"Art is messy." She leaned into his touch. "Especially when you suck at it, I guess."

"Were you enjoying it?"

"Very much. Mostly spending time with Nita and Maricela." She squinted at his wounded lip. "What about you?"

He rubbed her cheek again, soothing this time. "I've always been good at training people. I find it... satisfying. I think I can help the Riders become better fighters."

And they could help him discover what it was like to be part of a community. "Good."

"Gideon said you needed an escort to go to Sector Four this afternoon. I told him I could take you."

"Four—oh, my God." She'd forgotten all about it. "That's right, I gave my word."

A tiny furrow appeared between his brows. "Is something wrong?"

"Not at all." It seemed like forever since she'd promised Rachel that she would come back for the twins' one-month checkup. It was like her life had been neatly split by Ashwin's reappearance—there was ancient history, everything that came before, and there was *now*. "You'll like this visit. You'll get to see an old friend."

# seventeen

Ashwin didn't have the heart to tell Kora that the last time he'd seen Lorenzo Cruz, the man had shot him.

Perhaps he should have, though. Because when Cruz opened the door and caught sight of them, the man stiffened with a tension that Ashwin could only hope was imperceptible to Kora—the tension of a soldier trying not to lunge for a hidden weapon.

"Kora," Cruz said mildly, his watchful gaze still locked on Ashwin. "It's good to see you again. I know Rachel will be relieved you're here. Isaac's been keeping us all up with a cough."

"Babies make all kinds of noises," she said easily. "I'm sure it's nothing, but I'll be extra thorough."

"Is that Kora?" another voice called. Cruz let go of

the door as a second man pulled it wide. Ace Santana was leaner than his lover, with longer hair, a wicked glint in his eyes, and not a fraction of Cruz's self-control. "Holy shit, it's the crazy murder motherfucker."

Kora's expression froze.

"Ace." Cruz smiled. "Why don't you take Kora to the nursery so she can soothe Rachel's nerves? Ashwin and I can catch up."

Ashwin touched the small of Kora's back. "It's okay. I'll be right here in the hallway if you need me."

"I could say the same about the nursery," she muttered, then followed Ace down the hallway, her medical bag in her hand.

When she was gone, Cruz stepped into the hallway, crowding Ashwin back far enough to allow him to shut the door. Even knowing Cruz had done so to protect his two lovers and his newborn infants, Ashwin felt the familiar prickle of protective anger along his spine.

He didn't like having Kora on the other side of a closed door.

"So," Cruz said, his voice still mild. "You found her."

At Ashwin's lowest point during the war, he'd gone crawling to Cruz. The memory was uncomfortably vivid, even if the churn of desperate, unchecked emotions that had gripped him had the hazy distance of a dream. Everything had hurt then, and his instincts had driven him toward the one person he was sure could fix him.

But Cruz had hidden Kora away—at Ashwin's request—with the promise he wouldn't tell Ashwin where she was. And when Ashwin had come ready to beat the truth out of him, Cruz had calmly shot him in the leg.

There was every chance he'd do it again if Ashwin didn't appease him—which was, perversely, the reason Ashwin trusted him so much.

When Cruz promised to protect someone, he didn't renege.

"We crossed paths," Ashwin said finally. "Recently. After the war, I returned to the Base to undergo recalibration."

Cruz studied him for longer this time, as if searching for something. "You don't look recalibrated. Your stance is too relaxed. You touched Kora. You seem..."

The words trailed off, but Ashwin knew what he was thinking. Cruz had grown up on the Base, too. Not as a Makhai soldier, but one of their most elite. He was observant, intelligent. But not cruel enough to say the word.

So Ashwin did. "Human. I seem human."

"Yes." Cruz exhaled slowly, then frowned. He reached out to nudge Ashwin's sleeve out of the way, and his eyebrows shot up as it revealed his new tattoo. "Ashwin..."

"The Base sent me," Ashwin supplied, before he could ask. "Gideon knows that. So does Kora."

"The Base wanted you to join the Riders."

"Yes."

"Do you know why?"

Maybe he was developing a sense of humor, after all, because the question made him want to smile. "Do we ever?"

"No," Cruz admitted. "Not until they come down on us like a ton of bricks. Some days, I still expect them to pop back up and ask me why I haven't reported in for a new mission."

Cruz was a valuable resource, and the Base hated to lose those. But the generals weren't stupid men, nor were they short-sighted. They could haul Cruz back and try to make an example out of him, but they'd never have access to his skill set again. Worse, they'd enrage Dallas O'Kane, who had already shown himself capable of winning underdog rebellions against tremendous odds.

"I don't think they will," he told Cruz. "You're more valuable to them here. If they come at all, it will be to remind you how generous they were to let you walk away from your post...and to ask for your influence with Dallas."

"I'm sure he'll love that." Cruz shoved his fingers through his short hair and sighed. "Does that mean my debt to you is repaid?"

On the surface, the words were a request for Ashwin to absolve Cruz of his obligation, but his real meaning was just the opposite. Cruz was offering him approval. Acknowledgment. Reassurance that the Ashwin who was standing before him wasn't the same one who'd torn through a war zone to terrorize Kora.

It wasn't offered lightly, and knowing that lifted an invisible weight from Ashwin's shoulders. "Consider us even."

Cruz held out his hand. Ashwin hesitated only a moment before clasping it. He still didn't have handshakes down—he squeezed too hard and he knew it, but it didn't feel like a test he'd failed. Cruz just laughed and turned to push open the door. "Come on. We should save Kora. Ace will drive her crazy with questions."

Ashwin followed Cruz through a bedroom and the attached bathroom. On the other side he found Kora in a nursery, her face buried in a bundle of blankets in her arms.

She made a noise against the infant's belly, and the baby waved its arms and gurgled. Ace stood by, beaming as if gurgling and arm-waving was a clear portent of exceptional future aptitude. "See? Rosalía is kicking and babbling already. That's a *three*-month milestone."

Rachel shifted another baby in her arms as she looked on with indulgent humor. "All babies develop at different rates. You've read the same books—"

"You bite your tongue," Ace cut her off indignantly. "Our daughter is a goddamn genius."

"Ace." Cruz's rumble managed to be affectionate and exasperated at the same time. "At this rate, her first words are going to be *goddamn genius*."

"So? She should know it and own it."

"You're both right," Kora insisted, passing the baby back to Ace with a grin. "She's developing perfectly."

Ace tucked his daughter into the crook of his arm, but his triumphant smile faltered when the baby in Rachel's arms coughed.

"Let's see him." Kora took the child and began to examine him, stopping often to coo or make exaggerated, wide-eyed faces at him. Even Ashwin could read the yearning in every breath, and an odd feeling settled low in his gut. That *craving* that was both utterly rational and madly uncontrollable, the ultimate in survival instinct.

His DNA. Hers. And Ace thought *his* child was a genius. There was a definite possibility that any child with his and Kora's enhanced genes really would be able to read Zeke's mind.

It was probably something he should mention to Kora before he gave in to any regressive, instinct-driven fantasies of carrying her off to his safe house for sex with no contraceptives.

Finally, she pulled an oxygen sensor off the bottom of the baby's foot and gathered him in her arms. "His breathing is fine, lungs are fine, everything is fine. He's just stuffy because he has a cold."

Rachel smiled sheepishly. "That's what Dylan said."

"He's a good doctor, you know."

"We know," Cruz said. "And we trust him—"

"But our babies get the best of everything," Ace said firmly. "And you're the best."

On that, if little else, Ashwin and Ace could agree.

Ashwin had new scars.

Kora soaped her hands and finished rubbing them over his back, from the top of his neck down to where his Makhai tattoo disappeared into the scented water. She'd stopped trying to tell herself that she only noticed the scars because it had once been her job. That might account for a certain level of professional annoyance, but not this strange mixture of concern and wrath. Of tenderness and fury.

The tenderness won, mostly because if he thought she was upset, he'd haul her out of the tub before she had a chance to finish her exploration.

Ashwin tilted his head forward in obvious invitation, sighing in soft pleasure as she worked her hands back up to his neck. "I'm beginning to understand the point of wasting this much water for a bath."

"It isn't wasted." She tickled his earlobe. "It gets treated and used for irrigation."

"Of course it does." He huffed, a noise that sounded suspiciously like the start of a laugh. "Everything in this house is deceptive. The things that seem humble and rustic are expressions of wealth, and the things that seem like frivolous luxuries are ruthlessly practical."

"Welcome to Sector One." The bathtub was, like everything else in her suite, extravagantly oversized. She was ashamed to admit that she only noticed when she stopped to think about it. She'd been accustomed to opulence in the city, so the only difference for her was in the style. The giant bed was still simply a place to sleep, the bathroom somewhere she would brush her teeth and wash away the stresses of the day. The exquisite hand-built desk, a place to work. "I'm pretty sure Gideon hates it, but he can't build a new house just because the one he inherited from his grandfather doesn't suit him. Besides, people expect him to live in a palace. So he changes the invisible things."

Ashwin glanced back at her. "You think he hates it?"

"The extravagance? Yes. He's just..." It was hard to explain the dichotomy of a man who felt he deserved power but not the trappings of wealth that often went along with it. "If he had his way, I think he'd live in the barracks with the rest of you."

Ashwin seemed to consider that as he turned to face her. "He's difficult to read. Understanding people has never been my strongest skill, but I'm capable of recognizing common behavior patterns. I find him almost impossible to anticipate."

His irritation was palpable, and Kora laughed as she reached for the soap again. "I think he would consider that a compliment."

"Undoubtedly." Ashwin caught her wrist and plucked the soap from her fingers. He turned the action of soaping his hands into a slow, seductive movement—but it was nothing compared to when he slid them onto her shoulders and glided them down her arms. "I used to think I could anticipate you."

"Mmm, definitely a compliment." One of the scars she'd found bisected his left collarbone—light, barely noticeable, except to touch. "This one is new."

"From the final battle in the war." He smoothed

a path back up her arms and traced his way down her sides. "That one was a broken bottle. I misjudged whether or not an enemy was down for good. He wasn't."

*It's over*, she reminded herself, a past she couldn't erase or change. "I wish I'd known what you were going through." Then, because she couldn't contain the question, "Why didn't you tell me?"

His gaze fixed somewhere off to her right, and his fingers flexed uncertainly on her hips. "I..." Ashwin inhaled. Exhaled. "I've never been rational about you."

His words from the first night by the bonfire flashed through her mind, and her skin prickled as if he was whispering them into her ear now. *You know what happens to a Makhai soldier who lets himself become bothered.* "You think you were fixated on me."

"I *was* fixated on you." His gaze finally clashed with hers. "I am fixated on you."

"I don't like that word." The psychologists at the Base had ruined it for her forever, misapplying it to any emotion instead of the truly dangerous kind. "I don't think it's accurate."

"No?" Ashwin gripped her chin, holding her in place as he bent lower. "I watched you, Kora. For years. I knew every time you passed a security camera. Every surgery you performed, every date you went on. Everything. What word would you use?"

"I don't know." But maybe it would have been different if they hadn't trapped him in such a tiny cage. If he'd been allowed to embrace his feelings instead of shoving them down, hiding them like the forbidden things they were, then *watching* might have turned into something more. "If they had let you, you might have loved me."

"Love is subjective." He stroked down until his hand rested at the base of her throat, his thumb over her pulse. "I know I've lied for you. I've disobeyed direct orders, killed people who were trying to hurt you. I've committed treason for you. And I would die for you."

Her chest tightened until it was difficult to take a breath, and blood roared in her ears. "Do I make you *happy*?"

"You make me confused. You make me frantic. Overwhelmed and irritated and sometimes you make me feel like everything I ever learned about how the world works is turned upside down. You make me feel vulnerable." He leaned down until his forehead touched hers. "And I regret every minute I spend away from you. Because when you're touching me, I just feel you."

Everything else ceased to be—the water, the room. The world. She slid her arms around him and pulled him closer into this new, secret space where only the two of them existed. "Congratulations," she murmured, words nearly lost to his mouth. "I think you *do* love me."

He kissed her, and with his kiss he *showed* her. Action over words, objective truth. He kissed her deep and long, taking his time to tease her lips apart, taking longer to coax her tongue to tangle with his.

Not until she was gasping into his mouth did his hands begin to move. Her arms. Her hips. Her thighs. Trailing up to cup her breasts. The water made everything slow and slick, every movement setting off ripples that came back to tease over her heated skin.

She slipped one hand under the water, but he shook his head and turned her around so that her back pressed to his chest, trapping her arms between them. The water splashed as he settled on the tile seat on one side of the tub, his erection pressed against her ass.

Every movement was precise. Gentle but firm. He skimmed his hands down to her thighs and coaxed them apart. His middle finger settled over her clit, hard enough to spark electricity up her spine, but too light to satisfy the ache.

"This is what I need," he murmured against her ear. "This focus. Making you feel all the things that I couldn't. Do you have any idea how brave you are?"

She opened her mouth, but the question on her tongue vanished when he circled her clit again. His finger dipped lower, worked inside her with lazy thrusts that slowly filled her—and still left her so empty.

"This is the first thing that ever felt right," he continued, rocking his palm against her clit. The sensation jolted through her, but he wrapped his other arm around her to hold her in place. "Making you come."

Her wet hair clung to their skin as they rocked together, and Kora let herself fall into it. Into the rhythm and sway, into the steam rising around them, into the sensual spell he wove with his hands and voice. Into him.

And then, when he lifted her hips so that he could thrust into her, she fell into him.

They barely moved. Just his hands, one sliding up to cup her breast, the other finding her clit again to stroke. He held her in place so all she could do was rock in tiny, fitful movements as he forced her to feel every moment of the slow climb toward release.

His lips found her ear, his breath hot. "You're everything, Kora. And you're finally mine."

The water now seemed cool in comparison to the molten pleasure. It surged through her, ebbing and flowing until there was nothing else. It consumed her, shattering her as she came with a cry. And for once Ashwin didn't hold back from her. As her body clenched around him, he groaned against her ear and followed her.

The shivers went on forever, and Kora sank deeper into dizzy, quivering oblivion. She was only vaguely aware of moving, and of Ashwin sitting her on the cushioned seat beside the tub. He wrapped a warmed towel around her, intensifying the dreamy, weightless feeling.

Another towel rasped over her sensitive skin as he dried her, and then himself. He combed the damp strands of her hair with his fingers, his expression adorably serious. “Should I braid your hair for bed?”

It seemed like the last skill he would have picked up. “You know how?”

“Survival training.” His fingernails raked lightly over her scalp as he gathered her hair up. “You’d be surprised how many organic materials can be fashioned into makeshift rope.”

Of course. “I usually leave it down.”

“All right.” He ran the towel over his own short hair, leaving it rumpled and sticking up in tiny, chaotic spikes. Then he swept her up into his arms and carried her to bed.

The same sense of peace that suffused her radiated from him as well, and Kora basked in it. He was relaxed, easy in a way she wasn’t sure she’d ever seen in him before. Such a far cry from the unrelenting tension that had gripped him before, day in and day out, whether he was facing down an enemy or leading her by the hand into his room in the barracks.

She smiled into her pillow as he tucked the duvet around them. “Let’s stay here tomorrow. No one needs us.”

He kissed the back of her shoulder. “I would, but I promised Deacon I’d go to Sector Two with him. We’re doing some sort of construction on a soup kitchen, I think.”

"He can live without you for one day, can't he?"

"Probably." His hand settled on her hip, warm and possessive. "But I made a promise. I swore oaths. They matter to me...and I need them to matter."

He'd been devoted to her on some level for a long time. Now, she'd have to share him with the Riders and the rest of Sector One, but she didn't mind. He'd been forced for so long to keep himself separate from others, from *feeling*, and the only way for him to move beyond the habit was to break it, over and over. To care—about his brothers, his community, his home.

There was enough heart in him to go around.

"Fine." She snuggled back against him. "Just make sure you come back to me."

"I will," he whispered softly, and it sounded like more than a reassurance or even a promise.

It sounded like a vow.

# eighteen

Sector Two should have been a wasteland. Just under a year ago, Eden had ordered the Base to deploy a drone strike meant to send a message to the rest of the sectors: fall in line, or face the lethal consequences.

But instead of bombing a strategic military target, they'd wiped out an entire district of brothels, as well as the training houses where young girls learned to ply their trade. Civilians, women and children.

That decision had changed everything—not just in the sectors, which had shifted from simmering resentment to outright rebellion, but on the Base. Ashwin hadn't been there for the coup that had followed, but he had approved of the swift and decisive action that had removed officers blinded by corruption and severed their relationship with a city collapsing under the weight of its own greed and waste.

The last time Ashwin saw Sector Two, it was still a mess of collapsed buildings and precariously stacked rubble. Now, scarcely seven months later, Ashwin and Deacon maneuvered their motorcycles down clean roads lined with evidence of industrious construction.

Ashwin supposed the new leader of Two had several advantages when it came to cleaning up the mess her sector had been. Not only was she wealthy in her own right, with a controlling interest in many of the farms that provided food to the sectors and Eden, but she was an O'Kane, allied with the leaders of Sector Four, *and* in a relationship with Gideon's cousin.

Ashwin suspected the last advantage was the one that brought him and Deacon to her sector today. Gideon took family seriously, whether they shared his blood or not. But as tempting as it was to end his assessment there, Ashwin had to acknowledge the truth as he followed Deacon into the parking lot in front of a freshly constructed wooden building.

Gideon gave every indication that he actually cared about people, and not just the ones who paid into his coffers by tithing to his religion, or the ones who served his family by donating their time, skills, or labor.

All of the evidence Ashwin had collected pointed to Gideon simply...caring.

Deacon climbed off his bike, squinting against the morning sunlight as he began rolling up his sleeves. "Do you know anything about generators?"

"Enough." Ashwin set his helmet on the seat of his motorcycle. "I can't build one, but I can usually repair them, if I have the appropriate tools and parts."

"How about with decent tools and whatever parts we can scrounge together?"

"I'll assess it." He tilted his head and eyed Deacon. "Do you have any moral objection to getting parts on the black market in Eden? I can find anything we might need there."

Deacon muttered something under his breath, then rubbed a hand over his face. "That depends on a lot of things—who your contact is, what they're selling, how they got it." He paused. "I could go on."

Deacon cared about people, too—and not just when it was easy. "Charlotte is a city scavenger. She's spent years raiding Eden's recycle bins and bribing servants to pass her broken equipment. I can't promise she's entirely virtuous with the money she makes, but her vices seem limited to spoiling her nieces and buying pretty things for her wife."

"That's acceptable." Deacon unclipped a bag of tools from the back of his bike and swung the straps over his shoulder. "Do you know that much about everyone in Eden?"

"Only the ones who are breaking the law." Ashwin reached for his own tools. "I was head of Special Tasks for nearly a year. I was the one who decided when we moved in for an arrest and when we looked the other way. Educating myself on who they were seemed advisable."

"Sounds reasonable." He pulled a leather pouch from his pocket and tossed it at Ashwin. "Forget the tools. The generator needs a new charge controller. If you can find one, I'll be impressed."

"Consider it done."

As Deacon turned toward the building, Ashwin slid back onto his motorcycle and shoved his helmet into place. The ride from Sector One had been meandering, following the river that bisected the sector down to one of the few bridges spanning its width. Ashwin retraced his path to the bridge, but on the other side turned west instead of north.

Straight toward Eden.

The wall dividing Eden from Sector Two had been all but demolished. Just as in One, the stone had been harvested and put to better use—many of the newly reconstructed buildings closest to the city had that distinct white shine. The border between sector and city was mostly intangible now, marked by a lingering, unmanned checkpoint and the abrupt shift in architectural style.

Ashwin roared across the line and into a different world.

Without walls, Eden was even more incongruous. The city belonged in the reality that had existed before the Flares, a high-tech world of soaring skyscrapers and excess wealth. Gratuitous wealth, even—there was little efficiency in buildings that rose a hundred stories and seemed entirely made of glass. There were people whose whole lives were devoted to washing those windows day in and day out, a repetitive, thankless task that produced no tangible goods or commodities.

At least the new Council was reportedly paying them a fair wage. Rebellion had changed life for everyone, and mostly for the better.

Ashwin traversed the busy streets easily, weaving in and out of traffic and around silent black cars idling in front of buildings, no doubt waiting for the important people inside to finish their important tasks. He was glad for the helmet, all too aware that his face would be *very* recognizable to most of the people in those cars—and that few of them would remember him fondly.

If he was extremely fortunate, Kora would never know just how much blood stained his hands. If the ravens Gideon handed out for every kill were assigned retroactively, Ashwin might not have enough skin to carry the weight of his debt.

And yet, he had the nagging, irrational suspicion that Kora would still forgive him. That she'd lay her hands on either side of his face and tell him he was a hero, and he'd believe her the way he'd never believed anyone else. Without doubt, without hesitation, in the face of overwhelming evidence to the contrary.

He'd fallen asleep in her bed last night. Not the half-aware doze he was used to when he wasn't alone, but deep, restful sleep. He was even plagued by the vague notion that he might have dreamt—nothing solid that he could recall, but the sensation had lingered upon waking. Warm, sweet. Comfortable.

Maybe Kora had picked up Gideon's trick of bending reality.

Or maybe this was love.

A dangerous thought. Ashwin wasn't inside Gideon's alternate reality right now. He was driving into the most treacherous part of Eden, a neighborhood where inattention could get him killed. Gangs of street kids roamed the edges of the underground marketplace, looking for easy targets and a quick score.

For that reason, Ashwin pulled off into one of the nicer parking areas and paid the credits to stash his bike. Leaving it unattended for even the five minutes it would take to haggle over a charge controller was asking to have it stripped for parts.

He continued on foot, his hands in his pockets, staying alert for the sound of footsteps scampering behind him.

Instead, after two blocks, he heard the whisper of boots—military issue—and tensed before Samson appeared at the end of the street, looking deceptively casual as he leaned against the corner of a building.

"You're a hard man to find, Ashwin."

Samson was lying, and Ashwin didn't need to be able to sense the truth to know it. Samson was Makhai, one of the most cunning soldiers the Base had ever turned out, and he had the full resources of the Base at his disposal.

Ashwin had always considered him a friend. And he'd always been painfully aware of how swiftly *friend* could turn into *enemy* if two Makhai soldiers found themselves with opposing goals. "Samson."

"You look well. Very rested."

It could have been small talk. Unlike the other Makhai soldiers, Samson had always been good at it. But he knew Ashwin wasn't, and more than that...he knew Ashwin. He'd been there, helping Ashwin the night he'd flooded his veins with poison in an attempt to purge Kora from his thoughts.

He knew enough to endanger Kora.

Ashwin consciously controlled his muscles. Even a warning flex of his fingers could set off violence. He had the knife Del had gifted him on his belt, and a second in his boot. If he reached for either, only one of them would be leaving this alley. "Did the Base send you?"

"Not this time." Samson let the words—and their inherent warning—hang in the air for a moment. "I'm here as a friend."

If anything, that was more chilling. "Why?"

Samson moved, but what he pulled out of the inside of his jacket wasn't a weapon. It was a folder. "The Tech Division has been upgrading the drone sensors. The project started while you were incapacitated—" he uttered the word without a shred of emotion, "—and they just finished."

Ashwin accepted the folder, already uncomfortably sure he knew what lay inside. But he still forced himself to flip it open and stare at the surveillance photos showing aerial footage of Gideon's compound. In the first, he was visible as a bright-blue blob in the Riders' barracks. Kora was a red smudge in the wing of the mansion she'd claimed as her office.

In the second photo, they were together in the family wing, the edges of their blurry outlines merging into purple.

The time stamp read last night.

Ashwin closed the folder, looked up at Samson, and waited.

"I don't want to know," the man said mildly. "It's better that way for everyone, especially me. But in light of your past difficulties where little red blobs are concerned, I figured you should be...aware."

Ashwin stilled. He'd suspected what Kora was from the first time he'd met her. Something about her had always felt...familiar. Like recognizing like, though he'd understood even then that the feeling was illogical. Kora interacted with numerous Makhai soldiers, and none of them had seemed to realize she was more than merely human.

Then again, he'd never given any outward indication of his realization, either.

Of course, Ashwin had never trusted anything as subjective as feelings. It had been years since he'd hacked together his first makeshift isotope tracker to test his theory. Years since the first time he'd seen that bright-red smudge that had confirmed his suspicions and upended his world.

"How long have you known what she is?" he asked Samson, gripping the folder too tightly.

"I don't know anything. Or weren't you listening?"

"Dammit, Samson—" Ashwin bit off the next curse, aware that the lapse was too revealing. "Do *they* know who this is?"

"You're getting soft in your semiretirement, old friend. Or maybe you just don't want to think about the answer to your own question." Samson flicked the edge of the folder. "If they knew, you'd be dead. Or worse. Probably worse."

He didn't have to elaborate. Ashwin had already thought of a thousand scenarios far worse than his own death. The fact that he was stable would be fascinating enough. Undoubtedly there were other Makhai soldiers currently in various states of fracture. Too easy to imagine them trapping Kora in close proximity to see if she could provide the same stabilizing influence on them. He knew what a Makhai soldier in the midst of recalibration was like—made of enough cruelty to break Kora's body, and enough pain to break her heart.

And that was only the beginning. Ashwin had wondered what sort of children their combined DNA might produce, but the Base wouldn't stop at wondering, and they wouldn't wait for Kora's consent before harvesting her eggs for experimentation.

Even worse, Kora was old for a healer. The previous generation of Project Panacea subjects had begun destabilizing in their early twenties. Many had deserted the first time they were faced with an order that went against their ingrained instinct to heal. Those who stayed developed substance abuse problems that negated their usefulness. Even the deserters who were eventually recaptured were usually in terrible shape—worn down from the constant death and hopelessness in the world around them.

Kora's generation had been discarded when the project was terminated. If they realized what she was and how long she'd lasted—not just lasted but *thrived*—

She'd be lucky if they stuck to studying her. More

likely, they'd subject her to increasing psychological pressure in an attempt to find her limits. When that ran its course, they'd start the physical tests, carving off pieces of her until they understood what made her different. What made her useful.

No, Ashwin didn't want to think about the answer to his own question. Because then he'd have to decide whether to stash Kora in the trunk of a car for the second time in their lives. And this time, he wouldn't stop driving until he'd put the entire fucking continent between her and the Base.

"You're a smart man. Highly motivated." Samson leaned closer, his voice lowering to a growl. "*Fix it.*"

Then he was gone.

Ashwin barely noticed. The folder weighed a thousand pounds. The photos were damning, and he knew what would follow shortly—a communication from the Base demanding that he identify the Project Panacea healer and find a way to bring them in for evaluation.

He needed a plan. Now.

He folded the folder in half and shoved it into his jacket. He resumed walking, setting part of his attention to monitoring for danger while the bulk of it turned over the problem.

The safe house wasn't acceptable. It was within an hour's drive of Sector Eight, well within drone range for the Base. Anything inside of a hundred miles was too dangerous. To be truly safe, he'd have to get her through the mountains and into what remained of old California. There were coastal communities on the border with Mexico where they could easily disappear.

North was trickier. There were fewer communities up in the colder, harsher climate of what had once been Canada, but the ones that had sprung up would value a doctor of Kora's talent. And they were less likely to be trading with Eden than the surviving cities in the east and south of America—and trade was dangerous. Because if the wrong story got back to the Base...

So, southwest. Even the Base didn't cross the invisible line above Los Angeles—too many pre-Flare military outposts had set up their own territories along the coast between there and San Diego. If he could get Kora to the other side—

But Projects Makhai and Panacea had operated countrywide. They might retain tracking capabilities, which would put Kora at the same level of risk in a place where Ashwin was unfamiliar with the territory.

The only answer was to keep her off the grid. Away from people, where her skills would atrophy and the instincts inside her would twist into knots until she did something reckless. She'd done it before, walking out of Eden and into the devastated remains of Sector Two. She'd been driven by the call of pain, by the *need* to practice her skills.

If he tried to contract her life down to something safe, he'd be doing the same thing to her that the Base had done to him. Removing the social influences that kept her stable. Removing the opportunities to express her skills in a way that eased her heart.

The bonds of brotherhood offered by the Riders had given Ashwin the first solid ground he'd ever felt under his feet. Maybe that was what Sector One did for Kora, too. No other place in this broken world was better for a woman whose very sanity rested on the power to ease suffering. Gideon didn't just allow it. He encouraged it. Demanded it. Taking Kora away from her support structure might break her.

He needed a better plan.

The shady side of the market looked the same as always. Ashwin found Charlotte's little stand and waited for her to put on her usual act, pretending she didn't have the part he wanted. Two heavy coins—three times the value of the charge controller—cut through the game, and if she looked disappointed at the missed opportunity for a good, long haggle, Ashwin didn't care.

He tucked the prize into his pocket and retraced his steps, and by the time he reached his motorcycle he knew what he had to do.

He wasn't looking forward to it, but he knew.

The trip back to Sector Two passed in a blur. He found Deacon balanced precariously on the roof of the building, stripped down to his jeans and holding half a dozen nails between his teeth. He hammered shingles into place one by one, with no indication that a warrior of his caliber resented being assigned to mundane construction tasks.

When he reached the building, Ashwin held up the part. "I found what we needed."

Deacon grunted and vanished over the roofline. When he reappeared, he slid down the ladder propped at the edge of the roof, then held out his hand. "Took you long enough. Let's see it."

Ashwin surveyed the lot around them as he dropped the part into Deacon's outstretched hand. The handful of workers who had been there on his arrival seemed to have vanished, but activity buzzed around the building next to them, the wind bringing snatches of murmured voices and the occasional intelligible word.

Not secure enough for what needed to be said. "Is there anyone inside? I have to talk to you about something serious."

Deacon tilted his head toward the door, then led him through the large, open front room. In the back was the kitchen, an industrial one filled with stainless steel. It was deserted, so Deacon leaned one shoulder against a refrigerator and waited as Ashwin tried to decide where to start.

He could relay the meeting with Samson, but that wasn't the crux of the problem. The current threat was simply that—current. Unless he cut to the root of it, Kora would never be safe.

Ashwin pulled the folder from his jacket and unfolded it. It fell open, revealing the damning aerial surveillance. He smoothed the crease out of the middle and glanced at Deacon. "You know what these are."

Deacon stared at them for a moment. "Did someone in Eden give these to you?"

"A friend who wanted to warn me." Ashwin touched the blue smudge in the first picture. "Project Makhai shows up blue. Elite soldiers are purple. Regular enlisted are green." He shifted his finger to the hazy red dot outlined in pink. "And red... Red is Project Panacea."

"What the fuck is that?"

"A defunct experiment. They shut it down almost three decades ago because the subjects proved unstable and difficult to control." He forced himself to meet Deacon's gaze. "They were selected for intelligence, sensitivity, empathy. They were the most brilliant healers—"

Deacon cut him off with a vicious curse and slammed the folder shut. "She hid this from Gideon."

The urge to defend her was immediate and vicious. "No," he bit off harshly. "She did not."

"She sure as hell didn't tell..." He trailed off, and his hand twitched, like it ached to twist in the front of Ashwin's shirt. Or maybe slam across his jaw. "She doesn't know."

"There's no way she could." Ashwin shook his head.

"Decommissioned projects are buried deep and highly classified. I had to break most of the regulations on the Base to find information about the final project. Her group had thirty-seven infants, all listed as terminated. The man who raised her or someone connected to him must have smuggled her off the Base. Possibly to continue the experiment under different conditions."

"But you know." The words damned him, and they were meant to.

"I know." He couldn't meet Deacon's eyes anymore. For the first time in memory, he was the one who broke and looked away, unequipped to handle the judgment staring back at him. Because he cared now, and caring made him vulnerable.

It made him so vulnerable that he tried to rationalize it. "You don't know what it's like to live the way I do. To know that my mental stability has an expiration date that can only be extended for so long. Sixty-eight percent of the final adult generation of Project Panacea developed drug addictions. That was down from eighty-four in the previous group. And that's discounting the ones who killed themselves."

Deacon snorted, a derisive noise that dismissed his words without mercy. "You're full of shit."

"Those are objective statistics—"

"And they have jack to do with your real reason," Deacon cut in calmly. "You didn't tell her when you found out, so now you have to tell her why you've been lying."

Ashwin had heard the phrase *his blood chilled* before, but he'd never felt it so literally. It was the opposite of the time he'd injected himself with the drugs that burned like acid. It was gentler, a chill that seemed to slide through him and leach every bit of warmth from the world.

For all his analytical reasoning, even knowing he'd have to face Deacon and enlist his help, somehow Ashwin had envisioned the two of them working out a solution that left Kora blithely unaware of the danger she was in.

The look in Deacon's eyes smashed that illusion. And it was nothing compared to the look he'd see in Kora's eyes when he told her everything she knew about herself was a lie—one he'd allowed to stand for years.

He was going to hurt her. She was going to hate him.

And the worst part was that Deacon was right. Kora would want to know *why*. And Ashwin didn't know what to tell her.

Kora was halfway through a new supply list for her clinic when someone knocked on her bedroom door. It was past lunch, not yet time for dinner, and that couldn't be it, anyway. Maricela had proven, more than once, that if Kora forgot to eat, she had no compunctions about walking right in with a heated tray from the kitchen.

If she didn't finish this sentence, she'd forget all about it when she sat back down to complete her order. So she raised her voice enough to carry through the thick paneled door. "Come in."

The door clicked softly, the only sound until Ashwin's voice came from just behind her shoulder. "Are you busy?"

Her smile was immediate, automatic, a reflexive response to his presence. "Did you change your mind about staying in bed today?"

Silence answered her, so she turned to face him. He didn't look happy at all, and he definitely wasn't busy thinking of all the ways they could while away the next twenty-four hours in her bed.

The muscles in her neck and back tensed. "What's wrong?"

"Kora—" He shoved his fingers through his hair in

a rare nervous gesture. "This won't be easy to hear. But there are things I need to tell you. That I should have told you a long time ago. About where you come from."

It took her a moment to process his words, and when she did, they still didn't make sense. "I don't understand."

"Have you ever seen any reference to Project Panacea?"

"On the Base? No. Should I have?"

"It was something of a sister project to the Makhai initiative. One set out to genetically select the perfect soldier, and the other was meant to do the opposite. Produce superior healers."

It took her a moment to process his words, and her response was anything but articulate. "Um, no."

He just stared at her.

It stretched out before her, the only logical conclusion to be drawn from his nonsensical statements. Kora rejected it physically, rising to pace past him, to the other side of the room. "I had Special Clearance on the Base, Ashwin. In the *medical division*. I think I would know if a project like that existed."

"It was decommissioned. When you were eight months old."

A step too far, because he wasn't just saying that a project like this existed without her knowledge, or *had* existed, or anything else as inconsequential, and that was why she couldn't stop pacing, couldn't stand still and listen. His voice betrayed something personal, something *vital*. He was saying that she—

That she—

A strange calm settled over her, the detachment that allowed her to carry on in the face of emergencies. "The Base has project protocols. If this was true, then I'd be dead."

"You should be." Ashwin watched her, the crease between his brows betraying his worry. "I can only hypothesize that the man who raised you rescued you somehow. Or that someone meant to oversee project termination did."

The idea was more fantastical than the rest of it, that Ethan Middleton—staid, reserved *Dr. Middleton*, the man she couldn't even think of as *Dad* in the silence of her mind—had cared enough to save her, but not enough to love her. That he'd risked imprisonment or worse to spare her life, only to raise her directly beneath the watchful gaze of the Base administration.

It was just impossible enough to be true.

Slowly, Ashwin withdrew a bent manila folder from his jacket and offered it to her. "How it happened, we may never know. But you were tagged with the isotope, too. That's why you showed up in red on the tracking camera. People who haven't been tagged don't show up at all."

She kept her arms crossed over her chest as the first bit of hot pain lanced through the ice. "You told me everyone who wasn't tagged showed up red."

"No," he countered evenly. "I changed the subject."

The pain spiked. "I asked, and you let me believe it."

After a moment, he inclined his head and tossed the folder onto her desk. "I let the lie stand. I shouldn't have. But I hoped..."

She snatched up the folder and flipped through it. It was a couple of surveillance photographs, standard intelligence for the Base. All it showed her was what Ashwin's stolen drone already had, though she hadn't understood it at the time.

Then she froze. Because it *was* standard intel for

the Base—which meant they'd found her.

The ice cracked.

He'd hidden the truth from her, even though it was *her* truth, not his. More importantly—and maybe the only part that mattered—he had planned to keep hiding it from her. How long could he have done it? Shared her life, slept in her bed, all the while knowing the answers to the only questions that had ever truly haunted her?

Maybe forever.

She spoke past the lump in her throat. "You tracked my activity on the servers. You knew I was looking for answers."

"I did."

Perversely, the fact that he didn't try to deny it only made it hurt more. Tears burned her eyes, and she blinked them away. "How long?"

"I've known since your fourth week of service on the Base."

The heavy weight compressing her chest broke. She thought she might laugh, but what came out instead was a sharp, ragged sob. All of the disciplinary actions in her personnel file, all the heated arguments with the other doctors about how she knew the Makhai soldiers could feel just like any other human, she *knew* it—

She'd disproven her own theory. Because no one with a shred of empathy could have done this, even to someone they hated.

"Kora—" He took a step forward.

She held her ground, not out of invitation, but of challenge. "I have to tell Gideon. He'll have questions, and since you're the one who knows all about this, you should probably answer them."

His jaw tightened, and she knew she wouldn't like what he said next. "Deacon is telling Gideon now. So they can make arrangements to keep you safe."

"Of course he is." She couldn't muster any shock that Ashwin hadn't told her first. At this point, she was more surprised that she'd ever let herself believe that he honestly, truly cared about her.

Ashwin flexed his fingers. "It's dangerous information, Kora. I tried to contain it to protect you."

"From what?" She waved the folder. "From this thing that's happening anyway, you mean?" One of the photos slipped out, and the red smudge caught her eye. "They don't shut down successful projects. What happened to them?" *To us?*

"Kora, you don't need to know it all now—"

"No, I needed to know it yesterday. Or the day before that, or five years ago." But she already knew the truth, just not what form it would take. "Something went wrong. What was it?"

"Destabilization," he said reluctantly. "The main problem was burnout. Project Panacea healers were prone to emotional overstimulation. Many of them developed chemical dependencies as a coping strategy."

Now she understood all the nights she'd spent with her face trapped against her pillow—crying, *screaming*. Wondering if she just couldn't handle the work, or if she was losing her mind, if that was why it felt like her skin itched and the world was pressing in on her.

It had happened when Jaden died, too, and she'd run straight into Ashwin's arms. He'd soothed her, told her he knew exactly what she needed—and if she hadn't been so blinded by her infatuation with him, she might have realized the truth.

How stupid could one person be?

"You have to go now," she whispered. She didn't trust her voice anymore. She didn't trust *anything*. "Please."

He started to extend his hand, but froze when she shook her head. "I'm still going to keep you safe. I won't let the Base take you. I promise."

She'd dreamt about something that morning after—of wandering the desert and finding a rose, a single bit of life in the midst of the unending blankness. The moment she touched it, unbelievable pain had torn apart the world around her.

She'd dreamt about *Ashwin*. Somewhere, in the darker recesses of her apparently enhanced brain, she'd already seen the truth, even if her conscious mind couldn't accept it. He had hurt her, and he would hurt her again. Because it was all he could do.

"I'll be f—" Even now, she couldn't bring herself to lie. "It's not your problem to fix. It never was."

Plain blazed in his eyes, swiftly swallowed by blankness. He took a step toward her, then another, and she wanted to be scared of him. It would be smarter than the flutter in her belly, or the way her heart twisted with longing as he stared at her.

He stopped a foot away, looming over her for a silent, deadly moment. "I'll leave," he rasped finally. "But your safety will *always* be my concern."

He left, closing the door with absolute, perfect control behind him. He didn't even have the decency to slam it, to pretend that he was just as torn apart as she was.

Kora sank to the bed and reached blindly, automatically, for one of the plush pillows. She pressed her face against it, but the wracking sobs wouldn't come. Neither would the tears. Her eyes burned, but they remained dry as she stared at the far wall of her bedroom.

She didn't have time to fall apart, because the Base knew where she was. And they would want her back.

# nineteen

She hadn't even asked him *why*.

The thought was immaterial, unimportant, but it nagged at Ashwin as he sat at his desk in the Riders' barracks. On the papers in front of him, he'd roughed out a schematic of the Base from memory, and he needed all of his attention focused on figuring out a way to protect Kora.

It was good that she hadn't asked why. He still didn't have a reason, and if he had fumbled for one, it only would have made things worse. He'd tried to soften the blow, but he hadn't even understood where the hard edges were, much less how to blunt them. Every word had stabbed into her with such pain that he'd been ready to cut his own tongue from his mouth to stop it.

He wasn't built for protecting hearts. Just bodies.

The only way to protect Kora's was with a suicide mission. He'd highlighted his potential targets with little Xs on the map—the servers that housed the surveillance software, the warehouse that held the surveillance equipment, and the most probable location of the generals.

Killing enough of the generals to disrupt Base procedures was a long shot. They purposefully avoided congregating in the same location to avoid just such an eventuality—a habit they'd maintained with feverish dedication since the last coup. And in any case, an attack like that would only draw attention to what Ashwin was trying to hide.

Destroying the surveillance equipment had potential, especially if he could make it look like a negligent accident. It would take time for Sector Eight to replace the precious drones. But no doubt some had been requisitioned for fieldwork and would still be available, and the drones weren't the problem in any case.

She'd been safe before the software upgrade. Ashwin circled the X in the center of the compound, then frowned and drew new marks where the backup and redundant servers were placed. The Base wasn't reckless. The backups were hardwired and secure in their own closed network. He'd have to hit all three at once, which meant setting explosives without being detected and carefully coordinating the detonation.

Which wouldn't handle any additional copies he didn't know about. The programmers backed things up to data sticks all the time, even though it was technically against security protocol.

But it would slow them down. Give him time to...

What? None of this was worth a damn if he couldn't convince Kora to leave Sector One, and if he was going to separate her from the place that kept her stable, he shouldn't be bothering with complicated plans to assault the Base.

A sedative. A dark night. That was all he needed. Getting past the palace guards with an unconscious member of the royal family wouldn't be easy, but the eventuality had always hovered at the back of his mind. They could be over the mountains by the time she woke up.

She'd hate him forever for it, but at least she'd be alive to hate him.

Unless the hate destabilized her.

Frustration burned through him as he glared down at the impossible schematic, and the niggling thought worked its way back to the forefront of his mind.

*Why didn't you tell her?*

Deacon might have scoffed at the reason he'd given, but there was truth in it. Looking into Kora's eyes as he damned her to an uncertain future had been an agony worse than any recalibration. He'd have to retrieve the files he'd stored all those years ago and leave them with Gideon or Deacon. She would want them, but the bleak glimpse into her past might well turn into a self-fulfilling prophecy for her future.

It was a reason, but not enough of one. As loath as he was to hurt her, practicality should have forced his hand. He'd almost died multiple times during the war, and he could have left her without the tools she needed to diagnose potential problems that arose from her altered genes. It was reckless.

*He'd* been reckless. Thoughtless. Cruel.

The door swung open. Ashwin flowed to his feet, one hand closing around the back of his chair, his arm tensed and ready to smash it into the intruder's body.

Reyes stood there, leaning against the frame.

"What's up?"

Ashwin relaxed his hand, but only marginally. "Can I help you?"

"Hilarious. The way I hear it, you can't even help your own goddamn self right now." He stepped into the room and peered at the desk. "Making some big plans?"

Ashwin flipped the papers over. "How much did Deacon tell you?"

"Enough to figure out that you're a much bigger asshole than I thought." He paused. "I was kind of impressed, actually."

The words were incomprehensible, but whatever he meant, it didn't sound serious enough for this moment. "This isn't a joke. Kora is in danger, and quite frankly, so is everyone who has this information."

That quickly, something in Reyes's manner changed. His expression remained the same, but his eyes flashed with an almost predatory gleam. "Do I look like I'm fucking laughing?"

Lack of patience made him curt. "Then tell me what you want so I can get back to work."

Reyes shrugged. "All right. I came to relay a message, and also to give you something." Without warning, he hauled back, and Ashwin didn't have time to dodge the fist that landed *hard* across his jaw. "That's the something—"

Instinct kicked in. Intellect caught up only enough for Ashwin to open his hand and release the chair. Instead of breaking it across Reyes's face, he struck him with a punch of his own, knocking his head to the side and sending him stumbling back. Reyes dragged him along, and they crashed out into the hallway.

His face throbbed. His shoulder hit the wall, and he knew he'd have bruises—big, ugly ones that Kora would never fuss over. He embraced the pain and its stark simplicity. It was the punishment he wanted, the destruction he deserved for making Kora cry.

The pain would stop when the fight did, so he hit Reyes again.

Reyes planted a hand on his face and shoved his head back, one thumb perilously close to digging into Ashwin's eye. A dirty move that deserved a low response, so Ashwin twisted his head and bit the edge of Reyes's hand.

"*Ow*, you motherfucker—"

Ashwin shut him up with an elbow across the face. He shoved Reyes back hard enough to slam him into the opposite wall, but movement at the edge of his peripheral vision had him shifting to face a new opponent.

Except his new opponent had no intention of fighting. Zeke was standing at the end of the hallway, watching them with an entertained expression as he took a bite out of a donut. He chewed, swallowed, and waved his free hand. "Don't mind me. This was just getting good."

Reyes kicked the back of Ashwin's knee. Ashwin stumbled, catching himself against the wall and using the momentum to rebound into Reyes. He managed to land another glancing blow to Reyes's chin before taking a fist in the stomach.

"Poke him in the side," Zeke called around a mouthful of donut. "He's really fucking ticklish!"

"He can't listen to you." Reyes swiped a hand across his bleeding mouth. "Dumbass here is too busy planning his suicide strike on the Base."

"Well, that's disappointing. I thought he was supposed to be smart." Zeke finished off his pastry and jerked his head toward the stairs. "Lucio and I figured out how to save Kora, if you're interested. Or you could stay down here and keep punching Reyes. I mean, I get it. He's fun to punch."

Reyes tipped an imaginary hat, then winced as he rubbed his jaw.

Ashwin couldn't even feel the places where Reyes had struck him, because Zeke's verbal blow had landed so much harder. "You have a plan to protect Kora?"

"Yup." Zeke grinned as he turned. "Better get your ass up here, though, because it'll only work if you can pull off your part."

Zeke vanished. Ashwin licked his lips and tasted his own blood—Reyes's first punch had landed squarely. "Is that the message you came to relay?"

"Yeah, you're welcome."

"You could have told me instead of punching me."

Reyes grinned. "Where's the fun in that?"

Ashwin prodded at his split lip, embracing the mild sting. He couldn't say if it had been *fun*, but there had been definite catharsis in it. An outlet for the pressure building within, and without that pressure he could think more clearly.

He should have known the Riders wouldn't take a threat to Kora passively. She was a part of the royal family they'd vowed to protect, but more than that, they *cared* for her. She tended their scrapes and cuts and pieced them back together when someone tried to take them apart.

Protecting Kora would always be his priority. But he didn't have to do it alone anymore.

The bubbling fountain in the family courtyard usually soothed Kora. If the sound didn't work, then focusing on the swirling patterns of the pooling water did. It was random, and yet if you looked closely, you could find order in the flow of the water.

Today, it just reminded her of her bathtub.

She heard the footsteps on the tile before she caught a glimpse of Maricela in her peripheral vision. Greeting her was the natural thing to do, but right now even pleasantries seemed like a monumental task. She'd expended so much energy on remaining composed instead of breaking down, and she didn't have anything left over.

Maricela broke the silence. "Am I interrupting?" She spoke gently, as if she were trying not to startle a wild animal.

Kora didn't really want to talk to anyone—she didn't want to do anything but keep reminding herself to breathe—but avoiding it felt too much like hiding. Like *wallowing*. "If I wanted privacy, I'd have stayed locked in my room."

"I suppose," Maricela allowed, then smiled ruefully. "But that assumes that I wouldn't have walked in anyway, doesn't it?"

At least she understood the persistent, inexorable nature of her concern. Kora tried to return the smile, but it felt more like a grimace, so she patted the stone bench beside her. "Have a seat."

Maricela had been holding her arms tucked at the small of her back, but she produced a tattered, leather-bound book from behind her as she approached. "I brought you something. I don't know if it will help or not, but I wanted to share it with you."

She slipped the book into Kora's hands as she sat. The leather was old, scuffed and worn with areas that had both lightened and darkened with age. It had obviously been well used, softened by the frequent touch of many hands.

When Kora opened it, the faded, brittle pages that greeted her were filled with lives—names and dates and relationships. Anecdotes. Births and deaths, entire family histories codified in letters and numbers.

Kora's eyes burned. "What is this?"

"It's from the temple archives." Maricela shrugged one shoulder, the casual gesture at odds with the intensity of her gaze as she stared down at the book. "Nita was telling you about our genealogical records, right? The Rios family tree is plastered everywhere you look. So are all the other noble families. But everyone else gets recorded, too, in books like this."

So no one's past was ever lost. A tear slipped down Kora's cheek, and she barely managed to catch it with the back of her hand before it dripped onto the book. "I didn't know."

"Now you do." Maricela nudged the sheaf of pages, and the book fell open to one particular entry, as if it had often been opened to that spot. She trailed her finger over the page. "This is my listing, including my birth parents. He was a butcher, and she was an artist. They were killed during the unrest after the Prophet's death." Her voice cracked on the last word, but she took a deep breath and went on, stronger this time. "I was still a baby. They placed me in a temple-run orphanage, and that's where my mother found me."

She had her answers, all of the ones Kora had always longed for, and pain still radiated from her in sharp, discordant waves. "I'm so sorry, Maricela."

"For what? I was chosen by a new family, and I've had everything." Tears glittered on her lashes. "That's what they call it here—you're chosen, not adopted. We have that in common, Kora. Your father chose you, too."

*Did he?* She'd struggled with the inevitable question—*why*? Had Ethan Middleton been part of the project? Had he resented its closure? Viewed saving Kora as a way to continue the research on his own?

Or had he simply seen an innocent, doomed infant

and been moved to prevent another senseless death?

“Maricela.” Gideon’s voice came from the edge of the courtyard, firm but relentlessly gentle. “I need to speak to Kora, sweetheart. And I need you to stay within the residence for the rest of the day, please.”

“Bossy,” she muttered, the sharp edge of the word softened by the fondness in her tone. She accepted the record book from Kora, then paused to run a consoling hand over her hair. “It’ll be all right. I promise.”

A quick kiss on the cheek, and Maricela hurried into the house, the book clutched to her chest.

Gideon strolled toward the fountain but stopped a few paces away to study her. “I wish we had the time to sit and work through everything you’ve learned. We don’t. But I understand that right now you need to make your own choices. So I’d like to tell you about the plan Lucio came up with, and then I hope you’ll prioritize your safety by agreeing to it.”

She still hadn’t decided what to do—or how much she actually cared about her personal safety at the moment. “Did you know?”

“About your heritage?” He shook his head. “No, Kora. Of course not. That’s not something I would have held back from you.”

The hair rose on the back of her neck, a prickle of warning. “But you knew *something* you don’t want to tell me.”

“I knew the Base would be monitoring Ashwin.” Gideon folded his hands behind his back and watched the water tumble into the fountain. “Because they sent him here to monitor me.”

“They sent him to deal with the deserte—” The prickle turned into a shudder. “Oh God, Gideon. The deserters. *Jaden*.”

“No,” Gideon said forcefully. “Ashwin and I had a

very frank conversation about the deserters. I believe him when he said they were a problem that he turned into an opportunity. He took responsibility for Jaden's death, though, for the same reason I do. His failure to properly manage the situation."

His words allayed one fear—and stoked another. "Is that what I was? An opportunity?" she asked quietly. It hurt to look at him, but she made herself do it. "A pawn in whatever power game you and Ashwin were playing?"

Gideon met her gaze, not flinching away even though his sadness was thick enough to suffocate. "My intentions don't really matter. If I've made you feel like a pawn, that's the reality we're faced with. I'll have to earn back your trust on my own. But, Kora..." His tone softened. "Ashwin has only lied to me once, and that was when he tried to convince me he wasn't capable of caring about you. In any game Ashwin is playing, you'll always be the queen."

"I don't know if I can believe that." She twisted her fingers together until they ached, desperate for any distraction from the emotional pain. "I was thinking that maybe the smartest thing for me to do is go back to the Base."

Gideon stilled. Not like Ashwin could, with the absolute surcease of movement. Gideon vibrated with energy, carefully leashed, as if he was trying not to startle her. "They'd hurt you, Kora."

"I know. But I have to think about more than myself." The safety of an entire sector was at stake, because if there was one thing she'd learned in all her years of working for the Base, it was that they didn't suffer resistance gladly. If they wanted to find her, and anyone stood in their way, the resulting carnage would be considered reasonable collateral damage. "They can be relentless, Gideon. You don't even understand."

"Relentless, yes, but uncreative." One of his eyebrows quirked up. "They must not encourage flexible thinking, because you and Ashwin both drew a self-sacrificing line straight to the Base. I've always encouraged my Riders to think outside of limiting boxes. So if you're ready to listen...?"

"Are you?" She rose and faced him. "My whole life, people have been telling me what to do or trying to control me. I've done exactly *one thing* on my own—I left Eden. But even that turned into you keeping me here in One for my *safety*. I'm tired of it, Gideon. I'm tired of feeling like a spectator in my own goddamn life."

"Then take back your control." He turned back to the fountain. "I already made the call to the hospital in Three. Dylan has the necessary equipment. I don't understand all the medicine behind it the way you will, but from what I understand they can filter the tracking isotope out of your blood. Once it's gone, there's no way the Base will be able to track you again. And if you want to leave us after that...I won't let anyone stop you."

It was a chance, a *choice*. She could run away from the pain, the complications. From Ashwin. Start a whole new life, where no one knew. Be anyone. "I don't know where I would go," she admitted.

"Ah. Well, I'm afraid I can't be of much help to you there. I've never really had the option of leaving."

"You never thought about it?"

"A king who fantasizes about running away from all his wealth and privilege sounds like a selfish, spoiled child. Even in the silence of his own mind." Gideon glanced at her with a wry smile. "Some doors are best left closed."

She eased closer and slipped her hand into his. "I

don't think it sounds selfish. I think it sounds human."

He squeezed her hand. "I'm sorry, Kora. I'm sorry he hurt you. I made an unforgivable error in judgment. I truly believe he meant to protect you, but I, of all people, know how vast the gulf can be between our intentions and our outcomes."

"It doesn't matter." She couldn't put it all on him. Even if Gideon had rejected Ashwin's presence in One, Kora still would have felt the same way. She would have argued his case, fought for him—and maybe more. "Do you want to hear something stupid?"

"Always."

"I still love him. None of this has changed that." Her eyes were burning again, but this time they filled with tears. She let them build until they blurred her vision, then spilled down her face. "You said Lucio has a plan?"

"Something hemodialysis something something." Gideon pulled her to his side, his arm warm and comforting around her shoulders. "When we get to Three, the two of you can work it out with Dylan. But I have to say something, Kora. There's nothing stupid about having a heart big enough to love someone who doesn't know how to love you back. There's nothing stupid about love, period. He hurt you, and that's on *him*. Not you and your big, beautiful heart."

Maybe it was her programming. In a way, she was just as helpless as Ashwin when it came to emotion—he couldn't feel it, and she felt too much. Neither seemed like a healthy option. "He can't sacrifice himself for me. I don't think I could bear it."

"I know. That isn't in the plan." Gideon kissed the top of her head. "Deacon and Ivan have his back. Lucio and Reyes are waiting to have yours. Whether you stay or go tomorrow, today you're still family. And we take care of our own."

"Wait—" She touched the bar codes on the inside of her wrist without looking at them. If she was going to have the isotopes removed from her blood, it seemed like the perfect time to break from her past on the Base entirely. "Do you think Dylan can do something else for me?"

Gideon glanced down at her wrist and swallowed hard. "I think...he would be happy to help you."

"Then let's figure this out." If she could avoid the Base and still protect them all, including Ashwin, then she had to do it.

Whatever it took.

# twenty

The edge of the Base was a few dozen miles from the outskirts of One. Ashwin approached the familiar sprawl of concrete and steel buildings with the sun glaring so brightly overhead that the sand on either side of the road seemed to shimmer.

A massive fence surrounded the perimeter, with thick curls of razor wire lining the top. Ashwin drove alongside it until he reached the main gate, where he shoved up his jacket sleeve to scan his bar codes.

The *beep* had barely sounded before the rumble of gears started. The heavily armed man in the guard station didn't look at Ashwin as the gate swung open, no doubt staying as still as possible to avoid attracting any unnecessary attention from a Makhai soldier.

It had never stung this much to be fearfully

ignored before.

Inside, the feeling only grew worse. As soon as he'd parked his motorcycle and removed his helmet, the recognition started. Younger recruits scattered out of his way, whispering frantically to each other. Support staff altered their paths, disappearing down narrow passages between buildings or gritting their teeth to walk by him with the tension of someone easing past a feral dog.

The night the Riders had dragged him from temple to temple to endure hugs and kisses and a hero's welcome, the lack of fear had felt abnormal and off-putting. But it had taken so little time to grow accustomed to that easy, inexplicable warmth. Muscles he hadn't realized had relaxed were tightening again. His jaw ached from the effort not to clench it. His fingers trembled with the need to tighten into fists.

For so much of his life, Ashwin hadn't felt human. Now he understood the distinction. *He* had always been human.

But living like this was inhumane.

As much as he now loathed it, he supposed the palpable terror had its uses. By the time he reached the strategy center, a thin layer of icy rage coated his nerves like a shield. He scanned his bar codes again, and the lock opened with a soft *pop*.

A young corporal with closely shorn brown hair and a nervous expression saluted Ashwin with crisp precision. "General Wren is waiting for you, sir."

"Thank you, soldier." Ashwin moved past him, pretending he didn't see the young man flinch.

The surveillance room was in the reinforced basement, secure from anything but the most extreme drone or missile attack. The windowless rooms had walls covered with giant display screens, most of them currently dark. Undoubtedly they'd been cut off when Ashwin's scan at the door had alerted them to his presence—the Base trusted Makhai soldiers with a generous amount of autonomy, but not with unnecessary intel. The Makhai soldiers were too good at piecing together disparate pieces of information to form a picture of the Base's larger goals.

"Lieutenant Malhotra." General Wren was a lean man whose hair had been silver for most of Ashwin's life. The deep stress lines were newer—Wren had led the coup after the bombing in Sector Two. He waved a hand at Ashwin, who obediently stood at attention in front of the man's desk.

"Status of your mission, Lieutenant?"

A tinge of something that must be amusement stirred. If Kora ever talked to him again, she might appreciate this joke. The status of his mission was precarious—he was keenly aware of the small electronic device tucked into his boot. Outside the perimeter line, Deacon and Ivan would be covering Zeke as he got into position. Zeke swore he could bypass Base security if Ashwin got the gadget close enough to the surveillance servers—but it would take time.

Time Ashwin had to buy.

Ashwin had rehearsed his answer until he could deliver it with a semblance of his old detachment. "As expected, Gideon Rios was eager to recruit a soldier with my skill set, especially once we'd neutralized the threat of the deserters. I've been officially accepted as a Rider, with access to the royal family and household. My current focus is assessing the targets highlighted by the Base for possible subversion, particularly Fernando Reyes."

"Do you have any indication they suspect your true purpose?"

He could tell the truth, or a version of it. That he'd played on Gideon's desire to subvert him, and in turn had entrapped Sector One's leader with his own ego. But the perfect, simple lie was the easiest one—and it was a testament to how profoundly Kora had rattled him from the first moment that it had never occurred to him to use it on Gideon.

"No, sir. I told them I'd been honorably discharged in exchange for my service during the war. Gideon believes I'm looking for a quiet place to build a new life."

"Good." Moving with careful precision, Wren pulled out a folder and laid four pictures on the desk. Two were the photos Samson had shown him. The other two had time stamps from last night and early this morning. "Samson briefed you on the situation?"

"He showed me the photos."

"And?"

"I believe the data is flawed." Ashwin stepped forward and pointed to the photo showing him and Kora in her bedroom. "I can't speak to the rest, but if the time stamp on this one is correct, I was alone."

Wren's gaze narrowed, but Ashwin didn't flinch under his assessment. "Alone," the general repeated flatly.

"Yes, sir." Ashwin had never seen interior schematics in the files the Base kept on Gideon's compound, but just in case, he composed his lie carefully. "I was doing reconnaissance in the family wing while they were at dinner. I specifically chose a time when no one else would be present."

Wren's frown deepened as he leaned over and smashed his hand down on a speaker next to him. "Get North and Richards in here, now."

As they waited, Ashwin tracked the seconds on

his internal clock. Zeke would have started as soon as Ashwin got his device within range of the surveillance network. And as proficient as Ashwin was with network penetration, he'd doubted he'd be able to infiltrate the network this swiftly, much less pull off what Zeke had planned.

Deacon had sworn the man could get it done. But putting his life in the hands of a donut-obsessed criminal who lacked the capacity to take things seriously might be the least rational decision Ashwin had ever made.

Footsteps finally sounded in the hallway. The door opened, and Ashwin watched the two surveillance techs jostle almost imperceptibly for position, each one fighting to avoid being the first through the door. The tall redhead with freckles and crooked glasses—North—lost the struggle and slunk in, wilting visibly under General Wren's steely glaze. Richards followed, running a hand nervously through his dishwater-blond hair and looking anywhere but at Ashwin.

Wren snatched up the photo of Kora's bedroom and shook it at them. "Lieutenant Malhotra says he was alone when this was taken."

"Uh..." North adjusted his glasses and sidled around Ashwin, holding his arms tight to his body as if he was afraid Ashwin would snap one of them off. He gingerly took the surveillance photo and studied the time stamp, then glanced at the others spread out across the desk. "Uhm. Are—are all of the shots showing evidence of the Panacea isotope from the past forty-eight hours?"

"Yes," Wren rumbled. "Since your *enhancements* rolled out."

Richards came closer, curiosity temporarily overriding wariness as he snatched the picture from North's hands. “I told you,” he muttered, reaching for the next picture. “The sensitivity—”

“Was within reasonable parameters,” North snapped back.

“I *told* you we might be dealing with backscatter! The Special Projects isotopes—”

“Are sufficiently distinct!”

“At close range!”

Emboldened by the argument—clearly a long-standing one—North snatched the picture back and waved it at Ashwin. “Are you *sure* you were alone?”

The challenge was oddly comforting, and Ashwin vaguely regretted that he'd have to quash it. But a Makhai soldier would never tolerate insubordination from support staff, so he let the darkness gather behind his flat gaze—every life he'd taken, every life he'd shattered.

Especially Kora's.

North's bluster crumpled in seconds. His shoulders slumped, and his arm fell back to his side. He glanced at Richards—who was staring intently at the floor—and then at General Wren, who looked too irritated to intervene.

Fear crept into the man's hazel eyes. Ashwin didn't enjoy it, but it was necessary. He'd burn this Base to the ground if it would keep Kora safe. This tech could survive a little fear.

Finally, North opened his mouth. “Sorry, I—”

“I was alone,” Ashwin interrupted flatly. “I advise you to check your new software for bugs.”

North paled until his freckles stood out like scars on his face. “Yes, sir.”

General Wren wrapped his knuckles on his desk. “Richards, explain the backscatter.”

“Well—” Richards cleared his throat nervously. “I

can't say for certain that's what it is. There are plenty of things we can test for in controlled circumstances that don't replicate well in practical application. Topography, air haze, weather conditions, manmade structures—all of those can impact our sensors. Especially because there are so many naturally occurring isotopes, and when we mess with the sensitivity—"

"Explain it more concisely," Wren snapped.

Richards scrambled for the surveillance shots and held them up. "These were taken at over a thousand meters. At that range, it's possible that we're not picking up the Panacea isotope but a—a reflection of the Makhai isotope. Backscatter."

"So that's easy to test. We have drones on the roof." Wren pointed up, then pointed at Ashwin. "And a Makhai soldier right here. Take one up to a thousand meters and show me what you see."

"Yes, sir."

Ashwin moved aside so they wouldn't have to inch past him to reach the closest bank of computers. The screen on the wall above them flickered to life, showing a dead camera feed and the map and control schematics. Richards took a seat and started to type, his fingers flying.

The camera flickered to life, showing a blurry shot of the sky and the golden horizon before shooting upwards so fast that watching the image on the screen gave Ashwin temporary vertigo.

He was too tense. But this was the moment of truth, the moment where his reckless trust in Gideon's men would either save or damn him.

*950.*

*975.*

When the altitude tipped over a thousand meters, the drone jerked to an abrupt halt. With one keystroke,

Richards flipped the wide view of the desert over to the isotope filter.

Ashwin tried not to hold his breath.

Little splotches of color appeared on the screen. Blue and then red, directly in the middle of the screen. To the northeast three more blue dots appeared, echoed by red shadows at various distances. On the south edge of the screen, another appeared, so close to its red counterpart that they almost blurred together into purple.

The donut-eating fool had pulled it off.

"See?" Richards proclaimed triumphantly, jabbing his finger at the screen. "Backscatter. I *told* you we needed to test it more before rolling it out."

"I *did* test it," North protested, looking even paler. "On a Makhai soldier, an elite officer, and the regular enlisted infantry."

"At this altitude?" Richards pushed.

North hesitated just long enough, doubt shrouding his eyes, and Ashwin felt a prickle of sympathy. North had completed a deft bit of coding into which Zeke had simply inserted an error. When it was found, any protests North made claiming he hadn't been responsible for the bug would receive short shrift from command—the officers valued results, not excuses.

Not a kind thing to do to a man who had just been doing his job. But kinder than killing him.

"Fine," General Wren growled, waving his hand. "North, you're dismissed. Richards, you, too. But I want you to oversee a rollback. And make sure the next update is *thoroughly* tested."

Two voices exclaimed, "Yes, sir"—one significantly more dejected than the other. But neither man lingered once the drone was back on the ground, and Ashwin found himself alone again with General Wren.

Ashwin resumed his stance with his hands folded

behind his back. "Sir, may I request access to the mechanical resources inventory? I got away today by telling them I was going to find more generator parts."

"That's fine, requisition what you need." Wren gathered the photos and tucked them back into the folder. "I sent you on this mission because I trust your ethics, Malhotra. Your sense of right and wrong. Not all of your Makhai brothers share your...inner compass."

The words sounded like compliments, but there was a wariness in his tone that Ashwin wasn't sure how to reconcile. "Sir?"

"I also recognized that sending you was a risk." Wren tapped his fingers against the desk. "In the unlikely eventuality that Gideon Rios turned out to be the same man in private that he appears to be in public, I knew I risked losing you the way we lost Lorenzo Cruz."

Adrenaline surged, and it took all of Ashwin's self-control to stay still. One of Wren's hands was still tapping absently on the desk, but the other was in his lap.

Or reaching for a gun?

"This is between you and me, Lieutenant. And if you ever repeat the words, I'll deny them." Wren leaned forward. "I don't care if you come to respect Gideon Rios. I don't care if you come to believe your loyalties are conflicted. I want you there, standing next to him. Because if he ever becomes the monster his grandfather was, I know you would be the first person to put a bullet between his eyes, personal loyalty be damned."

Ashwin let the words sink into him, picking apart their meaning and implication. Wren was offering him a trade of sorts. A devil's bargain. If he accepted this charge, his mission in Sector One would be protracted. Potentially indefinite. There'd be no tension lingering in the back of his mind, warning him against getting too comfortable. No reason to expect he'd wake up one day and find himself recalled and reassigned.

Wren was offering him a permanent post in the only place he'd ever wanted to be. And, in exchange, he had to agree to kill the first man to believe that Ashwin could be more than an organic machine programmed for destruction.

But only if Gideon became a monster.

General Wren wasn't wrong. If Gideon began to abuse his power, Ashwin wouldn't be able to stand by and watch. His newfound sense of loyalty and protectiveness wouldn't allow it. The people most likely to be hurt in Gideon's fall were the people who had come to matter to Ashwin—Deacon and the Riders. Maricela and her eternal optimistic smiles.

Kora, who would let Gideon bleed her dry and blame herself for not stopping him, just as she'd done with Ashwin.

The vows he'd taken the night he'd become a Rider had been to protect Sector One and the royal family, and the easiest way to keep them was to make sure Gideon didn't give in to the temptations of power.

Gideon, Ashwin imagined, would be the first one to agree.

"Lieutenant?" General Wren prompted.

"I can make that promise," Ashwin said, keeping his voice even. "I don't think Gideon Rios is currently a threat to the Base. Given enough time to fully gain his trust, I believe I'll be in a position to ensure he will never be a threat to the Base."

"Excellent." Wren waved a hand at him. "You're dismissed, Lieutenant."

Ashwin saluted and turned, striding from the room. People hugged the walls as he passed, but he barely noticed this time. He made his way from the building and back toward his bike, stopping by the parts depot only long enough to snag the drive belt Zeke had been bitching about trying to find for his bike.

The smug bastard had earned it.

No one stopped him as he rode his bike back through the gates. He followed the road past the end of the razor wire fence and turned toward the old highway that connected to Eden. Five miles out of town, he crested a hill and saw Zeke, Ivan, and Deacon waiting for him at a dip in the road.

Zeke bounced his keys excitedly as Ashwin stopped and stripped off his helmet. "Well?" he demanded. "You're not riddled with bullets, and I didn't hear anything blow up. Did it work?"

Instead of answering, Ashwin took the drive belt from his pocket and offered it to him.

"Fuck, yeah!" Zeke plucked his prize from Ashwin's hand and waved it in the air. "In Noah Lennox's *face*. I'd like to see him pull that shit off."

Deacon was quieter in his questioning. "They bought it?"

"They bought it." Ashwin managed a smile, and it must not have been too off, because Zeke returned it. "Zeke was right. The techs were already fighting about the reliability of detection at that altitude."

"Told you." Zeke punched Ivan in the arm, so smug Ivan rolled his eyes and shoved him back. "Honestly, it was probably malfunctioning in other ways they hadn't caught before I tweaked the code. There was bound to be interference."

"Well, they've rolled it back now. And by the time they get another drone out..." Ashwin trailed off and glanced at Deacon. "Did Lucio tell you how long Kora's procedure will take?"

"I didn't ask." His expression made it clear that Ashwin wasn't allowed to, either.

The rebuke stung, but Ashwin didn't mind. The pain was well-deserved. Maybe, when they got back, he could convince Reyes to expand upon it by punching him a few more times.

Ivan picked up his helmet. "I don't know about the rest of you, but I'd like to get home. I don't like being this far from Gideon and the family."

"Agreed." Deacon squinted in the direction of the military compound, as if he expected to see a trail of armored trucks heading toward them. "Let's get the fuck out of here."

Ashwin donned his helmet and fell in beside Deacon as he roared down the road. But when they hit the south turnoff that led in the direction of Sector Three, it took everything in him to keep following the other Riders north to Sector One.

Kora would be in good hands at the hospital, safe and protected. Gideon had promised him that. And Deacon was right—Ashwin didn't get to ask after her. To go to her.

If he wanted that right back, somehow he'd have to earn it.

# twenty-one

Having your blood systematically removed, filtered, then replaced was surprisingly boring.

Mad had stayed for a while, and his easy Rios charm had distracted her from the intravenous lines running from her arm and neck. He'd told her stories about Gideon's childhood, and spent far too long admiring the newly bare skin on her wrist, where Dylan had used lasers to painstakingly remove her bar codes. Then he had to go, and Dylan had handed her a book.

She'd read it before. And it wasn't even a good one.

But it wasn't his fault. She couldn't stop thinking about what Gideon had explained about the other part of the plan—and Ashwin's role in it. There were so many variables, a hundred tiny things that could go wrong. If Zeke's software bug didn't work. If the general in charge of the operation didn't believe Ashwin.

If, if, *if*.

"Dr. Bellamy." Lorenzo Cruz pulled a chair up next to her bed and sank into it. "Mad told me you could use a visitor."

"Cruz." She handed him the book, and he set it aside. "How are the babies?"

"Good. You were right, Isaac's cough is clearing up." Cruz's usually stern face melted into a gentle smile. "Ace is still convinced our daughter is a genius. We're not arguing too hard with him. She's pretty amazing."

"He's probably right. But don't tell him I said so."

"I won't." Cruz sat back and laced his fingers together, resting them on his stomach. A casual, relaxed pose, but his words were careful. "Most people don't know why you're here, but Gideon told me. In case I want to have the isotope filtered out of my blood, too."

The Base had known where he was for the last year. If they'd wanted him back, they'd have him by now. But priorities had a way of shifting, and just because they hadn't come for him yet didn't mean they never would. "It's not a terrible idea."

"I'm going to do it." He lifted a shoulder. "Maybe it'll never matter. But if it does someday, I won't have time to fix it. And I've got a family to think about."

"Yes, you do." She twisted her fingers in the thin sheet covering her. It was rough compared to the linens at Gideon's house. "Ashwin went to the Base."

"I heard." Cruz reached out to cover her hand. "Ashwin spent months undercover in Eden. He can handle an hour on the—"

"Don't. You, of all people? You know." The generals didn't need proof of wrongdoing. All they needed was a hint of suspicion coupled with a reason to act. People far more innocent than Ashwin had suffered because of that.

Cruz sat back and studied her in silence for a long moment before changing the subject. "You've never said anything to me about the time he kidnapped you. You must have known when you showed up to help with Rachel's delivery and saw Ace. I half-expected you to turn right back around and walk out the door, but you didn't."

"I wouldn't do that. I couldn't." The tape securing the IV in her arm had curled up in one corner, and she smoothed it down. "The only thing I regret about any of it is that no one *asked* me to help."

"That would have been better," Cruz admitted ruefully. "I wasn't exactly in my right mind when I asked Ashwin for the favor. If I had been...I would have remembered the most important thing about him."

"What's that?"

"Have you ever heard that old saying? When all you have is a hammer, everything looks like a nail? That's how we are when we come out of the Base. We see a problem, and we look for a military solution. It took me *months* with the O'Kanes to understand that military solutions are fine when you're dealing with enemies, but they fuck everything up when you're dealing with friends."

"That's true. But you're not Makhai," she reminded him softly. "You're not Ashwin."

"Which is why it only took me months." Cruz rubbed his shoulder, his gaze unfocused. "I've been thinking a lot since you two came to Sector Four. Remembering the first time I met him. Did you know he pretty much saved my life?"

"No." Kora shifted on the bed, turning toward him as much as she could. Hungry for another tiny piece of the puzzle. "Tell me."

"It was my tenth birthday. I don't know how old

he was—eighteen, maybe? I'd just passed all my physical and mental evaluations and was wearing my new uniform, and a bunch of the older elite soldiers jumped me."

It wasn't an unusual sight in the common rooms on the Base. Everyone denied it when confronted, even the victims, and the generals never stopped it because they viewed it as another sort of test. "What happened?"

"Ashwin happened." His lips curled in a tiny smile at the memory. "He didn't have to haul them off me or wade into the fight. He just told them to run, and they did. Everyone was scared of the Makhai soldiers, and Ashwin was always the scariest."

As it turned out, she could still smile through the pain, after all. "Some things never change."

"That's what I thought. That Ashwin had never changed." He laughed softly. "I still remember what he said to me when I asked why he'd done it. Word for damn word. Because it was so...*Ashwin*. He said, 'You represent a massive investment of Base resources. You're small now, but within three to four years, your height will put you in the top percentile. It's inefficient to risk compromising your viability.'"

She burst out laughing. "That sounds like him." But just as quickly as the humor had hit her, it slid sideways into something sad. Desperate. "Do you think he meant it?"

"I think..." Cruz hesitated, as if he sensed her pain. As if he was trying not to add to it. "I think it's his tell, Kora. Efficiency. When he feels something he doesn't know how to process—compassion, caring, even just the urge to help someone—he has to rationalize it, so he claims he's just being efficient."

"Or maybe you're seeing what you want to see. What makes sense to you." She paused, unable to pinpoint exactly which parts of her agony she could share without laying her entire soul bare. “He had the perfect opportunity to tell me about Panacea, and he didn’t. Our entire acquaintance has been one long string of perfect opportunities, but he let me wonder, Cruz. Even though he knew it hurt.”

“Kora, there are things—” Cruz sat forward, his elbows on his knees, his expression suddenly deadly serious. “Hell. I don’t even know where to start with this, and you’re going to hate *me* after I say it.”

“I don’t hate people. It’s not in my programming, remember?”

Cruz scrubbed his hand over his face. “You didn’t see him during the war, not until that last battle. But before that he was...unhinged. Halfway to insane. And he came to me at one point and asked where you were. He wanted to take you to a safe house and hide you.”

“I know.” She’d spent too many quiet moments trying to imagine it. First, as a place filled with all sorts of things Ashwin knew she would like, and later as a utilitarian prison, because it felt like maybe he didn’t know her at all.

“I shot him. That’s how badly he scared me. I wasn’t sure I was going to get out of the situation alive, but then I told him...” He took a deep breath and met her eyes. “I told him that fear hurts. And that if he tried to take you anywhere in that emotional state, he’d hurt you.”

Now she understood the angry thread of self-blame running through his words. “It wasn’t your fault. All you’re guilty of is believing that what everyone told you was true.”

“Do you still think that everything they told us was wrong?”

That was the real question, wasn’t it? “I want to,” she confessed. “But that’s the problem. I’m not sure if I really believe I was right, or if I just need it too much."

"It's never easy to be sure." He leaned back in his chair. "When I got together with Rachel the first time, I was all twisted up inside. All the shit the Base and Eden had taught me about sex was fucked up. I didn't mean to hurt her, I just didn't know how *not* to hurt her. Still made it my fault. And I didn't *mean* to freak Ashwin out so bad he ran back to the Base for six months of recalibration. I didn't even know I could freak him out. Still makes it my fault."

It was a hopelessly tangled, snarled mess, and she could go around and around forever, trying to figure out what it all meant. Either Ashwin had made a mistake, one that would never happen again—not only because the situation was so unique, but because he had learned from it—or she'd spent the last few years of her life in complete, utter denial of reality.

She knew which option she preferred. But she didn't know if she could trust herself anymore.

Maybe she didn't have to, not yet. "What about you? Do you think everything they told you was wrong?"

"About me? I *know* they were wrong. About Ashwin?" Cruz lifted both hands. "He'd be the first to tell you that he makes the efficient, expedient choices. But if you watch him... He doesn't know how to care about people, but he tries. Sometimes by getting himself tortured, sometimes by hiding secrets. Sometimes by committing espionage and high treason. And even knowing that, I can't tell you to be the one to teach him, Kora. Whoever takes that on might be in for a lifetime of accidental hurt, however good his intentions."

It was the same thing she'd discussed with Maricela and Del the day she'd gotten her tattoo. An old question, one she was no closer to answering. But she was starting to think the real question wasn't whether Ashwin would hurt her or not, but whether what came between the hurts was worth it. If *he* was worth it.

And that answer was always, always *yes*.

By nightfall, Ashwin was missing the respectful terror he was shown on the Base.

*Lie.*

It was a lie, but not a large one. Every hour that ticked by without an update on Kora cranked the tension in his muscles tighter. Worse, gossip and rumor seemed to work far more efficiently here than on the Base. He got a few angry glares from servants who were particularly protective of Kora, but the Riders had rallied around him with such aggressive hope and relentless support that he found himself incapable of processing it.

Kora would have helped. A few minutes, even a few seconds. Just seeing her. Resting his head in her lap as she stroked his hair and performed whatever magic it was that eased the rawness that came with feeling too much. Or feeling at all.

But Kora was far away, and the Riders weren't helping.

They were *trying*. Reyes had offered to punch him again, and the exhausting sparring session had left Ashwin sufficiently bruised. Unfortunately, his brain had too many lingering connections between Kora and pain. What should have been satisfying only left him more on edge.

Bishop and Gabe tried to talk to him. Zeke brought him dinner from what he claimed was the best taco vendor in the sector, then expounded on how he'd chosen the top five until Ashwin ate the tacos just to make him stop. Ana mostly glared at him, which

Ashwin appreciated. He liked knowing someone was firmly on Kora's side.

Even Ivan made an overture, abrupt and surly, plopping an impressive collection of firearms onto the table in front of Ashwin to ask for his help cleaning them. It was a soothing ritual, with the familiar scent of gun oil and the rhythmic click of pieces sliding apart and back together.

But Ashwin could clean a gun in his sleep. It left his brain far too free to run through all the possible complications from Kora's procedure, all the ways she might still be in danger.

All the ways he couldn't protect her if she wouldn't see him anymore.

Deacon was the one who handed him an ice-cold beer, then dropped down beside him. "I wonder when the shit's gonna hit the fan."

Ashwin drained half of the beer, enjoying the chill bitterness. An acquired taste, but one he was starting to appreciate. "Which shit. Which fan."

"The big one. On both counts." Deacon eyed him balefully. "Orders aren't written in stone. You got out of that compound today with no holes in you because it wasn't the big showdown. Just a move in the middle of the game."

Ashwin rubbed his thumb over the cool glass of the bottle. "I don't think it will be soon, not unless there's another coup. General Wren said something to me today..."

Deacon grunted.

"Did you know Gideon's grandfather?"

"I never met the man."

"Neither did I, but I've read the files." Gideon's grandfather had started his career as the Prophet earnestly enough, preaching a religion of love and compassion to fight back against Eden's increasingly puritanical strictures. But as his power had increased, no doubt so had the temptation to misuse it.

Ashwin understood the way lies built now, how easy it was to rationalize something you wanted to do anyway. How difficult it was to detect—so difficult that he'd been doing it his whole life while smugly congratulating himself for being *too rational* to be susceptible to such folly.

"That's what they're afraid of," Ashwin continued quietly. "The refugees are joining Gideon's religion in massive numbers. His power is about to expand in ways he may not be prepared for. He wouldn't be the first man to fall victim to temptation."

"Mmm." Deacon remained silent for a moment, then waved his bottle in Ashwin's direction. "You know why I don't like you?"

"I came here under false pretenses, to potentially harm people you'd sworn to protect?"

"Exactly." Deacon grinned, but it was the kind of expression that evoked instinctive wariness, not humor. "You remind me of me."

It was the absolute last thing Ashwin had expected to hear. "I don't understand."

"Because you haven't asked me what I did before I became a Rider. It's okay—no one does. They all seem to think I was born with an armful of raven tattoos and a list of Gideon's directives tucked up my ass." He paused. "I was a mercenary. An assassin sent to murder Gideon. Hired by a man I'd never met."

The odd emphasis on the words wasn't an accident. Deacon was too precise. Too strategic.

*I never met the man.*

Deacon was implying that Gideon's grandfather had hired him. "What happened?"

"Gideon's father had taken over running the sector, but he wasn't very popular. There was...unrest. Half the people wanted the Prophet to come out of retirement, and the other half wanted Gideon to step up." Again, that chilling grin. "From what I hear, the old man never did like competition."

No, he wouldn't have. The psych profile on old Fernando Rios had identified intense narcissistic tendencies. Ashwin had never found that surprising. It took a very particular personality type to pronounce oneself the chosen of God. It took an even more specific type to truly believe it. "I've read similar assessments."

"When Gideon found out, he invited me to finish the job. Said a man of honor always keeps his word, which was just fucking laughable. There was no honor in that. In me." Deacon tipped his beer back, but the bottle was empty. He cradled it anyway, turning it over in his hands. "I was ready to die. I put the gun in Gideon's hand myself. Know what he did? He set it down on the table between us and asked me what in this world I considered worth fighting for."

And Ashwin thought Gideon had been reckless with *him*. And yet, he couldn't summon any surprise at the words. He'd been watching the man for weeks, and he couldn't imagine what a credible psych evaluation of him would look like. One minute he was earnestly humble, a man who didn't just pretend, but was of the people.

In the next, he gambled his life and the lives of everyone around him on his serene confidence that he could see the truth in another man's heart—a truth that man denied was even there.

Maybe he could.

All of Ashwin's equations had shared a similar base assumption: that any claim to be touched by the divine was just that. A claim. Fiction, even if the person believed it so fervently, so completely, that you couldn't classify it as a lie.

There was no evidence of the existence of any higher power, by God or any other name. But refusing to consider the possibility was as irrational as believing it without evidence. There didn't need to be a mystical component to his insights. Kora's genes had been altered in a way that honed her empathy into its own sense, almost as tangible to her as taste or touch.

The capacity was within humanity. Ashwin supposed it didn't matter if he believed Gideon derived it from a higher power or a mutation of genetics. It only mattered if he believed.

"What did you decide?" Ashwin asked, watching Deacon's severe expression. "What was worth fighting for?"

"I couldn't answer because I didn't know. So he offered me a way to find out."

"He made me a wager." Ashwin drained the rest of his beer. "He told me he could make me a believer."

Deacon grunted again. "Did he?"

Ashwin sidestepped the question with one of his own. "Did you ever figure out what's worth fighting for?"

"I'm here, aren't I?"

"So am I." Ashwin set aside his bottle. "Believe me or not...but you don't have to worry about me. Unless Gideon does something that endangers Kora, or starts turning into the kind of tyrant who would hire a mercenary to—"

Deacon waved the words away. "Gideon isn't your problem right now. Neither is the Base, or your orders, or me. You're the problem. And the solution."

"I don't understand."

"I know. That's why I'm here." He slapped his hands together, then braced them on his knees. "Kora is Gideon's sister, and you made her cry. You can fix it, but not for Kora's sake, and not because you can't stand to see her cry. You have to fix it because you need to. It's the only way it works."

"I don't know how." Ashwin laced his fingers together to avoid nervous fidgeting—evidence of how badly he needed to see her. "I *can't* stand to see her cry. It's intolerable. It makes me want to destroy whatever hurt her. How do I fix the problem when I'm the one that keeps hurting her?"

"You don't listen for shit," Deacon grumbled. "If you focus on never hurting her, it's a lost cause. It's not humanly possible. That's why the words *I'm sorry* exist."

It was so straightforward that it felt like cheating. It wasn't enough. The hurt he'd done to Kora had been deeper than words. A simple *I'm sorry* would be like all the times he'd sutured his own wounds in the field, serviceable and adequate, but not enough to heal. It always took more pain—a fresh cut—to open the wound again and avoid any lasting scars.

He could do it, start the hard work of making up for his mistake. But only if she'd see him. "What if she doesn't want my apologies?"

Deacon shrugged. "You can't make her. You accept her refusal, you respect it, and you carry on. But there's only one way to find out."

"I don't know if I can carry on." Ashwin caught himself clutching his knees, and because he was so agitated it was surfacing in telling gestures, he gave Deacon the blunt, horrifying truth. "I don't know if I'm sane without her. I could destabilize again. I could... become a threat to her."

"That won't happen, I promise you."

"You'll put a bullet in me?"

"Yeah, I will." Deacon grimaced. "If I don't decide to do it anyway because you're a pain in my ass."

It was the most affectionate threat Ashwin had ever been issued. Perversely, it eased a little of his internal pressure. Not as effectively as Kora could have, but the itching inside his skin was a prickle now. Like a limb waking up after blood flow was restored.

Fights with Reyes. Glares from Ana. Threats from Deacon. He was actually starting to like the perverse, irrational things that soothed him.

Being irrational made him feel human.

# twenty-two

Kora had wondered how long Ashwin would wait once she arrived home before coming to see her. If he would come at all. She got her answer while she was still peeling the pressure bandage off her arm.

He'd already been.

It was sitting on her bed, neatly and precisely placed in the very middle, its edges curled and worn, as if it had been handled often. A single manila folder, stuffed thick with pages. And inside, she was certain, were the answers she'd asked for. Demanded.

Part of her didn't want to open it. But nothing she learned from those pages could be worse than not knowing, so she slid onto the bed and flipped it open.

The words on the first page blurred together. She stared at it until the dark shapes resolved into letters, pictures, numbers.

If you put enough of them together, they told her story.

Her parents never met. They weren't even alive at the same time—her father died long before the Flares happened, before the lights went out and the world descended into chaos. He stared gravely up at her from an unsmiling photograph, proper and formal in a deep-blue uniform with brass buttons and red piping, his eyes almost hidden beneath the brim of a pristine white hat.

*Captain Christopher Thorne.* A decorated fighter pilot who had volunteered his DNA to a military study, not a genetic engineering project.

Her mother's picture looked less formal, like ones they took for personnel files and identification badges. But the mischievous tilt of her mouth and the glimmer in her eyes ruined the stern, professional effect. The papers listed her as Andrea Zellner, a Base engineer assigned to weapons research and development.

She died when Kora was nine years old.

There was more, pages and pages about Project Panacea, protocols and metrics and graphs and charts. But all Kora could focus on were those two names, the ones she'd been searching for her entire life.

Captain Christopher Thorne and Andrea Zellner.

She read the entries over and over, until she'd committed them to memory. The dry, factual information offered only scant glimpses into who these people were, but she could read between the lines, and she did. She read and she wept, rocking gently to ease the pain, until there were no more tears left for her to cry. But she kept rocking and reading, hoping for more than those scant glimpses.

A quick knock rattled the door, followed by

Ashwin's concerned voice. "Kora?"

She tried to answer, but the hoarse sound she made was barely audible, much less intelligible.

She heard the click of the latch and the whisper of his boots. Then he was there, beside the bed, his hand hovering over her shoulder. "Are you hurt?"

Emotion overwhelmed her, scraping at already raw nerves. Looking at him still hurt, like touching a hot pan and then keeping your hand on it instead of jerking away. But she was also relieved that he was there, and that she didn't have to go through this alone. He was *there.*

The only words that came were nonsensical. Inane. "I have my father's chin."

"You do," he replied gently, brushing his thumb over it before wiping the tears from her cheeks. "But you have your mother's nose. And her smile."

His touch soothed her, but it also dredged up the shame of their fight. "I'm sorry that I jumped to conclusions. You didn't deserve it. If it helps, I wasn't doubting you, not really. I was doubting myself."

"No, Kora—" He caught her face between both hands and tilted it up to his. "I should have told you sooner. And I should have told you *better*. I should have given you the file to begin with. I was so focused on the threat to you that I chose expediency at the expense of your feelings."

"I understand that now, with the tracking, but what about before?"

"I've asked myself that question. *Why*. And the only reason I can come up with seems..." he closed his eyes and finished softly, "...insufficient."

None of this meant anything if she couldn't *understand*. "I need it anyway, Ashwin."

"I don't like hurting you." The words all but

exploded out of him, rough and intense. "This is a terrible thing to know. I was trained from birth not to be impacted by the knowledge that my eventual fate is emotional destabilization followed by termination. And it's still...there. It's always there. That's why *feeling* terrifies us so much. Maybe it's a minor aberration, or maybe it's my turn to have the Base shoot me in the back of the head."

She'd been so focused on learning the truth of her origins, but finding out who her parents had been was just a fraction of that truth. Logically, she understood that Panacea had been dismantled because its subjects broke down—lost their control, their stability, their *minds*—but that didn't make it any easier to consider that potential fate hers. It was unfathomable. Unthinkable.

But not for Ashwin. He obviously thought about it all the time, not just for his own sake, but for hers, as well. "You've been worried about me?"

"Almost none of the project participants made it to your age without developing substance abuse problems or—" He broke off and took an unsteady breath. "What if you've done so well because you didn't know you should be falling apart?"

"You can protect me from a lot of things, Ashwin, but not from who I am." Even if she told him about the sobbing, sleepless nights, it wouldn't accomplish anything. Maybe someday she would try, but she wasn't sure it was possible to understand, not unless you'd lived through the helpless confusion. "All my life, I've thought I was weak. Everyone else seemed to handle things okay, but I struggled every single day. And if I had known—" Her voice failed her, and the pressure in her chest grew again until she could barely breathe, much less speak. But she had to. She *had* to. "If I'd known there was a reason things were so hard for me, it might have helped."

He released her face and silently gripped the blankets on either side of her hips. "I understand," he said. "I didn't give you the intel you needed to manage the situation. Worse, I could have died during the war. That file would have rotted away in one of my safe houses, and you never would have known. That's unacceptable."

Kora shook her head. Considering that possibility made her hands tremble—and not because she never would have seen her file. "You're here, and that's what matters. This is important to me, but not as important as you."

Finally, *finally*, he opened his eyes. "I'm sorry for not telling you. Maybe we were both right. All the ways they taught me to compartmentalize didn't make my emotions go away, but it twisted them. And I hurt you. And I can't promise I'll make the right choice next time. I'm still learning how much I've been lying to myself all along."

"So talk to me," she urged.

His fingers curled around the blankets. His gaze never left hers. "I think...I think the files were the first lie. Not yours. Mine."

The words were raw. Exposed. "You found your parents?"

"Mostly my mother. There wasn't as much about my father—just that he was Special Forces." He cleared his throat and looked away. "Rupali Malhotra was my mother's name. She was a scientific researcher in the mid-21st century. She held advanced degrees in mathematics, biochemistry, and philosophy. Some of her papers and books still exist in the restricted archives. She wrote extensively about the ethics of genetic engineering."

Kora touched his hand. "That can't be a coincidence, can it?"

"I doubt it." When he glanced back, there was a vulnerability in his eyes. "I was only fourteen when I found my genetic parents, so I didn't think about it much. But over the years I wondered if she changed her mind. Or if she joined the project to shape their ethics doctrine. Or if she even knew what her genes were used for. The woman who wrote those papers... She wouldn't have approved of my life."

Kora had a feeling she would have approved of Ashwin, though. "You took her name."

"Her surname." His hand relaxed slightly under her fingertips. "I tried to research naming conventions of the Indian subcontinent, but it was difficult to find reliable sources. So I took her father's first name, too. Ashwin."

"So you know," she whispered, "what it's like to need answers."

"I don't know. I told myself it was efficient. Logical. Even at fourteen, I could tell that names mattered to other people. Parents gave their children names that acknowledged their heritage, or their families, or where they came from before the Flares. I thought I would be less conspicuous if I had that sort of name."

"Efficient." She couldn't help but chuckle, though she tried to soften it with a kiss to his cheek.

His brow crinkled. "Is that funny?"

"Very, but you'll have to ask Cruz about it."

The confusion didn't disappear, but he pressed his forehead to hers. "It doesn't matter. I think you were right. When I reassess the choices I've made in my life, a statistically significant percentage indicate a subconscious need for connection. To family. To Cruz. To the other Makhai soldiers. To you. To the Riders." Now he made a sound almost like laughter. "And they've never been very efficient. The domestic handlers helped stabilize me, but it was like kicking dirt on the edges of a fire. When you touch me, all the air leaves the room. The only fire that can burn is the good kind."

The same way the world stopped spinning when he was holding her, and everything felt firm and solid. Made sense. Kora slid her arms around his neck and slipped into his lap. "Every time I fought with the Base administrators, it was because of you. I would close my eyes and see your face, and I had to try—to help you, to save you, I don't know. *Something.*"

"You did." He settled his chin on her head, tucking her snugly to his chest. "You helped me. You saved me."

She curled her fingers into his shirt. "I hope so, because you saved me, too."

"Kora?"

She wasn't ready to relinquish the steady thump of his heart beneath her cheek, but the gentle hope in his voice lifted her head.

"Will you teach me how to do this right?" His expression was so serious. So earnest. "How to love you?"

A person could live a thousand years and never be worthy of those simple whispered questions. "I can't," she admitted. "I've never been in love before. We just have to learn together."

He smiled—honest, open, without hesitation or artifice, and it was the most beautiful thing she'd ever witnessed. Her heart skipped, then started to race as he brushed his lips over hers.

Love could only exist when it was given freely, without reservation, but trust like this was another matter. She'd have to earn it, day after day, moment after moment, with every earth-shattering decision *and* the tiny, mundane details that made up a life.

And it would be worth every single second.

# twenty-three

Ashwin left Kora on the perimeter, tucked in a well-concealed hunting blind, and approached the safe house on foot.

It had been over eight months since the last time he'd seen it. The wood was weathered and cracked, and the doorframe had swollen. He slid his fingers along the edge of the jamb until he reached the spot where he'd applied a thin coat of invisible epoxy. Not enough for anyone to notice while trying to force the door, but enough to split apart if they did. His fingers found the smooth surface undisturbed.

Ashwin repeated the check at all five windows before returning to the front door. He'd already retrieved the key from beneath a small boulder five hundred yards to the north, but the keyhole was rusted. It took a few minutes to finesse it open, and a few more to run a sweep of the cabin to assure himself it was safe.

Only then did he go back to where Kora was hidden. “It’s all clear.”

She had her hand propped on her chin, and her elbow resting on a wooden crate he’d converted to a small table. “Was that really necessary?”

“I like taking precautions.” He smoothed back a lock of her hair, the curling piece at her temple that always seemed to work its way free of any braid or ponytail. “Especially with your safety.”

“Mm-hmm.” She slipped her hand into his. “Show me my palace, Ashwin.”

For someone who lived in a literal palace, the cabin wasn’t much to offer. The porch stairs creaked as they climbed them, and the rusty hinges on the front door wailed. Inside, the cabin was dark. Heavy curtains blocked out the daylight. There was no electricity. Even if he’d rigged the roof for solar power, they were too deep in the woods for reliable sunlight.

The table held a solar-powered lantern with a stash of batteries. He slipped one into place and turned the lantern on high. The gentle glow filled the main room, illuminating the wide bed with a brightly patterned quilt and an unnecessary number of fluffy, soft pillows. A bookshelf stood next to the bed, filled with a carefully curated selection of pre-Flare books. Novels and blank notebooks and big, glossy books with art on the cover, each one a treasure obtained on the black market at an impractical cost.

The opposite side of the cabin held a cookstove, sink, and a battery-powered refrigerator. The door behind the table stood open, revealing a bathroom dominated by a full copper tub. Another impractical detail, considering the fact that water would have to be pumped into the cabin and heated over the fire. But, like the pillows and the books, it was proof of what it had taken him years to admit.

He'd always loved Kora. Denying the possibility never changed the reality, only the expression.

She drifted to the bookshelf first, tilting her head as she ran one finger across the dusty spines. "Where did you even find these?"

"In shops and junk stores. Some I found in actual museums." He pulled out one with a cover dominated by a cheerful mountain landscape with fluffy whimsical clouds and bright blue flowers. "I remembered... you liked to visit the museum in Eden. You mentioned it once, while you were suturing one of my wounds." Later he'd cross-referenced the video footage of Eden's three art museums to discover how frequently she attended, and on his next trip past the deserted ruins of Reno, he'd side-tracked to break into the abandoned art museum and ransack its gift shop.

She stopped just shy of touching the book's cover, and her hand was trembling. "You got them for me."

She sounded so shocked, he realized he'd made another critical error. Actions were so clear to him. Definitive. But Kora needed words. "Of course. Everything in here was for you."

Her gaze tracked around the room, taking it all in with a growing expression of warmth and wonder. "Everything?"

As if it was so hard to imagine. As if she didn't deserve twice this, a thousand times this. He'd build her a palace with his bare hands, if she wanted, at least as decadent as Gideon's and filled with anything that pleased her.

But first he had a new mission: making her believe.

He stepped up behind her and nudged her hair

away from her ear. "The pillows certainly weren't for me. Or the giant copper bathtub. Transporting it to the middle of the woods was a logistical nightmare, but it will be worth it the first time I see you in it."

She turned in his arms, a smile curving her lips—and reached for his belt.

His pulse skipped.

He wasn't prepared for the feeling that roared up inside him. It was the wanting and the craving, the need and the desire. Emotions that were growing familiar, if not necessarily easier to manage.

What was new was the dark thrill of having her here, in the safe little bolthole he'd created for them. What was left of his intellect recognized the culmination of the most basic of instincts—food, shelter, and a mate. The caveman fantasy.

He'd never had so little intellect left. As her fingers tugged at his belt, her smile made of knowing mischief, every rational thought he'd ever claimed fled into the darkness, leaving him trembling in the grip of sudden certainty.

No matter how much the Riders grounded him in humanity, Ashwin would always be a bit of a monster. But he was *her* monster, utterly loyal, completely devoted. Loved—not in spite of his darkness, but because of who he had become by embracing it.

Kora left his belt hanging open and nipped gently at his chin. "I like pillows. And giant bathtubs. And books full of art." Another nip, this one close to his mouth. "And I love you."

The words hit him hard. Higher than his gut, somewhere in his chest—maybe that was his heart. He hoped the words never lost this magic, the power to make him *feel*, raw and wild, like it was the first time. He caught her mouth with his, kissing her hard, as if he could lick the taste of *I love you* from her tongue.

It tasted like joy.

Kora moaned, a low sound that he felt more than heard. She opened his pants, then broke the kiss to haul his shirt over his head. Then, instead of fusing her lips to his once more, she stepped back and kicked off her shoes.

He almost reached out to help, but there was something very deliberate in the way she stripped off her clothing. Slowly. Teasingly. Kora had always seen into him so clearly, even when he was lying to himself about what she might find. Maybe she could see this fantasy, too, the desperate, hungry need for her to be *his*.

Her shirt slipped to the scratched wooden floor. Her bra followed, baring breasts and nipples that tightened in the cool air of the cabin. He closed his hands into fists to keep from reaching for her as she toyed with the button on her jeans. When she popped it free, he was so attuned to her that the rasp of the zipper shattered through the room.

He held his breath as she coaxed her jeans and underwear down her legs, only to let it out in an explosive groan as she finally stepped free of the fabric. He started to reach for her then, but she slipped away to the bed and picked up a pillow.

And placed it at his feet.

Blood pounded in his ears. He couldn't remember ever being this aroused, and she'd barely touched him. But she was *here*, in the place where he'd channeled everything he wasn't supposed to have felt for her. Naked. Flushed.

Sinking to her knees with that same mischievous smile. But there was a vulnerability in her now, too, a tremor in her hands as she reached for his jeans.

She was offering herself to the monster. And it was the monster who stroked her disheveled hair and curled a lock of it around his finger. The monster who recognized his perfect mate, because she was just as inhuman as he was—*too* human. Impossibly, unbearably human.

And he would spend the rest of his life using every skill the Base had given him to protect her from every vulnerability they'd inflicted upon her.

She was his. Forever. "I love you, too."

She rubbed her cheek against his hip. "Say it again."

"I love—"

Kora parted her lips and closed them around the head of his cock, and the ability to speak joined his ability to reason. He groaned instead, rocked by the visual of her bright-blue eyes staring up at him as she took him deeper.

Not slowly or nervously this time. The tease of her tongue joined the heat of her mouth, and then her hand, gripping his shaft. And then *suction*, hot enough to make him lock his knees so he wouldn't stagger under the gut-punch pleasure of it.

Her free hand touched his, guided it to sink into her hair, and he knew what she wanted. What she *needed*, the slow twist of his fingers wrapping in her hair until the tug burned at her scalp. Sensation, enough to overwhelm the clamor of other people's pain, enough to purge it.

They both needed it. And now they *both* knew why.

He tightened his grip until her eyes watered, until she moaned in helpless arousal. And as beautiful as she was like this, on her knees, so sweet and willing—

It wasn't enough. Not for the monster.

The bed was dusty. So was the rickety table. But

Ashwin didn't need a surface. He reached down and hauled her up his body, lifting her until she scrambled to wrap her legs around his hips. Her pussy rubbed against his cock, wet and hot, and he gripped her ass and rocked her against him, grinding hard against her clit. "Do you trust me?"

"Always," she whispered. "With every breath."

A lifetime of physical training made it effortless to raise her higher, to align their hips perfectly. The first few seconds of pushing into her body almost rattled his control, but he ignored the tight grip of her pussy and the sweet noises she made as he exerted rigid command over his muscles and lowered her onto his cock.

When he was as deep as he could go, he brushed a kiss to the delicate point of her chin. "Close your eyes and tilt your head back."

She complied with a slow, blissful smile. "You're a resourceful man, Lieutenant."

He'd never been so grateful to be resourceful. Sex had always been a perfunctory way to scratch a physical itch, not an exercise in creativity. The list of places he wanted to explore the limits of their shared stamina had grown rapidly.

But this was the first. Here in this cabin, with her clinging to him like the only solid thing in the world. Because that's what he wanted to be for her—safe. Her strong foundation.

Maybe, someday, her world.

"Hold on," he whispered, lifting her hips until he was barely inside her.

Then he started to thrust.

It was bliss. Hot, clinging bliss. Her body was tight and sweet, her noises even better. She moaned and gasped, and when he tilted her hips a little and found the perfect angle, she cried out, her fingernails biting eight crescents into his shoulders. He shuddered at the sweetness of the pain and fucked her harder, until the sound of their bodies colliding made its own obscene music in counterpoint to her groans.

She came screaming his name, and the rush of satisfaction was so intense it overrode his need to follow her. Instead he lowered her to the floor and backed her toward the door, spinning her to press her hands against the flat surface.

It was more intense sliding into her like this, from behind, and she arched her back and let her head crash back against his shoulder. It put her neck right there, soft and exposed, and he timed his first bite with his fingers settling over her clit, relentless as he chased her pleasure.

He wanted her undone. Wrecked. *Destroyed.* He fucked her through her second orgasm, and then a third, holding her up when her knees started to buckle. "One more," he promised, whispering the words against her ear as she whimpered and shuddered. She was so wet his fingers slid easily, coaxing and commanding. "I love feeling you come around me."

Her parted lips moved, silently forming a plea.

It was enough. He felt the tremors, the soft flutters deep inside that cascaded until she was clenching around him so hard, his vision blurred. The hoarse crack of her voice was what tipped him over the edge, though.

His name. Broken and needy, just like he was.

When the blinding pleasure had faded and her shudders had stilled, he withdrew carefully, mindful of the way even that contact made her whimper. She was boneless as he lifted her in his arms and braced her weight long enough to tug the dusty comforter out of the way.

The sheets beneath where blissfully clean and cool under their overheated skin. Kora rolled toward him as if by instinct, seeking his embrace—and that was better than the orgasm. He cuddled her close and stroked her hair, still struggling to catch his breath.

Eventually, she turned her face from his shoulder and looked across the room. "You know...the tub looks big enough for two."

He imagined it—Kora, wet and soapy, her skin gliding over his as he held her trapped in place and rocked just enough to drive her wild. Someday, he would restrain her like that and see how long he could hold her on that edge, how fantastically she'd shatter when he finally let her come.

His cock stirred.

She wiggled against him with a husky laugh. "Really?"

Ashwin gripped her hip in warning. If she wiggled too much, he'd end up rolling her onto her stomach right here—or maybe rolling onto his back and pulling her on top of him. She'd look beautiful above him, her hair tousled from his fingers, her skin still flushed from her last orgasm, her eyes heavy and glazed with pleasure.

"You know," he murmured, "with your enhanced genetics, there's a high probability that you were given increased stamina, as well. We should test the theory. Extensively." He slid his hand down to dip between her thighs, teasing the soft skin there. "Sufficient experimentation is a priority."

Laughing, she nodded. "For science."

"Of course. What other rational reason is there to do it?"

"Funny, I can only think of one." Her hand grazed his side, lingering over his ribs. "Knock, knock."

A knock-knock joke. He could still remember the first time she'd tried to tell him one. How long ago it seemed—a different lifetime. A different *him*. "Who's there?"

Her foot inched up his leg. "Boo."

"Boo who?"

"Don't cry, soldier." She slipped her leg over his and stretched out on top of him. "It's not that bad."

It took a second for the ridiculousness of the play on words to sink in. And then Ashwin did something he'd never done before in his life.

He *laughed*.

It started deep in his chest, and it hurt a little. It got caught in his throat and came out choked, almost sputtering. But that was so absurd it happened again, and as if a broken circuit had finally been closed, he couldn't *stop*.

Kora laughed with him, cradling his face between her hands. "See? You're getting the hang of it."

Only because she was teaching him. It had taken all the years since that first joke for him to learn how to laugh. Learning how to love her the way she deserved would be a lifelong mission.

Luckily, Ashwin had always been mission-oriented.

# about the author

Kit Rocha is the pseudonym for co-writing team Donna Herren and Bree Bridges. After penning dozens of par-anormal novels, novellas and stories as Moira Rogers, they branched out into gritty, sexy dystopian romance.

The Beyond series has appeared on the New York Times and USA Today bestseller lists, and was honored with a 2013 RT Reviewer's Choice

# acknowledgments

We always have so many thanks to go around, but we always start with the team that makes these books happen. Our editor, Sasha Knight. Our proofreader, Sharon Muha. (She hasn't proofread this part, all mistakes are my own.) Lillie Applegarth, who maintains our timelines and series bible. Jay and Tracy, the original VIPs, who run our reader group and have made it the haven of sisterhood that it is. Gene Mollica, who brought Ashwin & Kora to life in the cover. And Angie Ramey, our assistant who keeps taking more and more off this process off our shoulders, which leaves us with more and more time to write books.

But as always, we end our thanks with our readers. Because without you, there would be no team. No books. You embraced the O'Kanes and became their family. I can't wait to see what your love does for Gideon and his rag-tag band of Riders. Because readers are the fuel for Happily Ever Afters.

Made in the USA
Columbia, SC
17 February 2019

**Connect with Tia:**

Website: www.authortialouise.com

Pinterest: pinterest.com/AuthorTiaLouise

Instagram (@AuthorTLouise)

Bookbub Author Page: www.bookbub.com/authors/tia-louise

Amazon Author Page: amzn.to/1jm2F2b

Goodreads: www.goodreads.com/author/show/7213961.Tia_Louise

Snapchat: bit.ly/24kDboV

**** On Facebook? ****

*Be a Mermaid!* Join Tia's **Reader Group** at
*"Tia's Books, Babes & Mermaids"!*
www.facebook.com/groups/TiasBooksandBabes

Keep up with the guys on their Facebook Page:
*The Alexander-Knight Files.*
www.facebook.com/pages/Alexander-Knight-Files/1446875125542823

www.AuthorTiaLouise.com
allnightreads@gmail.com

# ABOUT THE *Author*

Tia Louise is the *USA Today* best-selling, award-winning author of the "One to Hold" and "Dirty Players" series, and co-author of the #4 Amazon bestseller *The Last Guy*.

From Readers' Choice nominations, to *USA Today* "Happily Ever After" nods, to winning Favorite Erotica Author and the "Lady Boner Award" (LOL!), nothing makes her happier than communicating with fans and weaving new love stories that are smart, sassy, and very sexy.

A former journalist, Louise lives in the Midwest with her trophy husband, two teenage geniuses, and one grumpy cat.

**Signed Copies** of all books online at:
http://smarturl.it/SignedPBs

**eBOOKS ON ALL RETAILERS**

**THE DIRTY PLAYERS SERIES**

*The Prince & The Player* (#1), 2016

*A Player for a Princess* (#2), 2016

*Dirty Dealers* (#3), 2017

*Dirty Thief* (#4), 2017

**THE ONE TO HOLD SERIES**

*One to Hold* (#1 - Derek & Melissa)

*One to Keep* (#2 - Patrick & Elaine)

*One to Protect* (#3 - Derek & Melissa)

*One to Love* (#4 - Kenny & Slayde)

*One to Leave* (#5 - Stuart & Mariska)

*One to Save* (#6 - Derek & Melissa)

*One to Chase* (#7 - Marcus & Amy)

*One to Take* (#8 - Stuart & Mariska)

***Descriptions, teasers, excerpts and more are on my website!***

www.authortialouise.com

*Never miss a new release!*

Sign up for my New Release newsletter and get a FREE Tia Louise Story Bundle!

http://smarturl.it/TLMnews

# BOOKS BY TIA LOUISE

## BOOKS IN KINDLE UNLIMITED

### STAND-ALONE ROMANCES

*When We Kiss*, 2018

*Save Me*, 2018

*The Right Stud*, 2018*

*When We Touch, 2017*

*The Last Guy*, 2017*

(*co-written with Ilsa Madden-Mills)

### THE BRIGHT LIGHTS SERIES

*Under the Lights* (#1), 2018

*Under the Stars* (#2), 2018

*Hit Girl* (#3), 2018

### PARANORMAL ROMANCES

*One Immortal* (Derek & Melissa, vampires)

*One Insatiable* (Stitch & Mercy, shifters)

can say. I know how hard it is, and I just can't thank you enough.

Special thanks to Shannon of Shanoff Formats for the gorgeous cover and teasers... and for every single (Oh!) last-minute thing. I love you.

To my MERMAIDS and my INCREDIBLE Promo Team, *Thank You* for giving me a place to relax and be silly.

THANKS to ALL the bloggers who have made an art and a science of book loving. Sharing this book with the reading world would be impossible without you. I appreciate your help so much.

To everyone who picks up this book, reads it, loves it, and tells one person about it, you've made my day. I'm so grateful to you all. Without readers, there would be no writers.

So much love,
Stay sexy,
<3 *Tia*

# MAKE YOU Mine

*USA TODAY* BESTSELLING AUTHOR

TIA LOUISE

This book is a work of fiction. Names, characters, places, and incidents are products of the author's imagination or are used fictitiously. Any resemblance to actual events or locales or persons, living or dead, is entirely coincidental.

*Make You Mine*



Printed in the United States of America.
Cover design by Shanoff Formats
Photography by Wander Aguire
Interior Design/Formatting: Champagne Book Design

*"Lovers don't finally meet somewhere.*
*They're in each other all along."*
*—Rumi*

*For the true lovers.*

# Prologue

## Gray

I'VE HEARD PEOPLE CAN CHANGE OVERNIGHT.

I never believed it until that summer.

Gasoline, oil, dirty rags, grease, transmission fluid… the indelible scent of the garage. I don't even notice it anymore. I don't see the black under my fingernails that never completely washes clean. It's my life, and I'd never questioned it until that day.

"Hand me that socket wrench then get in the cab and spin it." A cigarette dangles from my uncle's lips, and the top of his overalls are tied around his waist.

I toss him the tool and climb into the cab of the ancient Chevy we're repairing. "Ready?"

My hand is on the key in the ignition. He holds up a finger, bending farther under the hood before stepping away and circling it in the air. I give it a crank, and it turns over instantly, settling into a low humming noise.

"There you go." Mack returns the cigarette to his lips and watches a few moments as the truck continues to idle. "Kill it."

I turn the engine off and climb out. "I'll write it up. Starter, alternator…"

"Just charge for the alternator. I got that starter off an old Mustang. They don't have to pay me for it."

Walking to the office, I call over my shoulder, "You'll never make money giving shit away."

"I'm too old to start worrying about money."

I shake my head and go into the tiny room off the side of the garage. It's all windows, so I have a clear view of the 1961 cherry red gunmetal Aston-hero Classic Jaguar rolling into the shop.

*Damn.* The sight of it gives me a semi. "Holy shit."

The words are a sacred whisper from my lips. I know who it is. I've been admiring this piece of machinery since I was a little kid. I can't believe it's right here in Mack's garage.

"Grayson?" Mack's voice snaps me out of my daze.

I snatch up the clipboard holding the workorder for the Chevy and head out to where my uncle stands beside the sexiest of all sportscars.

"What you need, Carl?" Mack steps back as the elegantly dressed man emerges from the low ride.

He gives my uncle a cold nod. *Asshole.* "Just a tune-up. I'm planning to drive out to the lake this weekend, and I don't want to end up on the side of the road."

Mack chuckles, but I stay back until I'm called.

Carl Harris is a strange and hateful man. The old ladies say he spends his days drinking whiskey and staring at the photograph of his dead wife. I wouldn't know. I've never been invited inside his house, even though he's my best friend Danny's dad.

Speak of the devil.

"Hey, grease monkey. Got any bananas for me?" Danny charges out of the passenger seat and runs around to grab me in a headlock. "Who won the Kentucky Derby?"

I'm taller than him and stronger, but it still takes a minute for

me to escape his grip.

"Charley Horse!" he cries.

I narrowly escape his elbow to my ribs. "Get off me, asshole."

Mr. Harris's voice is loud and sharp. "Daniel!"

My throat tightens. I didn't think he'd hear me swear. *Shit*.

"You're such an animal, Danny." That sweet voice gives me my second hard-on of the day.

Andrea "Drew" Harris walks around the back of the Jaguar dressed in tight white pants that show off her cute little ass and a top that stops right under her breasts, those small, luscious handfuls that seemed to grow overnight.

It also shows off the lines in her stomach, and I wonder what happened to the skinny little girl with stick-straight pigtails running around drinking Mountain Dew and bothering us.

It's like a sexy version of *Invasion of the Body Snatchers*. The aliens took little-kid Drew and replaced her with this grown-up bombshell, who now invades my dreams at night and leaves me with a tent in my sheets every morning.

I stand like an idiot beside Danny with my tongue figuratively hanging out as she walks up to us smiling.

"Shut up, Drew Poo," Danny yells before breaking into laughter.

Those four words flip the whole scene.

"You are such an asshole!" Drew yells, losing her cool.

I start to laugh. Even pissed, she's adorable.

"Andrea Rebecca Harris." Her dad's voice is another sharp command, but it doesn't deter Drew.

Her eyes are flaming fire. "I was three years old!"

"Didn't stop you from shitting on my carpet."

"I was potty training!"

"Drew Poo," he sing-songs.

My sex-kitten teenage-dream turns wildcat. She snatches up the socket wrench and starts chasing her older brother around

the plastic-covered cars.

"Stop this NOW!" Mr. Harris's face is beet red. He looks like he might have a heart attack. "Stop it!"

Danny dashes behind me, and I do the only thing I can. I grab Drew around the upper arms, holding her against my body as she struggles to get free. *Damn*, she feels so good.

She's soft in all the right places, and she smells like the beach and flowers and everything good. She does not smell like gasoline and oil and dirty rags.

I have to focus so my body doesn't betray how much I'm into her.

"Let me go, Grayson!"

"You can't swing tools around in the garage," I groan, giving her a shake. "Now drop it."

She struggles a moment longer before giving up the fight. The oversized wrench hits the concrete floor with a clatter. She twists in my arms and looks up at me, and for a minute, I'm lost in her blue eyes. I remember when she was four and a snake scared her in the brush behind her house.

She was crying, and I carried her in my arms to her mamma.

Fast forward eight years, and I remember comforting her after that pretty lady died. My mother died when I was even younger than her. It's what brought me to this town to live with my uncle in a garage.

This town where people treat us like dirt.

Holding her now, looking into her eyes, the way she's looking back at me, I'm struck by how much between us has changed.

"Boy!" Mr. Harris strides to where I stand with his daughter in my arms. "Let her go."

His tone breaks the spell. It banishes me all the way back to where I belong, outside his pristine world, hands off his princess daughter.

My arms relax, and Drew steps away from me. She's still

looking at me that way, but I have to ignore it.

"They were fighting..." My voice dies in the face of her father's cold disdain.

"How old are you?" His words drip with malice.

"Seventeen. Going on eighteen."

"You're leaving for college in the fall?"

My uncle steps up beside me. "Grayson got accepted to state as well as the military college." His voice is friendly, I'm sure he's doing his best to ease the tension.

It doesn't work.

Drew's messed-up dad steps closer to me, so close his warm breath is on my cheek. "Don't you *ever* touch my daughter again."

It's low, a veiled threat.

I've never been threatened before, but I know it when I hear it. This man has nothing to lose but his legacy, and he's not going to let me put my oil-stained hands anywhere near it.

"I don't think Gray meant any harm." My uncle puts his hand on my shoulder, ducking. It's a submissive response, cowering in the presence of this old lion.

An old lion with a useless crown.

King of a forest that doesn't exist anymore.

"As if you'd teach him not to touch what he can't have." He's talking to Mack, but he's glaring at me.

"Come on, Carl." Mack's voice is placating. "You know it wasn't like that."

The man lifts a trembling hand, and a sheen of perspiration is on his forehead. I don't know what they're talking about, but he looks like he needs a drink. Whatever's going on, I won't cower to Carl Harris.

He returns to his car, pointing for his children to get in the vehicle.

"Didn't you want that tune-up?" Mack calls after him.

"I changed my mind. We're not going anywhere."

He can say that again. I hold steady as he fumbles with the keys to start the engine. As if drawn by magnetism, my eyes move to the clear blue ones watching me from the back seat with a very different expression.

Drew smiles, and heat fills my lower body. I smile back, watching as she drives away.

"Finish up that work order." My uncle starts for the T-bird waiting under the plastic cover. "And don't chase after trouble."

I tear my eyes off the beautiful blonde in the sexy sports car. I know he's right. I should stay away from Drew Harris. Nothing good can come of getting mixed up with her.

It's too bad I'm not very good at doing what I should.

# CHAPTER *One*

## *Drew*

***Grayson Cole's eyes will stop your heart, but his lips will get it going again...***

*Four years later*

MY BROTHER IS SLAUGHTERING THE RIGHTEOUS BROTHERS AS WE walk through the door of my grandparents' lake house. "You never close your eyes anymore..."

"God, Danny is such a dork." Ruby wrinkles her tiny nose. "Four years, and he's still doing that *Top Gun* shit?"

Stick-straight, glossy black hair swishes around her ears. She's a sassy Constance Wu and my very best friend.

"He loves that song."

The roar of voices swallows my reply. I hate parties like this. I'd rather be home watching *Stranger Things* on Netflix in my pajamas. Only one person could get me to come here—or the sadness of saying goodbye to that one person.

"Your brother needs to get a life," she shouts, leading the way.

I can't argue. Danny's been doing this routine song since he

decided to join the Navy in high school. Now he's a Marine. It's four years later, and we're on the eve of his departure for God knows where (they won't tell us) with his best friend Grayson Cole.

*Gray, who has every nerve ending in my body buzzing with anticipation.*

The lake house technically belongs to my dad now, since my grandparents died, but he never comes here. After my mom passed ten years ago, he pretty much stopped leaving our big house in Oakville altogether. Danny and I are the only ones who come here. It's our summer escape, our winter retreat, and of course, Party HQ.

"It's sad, really." Ruby dodges a guy pushing out of the kitchen, red Solo cup in hand.

I strain my eyes for Gray as I answer. "How so?"

"Well… Danny never takes his eyes off Leslie, and Leslie never takes her eyes off Gray."

"Danny never takes his eyes off Leslie's boobs," I quip, real irritation in my voice.

Gray does not look at her.

He looks at me.

I want to say this out loud, but I know better. It's not worth the big scene, and I'm tense enough as it is.

We're approaching the door leading to the open living room, and the closer we get, the faster my heart beats, the shallower my breath gets. I'm about to see him again for the first time since last summer—fateful, memorable, hot as hell last summer—and we only have two days before he's gone again…

Will he even remember those days last year? Has he changed? Does he even care?

Swallowing the knot in my throat, I nervously play with the hem of my red dress. It stops mid-thigh, and has thin spaghetti straps, which means I'm not wearing a bra. My long blonde hair

hangs in waves down my back just like he always liked it, and my panties are tucked safely in my purse. *Surprise…*

This has to work.

His familiar voice carries across the space, and my body stills. He says he hates this song. I know he does. My brother ignores him as usual.

I round the corner, and there he is.

"You've lost that loving feeling…" Danny's muscled arm is thrown around Gray's neck, and my face gets hot.

Love like muscle memory squeezes my chest. My fingers curl wanting to touch him, my lips heat wanting to kiss him. The space between my thighs hums with need. Last summer feels so long ago, but I remember everything.

As predicted, Danny takes Leslie's hand, attempting to woo her. Leslie's a year older than me, and she's wearing a tight green dress that accentuates her Marilyn Monroe figure. Her eyes fix on Gray, who's laughing and pointing at someone in the crowd.

Straight, white teeth. A deep dimple pierces his cheek. He nods, his lips close, and the muscle in his square jaw moves. He reaches out to take a fresh beer, and his bicep flexes briefly. My brother grabs him again, and his shirt rises slightly, revealing the line of a V heading into his low-slung, faded jeans.

God, he's so fucking hot.

"Cut his mic!" Ruby yells. "Have some pride, man!"

Her voice draws Gray's attention to where we're standing. Our eyes lock, and emotion like electricity shoots through me, starting at my lower stomach and filtering through my limbs. His stormy eyes darken, and in that one look, I know he remembers.

Leslie watches us like a hawk.

A really pissed-off, green-eyed hawk.

My bestie is at my ear, breaking the moment. "How are you planning to get him alone with your brother hanging on his neck and that female vulture circling?"

Ruby and I are inseparable. She knows as well as I do Danny would shit twice and die if he knew how far Gray and I went before the guys returned to college last fall... and how many times.

I've held onto those memories like life.

Even after Gray told me I should date other guys.

*"Your daddy's right." He looked at me with tortured blue eyes that contradicted every word he said. "You're so young. You don't know what you want."*

I only kissed him again, crawled onto his lap again, put his hands on me and made us forget my disapproving father, my overprotective brother. Neither of them had been there for me the way Grayson always had.

*"I know what I want..."*

"Andrea Harris?" A nasal voice kills my memory, and Ruby spins to block me.

"Incoming!" she cries.

It's too late.

A skinny guy our age wearing plaid shorts and a mustard yellow shirt, steps around her to me. "I've been looking for you everywhere."

"I'm sure you have..." Ruby gives way.

"Ralph." I force a smile. Ralph Stern has been hounding me to go out with him all senior year. Too bad he's a mashup of Sheldon Cooper and Dwight Schrute...

Not to mention my heart's been gone a long time.

"I didn't see you today when I stopped by the shelter." Ralph smiles, revealing heavy silver braces on his teeth, bless his heart. "Did you catch a ride with Daniel and Grayson?"

Ralph's the only one of our friends who calls us by our regular names like he's part of the parent group.

"I left early to take a shower." I love my job at the animal shelter, but I didn't want to smell like kitty litter tonight. "Gray came straight from the airport. Danny's been here since Tuesday."

The serenade ends, and party guests immediately mob my brother and his best friend. Gray's head rises above the crowd. He's smiling and charming, but every few seconds, his eyes find mine in a sizzling wave of promise.

He inspects my outfit, stormy eyes passing over my skin leaving heat in their wake. I'm waiting for him to move away, toward the dark hall at the back of the room.

"Did you hear me?"

I force my attention to Ralph. "I'm sorry?"

"Mother said her ladies group is having a special luncheon for Daniel after church on Sunday. I'm supposed to invite you." Ralph's brown eyes cast to the side. "She said to bring your dad, but I figured—"

"Danny leaves Sunday afternoon." As I say the words, my heart sinks, because Gray will leave with him.

"It'll be right after church in the fellowship hall. To say goodbye. She said your grandmother would've wanted it."

"I'll mention it to him." Everyone in St. Stephen does things for the sake of my grandparents, the Oakville Harrises. You'd think we were royalty…

Except the Harris fortune has been disappearing since I was a child. My dad doesn't work, he drinks all the time, which means we're nearly broke. Pretty much all we have now is an old name, this lake house, the old house in town, and a few "priceless" antiques.

"In other news." Ralph straightens, tugging on his waistband. "I took a job with pest control, so I'll be visiting the clinic pretty regularly. Maybe we can go out to lunch sometime."

I see Gray drift to the back hall. My stomach is tight, and I clock the amount of time it'll take me to meet him without drawing unwanted attention.

"Wait, you remove pests?" Ruby's loud voice cuts in. "How ironic."

"It's mostly raccoons, but I had two ladies call with snakes in their swimming pools last week."

"Metaphorically speaking?" She's teasing, but I'm too distracted to play along.

"I don't understand." Ralph frowns at her. "They were water moccasins."

I give Ruby's arm a squeeze. "I have to use the restroom."

"I'll be here!" Ralph calls after me.

"I'll be at the keg." Ruby heads to the kitchen.

I plunge into the crowd of familiar faces, following him like a starving kitten. I smile and say hello to people I've known my whole life. It takes forever to pick my way through without seeming suspicious, and thanks to Ralph's water moccasin story, my mind has gone to the first time I ever saw Grayson Cole.

It's not a clear memory, only shadows and feelings...

*I was four years old, standing barefoot on the path leading behind our old neighborhood.*

Brown grasses taller than my head separated it from the wide canal that ran like a river all the way to Lake Mary. A shiny black snake with bright yellow spots had zipped across my feet, its thick body slippery and fast and forever long, and I screamed as loud as I could.

I screamed and screamed. I stood there screaming until Grayson appeared.

"What was it? A snake?"

I nodded rapidly, and he leaned down, inspecting my small feet and legs. He was only eight, but he seemed like a grown-up, so serious making sure I wasn't hurt.

The reptile was long gone, and I was just standing there, crying in my yellow-checkered romper, my white-blonde hair in two plaits on each side of my head.

Gray hesitated only a moment before wrapping his arms

around my waist and lifting me off the ground. He carried me up the path, jogging to the opening in the chain-link fence behind the big hydrangea bush at the back of Mr. Halley's garden.

I bounced wildly in his arms, and I held onto his skinny shoulders for dear life until I heard my mamma's panicked cries.

"Andrea!" Her hysterical voice made me cry more.

"She's not hurt, ma'am." Gray put me on my feet, and I flew into my mother's arms. "It was just a snake."

More panic ensued, and I was carried straight into the house and fussed at for leaving the yard, wandering off by myself. Everyone forgot my savior.

Everyone but me…

Eight years passed before he saved me again.

Ovarian cancer stole my mother's life, and I'd sneaked out of her funeral, hoping I could outrun the pain.

I ran and ran until I dropped to my hands and knees on that same dirt path. Grass stains ruined my fancy church dress, and I dug my nails into the damp earth, letting out another scream.

This time my screams were the pain of loss. My ribs cinched like a vise over my lungs. My body doubled with the pressure of my sobs, and I held onto that ground for dear life, convinced I'd never stop screaming, until a warm body appeared beside me.

Those same arms wrapped around me, and he held me on his lap, rocking me, rubbing my back, and saying quiet words of comfort. I don't remember what he said. I only remember holding on to him for dear life as grief ripped me apart.

Stormy eyes reflected my anguish back at me. Gray had come to our town to live with his uncle after his mother died. He knew my pain.

We didn't say much afterward. He went back to being Danny's best friend, and I went back to being Danny's little sister. Occasionally I'd catch his eyes on me, which meant my eyes were on him, but it wasn't until last summer our relationship changed

in a major way.

Danny and Gray were home from college, and we were all here at the lake house, hanging out. Ruby and I walked down to the pier where the boys were splashing and dunking each other in the brown water.

I took off my white cover-up to reveal a matching string bikini. My body had changed a lot in five years.

When I met Gray's eyes, they weren't frightened or sad. They were fire and lust, and every part of me lit up in response. He swam away from the guys to where we were sitting, and when he pushed out of the water, I learned a new kind of hunger.

The skinny shoulders from his past were now broad and strong. Lines cut across his torso, and his stomach rippled where his muscles flexed. His gaze was possessive, and my body answered with feelings I'd never had before.

When I was younger, he'd saved me from dangers I understood.

This was new and intoxicating.

It drew me to him like the ocean to the moon.

We kissed for the first time that night. We shared all my firsts that summer, and when he tried to slow us down, I learned my power over him.

Gray might have told me I was too young to decide, but I've been his since the day he carried me out of that brush...

The game room is cooler than the crowded upstairs. It's dim, and the only light is from the neon-blue Pabst Blue Ribbon sign over the pool table and the lamp post outside on the pier.

He sits on a barstool, reclining with his elbows on the leather edge. A casual grin is on his lips, but his steel-blue eyes are so intense, so heated as I walk through the door. "Hey, Drew-poo. How's high school?"

His manner, using my brother's silly nickname, it should put

me at ease, but his eyes contradict all of it.

"I hate that nickname." I try to be sassy, but my voice comes out soft and high. "Anyway, I graduated."

"That's right." He sits up and smiles, but no dimple appears. "You're headed to State with Ruby."

"How did you know?" I walk slowly toward him.

He shrugs. "Word gets around."

My fingers play with the hem of my skirt. "How's your uncle?"

"Same as always. Ornery. Complaining that he's tired all the time. Wanting to know when I'm coming back to work."

"But you got your degree." I don't want to disparage his uncle, at the same time…

"Yeah." He looks down, inspecting his palm. "Guess I'm too smart to be a mechanic now."

"I just meant you're good at so many things." *Like saving me, comforting me, touching me, kissing me…*

He straightens on the stool, sliding his palms down the tops of his thighs. "Got any new freckles for me?" The teasing is back, but the hurricane is still brewing in his eyes.

"I didn't think you cared."

"Why would you think that?"

"You didn't come to the house."

"Danny said to meet him here." His eyes flicker to my fingers, toying with my skirt, up my arm to my bare shoulders. My nipples tighten, tingling for his mouth. Last summer he would kiss them, suck on them. I would come so fast. "I figured you'd be busy."

"I'm not busy." I take another hesitant step forward.

"As pretty as you are?" Another fake smile. "You're not dating somebody?"

"I never wanted to date anybody." *But you…*

"Well, college is different. You'll have more options."

*Did he have options?* The thought makes my head hurt.

As pathetic as I sound, I can't help asking. "How many options did you have in college?"

Whatever the answer, I will not cry. *Oh, God, don't let me cry...*

He shifts on the stool again. "I was more... focused on my classes."

Nodding, I close the distance between us. "Danny said you graduated *cum laude*. So you didn't date?"

He shrugs. "Dating costs money."

He's not looking at me now. Where did Mr. Cocky go?

"Were you lonely?" *Did you miss me as much as I missed you?*

His hands tighten on the tops of his thighs. Strong hands. Strong arms. Broad shoulders and full lips. Dark hair that touches the top of his collar. I know how soft his hair is. I know how it feels to fall asleep in his arms.

I know so much I can't let go.

"Maybe." His blue eyes are focused.

Gray can be so focused.

The space between my thighs is hot and slippery. I can't wait any longer. I reach out and put my purse on the bar beside him. Then I place my hand on his.

He flinches as if shocked by the electricity humming through my skin. He turns his hand over and our fingers thread, pulling me closer, between his knees.

I step all the way into his chest, and my eyes close at the scent of warm cedar, fresh soap, leather, and *Gray*.

His voice is thick and rough when he speaks again. "I told you to find somebody closer to your age."

"No, thank you." I move my hands to his waist, slipping my fingers under his tee so I can touch his hot skin.

His breath quickens, and I'm buzzing with the heat surging between us. Lifting my chin, I place my lips against his muscled neck. The ice is melting. He's coming home to me, and when he

speaks, it's a husky whisper.

"You need to find someone who deserves you, Drew-baby."

My chest squeezes. That's the nickname I love.

"I found him."

Gray has been my hero since I was four. Now he's going away so everyone else will see him as a hero. I just want him to stay here and be my man.

Large hands trace my waist, sliding along my hips. I lean back so our eyes can meet. "Kiss me, Gray."

Blinking slowly, I'm drunk on his presence, on being exactly where I've dreamed of being all those nights. The muscle in his jaw moves, and the struggle in his eyes is clear.

But I know something else. He won't tell me no.

Leaning into his chest, I ask one last time. "Kiss me."

And my wish is granted…

# CHAPTER *Two*

*Gray*

KISSING DREW HARRIS IS LIKE SURFACING INTO WARM SUNSHINE, drawing a long breath after a deep dive. Her lips are so soft, and when my tongue finds hers, she tastes cool and sweet. Peppermint candy.

I hold her body against me, and she smells like heaven. She feels like forever.

All the shit disappears when I hold Drew. My body relaxes, the tension leaves my muscles…

I kiss her again, and she exhales a little noise of pleasure. It registers straight to my cock. Our lips chase each other's. Our tongues slip and slide together, hungry, eager, reunited at last.

I taught her to kiss this way. I taught her how to open to me. I taught her, but she also taught me. She took my hands and showed me how to touch her body. I was following her lead when she came alive the first time, full of wonder and surprise.

I learned every inch of her, every place that made her moan.

The idea of her doing what I said, of some other guy touching

her, sparks a dark possessiveness in me I don't want her to see. It would scare her if she knew what was in my heart for her.

Her soft lips move to my cheek and she melts into my chest. The tips of her nipples brush my skin through the thin fabric of our clothes. She's so fucking sexy. She's so fucking beautiful and sweet.

"I missed you," she whispers. "I missed how gentle you can be. I missed how rough you can be."

My stomach tightens, and I want to bend her over the pool table and take her hard while she screams for more. Her blue eyes are hot when they meet mine, and I place my palms on the sides of her head, smoothing her pretty blonde hair away.

The moment I saw her downstairs, the crowd disappeared. Everything faded away but her, only her. I don't know when or why my brain decided she was mine, but I've never been able to escape it—not that I want to.

"I dreamed about you every night." My confession makes her smile.

It's the truth. It's the only truth I know—if she's in danger, I'll carry her out. If she's crying, I hold her until she stops. If she wants me… I can't tell her no.

It's been that way since she was just a cute little kid. It's been this way since last summer when everything changed. I tried to fight it. She was only seventeen. I was almost twenty-one… Her daddy would've shot me dead and buried my body.

I tried to date… One time. It was a fucking disaster. I could only see her, taste her, want her. Only Drew gets me this way.

At night, I'd lie in bed and remember the first time we were together. Two triangles of white fabric covered her small breasts. I could see the curves at the bottoms and sides. They were perfect handfuls, high and pointed.

She looked at me as if she knew what she was doing to me in that white bikini. I'm sure I looked like an awestruck fool.

Then she blinked and tucked her chin into her shoulder, taunting me. Her hair swished down her back, ending at her slim waist. Her flat stomach led to round hips, long, silky legs. Her toenails were painted bright white, and I wanted to put them in my mouth. I've never wanted to do that.

I've never wanted to devour someone before.

My dick was so hard.

"I dreamed of you touching me." Her voice drips with desire, and just like that, I have a steel rod in my pants. "Will you touch me now?"

"Drew…" I should tell her no.

Being here with her is dangerous.

If Danny found out… He'd say what I know. I'm too old for her. She's too young. I should give her a chance to grow up. On top of that, I have nothing, no name, no status. I'm an orphan raised by a nobody.

I'm working to change it, but I haven't yet.

She takes my hand and places it on the top of her thigh, at the hem of her red dress. "Touch me here," she whispers, leaning into my ear.

She owns me in this moment, and she knows it.

She knows holding her is the greatest feeling in the world. It's like coming home.

Her hand guides mine higher, sliding up the smooth skin of her leg. I feel her body tremble, and when my fingers touch the soft folds of her sex, I almost come in my pants. She's not wearing underwear.

"Drew." My voice is a hungry noise, the growl of a starving man.

"Yes," she sighs. "Touch me, Gray."

Her nails cut into my shoulders as I trace my fingers along the damp slit, teasing the tiny strip of curls, dipping the tip of one finger into her tight, clenching core. One more, and she moans.

She's so wet. I want to taste her.

"Gray…" Her hands go to my waist, pulling at the button on my jeans. She has my pants undone, and my erection is pointing right at her.

"Hang on." I stand, fishing out my wallet, finding a condom.

I turn to the side to roll it on my aching dick.

As much as I dream of her carrying my baby, I know neither one of us is ready for that responsibility. Hell, I'm leaving for fucking Africa in less than two days. How I'll survive four years without her, I don't have a fucking clue, but I won't do what they say I will. I won't "ruin her" and run off.

My hands are on her again, lifting her by the ass and carrying her so her back is against the wall. Her mouth is on my neck, her soft tongue touching my hot skin as she kisses her way higher. I'm about to explode.

"I need you inside me." Her lips graze my ear before she kisses it, and I don't hesitate.

Lowering her onto my dick, my knees almost give out. My mind tilts at the sensation of her hot, tight, and clenching around my shaft. I have to hold still or I'll come. Her thighs tense around my waist, and she struggles to move, letting out a low moan.

"Gray…" I feel her tremble, her muscles spasm, and my brow tightens.

I raise my head to find her eyes. "Did you come?"

Her nose curls, and she stretches up and down on me. "I came when you touched me." She grips my shoulders, pulling up to kiss me. "Do it hard—the way you like it. I want to feel you. I want to remember you were here."

*Jesus*. My eyes close, and I lower my mouth to hers. Her lips part, and our tongues curl together. I start to move, a deep thrust, and there's no turning back.

"Drew…" It's a ragged groan, and her body breaks again.

I'm relentless, driven by a need that never lets me go. Her

small breasts bounce against my chest with every hard thrust. She moans, and her back arches, more clenching around my dick, pulling me farther in.

"Oh," she gasps, and I brace myself.

This is better than any drug. She's my crack cocaine.

My hands grip her hips, pulling us together again and again, until I break, pressing her to the wall, filling that condom with every pulse, the way I dream of filling her, of putting my baby into her, of having all the things I want with her, a home, a family.

I'm breathing hard. My eyes are closed, and her fingers trace my neck, thread into my hair. She kisses my jaw, my cheek. The sensations consume me, overpower me. I hold onto her as I fumble my way back to Earth. I got lost in heaven.

*Mine... Mine...* The word echoes in my ears on every heartbeat. *What will it take to make her mine?*

I've held Drew Harris in my arms so many times, and every time it feels right. She pulls my face into a slow, languorous kiss, and I savor what I can't yet have. What I have yet to earn.

"I can feel your heart beating," she whispers against my cheek.

It's trying to break out of my chest.

"I've been dreaming of that for months," I confess.

"And I came in less than sixty seconds."

"I came in two." That makes me laugh.

She laughs, and I slip out of her warmth.

"Shit." Stepping back, I grip the base of the condom, tie it off and toss it before jerking my pants over my hips.

She goes to the bar, opening her purse, and taking out a thin scrap of red lace. "You've changed in the last year."

She quickly pulls a thong over her hips, shaking her head as she straightens her skirt. I really wish we were alone, in a bedroom, naked...

Instead, I catch her around the waist, tracing a curl off her cheek. "How so?"

"You're a man now. You're ready to tell my daddy you don't give a shit what he thinks." I love it when she's sassy, but she's wrong.

"I do give a shit."

That makes her frown. "Why?"

Dropping onto the stool, I pull her between my knees. "Because your dad is an important part of your life. I don't want to fight with him. I want him to like me."

I want her dad to accept me, but I know he needs a reason. I'll never forget the way he spoke to me, the way he always looked at me like I was scum under his shoes. *Do I blame him?*

"If you were my daughter, I'd need a reason."

"You graduated with honors. You're going to fight for our country." She starts to pout. "You're leaving me again."

I hate it, too. "It's the deal I made for college."

"You could've just borrowed the money like everybody else does." She reaches behind me, over my shoulder, and I kiss her neck, inhaling the scent of flowers on her skin.

"I don't like being in debt."

She holds a coaster and a pen. "What guarantee do I have you'll come back?"

"I'll come back."

She writes on the thin cardboard, and I lean forward to read it. The words make me grin, and my eyes go from her slim hand to her shoulder, to her high cheekbones, to…

"You do have a new freckle." I kiss it on the side of her nose, right beside her eye.

"Sign it." She holds the pen out to me, but I'm distracted by the amber speck on her cute little face.

"Ned." I tap it lightly with my fingertip. "Ned the nose freckle."

Blue eyes roll, and she shakes the pen at me. "I'm not a baby anymore."

"You are definitely not a baby." My eyes are hungry, inspecting her gorgeous body.

My gaze drops briefly to her breasts, and her cheeks flush. She puts her hands on my thighs, and I try to remember if I have another condom... I should've bought a whole fucking box.

"Sign it."

"Waste of time. Nothing could keep me away." Still, I scribble my name real quick and shove it toward her, trading the pen for her slim waist and pulling her to me again.

"It's a binding, legal document." She shoves the round coaster into her purse. I lean forward to kiss her neck again, inhaling deeply.

Under the flowers is a sweet scent I only get from Drew's skin. I love it. Her shoulder rises and she laughs. "Tickles."

I want to taste her lips again. I want to spend some time with those perfect breasts. I want to tell her I love her, but the screech of the back door opening kills our moment.

Drew hops away from me, and I stand as her brother trips into the room, Leslie clutched under his arm.

"Here the fuck you are!" Danny's drunk. "I've been looking for your ass everywhere. What are you doing down here in the dark? Drew? Is that you?"

"I was just headed up to the party." Drew puts her purse under her arm. "Gray, you coming?"

"You'd better get back to the party." Danny's voice is sharp. "I don't want you messing around down here in the dark. You're just a kid."

"I'm eighteen now," she yells.

"Did you just talk back to me?"

Danny gets mean when he's drunk, and I want Drew upstairs before he tries anything. I'm not above putting him in a headlock.

"Hey." I step between him and his sister. "It's our party, right? What's next on the playlist?"

"Probably fucking Marvin Gaye. That's what you want to hear."

"Yeah, what's going on…" I sing, holding out my hand for a five.

He squints at me a moment, and my hand remains stationary, waiting for him to clap it. Leslie is there, glaring daggers at me. I ignore her. She'll suck Danny's dick then pretend like she wants to sleep with me. I'm no fool. She wants us both.

I only want Drew.

Danny finally decides to let go of whatever he's thinking and reaches up to slap my hand. "I'll be up in a minute."

My eyes drift to Leslie, and I know it'll be longer than a minute before he joins us again… with a red ring around the base of his shaft. If he doesn't pass out on her.

"Drew! I said go on," he barks loudly at her. It makes my jaw clench.

She pauses at the door and looks back at me. Our eyes meet, and hers are worried. I know what she's thinking, and I give her the smile I save just for her. The one that tells her how I feel. *Don't worry, I'll see you again before I go.*

"You don't have to leave, Grayson." Leslie's finger slides up my forearm.

My eyes flicker to her, and I take a step back. "It's our party. One of us should be up there."

Just like that, my cocky mask is in place again, the one I wear around this town to prove I don't care what they think of me.

I hustle up the back stairs, knowing when I get out, it's going to be different. I will be good enough. I will deserve her.

# CHAPTER Three

## Drew

"THE DAYS PASSED AND THE BEAST BECAME A BURDEN TOO GREAT to bear, but still the man carried on…"

Pastor Stemple drones on about a man and a cow, and I think he's trying to make a point about God's will for our lives. It's the same sermon he gave last year at graduation time, and I didn't understand it then either.

It's the special Sunday morning graduation service and at the end, they'll give us all new Bibles with our names stamped on the front and warn us against the evils of drunkenness, premarital sex, and paying too much attention to our professors. They want us to get our degrees, but they don't want us coming back with a bunch of wild ideas.

All I know is after last night, I'm having a hard time keeping my thoughts pure. Every time I shift in my seat, I feel where Gray was inside me, and my stomach does a flip. I'm dying slowly with the fear I won't see him again before he leaves today.

Danny surprised me by showing up for church, even though he smells like a liquor store. Ruby is flat out sleeping with her

head on her mother's shoulder in front of us.

"And when it came time to end the cow's life, he saw that it was God's will all along." Pastor's voice descends the scale as he says the words. "Let us pray."

My best friend snorts, lets out a yip, and jumps awake in her seat. Ruby's mom is a pincher, and I have to bend forward and hold my nose to keep from laughing.

A long prayer, the seniors all file forward to collect our shiny white Bibles, and we're released. Danny and I walk out onto the lawn separating the small sanctuary from the twin fellowship hall.

"Miracles never cease," I tease, turning to my brother as we wait for all the old ladies to appear. "I did not expect to see you in church this morning."

"I'm about to go to war, Andrea." Danny likes to use my full name when he's acting superior. "I'd like to be on everybody's good side."

"Including God's?"

Just then, Leslie Grant steps out of the sanctuary, and her green eyes fix on my brother in his navy suit. I guess he looks handsome… for my brother.

"Liar," I step forward and lower my voice, acting like I'm straightening his tie. "You wanted to see Leslie one more time."

Whiskey is on his breath, and he looks over my shoulder. "If I have to go to this old lady lunch, maybe I can get some dessert after."

"Ew." I'm about to say something, but my jaw drops.

Gray walks up dressed in a navy suit as well. His dark hair is messy, slightly damp on the ends. He's sexy as fuck, and when our eyes meet, I don't care about anything else. I want to kiss him.

"There he is." Danny steps away, leaving me to restart my heart. "Hey, man, thanks for coming."

"Won't turn down a free lunch." He only glances at my brother before turning that killer smile on me. "Good morning,

Drew, you look very pretty today."

My face heats right up, but Danny punches his shoulder. "Quit being a suck up. Come on."

I look down at my white dress. It's pretty basic, sleeveless with a giant yellow flower design all over it. It's my new favorite dress.

Gray waits for me, and when we file into the open hall, everyone starts clapping. A banner in the back reads "Good luck, Daniel," and weirdly, I almost start to cry.

"Why, Grayson, Ralph didn't say he'd invited you." Mrs. Stern hurries forward to meet us looking flustered. "We have to change the sign."

"It's okay. Danny invited me." Gray's voice is so strong and confident. I want to smack Ralph's mom for acting like he's intruding.

"I guess this is the last we'll see of you." Pastor Stemple places a hand on Gray's arm, and a knot forms in my throat.

"I don't know." Gray shakes the older man's extended hand.

"What?" The pastor only seems partly surprised. "I figured now that you have your degree, you'd head back east, to your own people."

My brow tightens with anger. *Why the hell would he do that?* Gray's lived here all his life. God, I hate this small town sometimes.

"I haven't had much contact with them since—"

"Still, it's more jobs, more opportunities."

I can't take it anymore. "Gray, can you help me in the kitchen? I think Mrs. B needs something."

Confused eyes meet mine, but the pastor releases him. "That's all right. You're a good man. Good luck to you."

"Thank you, sir."

Gray follows behind me, and I slip through the double doors, catching his wrist and pulling him into the narrow supply closet

before anybody notices us. I close the door fast and turn into his arms. His chest presses to mine, and his hands are on my waist. Our breath seems louder in the darkness.

"Hey, goat brains." I hear the smile in his voice. "What's going on?"

I reach up to find his cheeks. "I couldn't listen to him anymore, acting like you aren't even from here. You've been here since you were seven."

He leans down to kiss my cheek. "I was technically eight."

Warm breath whispers over my skin, and I lift my chin. "I want you to kiss me."

"You're so beautiful." His words thrill me and when our lips meet, everything is right.

Our tongues curl together, fresh mint fills my mouth. He smells like clean soap, and he's so warm. I want his hands on me. I want my panties off and his fingers inside. I want to hold him like I did last night… just one more time.

After Danny found us, we'd spent the rest of the party circling the room, giving each other smiles, touching hands when we got close enough, stealing quick kisses in dark corners. Until midnight, curfew, and Ruby and I had to go home.

The whole way back to town, I'd argued in my head how some things are worth breaking curfew. If only my daddy were less fragile…

He lifts his face, and I clutch his shirt, whimpering, "I don't want you to go."

That makes him laugh softly. "I should be saying that to you. You're going to college. You'll be meeting new people, going out, having fun."

"I won't have any fun without you."

"Yeah, but you will." He steps back and flicks on the light. I squint in the sudden brightness, and he pulls a giant can of lard off the shelf. "Might as well act like we're helping."

The door cracks open, and we both jump. It's only Ruby. "*Ni Hao*, love birds. I waited for the light to come on. Don't worry, I'm on guard."

My hand is on my chest. "You scared the shit out of me."

"What? No panties in church? Bless me Father, for I have sinned!" She waggles her eyebrows, and my face gets hot. Gray only laughs, which eggs her on. "Hey, handsome. My mom dug out her old Buddha statue to pray for you and Danny. I guess two gods are better than one, ay?"

"Thanks, Ruby."

My friend winks and leaves, but Gray's expression is different. It's a look I've never seen before.

I feel so stupid I never asked. "Are you afraid?"

It never occurred to me he could be afraid of anything.

He shrugs, and I go to him, placing my hand on his arm. "What are you afraid of?"

"You make it sound so dramatic." He puts the lard back on the shelf and wraps an arm around my shoulder. "I guess I'm most afraid of losing you."

"What?" I step away, facing him with my lips parted. "You would never lose me."

"Come on, Drew. You'll be away from home for the first time in your life."

"So?"

"So you'll grow up, move on, meet somebody with money, family, the right connections. Somebody with a name like yours."

"Oh my God, not that Harris name bullshit again. It doesn't mean anything outside of this town."

He shakes his head. "It means something."

"Well, I'm not interested in meeting anybody else. You can put that fear out of your mind."

A grin lifts his sexy lips, and he watches me with a mixture of pride and deep understanding. "I'm just mentally preparing.

You're going to be amazing. You already are."

My arms go around his waist again, and I press my chest to his firm one, smiling up into his eyes. "You've known me all my life. Do I ever go back on my word?"

He doesn't answer my question. Instead he places his hands on the sides of my head, smoothing my hair back. I love it when he does that. "You might change your mind."

"Not going to happen."

Leaning down, I get a slower, sweeter kiss. I pull his lips with mine, and I feel a rise in his pants.

He lifts his chin, eying the door and putting space between us. *Dammit*. "So what's your major anyway?"

Exhaling heavily, I try to think. "Psychology."

"What?" I love his dimpled grin. "I thought you'd say vet med."

Shrugging, I trace my nail along a huge box of cornmeal. So many conversations we never get to have. So much I know only he would understand.

"I like working at the shelter, with the puppies and kittens." My mind goes to my plans. "But when I grow up, I want to help people. Like be a counselor or a social worker."

He takes my hand, threading our fingers. "You always want to help somehow."

"I want to help my daddy."

Stormy eyes meet mine. He knows. He understands me, and it solidifies what I've known all my life. I can't wait to say it any longer. "Gray, I love you…"

The small door rattles. The handle turns, and Ruby's voice is loud. "Mrs. Stern! Can I get you something? I'm here to help!"

We step apart. I reach for the lard, and Gray turns to the other shelf, his back to me.

"When Mrs. Harris was alive, we didn't have any of this… flip flops in Sunday school. That can't be sanitary around the food."

Ralph's mom pushes into the supply closet. "Oh, here you are! I was looking for you, Andrea. What is that? Lard?"

"I thought you might need it... for the cooking."

She puts a hand on her chest, and laughs in a pitying way. "Bless your heart, you've never cooked a day in your life, have you?"

"I made pancakes once... and shrimp and grits."

"The food's already cooked, honey. You just come on out here and enjoy it with your brother. Oh, and Grayson."

She leads the way out, and I roll my eyes at her behind her back. We start to go, but Gray catches my face before we leave the small closet. He pulls me against his chest in a hug so tight, it brings tears to my eyes.

"I'll write to you." His voice is thick. He's telling me goodbye.

He kisses me long and hard returning all the love I told him I feel.

It's the final time we're alone before they board the plane.

It's the moment I'll live on, no matter what he thinks I'll do in college.

"Come back to me, Grayson," I whisper, watching him fly away. "I'll be waiting for you."

# CHAPTER *Four*

## *Gray*

*The Desert*

TIME IS REFRACTED HERE. IT SPEEDS UP AND SLOWS DOWN DEPENDING on the circumstance. When we're on base, the monotony and the loneliness wear on me. As much as I try not to, I can't help messaging Drew.

***Drew: Ruby is the worst roommate. She's a total slob! I'm always picking up her socks and underwear off the floor. She eats pizza and leaves the box in the bathtub.***

***Me: Don't tell me about Ruby's underwear.***

***Drew: You'd rather hear about mine? I couldn't decide between the red lace thong or the pink boy shorts. Want to help me?***

I hesitate, my fingers hovering over the letters. Sneaky girl. I walked right into that one. It makes me chuckle. Of course, I want to see Drew's underwear—more like her cute little ass wrapped in lace—or nothing at all. I push that down and do the right thing.

***Me: What's the dating situation like?***

***Drew: Ruby dates any boy who asks for her number. I've told her that's dangerous, especially when they start drinking.***

***Me: You know what I mean.***

***Drew: You really want to know?***

***Me: I asked.***

The little dots float in the gray bar, and my stomach tightens. My mouth is dry, and I try to swallow. I don't want to know she did what I said. I don't want to know some other guy is touching her, kissing her…

***Drew: I'm focusing on my studies. Maybe I'll graduate summa cum laude.***

A laugh bursts from my lips. God, I suck at being firm with her.

***Me: It's not a competition, Drew Poo.***

***Drew: If you ever call me that again***

***Me: (crying-laughing emoji)***

***Drew: I miss you.***

My stomach clenches.

***Me: I miss you, too, Drew-baby.***

***Drew: Much better. I love it when you call me that.***

*I love you.*

***Me: Gotta run.***

***Drew: Okay. Look after my idiot brother.***

***Me: Always.***

***Drew: Food for thought…***

A photo appears on my phone, and the blood rushes to my dick. I'm looking down into the V of Drew's shirt. One side is pulled lower, giving me a clear shot of her pink lace bra and the top of her dark areola.

*Fuck me.* I lean back, and just barely get my hand over my growing erection before a body dives into the bunk beside me.

"Who won the Kentucky Derby?" Danny punches me hard on the bicep. "Charley Horse."

"Shit!" I hold my upper arm. "Fuck off, Danny."

"You're getting slow, old man. What's that you're looking at? Porn?"

*Something even better*... I press the button to put my phone to sleep fast before he tries to take it. "Where have you been?"

He grins, putting his hands behind his head. "You wouldn't believe me if I told you."

The desert sun has bleached his hair out to pale blond, making him look younger than he is. His skin is golden and his hazel eyes glow green. The women in this country watch him like he's some kind of god or a prince, something rare, and he eats it up like a glutton.

I'm tanned as well, but my hair is dark. The only thing distinctive on me are my gray eyes, which appear wolfish in all the brown.

Danny leans forward whispering, "So you know how the internet said the girls here prefer anal so they can still be virgins on their wedding night?"

"No." Why would I know this?

He tosses a lecherous grin my way. "It's true."

"Ah, shit." I scrub my eyes with my fingers. "You're going to get us all killed."

"Took my first ass tonight. It was everything you imagine and hotter."

I won't lie and say I've never thought about anal. It's not something I'm planning to do here. "I hope you wrapped it."

"What do you think I am, an idiot?"

My eyes narrow, and he laughs, falling back on the bunk. "The next few years might not be so bad after all."

"You're a sick fucker. Don't get HIV."

It's how we pass the time when we're not doing drills or keeping watch. I do my best to give Drew space to grow up—and fail. Danny sticks his dick in any hole that will open to him, which

is a surprising number.

All of us are just trying to stay alive.

The days turn into weeks, the weeks months. Through it all, Drew is the bright light. She's the thing that keeps me going. Our texts and her occasional, sexy pictures are the high points of my life right now.

I'm pretty sure I'm addicted by how my pulse races when her name pops up on my phone.

*Drew: Sometimes I imagine you as Forrest Gump yelling YES, DRILL SEARGENT!!!!*

I snort a laugh when I read it.

*Me: Tell me what you really think of me.*

*Drew: I really think you're a stud in uniform. You're like Tom Cruise facing off against Jack Nicholson in A Few Good Men.*

*Me: You can't handle the truth.*

*Drew: I knew you'd say that.*

*Me: I'm so predictable.*

*Drew: What's your favorite military movie?*

*Me: Apocalypse Now, duh.*

*Drew: That's really Heart of Darkness.*

*Me: How's school going? Picked a major yet?*

*Drew: I decided to stay in Psychology. Still want to help people.*

*Me: You already do.*

*Drew: Help you to a boner?*

*Me: Your brother almost saw that last one.*

*Drew: I wish this is where your hand was...*

She sends a photograph of her palm sliding under the side of her short skirt. It gives me a glimpse of her red lace thong tracing over her slim hip. Damn, she's so sexy. I jump up and head to the showers to take care of the boner in my pants.

Like some old cliché, months turn into years, until three years have passed, and we're facing our last major campaign. I'm

starting to understand why some guys become career military. So much time has passed, being here has become my normal. I don't know what it will be like to be back in civilization, back around those people, back with Drew. I want to touch her so bad, it hurts…

As usual, her texts sweep my anxiety away.

***Drew: Why would anyone say The Beatles are better than The Rolling Stones?***

***Me: Not a Beatles fan?***

***Drew: I love them, but it's like comparing Barbara Kingsolver to Neal Stephenson. They're both great authors, but they're completely different genres.***

***Me: I'd compare Atwood to Stephenson.***

***Drew: Right! Except it's still sci-fi feminist fiction vs. traditional, male-dominated world building.***

***Me: Sounds like you're getting that summa cum laude.***

***Drew: Working on it.***

***Me: We're heading out in the morning.***

***Drew: Last time?***

***Me: That's what they tell us.***

***Drew: How long?***

***Me: Not sure.***

***Drew: Where?***

***Me: Classified.***

***Drew: Please be safe. I worry so much about you.***

My chest squeezes the air from my lungs.

***Me: I will, Drew-baby.***

***Drew: Take care of my idiot brother.***

***Me: Always.***

*Somewhere in North Africa*

My back is to the wall of the narrow tower. Looking out past the courtyard, I see the trucks are loaded and waiting to take us out of here. Men holding guns line the perimeter, watching us. They wear white robes, vests, and olive green *shemagh*, or head scarves. Occasionally a woman in a black burqa scurries across the yard.

After three weeks at this palace, we're pulling out, and I couldn't be more ready.

They don't trust us, and we don't trust them.

We spent the day yesterday sweeping the route for IEDs, and we're ready to go. My CO radioed for me to come down and join the others.

Still, I linger a moment longer, re-reading the words on the printed sheet of paper, looking at the small photograph one more time. In it, Drew is leaning forward, and her smile is so big, it makes me smile.

Her wavy blonde hair falls over one shoulder, and her arms are wrapped around her waist. She'd been looking at me when I took it, and the energy coming from her eyes tightens my chest. I turn it over, and the words she wrote hit me even harder.

The letter is worn from being opened and closed so many times. When we're in country, it's the only way I can ease my addiction to her messages. On these missions, we're completely cut off from civilization. No phones, no email, nothing.

These mementos keep her with me.

*At night I close my eyes, and I can feel your lips against mine. I feel the warmth of your hands on the sides of my face. I pretend I'm in your arms. They flex when you hold me, your chest is hard, and your heart beats so strong when I press my cheek against it...*

In these words, I'm with her, too. I feel her in my arms, soft and warm, smelling like flowers and the ocean and everything good.

As many times as I said we should stop, we've maintained contact the entire time I've been here, and as much as I try to downplay it, I count the seconds until I'm with her again.

She ignored my instruction to date other guys, and it fucking makes me happy as hell she did, despite what everyone thinks.

"Report to the staging area in zero nine hundred," Marten shouts into the small radio on my shoulder.

The wind pushes the paper in my hand, and I scan her words one more time before I tuck the photo inside. I can see her face, the way her nose curls, her pretty blue eyes blinking up at me. Her voice is pure and true.

"What the fuck are you doing? We're supposed to be heading down." Danny pushes into the small space, and I straighten, dropping the paper against my leg.

"Just trying to cool off." It's a lie. There's no escaping the heat here.

Everything is brown-beige sand, hot, and dusty. The heat I don't mind, but I never thought I'd miss trees so much in my life.

"You hiding out? It's time to go." Danny looks over his shoulder, and I see a red smudge on his collar.

"Is that blood?"

"What?" He jerks to look down as I reach, and just as fast he pulls away, pushing my hand aside.

"It's lipstick." My voice drops to a whisper. "Were you with Adara?"

His throat moves and he glances down. "What's that in your hand?"

I pull back at his deflection. Somehow, Drew and I have managed to keep our relationship from her brother this whole time. Danny and I are friends, but I expect he'll pull some over-protective, "my kid sister" bullshit.

"Quit changing the subject. Are you fucking that girl?"

"She's twenty-two. She's not a girl—"

"She's his youngest daughter." My mind flies through all we've learned about this place. "She could be stoned for not being a virgin."

"She's technically still a virgin, and trust me, she knows what she likes." He leans back against the wall, giving me a smug grin. "When she comes with my dick in her ass, she makes a noise like—"

"I don't want to hear it." I give him a shove, and the letter falls.

He bends fast to scoop it up. "Now… what secrets are *you* hiding? I knew it'd been too long—"

"Give it back."

"Oh, now I have to know." He laughs, opening the sheet.

Her photograph falls to the dirt floor and everything stops.

We both lunge at the same time but Danny gets to it first. "This is Drew." Frowning, his eyes meet mine. He speaks the words slowly, as understanding breaks across his face. "Why do you have a picture of my little sister?"

"It's old." As if that somehow makes it better.

He turns it over to read the back. "*My first*? What the fuck?"

My stomach is tight. I knew this was long overdue, but I hadn't intended to do it now, right before we pull out. "We'll talk about it later."

"We're talking about it now. How long has this been going on?"

"Your sister's back home, Danny. Nothing's going on."

He steps to me, pushing his arm against my chest. "When did she write this?"

Hazel eyes scan my expression, searching, studying my response. I've never been a great liar, and he knows how many girlfriends I've had.

"That last night at the lake house. We were talking downstairs."

"You said you never touched her."

"I never said that."

Anger flashes across his face. "You fucked my kid sister."

The words are a low growl. Danny has always been a hothead.

"It's not like that."

"Mother fucker. She's just a kid." He pulls his fist back to punch me, but I dodge, grabbing him around the chest.

"Calm down." My voice is louder, matching his.

"Let me go, asshole. I'm going to kick your ass."

"No." I hold him firmly against my chest. I'm stronger than he is, but not by much. "Settle down. I'm not going to fight you."

"You're three years older, and you fucked her. You ruined her and walked away just like my dad said you would."

"It was not like that. It was never like that."

"You worthless, good for nothing piece of shit. Drew is fucking royalty. She's so far out of your league, you can't even see her."

Like I said, I expected something like this, but it still pisses me off. Danny and I know each other better than anybody, and he knows I've never been a player. It's fucking hypocrisy, considering what he does, up to and including this week—putting our entire unit in jeopardy to screw around with the daughter of our host.

At the same time, I can't argue with him. "I told her to find somebody better."

"It didn't stop you from sleeping with her." He makes a sudden move, jerking to the left, and he's out of my grasp.

Before I can duck, light blasts behind my left eye as his fist slams into my cheekbone. I actually see stars.

"Fuck," I groan, staggering back and holding my face.

Pain radiates up through my skull, into my temple. He's worse off, shaking his hand.

"Fuck!" He yells louder.

I hope he broke it. "If you'd calm your ass down and talk to me—"

"Who else knows about this?"

It hurts when I shake my head. "Ruby…"

"Ruby." His jaw clenches. "Sounds like her. My sister would never go for some lowlife otherwise."

My teeth grind. Big brother or not, I've had enough. "We were together way before Ruby knew anything."

"Goddammit. Is that why she's not dating anybody?"

"How do you know that?"

"Because I asked Leslie to keep an eye on her."

*Leslie.* I rest my cheek against the cool barrel of my gun. "Speaking of, does Leslie know you're ass fucking every Arab chick who gives you the time of day?"

He lunges at me again, but I dodge, catching him around the waist and throwing him to the floor.

"Cut it out." I stand over him breathing hard. "What's your problem, anyway? We've been friends since we were kids. You know me."

"I won't stand by and watch you drag her down to some mechanic's shack, keeping her barefoot and pregnant. Drew was meant for better things. Finer things."

"I'll never stop Drew from doing what she wants." I step closer until our noses are practically touching. "But you listen up, if she wants me when we get back, I'm going to her. I don't give a fuck what you think."

"Over my dead body."

"If only I could be so lucky."

I'm pissed and I'm burning up with adrenaline, fighting, and the desert sun beating down. Still, even as I say the words, regret tickles at the back of my mind. I shove it away. I'm too angry to let him off the hook for what he said, calling me a lowlife. *Him.*

Our commanding officer blasts over my radio demanding to

know where we are, why we're not at the trucks. Danny and I are breathing hard, staring at each other with fire in our eyes. I grab my gun, snatch Drew's letter and photograph out of his hand and stuff them in my pocket.

"We're on our way," I say into the clip on my shoulder before turning and charging down the narrow stone staircase.

We're with the convoy in less than five minutes. I grab a helmet and throw my rifle onto my back. Our CO hands me a set of keys. "You're driving this one."

I don't even argue. I'm glad to take the wheel. It'll keep me from having to sit in the back staring at Danny and his stupid-ass face for the next several hours as we bump over hot, dry terrain.

Our truck is second in line, and I wait for the signal we're loaded up before heading out after the truck in front of me. Danny's words sting in my brain, as much because I grew up believing them as anything.

I don't need him telling me I don't deserve Drew. I know where I came from. I know my status in that fucking town. Small-minded bullshit aside, as pretty and sweet as Drew is, she could easily do so much better—marry a rich man, a man with a pedigree and a mansion, live out her life doing whatever the hell she wants.

The very thought of it causes bile to rise in my throat.

I've done my best to rise above my humble beginnings. I have my degree, and I'm serving our country. We've been here longer than two years, which means I'll go home with a medal, an honorable discharge. It's something to be proud of, and despite what Danny says, it does change things. If she chooses me, I will give her a better life, a life she deserves.

And I love her.

"Danny can fuck off," I growl under my breath.

My anger at him, my "best friend," his refusal to budge, acting just like all the assholes I grew up around in that town, it's a

hot ball of fire in my stomach. I don't know if I can forgive him for this.

I don't know if I want to.

"We're all on the road." The driver's voice ahead of me crackles through the radio. "Next stop, home base."

He's happy, because once we're back in camp, we can catch up with all our family and friends. It's a double-edged sword now. I'll be able to talk to Drew, but so will Danny. I don't know what he'll say to her. I don't know how it'll affect her, or if it'll change her mind about us. That thought turns my stomach. I've come to depend on her so much. I can't let her go. My anger toward him burns hotter, and my words float across my brain... *If only I could be so lucky...*

I didn't mean it.

*Did I?*

My cheek throbs, and my body is tight.

A clutch of goat herders on the side of the road draws my attention. Three men in white robes, olive green jackets and *shemaghs.* Only the militant wear the dark green headscarf. The civilians, the regular guys wear the more traditional *Keffiyeh,* which is red or black and white checked.

My heart beats faster. I look to the side, and I see a man standing alone. He's moving past the truck in front of me, closer to my vehicle.

Black eyes meet mine, sparking with hatred. My stomach clenches, he smirks, and I see in an instant what's about to happen. We have to turn around.

Easier said than done.

I jerk the wheel of the massive, four-ton transport vehicle, but it's too late.

"NO!" My shout fills the cab.

The blast deafens me.

The enormous vehicle I'm driving jolts into the air, front-end

first, and my head slams violently against the back glass. I'm wearing a helmet, but the impact is like a sledgehammer to my skull.

The vehicle twists in the air before slamming to the ground on the driver's side, jerking my head to the left. For several minutes, I lie there confused.

I stare blankly ahead.

A high-pitched shrill is in my ears.

Men shout all around me, running and pointing. Dust, smoke, and chaos surround us. I can't think.

I have to think. I'm trained for this.

I force my arms to move, force my fists to release the steering wheel. My fingers fumble as I try to unfasten my seatbelt. My movements are clumsy, disoriented, until finally it comes undone, and I drop against the door.

"Oof!" comes out of my mouth, but the ringing in my ears drowns out everything.

A hand grabs my arm, and I hear a voice like it's underwater. "Cole! Are you hurt? Can you move?"

I have to move. I nod, pushing against the door, doing my best to maneuver my legs under me so I can stand. I'm stunned and deaf and nausea roils in my stomach. The light blinds me. I have a concussion, I know it. From the haze of my memory, I recite the symptoms, which means I could also have brain swelling.

I could die.

I don't have time for that.

The door is open, and I crawl out onto the bright beige sand.

"God!" I yell and wince at the sound of my voice.

Every movement is another slice of pain through my brain. Still, I have to help my men. The other trucks have circled around us and snipers are up top covering us. I go to the back of my downed vehicle.

It's like a large animal lying on its side, the rest of the herd

surrounding us for protection.

"It was an IED," a man shouts.

"Impossible. We cleared these streets yesterday."

I don't have time to wait for the end of their argument. I have one thing on my mind, one person. Every time I signed off, I promised her I'd look out for him. I can't break my promise now.

Staggering down the length of the vehicle, I round the tailgate and pull back in horror. A severed half of a torso is on the ground in front of me, two legs apparently cut off from a body by the weight of the truck falling on it.

Medics run back and forth shouting and shoving past me. I'm still trying to clear my ears, trying to clear my vision. I'm seeing double.

"Lieutenant? I need you to sit down and let me check your vitals." A young woman pulls on my arm, but I shake her off.

"Danny?" My voice seems too quiet. "Danny?" I roar louder, wincing in pain.

"Cole!" Our CO is in my face. "What happened?"

I push past him. I can answer these questions later. Right now I have to find him. Drew would expect me to find him, make sure he's okay.

The chaos of emergency personnel shoves past me. The closer I get to the back of the truck, the worse the carnage. My fellow soldiers are lying on their sides, blood soaking through their uniforms.

"No." My voice is inaudible to me, but I know I said it.

Panic tightens in my chest, restricting my breathing. Through my double vision, I see his fair hair. His helmet is off. He's lying on his side with one arm twisted behind his body.

The fist he hit me with is swollen on his chest.

He's not moving.

"Danny!" I rush forward, but my head tilts. The nausea has caught up with me, and I stagger to the side to vomit. No food

comes up. It's only foam and mucus.

"You have a concussion..." Another set of hands grips me, but I shake them away.

I pull up, wiping my mouth with the back of my hand before falling to my knees. The noise of my ragged breathing is in my ears. It's a roar louder than the shrill of my blasted hearing.

Everything is chaos. Medics are dragging bodies out of the truck and lining them up on the sand for treatment. I strain my eyes to where I last saw him. I need to know if he's still alive.

"Gray." Something catches my leg as I try to pass, stopping me.

Looking down, I recognize Warren, one of the infantrymen in our squad. I drop to my knees, seeing at once his injuries are critical.

"Are you in pain?" I pull his torso in my arms, his back to my chest as I scan the area for a medic. "I'll take you to where they're treating the others."

"No..." His voice is breathless, and I can feel his body sagging. "It's not worth it. I'm not going to last much longer."

"Don't say that." I wrap my arms across his chest, squinting my eyes against the gaping wounds, the blood soaking his pants. "They can help you."

"Will you help me?"

"Of course. I'm trying to—"

"Just stay here a minute." He exhales heavily. "Just get me through. To the other side."

I hold him tighter against my chest, refusing to hear his words. The noise around us seems to fall back. It seems to dim and slow as I hold onto him through his final breaths.

Men jog past us, carrying stretchers and setting up triage. Nobody seems to notice as I hold a boy from Arkansas in my arms, sitting on the desert sand, watching as he takes his final breath miles and miles away from home.

His body goes slack, and I know he's gone. My eyes sting, and I look around. I have to find someone to take him into the truck, to take him home.

As gently as I can, I lie him down on the sand. My hand is on his chest, and I lean into his ear, even though he can't hear me anymore. "I'm getting help. I'll be back."

Dropping my head, I wipe my hand across my brow. I've never seen it this bad. I guess I've been lucky. I'm not sure I can get anybody to come check Warren, but I have to try. I have to let someone know about his death.

I take two steps when I collapse again. My head is getting heavier. It's pounding in my ears now, and I'm starting to feel weak. I'm at the back of the truck when I see him.

"Danny..." My voice breaks as I rush forward, dropping to one knee at the side of his body.

His hazel eyes stare at the sky, seeing nothing.

"No." My hands are on his chest as my insides splinter.

The last words I said to him fill my ears as a noise bubbles up in my chest. It's feral, howling like a wounded animal. The pressure expands upwards to my temples, inside my ears, blinding pain in my skull.

Two medics are beside me, taking me by the arms and pulling me to my feet, away from my friend. I try to struggle, fighting to get back to him, but they're too strong. The last glimpse I have is his straw hair in the dust, his vacant gaze open to the sky.

# CHAPTER *Five*

## *Drew*

*One year later*

"You can't keep this up. It's not healthy." My best friend is in my office fussing.

I arrange a small bouquet of bright yellow chrysanthemums on my desk and check the air freshener on my windowsill. Rose water and ivy, relaxing scents to help my patients feel at ease.

"Can't keep what up? My job?"

"This celibacy. It's been too long!" She shoves a lock of dark hair behind her ear. I'd never thought she could pull it off with her skin tone, but she's rocking it. "Flick your bean, hit the home button, rub one out."

"Are you talking about masturbation?" I roll my eyes, not even pretending to be surprised.

"Orgasms are scientifically proven to relieve stress, reduce migraines, cut down belly fat, improve sleep—"

"I have a vibrator." Leaning down to my computer, I check my next appointment.

Hunter McFee is waiting for me, and I lean back with a sigh. I've learned more about Watergate through his paranoid delusions and conspiracy theories.

"Wrap it up. Hunter's waiting—"

"It's been years. You need human contact. Skin on skin."

"I hug my dad every day."

"That's just gross."

I take her arm and walk her to my door. "It was actually a very popular mid-1970s public service campaign popularized by a Kentucky senator and the Mormon church aimed at decreasing juvenile delinquency through touch therapy. Remember, 'Have you hugged your child today?'"

"Okay, nerd. Stop using psychiatric history against me. We didn't all graduate with honors."

We stop, and I can't resist. "You're lucky that's the only thing you didn't get in college."

Her eyes narrow. "Are you calling me a slut?"

"Slut shaming is one of the most damaging forms of social control aimed at young women learning to explore their sexuality."

"Feminist theory 101?"

"Social cognition."

She nods, holding the door open before she leaves. "Will you let me know before you decide to quit this place and become a professor? I could use more clients."

Shaking my head, I start back for my desk. "Not interested. I'm here to help these people. Send in Hunter."

"What am I? Your secretary now?"

"You're my best friend since second grade. Now hurry up."

Hunter paces into the room seeming more agitated than usual. "Alexander Butterfield was not trying to be a whistle blower."

"Good morning, Hunter." I wait for him to get control.

He straightens, clearing his throat, but still blinking

rapidly. "Good morning, Miss Harris. How are you today?"

I respond with the practiced social cue. "Very well, thank you. Would you like to sit?"

"Yes, thank you." His hands clench in his lap, and he blinks fast at the floor.

"Now, why is Mr. Butterfield on your mind today?"

"He wasn't trying to be a whistle-blower. He decided he would only tell about President Nixon's White House taping system if asked directly."

Through the years, I've learned Hunter's anxiety flares up when he senses a confrontation.

Keeping my voice calm, I go back in his chart. "The last time you told me about Mr. Butterfield, you'd been putting trash bags in your neighbor's can."

"Mrs. Green never fills her can. She would never have known I'd done it if she hadn't asked me directly. I wasn't going to tell her."

Nodding, I look at my notes. "What happened when you told her it was you?"

"She said she wished I'd asked her."

This is good. "What else happened?"

"She said I could continue putting my bags in her can when mine was too full, and I offered to roll her can to the street with mine on trash days."

His face relaxes, and I smile. "Has something happened with Mrs. Green?"

He shakes his head. "I am not using any of her belongings."

"Okay." I hold my smile, waiting.

The clock ticks, but he deflects. "Have you ever heard of Martha Mitchell syndrome? Of course, you have. You're a therapist."

"I've heard of it. What does it mean to you?"

"Martha Mitchell syndrome is when you know what's

happening and no one will believe you." His fingers twist in his lap. "Martha Mitchell was the Cassandra of Watergate."

I don't answer. Sometimes asking questions moves Hunter farther away from what he needs to tell me. Instead, I make a note on the yellow legal pad. *Afraid I don't believe him. Martha Mitchell syndrome. Won't tell unless asked directly. Alexander Butterfield.*

We wait a few moments until I notice his time is running out. "I'm here to help you, Hunter. I want to believe you."

"*The X-Files* took the nickname 'Deep Throat' from Woodward and Bernstein's account of their mole during the Watergate investigation."

Another warm smile. "I actually knew that one."

"Fox Mulder wanted to believe. The question is, did he really?"

We're quiet again, and the clock winds down. Finally, I take a chance. "Is there something you need to tell me, Hunter? Do you know something?"

His breath hitches, and he blurts fast, "My neighbor steals yard ornaments and hides them in her garage. She does it every night. Hundreds and hundreds of them. She can't even park her car inside anymore. She takes them and keeps them a few days, then she returns them to the yards where they belong. Oh, God!" His cheeks are pink, and he covers his face with his hands, exhaling loudly. "I never should have told you. They shot down Dorothy Hunt's plane over Chicago because she knew too much. Are you planning any plane trips to Chicago, Miss Harris?"

"I'm not planning any plane trips." I place my palm on my upper chest and take a deep breath. "Look at me now. Let's practice our deep breathing. Inhale… Exhale…"

He's still agitated, and he's huffing like a train.

My voice is calm, steady. "Breathe with me, Hunter. It's going to be okay."

"It's not. First the trash bags and now this."

I lightly pat my chest to get his attention. "Deep breaths, okay? Can you breathe with me?" He's frowning, but at last he does what I'm saying, inhaling and exhaling. "Good job. Now let's think this through. Why would Mrs. Green want to steal yard ornaments?"

"She's implanting them with tracking devices to create a network of government surveillance all over town."

Nodding slowly, I continue breathing. "Or…?"

"Or she's a Russian spy gathering intel for the Soviets like in that show *The Americans*."

My lips tighten, but I do not react. I keep my voice steady. "How old is Mrs. Green?"

"Eighty-five, but don't be fooled. Russian intelligence agents are powerful until the day of their deaths. Did you see the movie *Red Sparrow*?"

"I did not." My voice is smooth. "Is Mrs. Green a creative person?"

"She has the most creative lawn of anyone in our neighborhood. She leaves big patches of uncut grass after she mows, and the wildflowers in her beds are out of control."

"Remember the last time you talked to Mrs. Green about a problem?" He nods, and I continue. "It worked out very well, and you learned she's really a nice neighbor."

"So is Kerri Russell."

I hear the outer door opening and closing, and I know our time is up. "For this next week, I'd like you to take a chance and ask Mrs. Green about the yard ornaments. She might have a very simple and reasonable explanation."

He stands and goes to the door, stopping just as he reaches it. "Will you come and visit me in the hospital?"

I almost forget myself and ask why. "Do you remember the crisis phone numbers?" He nods, and I smile. "Use them in case

of an emergency. We'll talk about this more at your next appointment."

His shoulders relax and he gives me a weak smile. "You really are kind, Miss Harris. I hope I haven't endangered your life."

"Remember your assignment. Try talking to Mrs. Green this week. Ask her about the yard ornaments."

"I'll try."

The door closes behind him, and I shake my head, smiling quietly to myself as I make a note of his progress and his assignment. He really is getting better at this, getting closer to confronting these fears. I lay the Mont Blanc pen on my notepad. It's the one gift my father gave me when I graduated with honors, with a concurrent master's degree, and became a licensed therapist.

My phone lies silent on the mahogany wood, and I pick it up, studying the face, allowing it to pull me back to my own emotional wound.

Tapping on the screen, I go to where his number is saved and pull it up in my messenger app. The last text I ever sent him waits, unanswered. I'd sent it a month after the funeral, when my dad sank farther into alcoholism, and I wasn't sure I could keep going. I wasn't sure I could put one foot in front of the other for one more day.

***I can't do this. I need you here. Please come home.***

The note it was delivered sits below it.

No reply.

He ghosted me just as sure as he became a ghost himself.

The only way I knew he was alive was through the list of soldiers who escaped the ambush. Not because he came back and told me himself in person what happened. Not because he was here for Danny's funeral.

"Ready?" Ruby's voice jumps me out of my unexpected trip down memory lane. She taps on the door before sticking her head inside. "Come on—I've got to hurry. I've got a date tonight."

"On a Wednesday? More Hookup4Luv?"

"Judgment from the girl who never dates? Yeah, I'm ashamed." Sarcasm drips from her tone as she waits for me to pack my laptop and notepad. "How was Hunter? Still convinced Mrs. Green is the real Deep Throat?"

"Russian spy." I pause to lock my door before walking with her down the short hall of the clinic. "He talked about Martha Mitchell syndrome today."

"I don't have my DSM…"

"Simply put, even paranoids have enemies. In his mind he's telling the truth, and I don't believe him."

She spins her car keys and laughs as we climb into her lime green Subaru. "Do you?"

Ruby got her master's this year and just started with me at the clinic. She's assisting while she waits for her licensing exam, sitting in with certain patients, and slowly building her practice.

"The Watergate conspiracy is a framework he uses to protect himself against unpleasant confrontations."

"So you don't believe him."

"I don't believe Mrs. Green is stealing yard ornaments and fitting them with government surveillance chips." My eyes drift out the window.

We pass Mack's garage with the closed sign still firmly in place. Mack left two years ago to stay with his sister in Delaware. She'd fallen ill and had no one to take care of her. He went and never came back.

Another ghost.

"I heard he died," my friend says as if reading my mind.

"What?"

"Mack. My mom read about it in the newspaper. Last month or something. I meant to tell you."

"Your mom is the only person in America who still reads the newspaper." The houses grow larger as we approach my parents'

place. "Did it list his survivors?"

"Don't know." We're quiet a moment, and I know she knows what I'm thinking. Besides the sister, Gray was Mack's only relative as far as we know. "So Mrs. Green stole my Dachshund sculpture? That ole klepto better bring him back. I miss my wiener."

She stops in the circle driveway of our enormous redbrick home with the massive white front entrance. Good thing it's mostly brick to hide how badly it's in need of repairs.

"Sounds to me like you get plenty of wiener." I grab my case and purse.

"Jealous much? I've tried to get you in on the game, but you won't play."

"No thanks. See you in the morning." I close the car door and step back as she zips out of the driveway, always going too fast for this neighborhood.

Walking slowly up the long side drive that leads to the back, I pause at the garage where the old Jaguar is covered in a thick canvass tarp. It hasn't been driven in years. I'd sell it and buy something more practical, but I'm pretty sure that would be the final nail for my dad.

I leave my bag and coat on the hook at the back door and take the narrow hallway that leads into the gourmet kitchen. It opens to a large living area with dark wood floors and white, wainscoted walls. The furniture is neat and the pillows are fluffed on the window seat. The fireplace is dark and empty, and the large flat screen television is black. No sign of life down here.

When I was a little girl we had housekeepers, but my dad's continued drinking and failure to return to work burned through all the money to pay them. Now it's just him and me.

My job keeps us fed and clothed and the lights turned on, and I spot-clean on the weekends. It helps that he hardly leaves his room, and I'm a relatively neat person.

Climbing the wooden stairs, I tap lightly on the oversized door leading to his study. He sits in a leather armchair looking out a massive window over the field behind our home. Off to the left is the fence separating our land from the creek where we used to play. It's the same one I sneaked away to when I met Gray for the first time, years ago.

"Hey, Dad, I'm home." I walk slowly to where he sits, holding an empty highball glass in his hand.

The ice cubes are still formed, but the whiskey is gone.

"Hm?" He stirs, looking up at me. "Good evening, Andrea."

His words are slurry, and I know he's more than half way to drunk.

"Have you eaten today?" I take the glass from his hand and set it on the side table. His blond hair has turned silver, and his blue eyes are lined and world weary. He's a shell of the person he was when I was a child. Or maybe everything just seemed bigger back then.

"I'm tired. I'm going to lie down."

"Did you go to your meeting?" After I got my degree, I thought it would make him listen to me more about attending Alcoholics Anonymous meetings, going to counseling sessions, taking control of his life.

It didn't.

"There's no such thing as anonymous in this town," he complains. "Everybody knows everybody."

He has a point. "We could find another group. Maybe something in Timmons?" I follow him onto the landing. "You can't keep living this way, Dad."

"Suits me fine. The sooner my body gives out the better. I've waited long enough."

It's not technically a threat of self-injury, still I don't like the implication of his words. As it is, I simply worry, nag, and try to distract myself with work. I'm a healer, but I can't heal him. I

think of the reason I went into this profession, and I feel like I've failed.

"I'm ordering Thai food. I'll let you know when it's here."

"If I'm asleep don't wake me."

The door closes, and my shoulders drop. I walk over to where he was sitting in the chair, and look at the framed photo on the end table. My mother was so pretty, with raven hair and black eyes. Her cheekbones were high and her smile knowing. This particular photo has always reminded me of Natalie Wood.

Neither Danny nor I got her dark features. We got her olive skin tone, but otherwise, we were both fair like my dad. Now it's only me. Stepping to the window, I place my palm against the glass. If I strain my eyes, I can see the tops of the marble monuments in our family cemetery over the hill and down a bit.

It's where he lies now.

We didn't know we'd lost Danny until weeks after it happened. I was at school when the soldiers came to the house with a flag and a letter signed by the President. I'm surprised my father even answered the door—he usually doesn't.

Stoicism is how he responded.

He smiled tightly, took the flag, accepted their condolences.

We organized the funeral with the help of the officers. They spoke, talking about my brother's stellar record of service. They presented us with his medals, and all I could think of was the carefree joker who loved to call me Drew Poo and who never stopped singing the Righteous Brothers.

How could someone so alive be dead?

I sat in that black dress on the front row next to my silent father feeling like a cannonball had been blasted through my chest. I didn't cry until Ruby's mother came to me with tears in her eyes.

She was so sorry she hadn't prayed to Jesus and the Buddha that day for my brother's protection. She had planned to do it as

soon as she got home from volunteering as church secretary. She felt so guilty.

I didn't have the heart to tell her my belief in such things had been blasted to kingdom come along with my brother's body.

Along with my heart.

The clouds glow neon pink in the setting sun and the pale blue sky stretches for miles over the trees, over the ocean.

I would text Gray every few weeks after it happened. When I was angry, I would demand to know why he wasn't here. How could he not come home when I needed him? When the pain felt like it was too much to bear, I would text him the simple words, *I miss you.*

My mind drifts to the earlier text I read, and with my forehead against the cool glass, I whisper, "How could you disappear on me, Gray? You promised..."

Three years I dreamed of him. One year, I sank into despair. I can't seem to let go. Maybe Ruby is right. Maybe I'm no different than my patients, cloaking myself in a failed relationship to save me from finding something new and real.

It sounds good.

God, is it time to move on? Is it possible I could do such a thing? My head says I should try. The only problem is my heart can't let him go.

Something in me knows he's coming back.

The feeling grows stronger with each passing day.

I'm simply waiting for it to happen.

And when it does...

# CHAPTER *Six*

## *Gray*

St. Margaret's smells like Lysol.

Not the pine-scented spray—don't get crazy. No, this place smells like that old-school concentrate in the little brown bottle. The kind that burns the shit out of your nose so it's impossible to name the fragrance other than *hospital*.

"She's having a good day today." Sister Constance wears a plain blue skirt and vest over a long-sleeved white shirt. Her hair is covered in a matching blue habit. "She told me about her first dance. She said it was with Timothy DuPont."

My aunt is lying in the bed with her eyes closed, and she doesn't appear to have moved in days.

"I guess it could've happened. How would we ever know?"

I came here from the reading of Mack's will. My heart is heavy, but I'm trying to focus on the good. His long battle with lung cancer is over, he's no longer gasping for breath, no longer in pain.

He left me the garage, and I came here to check on a woman

I barely know before heading south to face the past. My insides are twisting in knots. I'm agitated and impatient with this current errand, but it's time.

"Even if it didn't, her eyes lit up with joy. The way you look when you're in love."

My brow furrows as I glance at her. I guess it's possible nuns can be in love before they join an order.

"I brought this." I hand Constance a bouquet fragrant plants for fall, pine and tea olive.

"How lovely. You've been such a gift from God to her. And your uncle. You should be comforted he's at peace now."

She makes me sound more charitable than I feel. When I was honorably discharged with a purple heart and a medal of valor, I couldn't go back to Oakville. I was too broken. I'd wake in the night fighting, yelling, covered in sweat. I'd pass a man on the street and involuntarily recoil as if he'd left a bomb in my path—what they think might have happened on that road.

The road that changed my life.

After the accident, I stayed in the desert while they treated my injuries. I helped identify the men we'd lost. I attempted to recreate what happened. After six months, once everyone was gone and the base had been shut down, I came here to Dover.

My phone was destroyed in the blast. Uncle Mack was never one to use technology anyway. He sent me a letter telling me he'd closed the garage and moved back to take care of his sister. Her husband died, and she had dementia. He didn't tell me he was in the final stages of lung cancer.

I went from the desert sand to this lush, green city to try and get my head on straight. Then I nursed Mack until he was gone. Now I'm preparing to leave my Aunt Genevieve to the care of these ladies.

The nuns assure me she'll be fine, she has no idea where she is. I'm not sure she even remembers me. Looking down at my

hands, I decide to confess. She is a nun, after all.

"I won't be coming back for a while. I have to go back…" Is *home* the right word? "I have to check on my uncle's business."

I should say my business now.

Constance nods gently. "I guessed a man of your age would have unfinished business."

She says it as if she knows something.

"My uncle left his garage in my name. It's been sitting vacant for two years. I need to check on it and decide whether to keep it or sell it."

"You owe me no explanations. Do what you need to do." She goes to the window and slowly rolls up the blinds. "We'll take good care of your aunt."

"I'm not abandoning her. I'll be back. I just need to do this."

"I'm sure your friends are eager to welcome home a hero."

*I'm not so sure.* "I'm not a hero. I did my duty, the same as anyone would've done in those circumstances."

She gives me a placid smile. "I've found the greatest heroes are often the ones least interested in accepting the title."

I clear my throat, rubbing the back of my neck. "Anyway, I'm leaving for the airport now. If you'll let me know if she needs anything, I'll take care of it."

"She will be fine, and I will keep you informed." She hesitates, lifting a hand toward me. "How about you. Did you find the help you needed here?"

She's referencing my treatment. Constance was the first to diagnose my PTSD, and she referred me to a physician for meds, which I'm trying to stop taking.

"I'm… better." Not whole.

The woman nods. "I'll pray for you." Compassion is in her eyes. "Remember, it's not a sign of weakness to ask for help. It's a sign of strength."

Twenty minutes later, I'm going through the TSA pre-check

line. My entire body is tight, every muscle wound to the max. Seeing Danny's grave is something I've needed to do for a long time, but it doesn't lessen the dread I feel at returning home.

The trauma counselor said it was normal not to go straight home after what happened to me, but as time passed, it felt more and more like pressure I couldn't escape.

I have to go back and face it.

I have to face her.

I'll never be able to accept it wasn't my fault. I'll never have peace with what happened. It was my job to clear the road the day before we pulled out, and on top of that, I was driving the truck. I was one of the few surviving passengers.

"It's not your fault," they say over and over.

I'm not sure she's going to see it that way.

The silver step-side rumbles as I pull into the garage and kill the engine. The moon is out, and the town is quiet. I open the door, and the first thing that hits me is the smell—gasoline, oil, old rags, grease... The memories are close behind. God, I remember this place so well—the shame, the pressure, always being an outsider.

This garage was the only safe place.

This garage and her arms.

People call me a hero. I have my degree and my military training, my pension, and I own this shop. Mack said I could sell it if I wanted. He left me a small inheritance, but money's not on my mind.

I know what it means to have some kind of connection, some kind of name in this town. I might be returning in the dark of night, but I'm a different person all the way around from when I left.

Going to the garage door, I pull it down and close it. I take the closed sign out of the window. I called a few days ago and had

the utilities turned on. After everything that's happened, maybe focusing on something simple, internal combustion, would be therapeutic.

With a heavy sigh, I drop the plastic sign on the ground. Tomorrow, I'll sort out what happens next.

Inside the house, nothing has changed. The old linoleum table is against the wall under the window. The tiny kitchen is behind a half bar attached to the wall. It's a small place, a straight shot to the back bedroom. A bathroom is off to the side.

It smells dusty, but the lingering scent of Dawn dishwashing soap remains. It's the only thing that would take off the grease staining our fingernails.

Looking at my hands, I realize the telltale black smudges have been absent for eight years. I left for college thinking I'd never come back to this line of work. Now I don't want to do anything else.

Fixing cars feels like the perfect escape.

I'll put out a help wanted sign tomorrow.

I walk to the back of the house, dropping my bag on Uncle Mack's old bed. As a kid, I slept on a cot in the living room. It's not there anymore, much like all of Mack's clothes and pictures. All the mementos are gone.

He knew when he left he wouldn't be coming back here. He left the place clean for me. The bed is neatly made.

I pull the blanket off and the sheets. Even if he left it clean, it's been years. Everything is covered in dust. I'll wash these and see about getting a housekeeper in here to clean up.

Slowly, I take out my clothes. I put the jeans in the empty dresser, followed by socks, shirts, boxer briefs. I carry my few toiletries and my toothbrush to the bathroom across the hall. I don't have a lot of baggage.

At least not visible baggage.

I plug the phone I bought a few days ago into the wall. They

were able to give me my old number back, but everything from before had been lost. I'll have to start all over. All I have left from before is the piece of paper and the photograph I had in my pocket. It's tucked safely in the family Bible my uncle gave me before he died.

I take it from the pack and walk to the living room to put it on the coffee table. My fingers trace the worn leather, and I open it, allowing the sight of her smile to shred my insides again.

Even in the dark, I can't stop thinking of her. I can't stop thinking of what I need to do. Before I'd unpacked my clothes, I'd taken the bouquet of sunflowers out of my suitcase. They rode with me from the shop in Dover.

I take them off the counter and step into the garage again.

It's time.

# CHAPTER *Seven*

## *Drew*

MY PLATE OF NOODLES SITS HALF-EATEN ON THE BAR IN THE KITCHEN. Dad's is untouched. He never came down, and when I went up to knock and check on him, I heard him snoring.

A glass of wine sits on the counter in front of me, and I sip it when my phone buzzes.

Ruby's silly smile appears on the screen, and I scoop it up. "Awfully early for you to be calling it a night."

"Scratch Timber off the list." I hear the slamming of cabinets in the background and the squeak of a cork. "He wanted me to call him Falstaff."

"Because he's a fat alcoholic?"

"He says he's funny and a bad influence." The noise of sloshing fills my ear. "Cheers."

I hold up my glass. "Good timing. I finally opened that Pinot we bought in Napa."

"God, that was so long ago. Can we do that again? Now?"

"I think we have to give our patients two week's notice or something."

"Your patients," she grumbles.

"Hang in there. You'll build your practice."

"If I don't starve first."

"You live with your mother."

"Exactly."

I take the goblet over to the window seat and lean against the wall, looking out. "So Falstaff was a bust? I have to say, his reasoning doesn't sound too bad."

"He drank two whiskey doubles then started grabbing my ass every time he'd tell a joke." She sips loudly in my ear. "He was sweaty."

"Ew." I wrinkle my nose. "How did you leave him?"

"I told him I had to go to the bathroom."

"You sneaked out the window?"

"Walked out the front door." A ping sounds softly. "Look, he's texting me now."

"Need me to let you go?"

"I'll answer him on my laptop."

Clicking sounds fill the space. "Are you telling him he's a sweaty grabber?"

"He's asking where I went. He thought I went to the bathroom."

I tap my fingernail on the side of my glass waiting. "What are you saying?"

"Short and sweet. I am in the bathroom. The one at my house."

She exhales and flips her computer closed. "That's the fifth Timber date I've tried. I'm done with that app."

"What's left?"

"Let's see, I've tried Timber, Doodle, and RightyAphrodite."

I inhale so fast, I start to choke. "That's not… real…" I manage between coughs.

"Yes, that's a real name. Don't die on me."

Shaking my head, I blink the tears out of my eyes. "What happened with the other two?"

"How much time do you have?" I hear her flopping on her couch, and I can just see her swirling her glass as she thinks. "First there was the guy who started out by telling me he thought he might be gay, but he needed to have sex with a woman to be sure."

"You've got to be kidding." I take a long sip.

"I only wish. I'm pretty sure I saw him out last week." She pauses to take a drink.

"With a guy?"

"With another girl. It's like that's his go-to story for getting in a girl's pants."

"What a sleaze." I walk to the kitchen and pour another half glass. "It's like a reverse damsel in distress."

"You really are too smart for words." Muffled voices sound in the room behind her. "No, Ma. I ditched my date. He was sweaty and pinchy."

Fussing sounds come from the background, and she's back. "Where was I? Oh, there was the guy who said he didn't date Asians."

"Don't you have a profile picture?"

"I have a whole gallery of pictures. He thought it was a joke, like a cosplay or something."

"What's that?" My nose wrinkles.

"No, the fuck, way." I hear another, louder noise from her mom in the background. "Ma! I'm a grown woman! I just discovered something I know that smarty pants Drew doesn't know."

"Rude." I can't help laughing. "I guess your name isn't super Asian-sounding, Ruby Banks."

"It's a stripper name. I know. It's okay to say it."

Again, I almost snort pinot noir through my nose. "Trashy hooker."

"Oh, that reminds me of the guy who asked if I was a geisha."

"To which you replied you're Korean."

She barks a loud laugh in my ear. "As if that redneck would know the geisha are Japanese."

I take another sip of wine, thinking about what my dad said earlier. "How are you dating so many different people in Oakville?"

"I don't date guys from Oakville. These guys are all in Timmons and Fireside."

Nodding, I walk to the window, and my eye catches the flicker of lightning. "Hey, I'd better go."

"I know. The minute you see lightning, you're off the phone."

"You can get struck through the receiver!"

"And I thought you were smart. It's an old wives' tale."

"See you in the morning." I disconnect and go to the side door, sliding the glass open and stepping out onto the patio.

I'm facing the same field I observed from my father's study. Down the hill a little ways is the family cemetery. It's just a minute or two walk from here. The wind picks up, and I smell rain. I feel the change in the air. It's a little crisper, a little cooler. We're on the cusp of fall.

I don't like being cold. I much prefer baking in the hot sun, but it was Danny's favorite time of year. My throat tightens at the memory, and I take another, longer sip before setting the glass on the small picnic table.

My stomach is burning from the wine, and my head feels a little buzzy. I walk through the soft grass in my bare feet. I changed into jeans and a pale pink sweater that falls off one shoulder when I got home.

Another gust of wind carries the metallic taste of rain to my nose and tongue. Tightness is in my chest that moves up to my neck and shoulders. A dry ache is in my throat. It's a pain I can

never quite swallow away. I can never quite drink it away…

Or jog it away.

Or meditate it away.

Or deep-breathe it away.

Or any of the other therapeutic techniques I tell my patients.

As I walk, mist fills the air. It isn't rain, but it dampens my cheeks. It's cold on my face and in my hair as I get closer to the marble monuments standing in the flickering moonlight like sentinels, guarding the dead.

My pace slows the closer I get. In the back of the three-row cemetery is a small tree, a crepe myrtle. Under it is a white concrete bench.

"Oh!" My heart jumps and skitters like a rabbit.

Before the moon disappeared again behind the fast-moving cirrus clouds, I was sure I saw someone sitting there. Fear is somehow stronger than misery, and I freeze in place, waiting a few paces from my brother's grave for the light to return.

"Who's there?" My voice is a whisper, not quite loud enough to be heard.

I don't believe in ghosts, which leaves only one other option. Someone is lost, or a homeless person or a person with bad intentions is waiting out here. I should turn and run… but for whatever reason, I hesitate.

The dark form rises from the bench, and my insides lurch.

This time my voice isn't a whisper. "Who are you?"

No response, but the figure slowly walks in my direction. My lungs are like bellows pumping hard, forcing me to breathe. My head is light as I watch him move, as his shape draws closer.

I fight against what my memory is telling me.

It's been four years, but I still remember the way he moves, the way he walks.

I still remember the way he ducks his head when he's sad or unsure.

Danny's grave is steps in front of me, but I can't go any closer. The wind pushes my hair off my shoulders, and the clouds uncover the moon.

The moment I see his gray eyes, dark in this light, hot tears spill onto my cheeks.

"Gray." The word slips out on a broken whisper, loud enough so he can hear. "What are you doing here?"

His shoulders slump, and both hands are in his pockets. He blinks away from me and down to the headstone that reads, *In the hollow of God's hand…*

"I needed to see it."

The sound of his voice, the deep resonance, almost brings me to my knees. Another rush of hot tears spills down my cheeks.

I can't speak.

I can only shake my head. My body aches for his touch. My entire being aches for him, but he's holding back, defenses up.

"I didn't mean to see you."

My throat is so painfully tight, I can only utter one word. "Why?"

His eyebrows quirk up, and he takes a half-step away from me. "I didn't want to upset you."

"Were you hurt? They said it was an accident…"

We were told an IED, an improvised explosive device, took my brother's life and five other men in their unit. Many died horribly, limbs blown off, bodies severed by the weight of the truck collapsing on them. Not being next of kin, I couldn't get any details about Grayson Cole's injuries.

Danny was lucky, they said. He was bleeding pretty badly, but the medical report said he died instantly of a blow to the head.

"Nothing serious." He seems to trail off.

"Good." This is so hard.

I don't know why I'm being so formal. I want to run forward and hold him. I want to wrap my arms around his waist and

finally cry all my tears. I want him to comfort me like he did after my mom died when I was only twelve.

Something is different, though. He's not the same boy with open arms, ready to rush in and dry my tears. I don't understand, and it's breaking my heart.

I have to exhale slowly to stop my voice from shaking. "Are you back to stay?"

"I don't know yet." His eyes return to the headstone, and the muscle in his jaw moves. His hand twitches, almost like he wants to reach out. "I didn't mean to trespass."

"No. You're welcome here—"

"I'm not welcome here." His voice is harsh, and in this light, I can't see his face clearly. He passes a large hand over his mouth. "I'm sorry."

It's the last thing he says before turning his back and walking away from me, quickly to the road. I don't see a vehicle waiting. I can't tell if he walked all the way here from… town? Was he at his uncle's old place?

As much as I want to, I can't chase after him. My legs are frozen. I stand as hot tears wash my cheeks, as he grows smaller, moving farther away from me. A sharp inhale jerks me. It turns into a wail as my knees give out.

The clouds rush to cover the moon, leaving me on all fours in front of the grave, my back bowing as the muscles in my stomach pull me into a ball. Resting my forehead on my hands, I sob, sadness ripping through my throat as the rain soaks my hair and my clothes.

# CHAPTER *Eight*

## *Gray*

*THE FORCE OF THE BLAST SLAMS ME AGAINST THE WINDOW. MY EARS ARE full of cotton. I can't hear the men screaming. I only feel the thuds of feet running, the tremor of the truck engine.*

*A high-pitched shrill is in my head, and my heart beats out of my chest. I gasp for breath, struggling to get my bearings through the chaos.*

*The truck lies on the driver's side, where my head crashed against the window. I climb over the seat, doing my best to maneuver through the waves of concussion.*

*I climb out the passenger-side window and jump down. The moment I hit the ground, I fall to my hands and knees and vomit in the sand.*

*It's mostly foam and bile. I wipe it away with the back of my hand, with my sleeve, using the front bumper to drag me to my feet.*

*Where is he? I'm desperate looking for him everywhere. My heart beats faster, the pain becomes more intense.*

*"Danny!" I scream at the top of my lungs, the noise shatters through my skull, but it doesn't stop the shrill hiss. It's driving me crazy.*

*I clutch the sides of my head with both fists, but I hear him. Clear as a bell, through the fog in my head, through the nonstop* scree, *I hear him.*

*"Gray..." He's not shouting, he's calling me. "Help me, Gray..."*

*His voice is weak. It tightens my throat.*

*He's dying.*

*"Gray..."*

*"Danny!" I scream again, and again, the pain brings me to my knees. I've got to keep moving. I crawl forward, making it to standing.*

*I feel Warren's hand on my leg, but this time I shake him off me. I've got to get to Danny. I don't have time for a boy from Arkansas. My best friend, the guy who knows me about as good as anyone, the guy I promised to protect, is dying in the desert, millions of miles from home.*

*He's my focus.*

*He should be my focus.*

*I stagger along the length of the truck, around the back corner.*

*"Lieutenant, you have a concussion. You could have brain swelling!" I push the medic away.*

*Danny's voice is still calling me. It's weaker, but I hear it.*

*"Gray..." It's the last time he'll call. I've been here before.*

*The bodies part, and there he is, lying on his back, his blond hair spread around him in the sand, hazel eyes staring at the sky.*

*I try to rush forward, but I fall and vomit again. The medic is at my arm, but I push him off me.*

*"Danny..." My voice grows louder until his name tears like claws through my throat. "Danny... Danny..."*

I wake with a jerk, sitting straight up. I'm covered in sweat, my throat aches, and I'm lying on the floor in the living room.

The sun blasts through the blinds, and I'm disoriented.

It happened again.

Standing on shaky legs, I go to the kitchen where the bottle of meds sits, the PTSD medication. I've been trying to wean

myself off it. I've been trying to follow the self-help steps.

Last night was a setback.

I came home, had a few stiff drinks, then collapsed on my uncle's unmade bed with visions of Drew swirling in my brain. She was so beautiful standing there in the mist, tears in her gorgeous blue eyes. Her hair hung in those long waves I used to bury my face in and inhale deeply, taking in her scent and committing it to memory. The jeans she wore hugged her curves, and even though she wore a baggy sweater, I could tell her body was the same as I remembered, soft in the right places, molding to mine.

She was miserable. She was crying.

The pain of what I've done, of what's become of me, had crashed down on my head, forcing up the walls, and pushing me away from her.

As I lay on the bed, waves of exhaustion rolled over me, forcing my eyes closed. It was a killer cocktail of grief mixed with anxiety mixed with regret. I'd known it would be this way since the day I decided to come back. Still, I had to do it.

I needed to see his grave. I needed to ask for forgiveness even though his ears would never hear it. I needed to come here so I could try to forgive myself.

I'd hated him for what he'd said that day. I'd hated him almost as much as I'd hated their father for saying it years before. I'd worked so hard to prove I was good enough, but he would never let me be.

Then Danny had shown he felt the same way.

Maybe I did want him to die for those few minutes.

I never believed it would happen.

All that anger. All that hatred. Years and years of bad feelings pent up in my chest… Now it's only emptiness.

She wasn't supposed to be there, taunting me with memories.

I had planned to pay my respects at his grave, tell him I was

sorry for my words, for my feelings, for driving that truck, for not keeping my promise to look out for him… For not wanting to keep it.

Then I saw Drew, and everything slammed into me like a freight train, like the force of the blast that blew us off the road.

I hadn't just made the promise to Danny. I'd made it to her as well. Every time I signed off on a text, I told her I'd protect him.

In that moment I knew the truth: Forgiveness is going to be a long road.

I came back here, went to sleep, and I was right back there again.

Staggering into the kitchen, I flick on the old drip pot my uncle had since the stone age. I open the drawer and find filters still waiting. A canister of coffee is on the counter behind the pot. Opening the stainless lid, I take a sniff. No scent. It's got to be two years old.

"Old coffee is better than no coffee." My voice sounds like gravel.

My mouth is dry, and I note the empty bottle of tequila on the counter. It was only half-full when I got here. I feel like shit. Probably how I ended up on the floor in the living room. I started in my uncle's bed then sometime in the night, I tried to return to my old quarters.

As the coffee drips, I take a quick shower. I'm just having my first mug when a knock on the door sends my insides into turmoil. Drew wouldn't come here…

I'm not sure.

A pair of faded jeans hangs around my hips, and I snatch my old tee off the back of the chair, pulling it over my head before opening the door.

I step back when I see a skinny kid with long, shaggy brown hair hanging to his collar. Long bangs, parted in the middle are in his eyes. His black sleeveless tee has Metallica across the front.

"Who are you?" My deep voice is sharper than I intended, but the kid doesn't seem fazed.

"Name's Billy. I heard you were looking for help." He looks at my shoes. "I need a job."

"How did you hear that?" Shit, I haven't even put the word out yet. I haven't even been in town twenty-four hours.

"My neighbor said you'd turned the power back on. I figured you'd need help."

I forgot how fucking nosey this place is. Nothing gets by these assholes. "How old are you Billy?"

"Twenty-one."

"Last name?"

"James."

"Billy James." I scratch my jaw, thinking. Then I realize I probably look as old as my uncle right now, even though I'm only five years older than this guy. "You new in town?"

"I grew up over in Pintoville."

"Oh." *Shit*. I don't say that part out loud. *Pintoville* is the racist nickname for the part of Oakville where most of the Mexicans live.

I thought I was an outcast, but it was nothing compared to the way these guys are treated.

"Did you go to school? I don't remember seeing you around."

"My daddy sent me to the school in Raymond. He had a friend who could drive me. Thought I'd get in less trouble there."

"Are you a troublemaker?"

His stick-straight hair sweeps around his neck when he shakes his head. "I've never been in a fight. I don't want to fight. I just like working on cars. I graduated top of my class at the trade school."

"I'm not really open yet. I'm not sure how much business I'll get. How about you come around in a week?"

He nods, glancing up at me with serious, black eyes. "You going to hire somebody else?"

My brow furrows, and it only takes me a moment to decide. "Nope. The job's yours if I can keep you busy."

He nods. "I work cheap."

"I'll remember that." He extends his hand, and I catch it, giving him a firm shake. "It's a deal. Next week."

He walks away, hands shoved in the front pockets of his jeans. A heavy silver chain dances in a loop from his belt to what I guess is his wallet in the back pocket. It was never my look, but it's pretty classic grease monkey. I wince at the memory. Danny had nicknames for everybody.

Clearing the sudden thickness from my throat, I walk to the overhead door and pull it open. If they all know I'm back and open for business, no use hiding it. I confess, I'm curious to see who all's got their eye on this place.

It doesn't take long to find out.

# CHAPTER *Nine*

## *Drew*

I PULL DARK SHADES OVER MY EYES BEFORE RUNNING OUT TO MEET RUBY. The only things that got me out of bed this morning were making sure my dad ate some pancakes for breakfast and my patients.

I lost track of how long I cried last night. Seeing Gray after waiting so long, feeling how distant and guarded he was, had been worse than when he was only a ghost. Now it's like the hole in my chest has been stuffed full of shards of glass.

"Nice look, Jackie O," Ruby quips as I climb in the car. "I thought about it all night. What I need is one of those insanely rich Asian men to come and sweep me away to his mansion in Singapore on his extravagantly lush jet airline."

"I think you mean crazy rich." Thank God my voice doesn't sound as fragile as I feel. Maybe I will survive this day.

Ruby's voice drops to a conspiratorial whisper. "I thought we didn't like that word."

"What? Crazy?" I shake my head, flipping down the visor to check my face. Less puffy than an hour ago. "Just don't use it

when you're talking about patients."

We're just entering town, K-pop playing on the radio, when my broken glass-filled chest squeezes tighter. We're getting close to—

"Holy shit!" Ruby lunges forward in her seat, craning her neck so much, I reach for the steering wheel.

"Careful!"

"Is that… Mack's garage is open!" she stage-whispers.

I guess that answers my question. He didn't say he'd open the garage, but he didn't say much of anything.

My quiet reaction gives me away.

"You knew!" Ruby cries, whipping her head back to me. "How long have you known? What have you not told me?"

"I didn't know the garage was open."

"But you knew he was back in town." She's studying my face hard. "Take off those sunglasses and prove me wrong."

"I have nothing to prove." I take off my sunglasses, and her face goes from triumphant to sad. It irritates me. "Don't look at me that way. I hate it."

"You know, anger is a common defense against depression."

"Oh, now you know so much about psychoanalytical theory?"

"Need me to cover your appointments today?"

"No." I have to pack these feelings down into a tight little ball and put them away and do my job.

I can't believe I just thought that.

She pulls into the parking lot of Friends Care, and I charge out before she can ask any more questions. I almost wish I'd stayed home when I walk inside and nearly collide with Dotty.

In addition to being our part-time receptionist, Dotty Magee is the town's busiest busybody. She's holding a cardboard tray of coffees, and her cheeks are so red, I'm afraid she'll explode.

"I didn't think you'd ever get here," she cries, and I know the

look of hot gossip.

I keep walking, straight to my office. "Sorry, Dotty, no time to chat. Is Darlene in yet?"

"She's not on the schedule til nine. You've got fifteen minutes."

"Dotty! Coffee, stat!" Ruby cries, charging into my office right behind her. "Which is the low-fat soy?"

Dotty turns the tray, and Ruby takes the paper cup with the black *R* marked on it. Dotty hurries to my desk. "I asked them to add a little cinnamon to yours today."

"Thank you, Dotty." I'm doing my best to wake up my computer quickly.

The last thing I need is to be armchair analyzed by the staff. Still, they're both standing on the other side of my desk watching me with wide eyes.

I give up. "Okay, let's get it over with."

"Grayson Cole is back and he's re-opened his uncle's garage. I sent that young man Billy James, you know the one of Hispanic descent? I sent him over first thing this morning."

"He's Mexican, Dotty," Ruby jumps in. "It's okay to say he's Mexican."

Dotty's worried eyes fly to her. "I wasn't trying to be provocative."

I scrub a hand over my eyes. This entire conversation is provocative. "You sent Billy to the garage? Why?"

"He's been hanging around here, butchering the lawn and pulling the flowers instead of weeds. I confess, I was shocked at what a terrible landscaper he is. He leaves big patches of uncut grass..."

"Dotty, seriously. You have got to evolve." Rolling my eyes at the overt stereotype from Miss Non-Provocative, I remember Hunter's observations. "Hang on, does Billy cut Mrs. Green's lawn?"

"I'm not sure, but I can ask him."

My eyes go to Ruby's, but she's confused. "Maybe Billy's taking the yard ornaments!"

"Well, I'll be dogged," Dotty whispers. "I never thought he stole anything."

"I did not say *stealing*." Shaking my hand, I wave her away.

Dotty's eyes are wide as she looks from me to Ruby. "Maybe he's selling them on the black market. I heard about that dark web on the Today show..."

"My poor wiener!" Ruby cries, playfully. "He's being trafficked!"

"Nobody's selling anything." This is how rumors get started. "I'm sure there's a logical explanation." I'm checking the clock. *Where's Darlene?*

But Ruby's into it now. "So you sent Billy to the garage. What did he say when he came back?"

Dotty gives me another worried look. "Gray told Billy he'd give him a job. Billy was real excited about it. Said he'd start next week."

So he's planning to stay a week. My lips tighten, and I fight against the knots tying up my stomach. *Push it down. Compartmentalize.*

"I know!" Ruby jumps up, suddenly inspired. "We should have a welcome home party for him."

"No!" It's an involuntary cry, but if I were any closer, I'd kick her in the shin.

"Why not? He's a hero. We should welcome him home."

Dotty's entire demeanor changes. "I love it! We can have it at the church, invite everybody, and get the story straight from the horse's mouth!"

The vein in my left temple starts to pound. "This is a terrible idea... Gray doesn't like big parties."

I'm grasping at straws. The last thing I need is the entire town

being there to witness me breaking down in front of him.

Ruby nods, slowly pacing my office, arms crossed. "You make a point. Gray never was as outgoing as Danny. Something smaller, more intimate is his speed. I'll talk to Ma and do something at our house."

The bell on the front door rings, and Dotty hops to my door. "Darlene is here. I'll check her in then we can start planning."

"Saved by the bell." I take out my notepad.

"You know, my daddy was never the same after Vietnam. Back then they called it shell shock…" She continues down the hall discussing Gray, and my brow furrows.

As much as I hate gossip, I've lived here long enough to know there's often a kernel of truth in what they say. Now in addition to my insides stuffed with glass and my stomach in knots, my heart aches at the idea of Gray suffering from trauma.

I don't have time to dwell on it before Darlene enters my office dressed in ripped black skinny jeans and a tank.

She flops on my couch with a heavy exhale.

"Good morning, Darlene." I take out my notebook.

"What's up, doc?"

"I've told you, I'm not a doctor." Scanning her file on my computer, I refresh my memory of our last session—something I should have done before she arrived instead of being pulled down Crazy Lane.

We don't use that word.

"How was the road trip with your mom? Did you tell her your memory of the neighbor?"

Darlene's family doesn't live in Oakville. She was referred to me from the university. "We drove all the way to Burnside listening to sad 80s music."

I look back a few dates. "That's where your mother grew up?"

"I guess." She studies her black fingernails. "We went through a prison area. It had a sign that said 'Do not pick up hitchhikers.'"

"Okay." I pick up my pen to make notes—which I transfer to the computer in the evenings.

"After she went to bed, I got up and took the car. I went back and just drove up and down the road, looking for one."

My brow furrows. "One what?"

Brown eyes snap up to mine. "Hitchhiker. I drove past every night, back and forth, over and over slowly. Watching."

"You told me the neighbor you believe touched you is in prison now." I make a note on the legal pad. "Do you think he might be there?"

She blows air through her lips and arches her back. "I don't know! I don't care about him. I want to find a young Brad Pitt ex-con and pick him up and see what happens. I watched *Thelma and Louise* every day while we were there."

"You didn't talk to your mother." It's not a question. I make another note on my pad.

"What difference will it make? He's in prison. It's done."

My lips press together, and I inhale slowly. "Engaging in risky behavior won't make the pain go away. We've talked about this."

She flips on her side, tracing a fingernail over the seam of the cushion.

"Darlene?" She doesn't look up. "Have you been sleeping?"

"I slept last night."

"Did you sleep while you were with your mother?"

"No." She glares at me, challenging, and I dial it back.

I give her a warm smile. "We're working on healing here, avoiding triggering situations. You've come a long way."

The defensiveness melts away, and I take out my assignment pad. "I want you to keep a thought log this week. Keep a record of how you think about yourself..."

"We did that in the beginning."

"I still have it. We'll compare next time and see how much progress you've made."

Our time is up, and she stands, walking over to take the slip of white paper. "I'll try. If I have time."

Focus on the small wins. "And no more driving past prisons looking for hitchhikers. Brad Pitt's not in prison."

She exhales a huff and shrugs. "It was worth a shot. You never know when that dream might come true."

"Not all dreams turn out the way you hope."

My words hang in my ears after she's gone, and I look out the window in the direction of the garage. My dream has certainly not turned out how I had hoped.

He'll be here at least a week. I wonder if that's enough time to find the answers I need.

# CHAPTER *Ten*

THE BEAT-UP OLD STATION WAGON PULLS INTO THE GARAGE AND SYLVIA Green steps out. "You open for business?"

Her gray hair is tucked under a cotton cap. I'm pretty sure she looks exactly the same as she did when I left here four years ago—scowling, dressed in denim overalls.

I walk over to where she's waiting. "The garage is open for now."

"It's about time." Her blue eyes bore into mine like she's looking for answers. "I've been driving halfway to Charleston every time I need an oil change for the last two years."

"You need an oil change?"

"And rotate the tires while you're at it."

She drove through the rolling steel door I'd opened this morning, right over the car lift. It's just how my uncle designed the place. I walk over to the supply cabinet and open it. Sure enough, Mack has a stock of oil filters just for this old lady's car. He was like that, remembering what people needed.

Hitting the button on the wall, the steel pads go under the axels and raise the old body to the height of my head then muscle memory takes over. I step under the car and loosen the drain plug, allowing the oil to stream down into the trap under the floor. Just like riding a bike.

She watches me the entire time with those eagle eyes. "You doing everything by yourself now?"

We both glance out at the road where the occasional car slows down, curious eyes peer into the shop, and I shrug. "Had a kid stop by this morning looking for a job."

"Did you hire him?"

"Pretty much." I go to the lines of brake fluid, transmission fluid, washer fluid, coolant, and oil.

I give them a test to see if they're still functioning. Looks good. Uncle Mack left everything sealed up tight, and the garage is cool and dry. These lubricants should be ready to do their job.

"Who is he?" She looks around the space. "More importantly, where is he?"

Fluids topped off, oil filter replaced, I lift the car back up to replace the drain plug before taking out the impact wrench and quickly spinning off the lug nuts on her tires, letting the heavy wheels bounce on the concrete floor. It's familiar work, soothing and uncomplicated. It occupies my mind, drowning out my memories, the long blonde hair, the soft lips.

It distracts me from my guilt until my hand catches my eye. It's smeared in grease, black at the fingernails. *Grease monkey.*

"He'll be here tomorrow."

"Good." She nods as if approving my unspoken decision. "We need you here."

I give her a quick glance. "What?"

"The town needs a good mechanic, a garage that isn't thirty miles away."

"Oh." I lift the heavy tires, powering the lug nuts back on.

"Don't torque those too hard. You'll strip 'em."

Shaking my head, I don't even answer. She continues. "Towns change. The old people like me die, and hopefully the new ones do better. The crazies are always with us."

"Okay." It's the only answer that I can give her. The problems I have here are all still alive and well. "Anything else?"

Her tires are all on. I hit the switch to lower it all the way before grabbing the hose to refill the oil.

"Nope." She follows me to the counter, where I write up the work order, take her cash, and drop it in the box.

"Thanks."

"I'll be back." She's walking back to her car when a lime green Subaru pulls into the open bay.

I take the shop cloth and wipe my hands, wishing I'd gotten Billy's number. If Mrs. Green is right, I'm going to need help right away. Two cars, and I'm already falling behind. When the driver steps out, I take a step back.

"Look what the cat dragged in!" Ruby Banks is as bold as she ever was, and she's Drew's best friend.

I brace myself. Ruby always has a lot to say. "How's it going?"

"I'd say the same as always, but things just got really interesting all of a sudden." She closes the space between us, brown eyes leveled on mine. "So are you back or are you just wrapping things up before you leave again?"

My hands are still dirty, despite my attempts to clean them. I decide to own it. It's fucking symbolic.

"I'm planning to stay for a little while."

Her eyebrows rise. "Good! I've put together a little welcome home party for you—"

"No." I turn and head for the office, but she's right behind me.

"You can't say no. It's at my place, and I've only invited a

handful of your friends. Remember those pesky things called friends?"

"I said no. I'm not here for parties."

"What are you here for?" She stands at the door with her arms crossed over her chest.

Inhaling, I think about it. I wanted to come back to pay my respects. Now… "I'm not really sure."

"You're over-educated to be working in a garage."

"I own the garage." My eyes roam over the neat, open area. "It's honest work I enjoy."

Both her hands go up in surrender. "Far be it from me to knock what somebody loves. I happen to love throwing parties. I've put together a really nice, intimate gathering for you. Are you going to disappoint your friends?"

"I don't need you to throw a party for me."

"And to think, my mother prayed to Jesus *and* Buddha for your protection every single day for three years, and here you are, as ungrateful as ever." She shakes her straight black hair. "You're going to break her heart."

My jaw tightens. I don't like manipulation, but she has a point. Mrs. Banks did stand up for me back when I lived here. She never treated me like the other church ladies, people like Stern… Probably because being Korean, she was an outsider, too.

I pass my hand over my mouth. I know if I go to Ruby's party, I'm going to have to face Drew again. Hell, being in this town, I'm going to have to face Drew again.

"Your mom's going to be there?"

"She helped me plan the whole thing! She's making those spicy dumplings you like with Kimchi."

It's been a while since I had authentic Asian food. My stomach starts to growl, and I glance at the clock. It's after noon.

"What time?"

Ruby does a little squeal and claps her hands. "It's tonight at seven. We won't go too late since it's a school night…"

"At your mom's house?"

"Yep!" She hops over to her car, and I wave.

"Did you need anything for your car?"

"Oh, no, but I'll be back when I do. I've got to go get ready. See you tonight!"

She pulls out, and I'm left standing wondering what the hell I've just agreed to do.

# CHAPTER Eleven

## Drew

When the braces came off Ralph Stern's teeth, he got contact lenses, stopped dressing like a geek, and got his degree in business. He never lost his crush on me, but at least now he's not so creepy. He's actually what most girls would consider handsome.

Most girls who've never met him.

"It will revolutionize the economy of Oakville." He pulls a hand from the pocket of his dark jeans and opens it. "Hall's Hardy almond trees produce excellent nuts, and they're very cold hardy."

I look at the pale nut sitting on his palm and nod, falling back on a Dotty-ism. "I'll be dogged."

"Yes, you will!" His eyes flash with excitement. "Who says California should have the market cornered on these little guys? We're going to give them a run for their money right here in South Carolina."

"Well, all right, then." I force a smile and take a sip of the warm cider, wishing it was spiked.

Ralph's expression turns serious. "How are things down at the clinic?"

I wave my hand. "You know I can't really talk about my patients, Ralph."

"You should be at a hospital or in private practice. Not in that rinky dink little store front."

"Friends Care is exactly what I had in mind when I got my degree. It's small, affordable, catering to people who otherwise wouldn't get help."

"Your heart's too big." He clears his throat. "Speaking of, I heard Grayson might need your services."

I inhale my sip, and start to choke. My eyes fill with water, and I cover my mouth as Ralph slaps me on the back.

"You okay?"

"Sorry," I mange to squeak out. "I don't know what you mean."

"Oh, those boys always come back with problems. PTSD or survivor's guilt or something like that. They're never the same."

"Ahh..." *What an asshole!* Like he knows anything about what Gray is like or what he's been through.

I'm about to ask when he's ever put his life on the line for someone else when Ruby comes out and grabs my arm.

"Drew! Ma needs our help in the kitchen." I sometimes think my best friend has a sixth sense for when I'm about to go off.

"Sure." My smile is tight, teeth clenched.

We push through the door, and she lets out a nervous giggle. "That was close."

"Why did you invite Ralph Stern again?" I do some deep breathing as I lean against the ceramic counter.

"Mom feels sorry for him. She says he didn't have enough friends growing up."

"We had our reasons."

Voices rise in the other room, and my insides jump. I've been

wired and edgy since I walked in the door. What will I do when I see him again?

"Ralph is a nice boy." Mrs. Banks pats me on the arm to move.

"If you say so, Mrs. B."

She lifts the lid on a bamboo steamer. "Good."

I watch as she turns the dumplings over quickly, and my mouth waters. Ruby's mom is one of the best cooks in town, and I've been living on takeout for weeks.

"Maybe you should go out with Ralph." I elbow my friend in the waist. "He's not Asian, but if that almond deal works out, it could revolutionize the town." I imitate his voice.

"Do not even say it. You are evil." My best friend scowls at me. "Anyway, I don't date men that inexperienced."

"You could coach him in the ways of love. Be his naughty nanny."

"Ew." But then she pauses. "Hang on, that gives me an idea. Maybe I could be a nanny…"

"You know nothing about kids."

Her eyes narrow. "I have a master's degree in psychology."

"And zero experience."

"How hard can it be? I was a kid once. And I could use the extra money."

"Oh, this sounds like a great idea." I tease, lifting my mug for another sip of cider.

My shaking hand gives me away, and she grabs my arm, dragging me to the opposite side of the room, away from her mother.

"How are you doing?" She glances over my shoulder before turning to the side and whipping out a flask. "Here… liquid courage."

She pours half the flask into my cup. "Stop," I hiss. "I can't be drunk."

"Don't slug it. Just sip it."

Ruby's mom comes up behind us. "Girls! Help me plate the food!"

I yelp and jump a foot in the air, and Ruby pinches my arm. She grabs a platter of dumplings and one of Kimchi. I take a long sip of straight whiskey then grab a platter of rolls and a cheese board, complete with more traditional meats.

When we enter the room, I almost drop both. Gray stands in the foyer looking like he stepped out of a *GQ* magazine. He's wearing black jeans and a gray tee with a plaid shirt unbuttoned on top. His dark hair flops to one side on his forehead the way it always has, and when his eyes meet mine, my stomach plunges to the floor.

I swallow the knot in my throat. I'm not sure I can move.

"Grayson!" Mrs. Banks crosses the room to hug him. "Welcome home, our hero. I prayed for you every day you were gone. Jesus and the Buddha brought you back to us safely."

His eyes are still on me, and every hair on my body stands at attention. My nipples tighten inside my bra, and I'm glad I'm wearing a blazer on top of the thin, olive green cropped tee. It stops at the top of my high-waisted black leggings, and it's so thin, he'd know immediately how my body still responds to him.

"Grayson Cole, welcome home." Ralph walks up beside me and puts his hand on my lower back. It makes me jump. He's never touched me like that. "Andrea, can I help you with those platters?"

"Uh… no." I turn to the table, which is set for eight and quickly put the food in the center. "I forgot my mug in the kitchen."

I hurry away from Gray's searing gaze. I need one more shot of whiskey if I'm going to get through this dinner.

When I return everyone has taken a seat, and I'm left beside Ralph and across from Gray. I won't be able to eat a thing.

Instead, I grab my mug.

Mrs. Banks says a quick prayer of thanks, then the platters start making the rounds. Ralph hands me the cheese plate, and I take a slice.

"You should eat more than that, Andrea," he says, and I try not to gag at his fatherly tone. I don't know why he acts so parental all the time, calling me Andrea. That's his problem.

I might be feeling the whiskey…

A glance, and I see Gray staring pointedly at Ralph from across the table. If I didn't know better, I'd say he wanted to grab him by the collar.

"So Gray," Mrs. Banks calls. "Ruby says you opened your uncle's garage again. I'm so glad. I hope that means you're planning to stay?"

My eyes are fixed on the roll Ralph put on my plate, but I can feel Gray watching us. "For a little while." His deep voice sends fireworks fizzing through my stomach.

"I sent Billy James over to ask about a job," Dotty joins the conversation. "Did you meet him?"

In my peripheral vision I can tell that got his attention. He looks at her, and I sneak a peek at him. His square jaw is clean-shaven, and his profile is as perfect as it ever was, straight nose, high cheekbones.

"You know how to reach Billy?"

"I sure do. He lives right over in Pintoville."

"Dorothy Magee!" Mrs. Banks's snaps at her. "I do not approve of that word."

Dotty looks down at her plate. "Sorry, Mrs. B. We've just always called it that."

"That doesn't make it right."

Gray picks up the conversation. "If you could tell him to come on back. I'd told him I wasn't sure if I had enough work, but I do."

She nods, still seeming embarrassed. "I'll tell him as soon as I see him. I usually drive through… east Oakville on the way home."

"You should probably take Dagwood with you." Ralph says, nodding to Dotty's husband Steve, a.k.a.,"Dagwood." He got the nickname from the school lunches he used to bring. "Have you heard about my almond tree idea, Gray?"

Ralph dominates the conversation explaining to Gray about the amount of rain we get in the Carolinas, and how we shouldn't allow the California growers to corner the market. Ruby talks to Dotty and Dagwood at the other end of the table about her last dating disaster, and Mrs. Banks seems fascinated by growing zones and nut trees.

I push the food around my plate and try to do personal therapy, deep breathing, distracting my thoughts. It doesn't work. Every time I steal a glance at Gray, my eyes go to his lips, and I remember how good they feel touching my skin, tracing kisses down my neck, pulling on my nipples.

The space between my thighs is hot and needy by the time I realize I've finished my mug of whiskey, and I haven't eaten a thing. I grab a roll and stuff it in my mouth.

"Are you feeling okay, Andrea?" Ralph places his hand on my arm, and everyone at the table looks my way. I'm mortified.

"Of course!" I do a little laugh and rise to my feet. "I was just thinking about work tomorrow. I'd better be getting home."

Taking my plate, I start for the kitchen, bumping into the corner of the bar on my journey. I'd better scarf down some dumplings real quick. The door doesn't close behind me, and I realize I'm not alone.

"Are you okay?" Gray's voice is the same quiet tone that warms my entire body.

My throat hurts. It makes me want to cry. It makes me want to rush into his arms, but I suck it up until I face him. His eyes are

burning, studying me.

"I'm fine," I manage to smile, even though it's shaky. "I can't remember if I told you welcome home the other night."

"It was late, and we were... unprepared."

I'm not sure what that means. "I didn't think you liked working at the garage. You have money now. You could sell it."

"It's what I want to do. And you're dating Ralph Stern now?" The sudden edge in his voice takes me by surprise.

My jaw drops open, and I don't say what I should. I don't say *no*. Instead, I snap at him.

"Isn't that what you kept telling me I should do? Date other people?"

He disappears without a word for a year, then comes back angry because I didn't sit around waiting?

...only I did.

His blue eyes are storm clouds and thunder, and the muscle in his jaw moves back and forth. The air between us seems to crackle. He starts to go, but I throw caution to the wind. I reach out and grab his arm.

"Why didn't you come to the funeral?" I don't say the rest. *He was your best friend. I was so lost and confused, so lonely.*

He doesn't meet my eyes. "I said goodbye before they brought him home."

"Funerals are for the survivors, Gray." My voice is trembling. "You should have come home for me."

His brow furrows over those stormy eyes, and when they meet mine, I can't hold back. I step forward, pulling my body into his, letting his familiar scent of cedar, soap, and *Gray* engulf me.

Strong arms go around me, and I almost cry. My body melts, I grip his shirt. It's so right where I belong, but it's cut short. His back stiffens and he pulls away, gripping my upper arms in both hands.

"We can't do this."

The shards of glass make it to my heart, cutting painfully. "What happened?"

His chin drops. "I'm not the same person anymore."

"Well, I am." Tears are in my voice. "Didn't you get any of my texts?"

The lines around his eyes deepen. "The accident… busted my phone. I didn't get a new one until a month ago."

Frustration burns my insides. I can't stand this pain. "Do you still have my number?"

He hesitates too long before admitting. "Yes."

I can't stand here anymore. Grabbing the door, I'm ready to leave this place when Gray stops me.

"Ralph seems like a nice guy now. You're right to move on, forget about me." Bitterness is in his voice, like he doesn't mean a word of it.

I look to the door, frowning. "If that's how you feel, why did you come back?"

Another long pause, then finally. "I don't know."

"Not that it's your business, but I'm not dating Ralph. We're just friends."

His lips tighten, but I refuse to stay and see the relief in his eyes. I'm through the door, and of course Ralph meets me as soon as we exit the kitchen.

"I was telling Dotty about the health benefits of almonds," he starts. "Gray, your degree is in civil engineering, right?"

Gray makes a noise behind me.

"Well, when you get serious and stop wasting your time in that garage, I could use you on my team. Help me run my logistics."

He puts his arm around my shoulders and gives me a squeeze. "Isn't that right, Andrea?"

A shadow of anger flashes across Gray's face, but it's gone so fast, I'm sure I'm the only one who saw it. I'm the only one who

knows him well enough.

"I'm good for now." He goes to where Mrs. Banks sits with Ruby. "Thank you for inviting me here and for all your prayers. I appreciate it."

"You're not leaving!" Mrs. Banks clasps his hand. "We've barely had a chance to talk."

"I have to work in the morning."

Dotty waves at me. "I'll tell Billy to stop by tomorrow."

When he reaches the door he pauses, and my chest squeezes. I wait to see if he'll look back at me one more time before he leaves…

At the last second, he doesn't. He walks out, closing the door behind him.

"Well, that was weird." Dotty raises her eyebrows, giving Ruby a knowing look.

"Who would want to be a mechanic when you could get in on the ground floor with almonds?" Ralph is truly astounded, and completely oblivious.

"I'd better go, too." I step over to Ruby's mom and give her a hug. "It was a wonderful dinner. Thank you, Mrs. B."

My best friend hops up from where she sits beside Dagwood on the couch. "I'll walk you out."

As soon as the door closes, she grips my arm. "Did you see that? He could barely keep his eyes off you."

"Don't, Ruby." I'm doing my best to hold back fresh tears.

"What?" she cries. "I'm pretty sure he wanted to break Ralph's neck at least twice tonight, not that I'd have stopped him. Now that he's a veteran, he's probably got massive GI Joe-type skills."

"I think everybody wanted to break Ralph's neck. He was driving us crazy with all that almond talk. Then he suggested Gray was wasting his time at the garage. What business is that of Ralph's?" Despite it all, my protectiveness of him is strong as ever.

Ruby's head tilts to the side. "I have an idea about that."

She walks with me down the sidewalk toward my house the same way we used to do when we were girls. Ruby would walk me halfway to my house, then she'd turn around, and I'd walk the rest of the way alone. We haven't done it since she got a car.

"If this is about me using one of your dating apps again—"

"Isn't it time you had a car to drive?"

Embarrassment joins the overload of emotions swirling in my chest. "You know I can't afford to buy a car, much less pay for the insurance. Anyway, I don't need one. I can practically walk to work."

"Hello?" She pretends to knock on my skull, and I bat her hand away. "Your dad has that gorgeous Jaguar just rotting in the garage. The man of your dreams returns, and he owns a garage…"

She gives me a look that says *Wake up, stupid*, and I wrinkle my nose. "That doesn't seem too… obvious?"

"You need transportation, right?"

Twisting my lips, I think about it. "It would be nice not to walk everywhere. Or depend on you."

"It would be even nicer to drive a sexy, classic Jag over to your ex lover's garage and see what happens."

"Ruby!" I grab her hand, as if anyone is around to hear her at this time of night. I confess, the suggestion makes me nervous and excited and scared and horny all at the same time. "I'll think about it."

# CHAPTER *Twelve*

*Gray*

ANOTHER RESTLESS NIGHT, AND AGAIN, I WAKE UP ON THE COUCH. Something about sleeping in Mack's bed isn't registering with my brain. I got new sheets, new pillows. I rearranged the furniture. Nothing works.

It probably didn't help that I had to drink Drew away again last night. Seeing her there, so pretty, those black leggings hugging her curves, and Ralph Stern talking to her, touching her like he owns her. I remember all the times I encouraged her to date other guys, and I want to kick my own ass.

She said she's not dating him. Did she ever? He seems awfully familiar. She asked me if I'd seen her texts. Was she trying to tell me about him while I was hiding in Dover, taking care of my uncle?

Everything about last night swirls in a tornado of anger and frustration in my mind. Ralph Stern lost the creepy-nerd with braces vibe, and he actually looks like the kind of guy Drew's dad would approve for her. He's got the name and his church-lady mom, who always looked down on me.

Don't forget he has that almond orchard he won't shut up about, and he calls her *Andrea*. Nobody our age calls her Andrea. He sounded exactly like his judgy mother, and it was all I could do not to punch him in the face at Mrs. B's table.

It's the same way they all treated my uncle back in the day, and he was a fucking small-business owner. Now I am.

I have a degree I'll use when I'm good and ready, I'm a veteran, and I'm still dealing with this shit. Talk about nothing ever changing.

Drew was right. What the fuck am I doing here? I thought I came back to make peace beside Danny's grave. *Done*. Now why?

It's more than that. I know. I'm still here because I want to be sure she's okay.

She seems to have a good job. She has a nice, pedigreed guy who's as boring as watching paint dry just waiting for her to notice him. A growl rumbles in my chest, and I know the truth in that moment.

Last night, I held her in my arms. Even if it was less than thirty seconds, my whole body moved to hers. I was home again, safe and comforted. If Drew married someone else, it would kill me. But how can I be with her after what I've done, what I've become? I'm still so fucked up.

A mug of coffee is in my hand, and I nearly toss it when I open the garage door to find Billy standing right there. He's again wearing black skinny jeans and a sleeveless black tee with *Pink Floyd* across the front. In his hand is a stick about two inches in diameter and a short-bladed knife with a thick handle.

He squints up at me. "Hey."

"Dotty give you my message?"

"She stopped by last night with her husband. Said you needed me to come back today."

I motion for him to follow me inside. "What's that in your hand?"

Glancing down, he turns the stick over, revealing deep rivets cut in a pattern along one side. "It's just something I do to pass the time."

"That's pretty good. What's it going to be?"

He shrugs it off like it's no big deal. "Don't know yet."

"Here." I open a locker in the back corner and take out the old work shirt I used to wear. It's thick canvass and has Mack's Garage in a patch on the front pocket along with my name. "Wear this for now, while you're working."

"Do you need me to sign something or anything?" He looks around.

"I can pay you in cash if you need me to." It's not my business to ask questions.

"I got my social security card. I'm not doing anything illegal."

Apparently I'm the asshole making assumptions as well.

"Sorry. I didn't mean... Hang on." I take a step toward the office. "I think Mack had an application somewhere you can fill out. Give me a second."

I go into the glass-encased office just as a yellow Miata pulls in front of the first bay. Billy walks slowly to greet whoever it is, while I dig through my uncle's old files. It was always just the two of us, but I vaguely remember filling out a W-9.

My fingers land on the off-centered copy, and I grab the old clipboard holding work orders. I'm just walking back into the garage, when a woman rushing up to give me a hug makes me stop.

"I didn't think you'd ever come back." I'm surrounded by the familiar scent of perfume and hairspray, and I pull back to see Leslie Grant blinking up at me.

She's wearing a silky red dress that plunges low in the front, showing off her cleavage, and on one arm is an oversized basket. Billy's looking at her like she's one of those old vintage Playboy calendars hanging in the bathroom come to life.

I clear my throat and step back. "Leslie. I didn't know you

were still in Oakville."

"Where else would I be?" She laughs, and pulls the basket around in front of her.

The movement squeezes her breasts closer together and Billy exhales a little noise.

I slap the clipboard against his chest. "Take that and fill it out. Leave it on my desk."

"Yes, sir," he says, slowly walking away but not taking his eyes off our visitor.

Leslie's green eyes don't stray from mine. "I brought a little breakfast. Dotty said you just got back in town, and I figured you could use some groceries. Muffin?" She pulls back the cloth cover and inside are purplish-tinted muffins. "They go great with coffee. Do you have some?"

"Ah, yeah, I just made a pot in the house." I hold out a hand and we start toward the small cottage.

She follows me through the door into the miniscule dining area with the old linoleum table and only two chairs.

"Not much has changed, has it?" She looks around before flashing me a big smile. "I'm sure you'll fix it up."

The basket is on the table and she walks to the kitchen, opening cabinets until she finds plates over the sink. She reaches for them, and I glance away from her round ass straining in that dress.

"I might have to make some more coffee if you'd like some." Going to the pot, I pull out the carafe and tilt it to the side.

"Don't you dare!" Leslie pats my arm like she's scolding me playfully. "I didn't come here to make you work. I came here to take care of you."

Something about the way she says it makes my stomach tighten. Leslie was always playing games like this, making eyes at me over Danny's shoulder. Then I'd catch them in the back room either with Danny's dick in her mouth or doing it doggy style against the wall.

She sets the old beige plate in front of me and pours a cup of coffee. "How are you doing… really?" She leans forward, giving me a straight shot down the front of her dress.

I pull up and take a step back. I might be conflicted over what to do about Drew, but I'm sure as hell not conflicted enough to get tangled in this web.

"I'm doing okay," I lie, taking the mug and holding it between us. "Thanks for the muffins. I'd better get out and check on things. It's Billy's first day."

She puts her hand on my waist. "Grayson. You can talk to me. We all know you were there when Danny died. You must be devastated."

Normally, conversations like this cause my anxiety to rise, but I don't have time for involuntary responses. A loud knocking on the door interrupts us, and Billy is outside calling through the door.

"Mr. Cole? I'm sorry to interrupt, but a customer is here asking for you."

I pat Leslie on the shoulder. "Thanks again. I really do have to get to work."

Setting the coffee on the counter, I charge out the door into the garage, curious as to who might be here so early.

A knot forms in my throat, and I'm not sure if I should be thrilled or alarmed when I see the car of my dreams, Carl Harris's cherry red Jaguar, sparkling in the sun.

Drew stands just inside finishing up with the tow truck driver. She looks better than any vintage pinup in jeans and a basic tee. Her hair is done in a loose braid that hangs over one shoulder. My chest tightens at the sight of her when she turns and walks up beside her father's car. I'll never forget the day he brought it here… or how that day ended.

I do my best to act casual. "What's going on?"

"Hey, there." Drew gives me a dazzling white smile, and

I have the sudden urge to kiss her. She seems to have forgotten whatever was bothering her last night. "I need a car, and Ruby suggested you might get this one going for me. At least I know you'll be careful with it."

I walk around the vehicle, inspecting the perfect chassis, the shining chrome, the pristine leather seats. "Yes, I will."

Billy walks up beside me and lets out a low whistle. "When was the last time you drove it?"

"I've never driven it." Her chin drops, and she scuffs her brown cowboy boot on the pavement. "But to answer your question, I can't remember the last time Dad took it out. Maybe ten years ago?"

"That long?" Billy's face is total astonishment. "Why?"

I know she doesn't want to answer that question. "Billy, get behind it and push it in here over the lift." I step forward and put the gearshift into neutral.

Holding the steering wheel, I guide the car into the bay with Drew right behind us just as Leslie emerges from the door leading to the cottage. I don't miss the flash of confusion mixed with anger in Drew's eyes.

"Well, good morning, Drew!" Leslie crosses her arms under her breasts and stands a little to close to me. "What brings you here so early?"

Drew steps back, hands on her hips, doing her best to smile. "I'm getting Dad's old car checked out. What are you doing?"

"Oh, you know, men need a good breakfast. I was just making sure Gray had something to eat." Her voice is sending a message I don't like.

I especially don't like the way she touches my bicep.

"I've got to get to the clinic." Drew spins on her heel and heads for the door.

I take off after her. "I'll give you a call once I've checked everything."

My voice is low, professional. Nothing is going on here, and I'm not trying to send any wrong messages.

"I can stop by after work." She's not slowing down, so I reach out and catch her arm.

"Hang on." It stops her, but she's still mad. I know my girl. "I'll probably have to order some parts. I expect if it hasn't been driven in ten years, I'll need to check the brakes, steering, suspension… the electrical systems."

I'm stalling, trying to keep her close until she's less pissed.

"Just do what you need to do."

"Okay." I want to say something more, but she jerks her chin toward Leslie.

"Does that include her?"

"She just showed up a few minutes ago." My grip turns into a stroke down the length of her arm. I want to thread her fingers with mine. I want to tell her she has nothing to worry about. *Nothing.*

I might be broken, guilty, undeserving of her… it doesn't change the fact she still owns my heart.

She wavers a moment, her pretty blue eyes flickering to where Leslie waits inside the garage with Billy before returning to mine. The electricity between us sizzles like always. It never went away.

Her voice is less angry when she speaks. "I'll wait to hear from you."

"You'll hear from me. I have your number."

"I know you do." She turns, and I watch a few moments as she crosses the street and heads up the sidewalk, her sassy stride making me smile in spite of my good intentions.

# CHAPTER *Thirteen*

## *Drew*

"BUT YOU DIDN'T HAVE SEX WITH THE BABYSITTER?" I CLARIFY, making notes on the legal pad.

Riley Sturgiss is a new patient, a petite older teen, with bright red hair and dark eyes. She disclosed her issue is social anxiety, but I'm starting to think it might be more like compulsive lying.

Also, I'm still really pissed about whatever the hell was going on at Mack's garage this morning.

Or I guess it's Gray's garage now.

Her cheeks turn pink, and she shakes her head. "I didn't want to go to the open house, and I knew if I was grounded, I'd have to stay home."

"You might have jeopardized your babysitter's reputation… or worse. Could it have been construed as statutory rape?"

"Oh my gosh!" Her brown eyes widen. "I don't think so?"

"Then you told your boss at Hamburger Heaven you used to be a man?" I give her a compassionate smile. "Are you a trans female?"

Riley chews her bottom lip. "Does it matter?"

"I'd say yes, it matters a lot."

Her voice is quiet, apologetic. "I'm not."

I make another note. "How would telling him you're trans help you?"

"I thought he might hit on me."

My brow furrows. "Has he made inappropriate advances toward you in the workplace before?"

Her chin drops. "No."

My voice is calm, measured. "So if it wasn't to protect yourself from sexual harassment…"

I wait, seconds tick, finally she answers. "I did it to get out of corporate training. They don't have unisex bathrooms."

"I see." It's starting to make sense now.

"I can't stand around in groups."

"Why do you say that?"

We wait. She wavers. It's okay. I smile kindly.

Then it breaks, words gushing like water. "I stand there and it always gets to that point where everybody's looking at me, waiting. The pressure keeps building. They're all waiting for me to say something, and if I don't they all think I'm a bitch or I'm unfriendly and they won't ever talk to me again."

I make a new note on my legal pad. "Were you quiet as a child?"

She shrugs. "I guess… I just… I never knew what to say to people."

"Were you punished for it?"

She doesn't answer. She studies her fingernails, blinking quickly. My heart breaks a little, but I'm not trying to make her cry.

"It's okay. We're here to find answers, right?" Ducking my head, I catch her eye and give her another smile.

She gives me a very brief grimace in return.

"I have a little assignment for you to try." I take out my white notepad. "I want you to write down the times you told a fib. More importantly, I want you to think about what happened right before that. Maybe we can find other ways to handle these situations. Ways that won't get you or anybody else in trouble."

I tear off the slip of paper and hand it to her. She takes it, reading slowly as I show her out. Despite the personal crap in my life, we made a little breakthrough here. I make a note. *Riley is very sensitive*. I don't want to be frustrated or on edge when I meet with her next time.

Once she's made it to reception, I step across the hall where Ruby is at the copy machine. My stomach is burning thinking about Gray with Leslie, seeing him so relaxed and familiar with her. "It doesn't make any sense."

"What doesn't?" She doesn't look up from punching numbers.

"He was so broken, talking about how he isn't the same person anymore."

My friend's eyes flicker up to mine. "Hang on." She hops over and shuts the door, quickly twisting the wands to close the mini blinds. "What happened? Why are you so upset?"

"It makes no sense. Lies make no sense."

"Need me to take the new patient?"

I shake my head, although I probably should have postponed my appointments for today. I can't do that. I have to be a professional.

Still… "I thought he needed space to heal. I was giving him space. I was waiting… like always." I'm pacing the break room fuming. "Then I find him over there healing with Leslie Grant."

"That whore. Of course, she's going to rush right in the minute he returns. She always had her eye on him when they were in school."

I'm chewing on my lip when Ruby hands me a cold soda.

"Drink this. It'll help you cool off."

"I'm cool. I'm better than cool. I'm so cool…" I'm like Riley. I'm having a breakthrough. "I'm not crying anymore. I'm not waiting around anymore. I'm going on a date."

"Oh!" Ruby bounces on the balls of her feet. "Let me set you up on Bumble!"

Shaking my head, I hold up a hand. "I'm going out with Ralph Stern."

"No!" My best friend draws back in shock. "Not the almond king! Try a dating app first."

"After all the horror stories you've told me? No thank you. At least I know what to expect with Ralph."

"You expect to age a hundred years in an hour? To die a slow, painful death of massive boredom covered in almond milk?"

"Ralph is not that bad."

"Ralph is that bad." She slaps her hand against her forehead. "Sure, he lost the braces and grew two feet and got better looking, but he would never find your clit. Not even if it had an almond on it."

She's probably right, but I'm not in the mood to defend Ralph. My mind is too busy brooding over my morning. Also, I am not having sex with Ralph Stern. Ew.

"If he's having survivor guilt, why won't he talk to me?" I cross my arms over my stomach. "Nobody knows Gray like I do. I'm a therapist…"

"Maybe… But didn't we learn it's not always a good idea to treat close friends or family?" Ruby takes her copies off the machine. "Like how surgeons don't do surgery on their own loved ones?"

"Now you suddenly remember what we learned in college."

"Don't be shitty. I'm trying to help you."

"Whatever. It doesn't matter now. I'm moving on!"

"You're moving in the wrong direction."

"Maybe. Maybe not." I take a deep breath. "I'm not sitting around waiting to find out anymore.

Feeling energized, I return to my office. I have two more clients to see today, and I'm not letting a man mess up my career. Especially not a man with as little loyalty as Grayson Cole.

I'm exhausted from fighting thoughts about Gray all day when my last client leaves. It's five o'clock, and I have a text waiting on my cell. Of course, it's him.

***Gray: Car's ready for pickup. Good and bad news.***

He's got a lot of nerve texting me about my car, I mentally huff. Although, I suppose it's what a mechanic is supposed to do when he's working on your car. Still, I'm not ready to let Gray off the hook.

When I arrive at the garage, the doors are closed, but I hear voices coming from inside. Thankfully, they're both male voices. I wonder if I should knock. Instead, I just open the door. It is a place of business, after all.

Gray's eyes light up briefly when they meet mine, and I shove down the rise in my stomach at the sight of it.

I don't care.

"I'm here to pick up my car." I stop just inside the door and wait as Billy slides off the chair where he was sitting and goes to the rack of keys.

"Right." Gray clears his throat, clears away his obvious interest. Whatever. "So the engine turns over. The electrical system checks out, and the cooling and lubrication systems are all working and leak free."

I take the keys from Billy when he hands them to me. "You said there was bad news?"

He takes a pair of heavy black glasses out of his pocket before he reads the clipboard. I'm not prepared for how my insides react to this new bit of information. *He needs glasses?* Also, he looks

damn sexy with this new sexy-nerdy thing going on.

"The transmission will need to be replaced. Also, the brake pads are pretty worn, and it needs new tires." Blue eyes blink up at me behind those glasses.

It takes me a blink to remember how to speak. "So I can't drive it?"

"You can drive it, but I wouldn't wait too long. You need to bring it back in a day or two and let me finish working on it."

In my head, I do some quick math, my stomach sinking at the thought. "How much is all of this going to cost?"

Billy starts to answer. "Transmission can run you at least eight—"

"Don't worry about that right now." Gray takes off those glasses and returns them to his shirt pocket. "I've always wanted to work on this car."

The genuine warmth in his tone almost makes me forget how angry I've been at him all day. It's so much like how he used to be, optimistic, excited. I want to reach out and touch his hand, hold him, but his signals are so mixed, I don't.

"I can bring it back in the morning if that's okay?" I manage to give him a little smile, a sign I'm still here, waiting.

He takes a step back, almost like he's guarding a wound. "I'll have to order parts for the transmission and tires—"

"We can work on the brakes tomorrow." Billy has been hanging back, following his new boss's lead, but I can tell he's pretty smart with cars. "We have what we need for that."

Gray nods. "If you want to do that, we can keep things moving."

"Thanks." A little smile, and I slide into the seat, amazed at how smoothly the engine turns over. The car sounds like it used to.

It gives me an unexpected sense of hope, of bringing something back that was broken. It just needed a little TLC.

My hope turns to sadness when I get home and find my dad in the same place I left him this morning. He's in that same chair, holding that same empty tumbler of scotch.

"The Jag is almost back to perfect," I say, taking the glass from his hand.

He sniffs as if I've startled him out of a trance. "Drew. Don't you need to go to work today?"

His question makes my heart hurt. "I did go to work, Dad. I'm just getting home."

"What?" He looks around the room confused.

"Did you sit here all day?" I take the chair across from him, inspecting his clothing. "It's not good not to move all day."

"Danny never moves now. Your mother never moves." He looks out the window again, and I'm at a loss.

I know this is all part of his addiction. The alcohol feeds the depression, and the more he drinks, the less grasp on reality he has. I'm starting to despair at my inability to help anyone I care about.

I decide to change my approach. "You know, Ruby likes to use dating apps to find guys to go out with."

He leans his head back, frowning at me. "A dating… *app*? I don't know what that is."

Shifting in my seat, I do my best to stay positive. "It's a computer program that matches your personality with other people's personalities. Anyway, that's not really the point I was trying to make."

"I'm not looking to date anyone." He puts his hands on the arms of his chair and starts to stand. "I'm really tired."

"No, wait. I didn't mean for you to date someone." I scoot forward, catching his hand. "I was thinking about what you said. About nothing being anonymous in Oakville."

He straightens to his full height, looking down on me with disdain. "I hope this isn't more of your harping on me to attend

those *meetings*."

The way he says the word lets me know I'm losing the fight once again. I stand as well, even though my head only reaches the top of his shoulder.

"Dad…" I do my best to carefully choose my words. "I know you feel sad because of Danny, because of Mom. I know it feels like you have nothing left… But you still have me."

His expression softens a bit, and he almost smiles. "Yes, and one day, you'll leave me, too. Live your life, Drew. Don't spend it worrying about me."

He takes his first slow, staggering steps toward the door, and I hurry up beside him. "I'll never stop worrying about you, Dad. I want you to be well."

I stop short of saying he has so much to live for. That's a bridge we'll have to cross when he finally gets sober.

If he ever gets sober.

If his liver and his pancreas don't give out first.

"I'm well knowing you're well." He continues, pausing at the door to adjust his posture. His proud posture, ingrained from childhood.

We don't have much left to make us proud.

"I'm making shrimp and grits tonight. It's your favorite."

"Don't wake me if I'm sleeping."

He leaves me alone, and I slowly make my way down the stairs to the large kitchen. I take the bag of shrimp I picked up on the way home out of the refrigerator and start the water to boil for the grits.

A canister of the dry hominy sits behind the coffee maker. I only remember a few recipes from when my mom was still alive. She taught me to make grits the old-fashioned way, boiling them on the stove top. Any good southerner knows how to do that, and anyone who lives along the coast knows how to boil shrimp.

I take out a package of corn, sausage, and different colored

bell peppers. While I slice them, I put the streaming music on a Motown mix. Gray got me interested in artists like Sam Cooke, Marvin Gaye, and Al Green. He would hum the words in my ear when we slow-danced. The memory makes my skin hum.

Once the peppers are chopped and the water is boiling, I close my eyes and remember him singing "Mercy, Mercy Me" in my ear as he held my body close to his. I can't stop what I do next. It's an addiction I'll never get over.

***Me: I'm making shrimp n grits tonight.***

My chest is tight as I stir the pot waiting, wondering if he'll even respond. The grits are thickening, and I slide them to the low heat when my phone buzzes on the counter. My heart jumps, and I pick it up.

***Gray: It's your signature dish.***

***Me: The only thing I know how to make.***

***Gray: Your pancakes are good.***

***Me: Sam Cooke is on Spotify.***

***Gray: My favorite kind of night.***

My heart is beating so fast, the blood races in my veins. He's like a drug.

***Me: You wear glasses now?***

***Gray: Just for reading. Concussion weakened my eyes.***

That makes me frown.

***Me: I didn't know you had a concussion.***

***Gray: I hit my head in the blast. It left me pretty messed up for weeks.***

My chest hurts thinking of him alone after the accident, injured and so far away from home.

***Me: Are you better now?***

***Gray: Somewhat. Not as many bad days.***

*Not as many…* I remember what he said about being changed.

***Me: Is this why you stayed away?***

***Gray: Partly. I needed to heal.***

*Let me help you heal.* I don't type it.

The song changes to Marvin Gaye, and I want to sing it to him. I want to be secure in his arms, press my cheek to his chest. Instead, I slide my finger over the screen, wishing it were his face.

***Me: I'll see you in the morning.***

***Gray: Night, Drew baby.***

I don't even realize I'm crying until my eyes close, and a hot tear hits my cheek.

# CHAPTER Fourteen

## Gray

I MANAGE TO SLEEP WITHOUT TAKING THE PILLS. TEXTING WITH DREW wasn't a trigger like I'd feared it might be. It actually soothed the ache in my chest and warmed my insides. It reminded me of better days, the days before the accident. When we were happy.

When I wake in the morning, I'm still in the bed—not face down on the floor in the living room or on the couch. I know it's only baby steps, but at this point, I'm ready to take all the encouragement I can get.

Coffee made, I walk out to find Billy in the shop waiting, that knife and stick of wood in his hands.

"You drink coffee?" I ask, holding out the mug.

"Nah." He shakes his head. "I just had a Coke before I came in."

He's digging that knife into the stick of wood, creating a line.

"What you got there?"

"It's nothing." He opens his hand, and I see the stick is now a smooth, yellow wooden carving of a whale.

One of those old-timey whales like Moby Dick, but still a whale. I'm actually impressed.

"That's pretty damn good." I hold out my hand, and he gives it to me. "Do you sell these or something?"

"Hell no." Billy laughs, taking it back. "Nobody wants to buy this shit."

"They might." I take the shop cloth off the peg and tuck it into the back of my jeans. "How'd you learn to do that?"

"My old man." He follows me to the key box where a few cars left overnight are waiting. "He was in some of the fighting along the border when I was a kid. Messed him up pretty bad."

"That so?" I'm reading the work order on the envelopes containing the keys, but this catches my attention.

"Yeah, he'd have bad memories, dreams. It was the only thing that calmed him down."

I take another look at the stick in his hand. "What do you use it for?"

"Just to pass the time, mostly."

Nodding, I hand him two of the envelopes. "Bring these inside. Got an oil change and a brake job."

Billy's hand is on the envelopes when his eyes move to something over my shoulder. He mutters words in Spanish I don't understand, but I understand the tone. It's pure lust.

"Good morning, guys, who's ready for breakfast?" The sultry voice causes me to turn, and Leslie is back again.

Today she's wearing tight jeans and a shirt tied up so her stomach shows. Leslie always had a banging body, and in this get-up, it's practically on full display. In her hands is a plastic container.

"Hey, Leslie." It's pretty lame, but I'm not sure what to say. I didn't ask her to bring us breakfast every day.

"Don't just stand there. Come eat!" She grins and winks, walking over to put the container on the worktable. "I made your favorite, cheesy biscuits with sausage crumbles."

The savory odor fills the garage, cancelling out the odor of grease and making my stomach growl. "Smells good."

Billy hustles over, and she hands him one of the round pieces of bread. He thanks her and heads out to bring in the cars. I walk slowly to where she's leaning against the counter. Her back is arched, and she's giving me that look I remember.

"You don't have to make us breakfast." I take the small parcel she holds out to me.

"I'm going to take that as a thank you." She winks at me, turning to dig something out of her purse. It points her round ass right at me. "It's just my way of welcoming home a hero. Since I was left off the guest list for Mrs. B's party."

I rub the back of my neck. I've never been good with this kind of stuff. "Ruby said she was keeping it small."

"It doesn't matter. Ruby never liked me." When she turns around again, she's holding a set of keys. "I found this roll of film at the house. I'm not sure where you can get it developed, but I thought you'd want it."

"Thanks." I guess. I'm not sure I'm up to seeing what this small, black cylinder might contain. "Film is pretty old-school."

"I thought for a while I might be a photographer." Her eyes travel around the garage before meeting mine. "We don't always get to do what we want, do we?"

"More like we never know where the road's going to lead."

She smiles and steps forward, placing her hand my forearm. "Maybe the road will lead you somewhere new."

My eyes flicker to where her breasts almost touch my chest and back to her green eyes. Leslie never was one for subtlety. I'm about to ease my arm away when a high voice slices the air.

"Am I interrupting something?"

I pull away, turning to where Drew stands, arms crossed, looking feisty and gorgeous as ever. She's wearing a short skirt, and her long legs are smooth and tempting. Her button-up shirt is

cuffed, and her slim fingers tap on her upper arms.

She is not smiling.

"Drew. What a surprise." Leslie returns to her bag and lifts it over her shoulder. "Aren't you supposed to be at the clinic?"

My girl fires right back. "Aren't you supposed to be at the salon?"

Leslie acts bored, pushing her hair off her shoulder as she walks slowly toward the door. "I set my own hours. See you later, Gray."

Clearing my throat, I try to salvage this situation. "Thanks for the breakfast. You really don't have to keep doing—"

"I told you, I'm happy to give you whatever you need." She does a little wink and steps out the door.

Drew's blue eyes are fire when she looks at me. "Whatever you need?"

"I don't know why she keeps coming here."

"I do." Her tone is hard, but she shakes her head. "You know what? It's not my business. I just brought the car back like you asked."

I want to argue with her, tell her nothing is going on with Leslie, it is her business. But what am I thinking? We haven't had the talk we need. I haven't told her what she needs to know about me, about Danny, about all of it. I haven't had a chance to make peace with my demons. I'm still all fucked up.

"What did your dad think?" The biggest demon of all.

Her slim brows pull together, and I can tell my question hurts her somehow. "He didn't see it. He was… tired when I got home, so he went to bed."

"He didn't have any shrimp and grits?" I hope bringing up our text conversation lightens the mood.

It doesn't.

"Will this be done by tonight? I'd like to use the car this weekend."

"You have plans?"

Her eyes flash at me. "Is that *your* business?"

My jaw tightens, and I know the answer. It's not. I don't have any right to ask her these things. Not after the way I've been.

I can't help it. "Do you have a date?"

Her arms cross. "Maybe."

Anger flashes in my chest. It's the same feeling I had the night I thought she might marry someone. I might be holding back, but I'm not ready to let go. I'm a bastard.

An edge is in my voice now. "Who with?"

"Like I said before, it's none of your business." She leans forward and says the words slowly, her full pink lips taunting me.

My fingers curl against my instinct to grab her and kiss her hard. Instead, I redirect my thoughts, extend my hand. "I'll work on it today. If anything comes up, I'll give you a call."

She drops the keys in my palm. "I won't be waiting by the phone."

Turning on her heel, she storms out the door, long hair swaying down her back. She's so fucking beautiful. I'm so fucking screwed.

# CHAPTER Fifteen

## Drew

I'M SO MAD I COULD KICK LESLIE GRANT IN THE CROTCH.

Dotty is waiting with our coffees when I storm through the glass door of the clinic, but I don't even stop to take mine. I go straight to my office. Naturally Ruby is right behind me.

"Oh boy." My best friend is too excited. "I haven't seen you this mad since Rita Puckett picked Leslie's pancakes over yours in the Junior Class cook-off!"

"She hasn't changed a bit." I throw my purse on my desk and snatch up my telephone. "What's Ralph's number?"

"Noooo…" Ruby hisses. "Try the app first. I've been really happy with Bumble."

"Weren't you using Bumble when the guy farted really loud then went to the bathroom and never came back?" I level my eyes on hers.

"You know, that could have been a health issue. I'm not ready to give up on Bumble."

I grab my cell and do a quick search. "I'm not looking for a health issue. I'm looking for a wake-up call. Here it is."

I type the numbers into my office phone and wait as it rings.

"Sternwood Orchard. This is Sandra." The female voice is only moderately perky. I wonder if she's heard all the benefits of almonds as many times as I have.

"Hi, Sandra, I'm calling for Ralph. This is Drew Harris."

"One moment please." The hold music is some weird, atmospheric sounding techno.

I wait through an entire loop before Ralph finally comes on the line. "Hello, Andrea? Is everything okay?"

"Hi, Ralph, I'm fine. I was just wondering what you're doing tonight for dinner?"

"What?" He does a sputtering cough, and I imagine a spit take. "You mean for like a group-type thing?"

"Not in a group. Just you and me."

It sounds like he might have fallen out of his chair.

Ruby stands in front of my desk making pleading eyes. "Think this through, girlfriend. You have so much to live for. You're just pissed."

I cover the receiver with my hand. "I'm interested to know why everyone thinks I should go out with him. Gray included."

Ralph is talking when I come back to the line. "...up around eight?"

"Sorry, you want to pick me up at eight? Would seven be okay?"

"Sure!" His voice sounds like it did in high school—a sudden tenor. "I can pick you up at your house?"

"I think I'd rather meet you at the restaurant. Would that work?"

"Of course. I'll see you at the Watermark at seven."

"The Watermark at seven. See you then."

We disconnect the call, and Ruby closes her eyes. "This is a terrible idea!"

"Stop being so negative. Dating is about meeting other

people, trying them on to see if they fit." I grab my mouse and pull up my schedule for the day. "You of all people should know that, as many dates as you go on."

"Don't slut-shame me. You're going out with a guy for the first time in almost two years, and it's with Ralph the almond king."

"At least the Watermark is a nice place." I lift my chin in defiance. "I'm keeping my mind open. I'm open to the universe!"

"Just keep your knees closed. And your lips."

"My first appointment is here."

The Jag is parked in the lot when I arrive to pick it up at the garage. I see Gray and Billy inside, standing around the worktable. I assume they're finished for the day. A quick scan tells me Leslie isn't back.

"It's really good," Gray is saying. I can't see what they're looking at. "You should try selling them online or something. Maybe Dotty can help you."

"Maybe I can make some money. Get a hot babe to bring me breakfast too?"

"I still haven't figured out how to make that happen. Or to make it stop."

He's joking, but their conversation about Leslie pisses me off.

"Is my car ready?" I interrupt using my very best *I don't give a shit about you* tone.

They both straighten, and Gray's eyes sweep me from head to toe. I hate that my body responds every time he does that.

"Yes, ma'am." Billy hustles over to the key rack. "I changed the brake pads and checked the lines. They look good to me."

"Thank you." I take the keys from the guy's hand. "How much do I owe you?"

Sliding my purse off my arm, I do my best to stay calm when Gray closes the space between us.

"We still have more work to do." His low voice makes my stomach clench. "Just wait and we can settle up when it's done."

"I don't like running up a big bill." My voice is soft. "It could end up more than I can afford."

"I'm looking out for you."

*Don't look in his eyes. Don't look in his eyes...*

I look, and it's a lightning strike straight to my core. "I still like to know what I'm getting into."

"I know." He smiles, and I turn my back, ready to leave this place.

I can't take his hot and cold anymore. It's confusing and frustrating.

"Hang on." He catches my arm. "Where are you going tonight?"

I pull my arm out of his grip. "I'm not going through this again with you."

"I just mean... the tread on those tires is pretty worn, and it looks like rain tonight. Or maybe you're not driving?"

Fine. If he wants to play this nosey game, I'll give him what he thinks he wants. "I'm meeting Ralph at the Watermark. I'll be driving myself."

His expression tightens, but his tone remains steady. "You should be okay to make that short drive. Call my cell if you have any problems. I'll come get you."

"I'm pretty sure Dad still has roadside assistance on the car. I'll call them."

I start to go out the door, but he puts his palm against the jamb, blocking my exit. "Those guys can take forever to find you on these little country roads. If you have any trouble, call me."

"Do you mind?" I give him a hard glare, and he eases back, allowing his hand to slide down the door.

I take that opportunity to leave.

He can give the possessive act a rest.

I check in with my dad, making sure he eats some leftover shrimp and grits before I leave to meet my date. Since the Watermark is on the lake, I plan to spend the night at my grandparents' old place, depending on how late we stay. Dad seems to be stable, and he promises me he'll eat something. And get out of that damn chair.

I can't sit at home forever tending to him.

While I dress and brush my hair, I try to remember the last time I even went on a date. I want to dispute Ruby's claim, but she's right. The last time was with a guy from school… Brent something. He escorted me to a college graduation banquet, some honors recognition. Romance was not involved. I was home by ten.

Tonight I stand facing the full-length mirror, inspecting the dark green silk dress I'm wearing. It has spaghetti straps and swishes around my thighs when I move. At the last minute I grab a thin, white cardigan in case it's cool in the Watermark.

Shaking my head, I do my best independent-lady face.

"I'm not waiting on you anymore, Grayson Cole. It's over." My heart isn't in the words, so I straighten my shoulders and say it slightly differently. "I've waited for you long enough."

That sounds more convincing.

The Watermark is a long, wooden house, right on the banks of Lake Mary. It has porch views overlooking the enormous body of water and a full seafood menu. It's about as fancy as local restaurants get around Oakville.

My hair sways over my shoulders and down my back in the light breeze as I walk. The cardigan is over my arm, and the hostess guides me to the patio table where my date waits. Across the railing, a long boardwalk extends over the lake, and the sun is just starting to set.

Ralph jumps out of his seat as I approach. "Andrea, you are as beautiful as ever."

He leans forward to kiss my cheek, but the moment his lips touch my skin, my stomach turns.

He doesn't smell right.

He doesn't feel right.

Gah, Ruby was right—this is a horrible idea. What am I doing here?

I shake the doubts away. I'm an independent lady enjoying a nice dinner with a friend, not sitting at home waiting on a guy.

"Thank you, Ralph, and thanks for joining me tonight. It was such a pretty day, I just felt like doing something special."

I try to create a friendly distance between us, a way out of this situation for later. Ralph's not budging an inch.

He smiles, reaching for my hand. "And you thought of me. I can't tell you how happy that makes me. I've waited so long for this."

*Distance-creation fail. Shit.*

"We've been friends a long time, haven't we?"

*Remember the Friend Zone? You're still in it.*

But Ralph is like a duck on a june-bug. He's determined to get me. "Yes we have, a long time. I'm so ready to take it to the next level."

Thankfully our waiter appears. It's Kenny Hartnett, one of the kids from the high school. "Good evening, Mr. Stern, Miss. Harris. Can I start you out with some drinks?"

"I'd like a margarita. A double if you have it."

"We certainly do, and for you, Mr. Stern?"

Ralph gives me an adoring gaze. "I'll have what my lovely date is having."

*Oh, brother.*

"I'll have Sasha bring those out for you. Any appetizers?"

We decline, and the fellow takes off. Ralph reaches for my hand again, and I wonder how long it takes to mix up two drinks. I manage to dodge the hand holding by picking up my menu.

"Looks like they've changed their entrées."

Ralph frowns, opening his menu. "It looks the same to me. When is the last time you've been here? You never leave the house."

He doesn't have to be rude about it.

"I guess I don't get out as much. I'm usually home taking care of my dad. You know, making dinner and stuff."

*Pining over Gray.*

*Like an idiot.*

"How is your father these days? I often think of you alone in that big old place, chained to him like Estella to an aging Miss Havisham." He shakes his head, looking down. "Such a waste."

Ralph is starting to annoy me. I'm not interested in his pity, and that analogy is as weird as he is… Even if it is slightly true. An older girl returns with our drinks, and I scoop mine up quick, taking a long sip of tangy lime.

"You know, Dad's not that bad." I take another sip, spinning what's basically a big fat lie. "He's doing some self-help stuff, and I'm working on grief therapy with him."

*Take that, Ralph Stern,* I think, slurping more margarita.

Kenny is back at the table asking if we're ready to order. Ralph gets the trout almandine, no surprise, but I go for the spicy, grilled shrimp salad.

"I'm glad to hear your dad's doing better." Ralph looks out across the room. "Would you like to dance?"

A live band is starting up on the other side of the patio. They're playing slow beach music, Buffett and Marley. The last thing I want to do is hug up against Ralph. I only want one person's arms around me.

No.

I am not letting my mind sabotage what could be a nice evening. Ralph is here, being somewhat tolerable, and I intend to enjoy my dinner.

"Maybe after we eat." After I see how the rest of the meal goes.

A busboy helps Kenny bring out our entrées. Ralph orders us another round of drinks, and I dig into the salad. I'm going to have to ease off the tequila if I plan to drive myself to the lake house. It's not far, but I won't drive drunk.

I glance at Ralph's almond-encrusted fish. "What got you interested in tree nuts anyway?"

Yes, I went there, but discussing almonds is better than analyzing my home life.

"I wanted to work in the food industry, but not necessarily restaurants." He slices the flaky white fish and puts a piece in his mouth, tilting his head to the side as if testing it.

I wait as he finishes. "Good?"

He nods. "Did you know you only have to eat fifteen almonds a day to get the health benefits? You actually shouldn't eat more, because you can overdose on the good nutrients."

I've just crammed a giant grilled shrimp in my mouth, so I nod my head, doing my best to act interested.

"The old adage 'an apple a day keeps the doctor away' should be modified to 'an apple spread with almond butter.'"

"That must be great for your business." I imagine if Dotty were here, she'd say *Well, I'll be dogged*. Ruby would groan and say she's aged fifteen years.

"But you don't want to talk about almonds." He smiles in a suggestive way that makes me cringe.

"You're so wrong!" I place my hand on my chest, leaning forward. "I find almonds fascinating. It's why I wanted to talk with you more. Maybe I should prescribe them to my patients."

It's the first time I've seen Ralph disappointed by his favorite edible. "I'm not sure they've been tested for clinical use."

"Still, the health benefits are outstanding. Didn't you say that?"

"I suppose." He looks down at his fish, cutting another piece while I stab my last giant shrimp. "It's primarily in the areas of heart disease and eye health."

"Didn't you say almonds help with diabetes?"

"And lowering blood pressure. It's mostly vascular benefits." He's finishing off his fish, and the band is back from their break.

I've had my last bite of salad, and Kenny returns to the table. "Save room for desserts or coffee?"

I glance at my untouched second margarita and decline. Ralph does the same. I'm about to take this as a cue to make my escape, when he finally manages to catch my hand in his.

"Let's have that dance now."

"Oh… well… I don't know. Aren't you supposed to wait twenty minutes after eating?"

"That's swimming."

He drags me out onto the floor amidst a crowd of couples paired up and moving slow. The band plays Jimmy Buffet's "Treat Her Like a Lady," and I hope Ralph takes it as a sign, even if it is about the ocean and not a girl.

He puts one hand on my waist and pulls me close, holding my other in his. His cheek is against my temple, and he leans close. "You should always be treated like a lady, Andrea."

My nose wrinkles as we sway side to side. "Thanks."

While I endure the dance, I look over Ralph's shoulder at the sun, disappearing on the horizon. The sky is streaked in dark blue, purple, neon orange, and pink. It's really beautiful with the clouds sliding in across the face, although as I watch them, they look pretty dark.

"You think it's going to rain?" I'm thinking about the convertible Jag. I left the top down…

"I hope not. We've had enough rain for this season." Ralph actually stiffens and turns us so he can look at the sky.

I'm now facing the bar area, and as I blink absently to the

crowd. Like a magnet, my eyes are drawn to another set of equally stormy ones watching us. I lean forward to get a better look, and my stomach flips.

Gray is sitting at the bar, eyes fixed on me and scowling. His jaw tightens as he traces our movements, Ralph's hands on my body.

I try to jump back, but I've unintentionally moved closer to my date. "Andrea," he groans. His arm tightens around my waist. "Let me hold you closer."

"Oh, I'm sorry!" I struggle to move away, putting my hand against his chest. "I was just looking at something. I didn't mean to—"

"I'm sure you're nervous. It's been a long time since you were with a man, but I'll be gentle."

My eyebrows shoot up to my hairline. "Hang on a second, Ralph. I didn't mean to send the wrong message."

"No need to apologize." He leans down, pressing his lips to my head. "We were meant to be together, to merge our two families in the creation of a new one. An almond dynasty in the heart of Oakville."

"Excuse me." The deep voice startles both of us. "I'm cutting in."

Gray stands at my shoulder, glaring down at my dance partner, or should I say my pet octopus, with angry eyes.

"You may not." Ralph straightens, finally giving me room to breathe. Still, he clutches my hand and waist. "This isn't that kind of dance."

"They're all that kind of dance, now beat it, Stern." Gray reaches for me, but I step away from both of them.

"I'm tired of dancing." No lie. I'm tired of being in Ralph's arms, and there's no way I can jump back into Gray's. I'm tired of playing games. "Thank you for a lovely evening, Ralph. I'll leave my share of the check on the table."

Shaking my hands, I walk off the dance floor to where my purse hangs on the back of my chair. I've just found my wallet when Gray appears at my side.

"Here." He tosses a few twenties on the table and tries to take my arm.

I pull away again. "You're not paying for my dinner with Ralph." I try to scoop up the twenties and give them back to him, but he slips the money from my fingers and puts it on the table again.

"We need to talk."

"I can't talk to you right now." My insides are all twisted up, and my head is buzzing.

The prospect of dancing with him, of him holding me in his arms made the entire world tilt, and it's not fair after the way he's been acting since returning to Oakville. He's hot one minute then distant and pushing me away the next. I'm through getting whiplash.

"Where are you going? You can't drive."

"I'm perfectly fine to drive." I've only had one margarita. I didn't even touch the second.

We're outside the restaurant now, walking toward the boardwalk that extends over the lake. He's following me, more like walking right beside me. Tension rolls off him in waves, and I'm wondering if he'll seriously try and take my keys.

"Why are you here, Gray?" I spin around to face him. It's a huge mistake. His blue eyes are so intense. *God, please don't let me cry in front of him.*

"I was worried about the car. Those tires are old, and the transmission could go out at any moment."

"I don't believe you." My arms cross over my waist, like I'm hugging myself, holding me together. "You'd have never let me drive it off the lot."

This is a bad idea. I shouldn't be here alone with him. I need

to go to the lake house and go to bed.

He shrugs. "I also wanted to be sure Ralph didn't get too… handsy."

"I met Ralph tonight because we can't be together anymore. You're no good for me. Remember?" The words are like acid on my tongue, but they're his words. He needs to hear them again and decide if they're true.

His brow tightens, and he looks down. "I remember."

A drop of rain hits my cheek, and I wipe it away angrily. "How dare you come back here, acting like there's nothing between us, then get jealous because I'm on a date?"

"I don't like you putting yourself in danger."

I've had enough. "I'm not doing this," I say, pushing past him. "I'm leaving."

He catches my arm. "Not yet."

"Stop it." I'm losing my fight against the tears. "You left me. I was right here, and you left like you forgot all about us."

He moves in closer, heat in his tone. "I remember every detail of us."

"Prove it."

Fire is in his eyes, those stormy eyes I love, but he's still holding back, fighting me. I'm out of patience.

Raindrops fall faster on my arms. "It's starting to rain."

A flash of light in the sky distracts him, and I take the opportunity to pull away, jogging to where the Jag is parked. The top is down, so I throw my bag inside and jump behind the wheel.

"Drew, wait!" Gray jogs after me, but I floor it, throwing rocks as I rush out of the gravel parking lot. I've had it with the games. I'm not a yo-yo.

The raindrops are like pellets hitting my cheeks, and I lean forward to protect my face. It's less than two miles to the lake house, but the road is curvy and dark. This is all Gray's fault. If he hadn't been so damn pushy, I'd have been able to put the top up.

Now I'm getting soaked, my purse is getting soaked, the inside of the car…

I'm rounding the last curve when my headlights land on a small animal, a dog or a raccoon, in the middle of the road. I scream and slam on the brakes, jerking the wheel and causing the car to skid off on the gravel shoulder.

"No!" I scream again, pressing harder on the brakes.

It's too late, I spin out in the loose gravel, and the front end goes down, straight into a ditch.

"Oh!" I cry. The collision is loud, and I'm a little dazed at first.

The rain is getting harder, and I'm not getting the car out of this tonight. It's still running, so I hit the button to close the convertible top. When it's finally close enough to the windshield, I pull and jerk it into place. I snatch the keys out of the ignition, grab my purse, and slip off my shoes. Then I dash out into the brush, jogging up to the highway toward the lake house.

It doesn't take long to get there, still, I'm soaked through. Unlocking the back door, I stand in the mudroom, dripping, and searching everywhere for towels, dry clothes. I can't find anything.

We stopped coming here after Danny died. Well, my dad stopped coming after my mom died, but once Danny was gone and Gray never came back, I couldn't stand all the memories in this place. I'm not sure why I thought I could stand them tonight.

"It was a complete disaster," I grumble, stripping off my wet dress, bra, and panties, and leaving everything on the floor where I entered.

I dash through the house to my bedroom upstairs, where a thick, white robe hangs on the door of my bathroom. I pull it over my naked body and use a hand towel to catch the water from my hair.

Then I take my cardigan, dress, panties, and bra off the floor, walking slowly to the clothes drier in the back room.

Once they're started, I go to the kitchen and pour a big glass of wine while I try to salvage the contents of my purse.

My heart is a lead weight in my chest, and no matter how much I want to deny it, I loved the way Gray charged onto the dance floor tonight and told Ralph to let me go. I love his possessiveness. It's what I've been waiting for him to do since he reappeared at the grave that night.

Walking to the couch, I rub my fingers over my eyes. "What am I going to do?"

My whole body is heavy with emotions, with aching and longing for my man. I watch the lightning crawl across the sky through the tall windows facing the lake, and I sit, pulling my knees to my chest. The rain beats like a drum against the glass, and I rest my forehead on my knees.

I'm out of options. I don't know what to do anymore. Nothing will make me stop loving Gray, but how can I tear down the walls he's built around his heart?

He wants out of that prison he's constructed. I can feel it every time we're together. I can tell by the way he came for me tonight. Still, it's not something I can force him to do. As much as I know about the human mind, I know this battle is one he'll have to fight on his own.

He has to make the decision…

# CHAPTER Sixteen

## Gray

WATCHING DREW FLY OUT OF THE PARKING LOT DOES SOMETHING to my insides.

The transmission is on its last leg, those old tires need to be replaced, it's starting to rain, and she drank that margarita way too fast. I watched her do it, and my frustration at her behavior made my skin hot. I wanted to charge across the restaurant, pick her up, and take her home like some goddamn cave man.

Drew is small, and she's a girl. She shouldn't be drinking like that, and she sure as hell shouldn't be driving on a night like this.

My chest tightens, and I jog to my truck, snatching the visor down and catching the keys. I'm breathing fast as I race through the streets trying to find her. That Jag has a freakin V8 engine, and I'm driving an old-assed Chevy. She's long gone. *Fuck.*

Tension radiates through my brain, conjuring unwanted images.

These roads are dangerous.

I see the broken bodies, the blood. The screams echo in my

head. *Stop*. I do my deep breathing. I remind myself I'm in a different situation. I'm not in Africa. This is not a war zone.

Drew is in South Carolina driving too fast on a rainy night.

In a car in desperate need of new tires.

*Fuck*.

I have to get a handle on my anxiety. I came here tonight because I didn't want her alone in that car… I didn't want her alone with Ralph Stern. Not after the way he put his hands on her body at Ruby's party, touching her lower back, guiding her around the room like he owned her.

He did it again tonight on the dance floor. She tried to push away from him, and he held tighter. I should have punched him in the face, flattened him right there in front of God and everybody.

My heart beats faster, and I rub the back of my neck, trying to calm down. I need to think rationally. What am I going to do when I catch up to her? I'm going to be sure she made it there safely, then I'm going to turn this truck around and go back to Oakville. I'm going to get in my bed and sleep and keep making progress.

Only, why am I making progress here?

Why am I still in this fucking town if not for her?

It's not the garage. It's not Danny.

I'd better figure it out quick, because I'm almost to the house. It's time to make a decision.

Easing off the accelerator, I allow the truck to cruise around the big, final curve. I remember it so well from when we were kids, driving out here every weekend in the summer. I know it by heart. This curve can be tricky if you take it too fast, and it's blind. An animal or even a jogger or a biker could be in the path ahead.

My headlights illuminate the pavement, and the first thing I notice are fresh skid marks.

"What the hell?" The words slip from my lips as my throat tightens.

Putting a little more pressure on the brakes, I trace the black marks off the side of the road onto the shoulder and into the ditch.

"No…" The world tilts, and I hit my brakes hard, stopping the truck.

My headlights shine on the rear of the Jag sticking out from a deep ditch.

"Drew!" I shout, flying out of my vehicle, doing my best to breathe through the panic strangling me.

Rain pelts my face, but I rush forward, jerking on the door handle so hard my hand slips off. It's locked. The top is on, and I have to cup my hands on the windows to peer inside.

"Drew?" I don't see any blood. I don't see any broken glass or anything.

Still, these old cars don't have air bags. She could have hit that ditch and hit her head. She could be wandering in the woods with a concussion or passed out beside a tree in the pouring rain.

My chest seizes at the thought. "Drew!" I shout as loud as I can into the darkness.

I look everywhere, but I don't see signs of her going into the woods. The grasses aren't broken, and there are no tracks. I shut off the truck and shove the keys in my pocket, leaving it parked on the shoulder where she went into the ditch. Then I take off on foot toward the house.

"Drew!" I shout as loud as I can, scanning everywhere, the shoulder, the trees, the road ahead, for any signs of her collapsed or injured. "God, no. No…"

I'm having trouble breathing. I feel like my skull is coming apart. If anything happened to her… An image of Danny lying on the sand, empty hazel eyes staring at the sky flashes across my mind, and my stomach grabs.

No.

That cannot happen.

"DREW!" I scream again, running faster toward the house.

The rain drenches me, preventing me from being able to see. I wipe the rivulets off my brow, blotting my eyes with my wet sleeve, trying to avoid falling myself.

The house rises in the night ahead of me, and I run faster when I see the lights on downstairs. Could she be okay? I dig in with my heels, pushing faster as I run to the house.

The back door is locked, and I beat on it with my fist, twisting the handle. "DREW!" I'm shouting at the top of my lungs. "DREW!"

A flurry of noise comes from inside, and I see a shadow running to the door. It flies open, and I stagger back, using my hands to wipe away the rain mixed with heat from my eyes. God, am I crying? My throat is raw from screaming her name.

"Gray?" Her eyes are wide, terrified, I'm sure, at the sight of me.

I don't even hesitate. I can't.

Rushing forward, I grab her to me, hugging her tiny body so close against mine. "Drew… Are you okay? Are you hurt?"

I'm breathing so hard, but my cheek is against hers. My nose is in her hair. I'm holding her to me, holding her body to mine like it's the last thing on Earth. It's the only thing I have to keep my broken self alive. I need to know she's whole if only to keep putting one foot in front of the other.

"I'm okay." Her small hands are on my waist. She reaches up to wrap her arms around my neck as I lift her off her feet. "Are you okay?"

"Drew." I can't stop saying her name. I'm shaking with adrenaline, and I might be a little crazy right now.

She's safe in my arms, and it's hitting me hard. I've needed to be in this place, holding her, since the day that truck exploded. Since before that truck exploded. Drew's the only one who can heal my soul.

"It's okay, Gray. I just skidded off the shoulder. A raccoon or something was in the road… Anyway, I'm not hurt. I'm okay."

My arms are tight around her, and her fingers thread in my hair, stroking the pain away, holding me just as tightly as I'm holding her. I force my grip to relax. I try to let her go and step back, but the robe she's wearing slips open.

She's still in my arms, when I notice she's completely nude underneath. Her perfect breasts, those perfect little nipples, strain at me. Her legs cross, and she's every dream I've ever had standing right here. My erection is alive and straining in my pants.

I groan with the forces surging through my belly. "Drew." It's a broken noise. "You're so beautiful."

Her hair hangs in damp waves around her cheeks, and her crystal blue eyes sparkle with tears. She blinks, and one falls down her face. "I need you, Gray. I've needed you so long. Please don't leave me again."

My lips crash into hers with a low noise. She's off her feet, and I carry her forward into the kitchen, pushing her ass onto the small table under the window.

Her hands are on me, moving just as fast, pulling at the hem of my shirt, jerking it higher until I pause to rip it off my body.

We both let out a low moan of satisfaction when our bare chests meet. Her soft breasts flatten against my hard body. It's heaven.

"Drew…" The word escapes on a ragged whisper.

Her hands are on my cheeks, guiding my lips back to hers, which I hungrily take. I'm kissing her hard, pulling her lips with mine. She moans, and my erection aches. I need to be inside her. I need to feel her all around me.

Water drips off my hair onto her neck, onto her shoulders, I put my mouth on her beautiful skin and kiss, bite, suck.

"Yes," she hisses as I move lower, taking a tight nipple into my mouth.

I flick my tongue back and forth over that hard little bud and her body rises up to meet mine.

"Gray, yes... please." Her body undulates beneath mine like the rhythm of some primal music, and I feel her fingers pulling at my waistband.

My hands only leave her long enough to unfasten my wet jeans. I shove them down, low enough to allow my erection to spring free. Her cool fingers wrap around me, and she guides me to her core.

"Are you sure?" I groan, dying inside. If she says no, I don't know how I'll survive.

"Yes," she moans.

Our mouths fuse together, tongues entwining as I push into her slippery core. It's so hot and tight, gripping my dick. My hand slams onto the table. I break away with a low groan, sparks flashing behind my lids.

Her hands are on my ass, pulling me closer. Her pelvis bucks, and I rock my hips, thrusting harder, pumping faster. She moans, her fingernails scratching the skin of my hips, my thighs, as she pulls me, moving her body with mine, driving me deeper into her core.

"Drew..." It's a desperate prayer.

I can't hold out. It would take more strength than I could ever possess to prolong this, not after how long we've been apart.

The orgasm snakes up my legs, and my back stiffens. I arch, letting go with a loud moan, pulsing into her beautiful body. She shudders, thighs tightening around my waist, her pussy pulling, milking me.

"Gray." Her voice is a breathy cry.

I brace my body just above hers, so as not to crush her. The waves of pleasure blanket my mind. Her beautiful scent, her beautiful body, her beautiful eyes, lips, breasts. Her hands glide over my shoulders, my neck, my cheeks.

"Drew." I've gone from prayer to worship.

Another pulse. The orgasm pours my soul into hers. We were made to be this way. She was made to be my mate. *I love her…*

I can't deny the words or what they do to my soul.

It takes a few moments for us to fumble our way back to reality. I haven't let her go since I broke through that door, panicked and desperate to know she was okay.

Drew pushes up to sitting, and I release her, allowing her to rise. Even though I've let her go, my arms are still beside her. I still want to hold her close.

She reaches out to touch my neck, resting her sweet face against my chest. I can't deny us what we need. My arms are around her again.

# CHAPTER Seventeen

## Drew

My insides throb from Gray's invasion like a deep longing has finally been filled. My thighs burn from exertion, and my breasts are sore from his kisses and sucks. If I looked in the mirror, I'm sure I'd see red marks all over my skin.

He was like a wild animal when I opened the door. It broke my heart, but it also filled it with desire. He was desperate, determined to find me, to save me… then to fuck me.

Finally.

I lift my cheek off his bare chest and cup his face. "Will you spend the night?"

The muscle in his jaw moves as if a shred of resistance still lingers. A trickle of fear moves through my chest, until he nods. I watch as he pushes the wet jeans down his legs and gathers them along with his shirt.

His ass is so fine, tight and square. I chew my lip as I watch him walk to the back room where the washer-dryer set is located. When he comes back, I rub my legs together, admiring the lines in his chest, in his stomach. The way his dick sways, long and heavy

between his muscular thighs, coming back to life when our eyes meet. I don't even try to hide the lust on my face. I want him again.

"Come with me." He takes my hand, and I slide off the table.

The robe is still on my shoulders, but it's open. I want him to see my body. I take a step toward him, and thick wetness drips onto my inner thighs. His eyes darken at the sight.

My lip goes under my teeth. "You didn't use a condom."

"I haven't been with anyone but you."

Another wave of joy hits me so hard, I almost sit down. I'd wanted it to be true, but I was afraid to ask.

"Me either." It's a quiet confession, almost shy.

He lifts me off my feet, carrying me to the stairs. His expression is set, determined, and I put my arms around his neck again, resting my face on his shoulder.

My body hums with excitement, and he doesn't stop until we're in my bathroom, where he sets me down again, picking up a washcloth. It's damp, and he uses it to clean me. I'm not sure why, since his cock is like a steel rod pointing at me.

Tossing the cloth aside, he straightens, placing his thumb under my jaw and lifting my face to his. "I want to kiss you again."

Without a word, I rise onto my toes, holding his shoulders and pressing my lips to his. His warm mouth opens mine, and his tongue sweeps inside. Another wave of happiness fills my chest. My eyes are closed, and I cling to him. He's my stability through this overwhelming reunion.

I'm off my feet again. His strong hands grip my ass, and I wrap my legs around his waist as he walks us to my bedroom. I hug him close, pressing my breasts against his rock-hard chest.

"I want to be inside you again." It's a low vibration against my cheek.

"Please." I whisper, sliding my lips along his jaw, up to his ear. I lean closer so my lips can graze his skin. "I've missed you so much."

His grip on my ass tightens, and it's thrilling and intoxicating. I'm on my back, and he slides into the bed beside me, his palm flat against my stomach, gliding higher to cup my breast.

"I dreamed of this every night." He leans down to kiss my lips, my jaw, my neck, before pulling a nipple into his mouth.

The sensation registers straight to my core, making me moan. "I told you how I felt, how I would dream of you."

His hand slides down my stomach, moving to my inner thigh before changing direction. It glides higher until he's touching me, teasing that sensitive bud with gentle strokes.

My back arches, and I press into him. "Yes…" I whisper.

In one smooth movement, he parts my legs, moving between my thighs, and gliding his cock into my slippery core. His arms are on both sides of me, holding me against him as we rock. Our mouths meet, and it's hungry. Our kisses chase each other, lips pulling, teeth nipping.

This time we're going slower, our bodies swaying in time, like waves on the ocean. We're kissing, touching, exploring, until at some point, we reach the tipping point. He places a hand on the bed beside me and starts moving faster, harder, with fierce determination.

I lift my hips so he can drive deeper, rolling my eyes closed as I feel him hit that spot deep inside. It registers like a shock of pleasure to the base of my spine.

"Gray… oh…" My insides erupt in a shower of orgasm, fluttering and gripping.

"Drew," he groans, thrusting faster.

He's right there with me, rocking deeper until his muscles flex. His body goes rigid, and he holds, pulsing, groaning even deeper. It's so sexy, another flutter of orgasm breaks through my insides.

His lips are on my cheek, pulling the skin in a kiss. He moves higher, behind my ear, and I moan, my back arches as waves of

bliss flood my lower stomach.

I feel his cheeks lift in a smile. "That spot still works."

Warmth fills my chest at his smile, at having him here with me, inside me, remembering where to touch me, kiss me. I hold him closer, smiling so big my cheeks ache. "You know all the places I love. You found them all."

He pulls away, lifting onto an elbow and gazing down at my face with so much affection. "Any new freckles?"

My stomach squeezes at his question. My eyes heat, and I have to blink away the mist. I don't want to cry. I'm so happy.

"I don't know. You have to check." Lifting my chin I turn my face side to side in the light of my bedside lamp.

"Ned is still there." His finger traces the side of my nose. "What's this?"

"What?"

His lips touch my temple. "A new one."

My eyes slide to the side. "You're kidding."

"We have a new freckle right here. Tanya the temple freckle."

"I'm not sure that one's new."

"Are you trying to say I don't know every freckle on your face?"

I can't help it, I start to laugh. I'm too happy to hold it back, only it pushes him out. We both make a sad noise, which makes me laugh more. When I catch his eyes, he's smiling, gathering me closer in his arms and kissing my lips.

"We need to get you cleaned up." He pushes off the bed, taking that fine ass into my bathroom again.

I lay there listening as he runs water in the tub. "I don't think we can both fit in there," I call.

He's back, ignoring my concerns. That cloth is in his hand again, and he touches me gently with it before lifting me in his arms. "Come on."

In the bathroom, he lowers me to my feet, and I watch as he

steps into the foamy water.

"Where did you find bubbles?" I look around and see an old bottle of spa gel. "I'm pretty sure that's three years old."

"Still smells good." He sits with his back to the wall.

I step into the tub, between his legs. "How are we doing this?"

The fixture is just wide enough for him. I'm about to laugh, but he guides me down to sitting, facing him. A fresh cloth is in his hands, and he swirls a bar of soap in it, creating lather before smoothing it along the tops of my shoulders, down my arms, softly over my breasts.

His eyes are so serious as he follows the path of his hands. He looks at me as if I'm something so precious. I reach out and touch his cheek, tracing my fingers over his lips, which pucker out to kiss them.

"What happened tonight?" I ask in a soft voice.

His eyes wince ever so slightly, like I pressed a tender spot. I'm afraid he won't tell me, but he does.

"This body is so precious to me." His voice is quiet, thick. "I couldn't stop seeing it broken, bleeding. I couldn't stop seeing you hurt."

The pain in his voice aches in my chest. I reach out to hold his neck, putting my forehead against his. "I'm sorry. I shouldn't have run away from you."

His hands stop washing me, and go to my waist. Palms against skin, we hold each other, and for a moment, we're quiet, breathing each other's breath, knowing we're here together.

Until he clears his throat and straightens. His blue eyes are stormy again, pulling away. "I guess I overreacted."

My brow furrows. I want to stop him from saying these things. I want to tell him if he's suffering from PTSD, it's nothing to be ashamed of. I can help him, or help him find help. He doesn't give me the chance.

Scooping water in his hands, he washes the foam away. Next

he takes both my palms and helps us stand, catching a thick towel off the lavatory.

"Are you hungry?" He quickly dries his body before passing it to me. "I'm starving."

"Did you sit at the bar the whole time just watching us?"

"I kept wanting to leave, but shit kept happening."

I think back over the evening as I slip into a pair of lacy boy shorts. "Nothing happened. We talked about almonds."

His loud laugh makes me smile and look up. The towel is tied around his waist, and he's just so delicious. I walk over and put my hand on his stomach.

"I missed your laugh."

He covers my hand with his, lifting it to his lips for a kiss. "Let's eat before I get other ideas."

"I don't mind other ideas." My voice is a little pouty, although, to be honest, I have worked up an appetite.

Gray is out of the bathroom and across the hall. "Any chance I left any clothes here from before?"

I'm in my bedroom, pulling out an oversized long-sleeved button-up shirt. The closer I look, I'm sure it probably once belonged to either Gray or Danny.

"You're bigger now than when you left." I walk out to the hallway, trying to think. All of our clothes are in the dryer. "My dad might have something that would fit you."

"It'd be pretty old." He follows me to the other side of the second floor, to a room that hasn't been used in ages.

I open the drawer, and the scent of ancient cologne meets my nose. It's something from another time. I shuffle through, only finding a few pair of old socks and a cummerbund.

"What in the world?" My voice trails off, but Gray interrupts me.

"Check this out." He pulls out a shirt that has a big Fayz logo on the front. "I think this will fit."

He pulls it on, and I dig out a pair of gray sweatpants. "Try these."

"Perfect." He steps back, and I have to agree.

The tee is just snug enough to show off his muscles, and I'm not sure those sweatpants can be legal the way his junk swings low in them.

"You'd better stop looking at me like that." He chuckles, catching my chin and kissing me quickly on the lips. "I'm going to see what's left here to eat."

"I ordered some groceries earlier today. They should have been delivered."

He heads out of the bedroom, and I run back to grab a pair of micro cutoffs before following him downstairs. I straighten the bed and put the towels on the rack, and when I arrive in the kitchen, he's opened a bottle of red wine and poured two glasses.

"I see you found them."

A loaf of bread is on the counter, and he's in the refrigerator, pulling out a block of cheese and butter.

"This all seems pretty fresh."

"Yeah, I was saying they were delivered earlier today."

He nods, clicking on the stovetop. "Smart."

I lean against the counter. The wine is in my hand, and I take a sip, nodding at the flavor. "It's good, ripe cherries."

He has four pieces of bread arranged in a square and quickly covers them with thick slices of cheese. I walk over to the speaker and turn on the music. It's Marvin Gaye, and he glances up, giving me a sly smile before arranging our food in the frying pan.

The delicious aroma of warm butter and melting cheese makes my stomach growl, and I take another sip of wine. It's so homey and warm, watching him make us supper. I have so many questions to ask him, so much I want to know, but tonight we're taking it slow.

"Tell me about Dover." I sit on the edge of the bar, watching

him work. "Is it pretty? I've never been."

He leans down to check the food, and his dark hair falls over his brow. I want to curl it around my finger. He straightens and our eyes meet. It makes my stomach flutter.

"I guess. It's historic, old." He shrugs and uses the spatula to flip the sandwiches. "We weren't really in the city proper. Their place is a little north, on the coast."

"It sounds pretty."

"I didn't get around much. I was mostly at the hospital."

"Oh." I let the questions go.

I want to let him open to me in his own time. Now it feels like I was digging into his past. He scoops the sandwiches onto a plate and cuts them in half. Then he switches off the heat, moving the cooking utensils into the sink.

I'm waiting, sitting on the bar when he walks over to me, smiling and holding the plate. "See what you think."

He sets the plate beside me, and I lift a hot, drippy triangle of bread. He does the same. We both take careful bites from the corners, and my mouth fills with tangy, warm, comforting grilled cheese.

I make a little groan as I drop the hot slice on the plate again. "It's so good!"

He nods, grinning, then sets his piece on the plate again, stepping between my legs and wrapping his arms around my waist. It's so sudden and unexpected, my breath catches. I wrap my arms around his shoulders and hold him.

Our chests are together, and I can feel his heart beating strong. It's only a momentary hug. He steps away, smiling into my eyes as he lets me go and picks up his sandwich again.

I feel a little wobbly from his display of affection. "What was that for?"

He takes another, bigger bite. "Just needed to feel you in my arms again."

My entire body melts at his words, at his touch. I'm a pillar of sensation, waiting for another hit of my favorite drug. It's so seductive.

Al Green sings softly in the background about staying together, and Gray finishes his sandwich in three bites. He takes a long sip of wine, and puts the glass down.

"It's your favorite song." I've only eaten half of my sandwich. My stomach is so tingly, I'm not sure I can eat, even thought my shrimp salad abandoned me an hour ago.

"One of them." He smiles down at me. "Finished?"

"For now."

He takes the plates and puts them in the sink. While his back is turned, I unbutton another button on my shirt, so it can easily slip off one shoulder.

When he's done, he returns to where I sit, standing between my thighs again. I put a hand on his shoulder, watching him, mesmerized by him like always. His eyes trace the line of my collar bone, and my breath is a little faster.

He clinks the wine glass in my hand. "Cheers."

We both take another sip, and his brows pull together. They always do that when he's focusing on something. Gray can be so focused.

"What are you thinking about?" I ask, hoping he might open up more, let me all the way inside those walls.

"What happened to your dad?"

It's not the question I expected and not a topic I really want to discuss. Still, if I want him to open up to me…

"He never was right after Mamma died." I tilt the wine glass side to side, choosing my words. "You know that."

"I remember he didn't like to leave the house." His warm hand is on my bare leg, sliding up and down in a soothing way.

"He started drinking more after Danny died. He kind of went on a bender. I think he was trying to kill himself."

Gray's eyes wince as if I kicked him really hard in the stomach. He's quiet. He takes another sip of wine.

Finally, he speaks. "He never liked me."

"I'm not sure that's exactly right. He was just over protective about me. After Mamma."

He shakes his head. "He said I'd ruin you and run off."

"Well, it's too late for that." I smile, resting my hand on the top of his. "I'm already ruined."

His smile doesn't reach his eyes. "You used to say you wanted to help him. Have you?"

My chin drops, and I hate telling him the truth. "Not as much as I'd like. He's pretty resistant to change."

"I'm sure this, what we're doing here," He waves a finger back and forth between us. "Wouldn't make him happy at all."

I catch his finger in my fist and hold it against my chest. "The demons my daddy is fighting were around way before I met you. He needs help. "

He twists his finger so my hand is in his. "It's late. Let's get some rest."

"Will the truck and the Jag be okay tonight?" I look up at the clock and see it's after midnight.

"Don't worry about anything tonight."

He helps me off the bar, and in my bare feet, my head comes to the center of his chest. I loosen one more button before reaching to put my hand on his neck. It causes my shirt to fall back, open more, showing off my lace bra underneath.

He's so strong. His body has filled out, and he's a man now, a sexy man I want to seduce. I slide my fingers down the muscles in his neck.

"Take me to bed," I whisper.

He doesn't make me ask twice.

# CHAPTER Eighteen

## Gray

LYING IN THE COOL NIGHT, THE LIGHT OF A FULL MOON CASTS THE room in silver, and I trace my finger down the line of Drew's back. Her skin is like silk, it's creamy and pale like the exposed pine beams in the vaulted ceiling over our heads.

This old place was built well. It's a classic structure, sturdy and strong. But even it's showing age, cracks in need of repair. It reminds me of myself, another cracked thing in her life. Drew is a princess, but her kingdom needs so much work. The men who should be her heroes are all broken.

Her daddy.

Me…

My mind returns to my breakdown earlier when I found her car on the side of the road. Waves of shame filter through my stomach at the memory of how messed up I was.

I couldn't stop the flashes of fear, the abject terror I might find her the way I found all of those men in my unit. It shook me to the core to think of this beautiful body broken.

I was so fucking out of control. I barely remember running to this house. I do remember scanning the road, the woods, the grass, frantically searching for any sign she might have lost her way, for any signs of blood.

Another flash of worry hits my chest. When I found her here… I held her so tightly, I'm surprised I didn't crush her. God, I was shaking in her arms. My brow tenses. I can't burden her with this mess I've become. I can't make her take care of me, too.

Her dad said I would ruin her life, but I don't think he meant by being a burden on her. I should be able to take care of her, not the other way around.

Then she asked me not to walk away.

I've never been able to tell Drew no, but I'm not sure either of us expected our yes to be so primitive. After so much time apart, when I saw her body, the way she's matured and changed… I was demanding, possessive, and wild. I couldn't get enough. All my fears took a back seat to claiming her again.

Even tonight, after everything we'd done, I wanted more. I wanted to taste her. She asked me to take her to bed, and I lifted her in my arms, carrying her upstairs to this bedroom. Those cut-offs had been taunting me all through dinner, exposing the lower curve over her cute little ass.

I took my time sliding them down her long legs, before kissing my way up them again, moving between them, sliding my tongue up, down, around, and all over that tight little bud that makes her scream.

I love the way she comes on my mouth, her back arched, and her thighs trembling, her fingers fisting the sheets, my hair. She moans my name like she's casting a spell. I'm under her spell.

I went to heaven when I sank into her again, so hot and soft and clenching.

Lying in the dark, holding her now, the guilt fights back with every heartbeat. Her daddy is even sicker than when I left, and

it's because of Danny. I have to tell her I was driving the truck. I have to tell her about the fight we had, and how I didn't go to him right away. I let him die on the desert sand alone.

Every one of those men whose lives were in my care as I drove that truck died.

"Gray?" Drew's soft voice cuts through my self-flagellation. Her sweet hand caresses my cheek. "Can't you sleep?"

I reach up and cover her hand with mine. Once again, she's saving me from myself. "I'll sleep."

"Okay." She moves her cheek against my chest, and I hold her closer in my arms.

Her breath evens out to a warm whisper across my skin. She's so beautiful, so perfect in my arms.

I want to pretend there's nothing more to say, nothing that might cause her to blame me, to hate me. I want to pretend I'm not broken, half the man I used to be. But I am broken.

Somehow I've got to get free of this pain, this prison I'm living in every day. Only then can I come to her like I should be, whole, and ask her forgiveness.

# CHAPTER *Nineteen*

## *Drew*

A COOL BREEZE PUSHES THROUGH THE OPEN WINDOW OF GRAY'S truck as he drives us back to town. I look over at his dark hair flickering across his steel blue eyes, and when those pretty, pretty eyes meet mine, he gives me a little grin. A swirl of warmth surrounds me.

Everything changed this weekend, from his appearance at my door, wild desire and relief in his eyes, all the way to this morning, when he woke me before dawn, sinking deep between my thighs.

He reaches out to place his hand on my leg. I'm wearing my cutoffs again, and his palm rests so casually, so close to the part of me still tender from every time we made love. Goose bumps skate across my skin, and I lay my hand over his, threading our fingers, welcoming his touch.

His protective possession is so familiar—he feels the same, he smells the same—but I can tell he's holding something back. I still haven't made it completely inside the walls.

What will it take for him to be fully mine again?

"I'll drop you off at your house, then I'll head back to take care of the Jag." He gives me a brief glance before returning his eyes to the road. "Hopefully, there's not much damage."

"Can you fix it if there is?" I hate the thought of telling my dad I bent his precious car.

"Depends. If it's just a part that needs to be replaced, probably." The muscle in his jaw moves as he thinks. "I don't do body work, but I can find someone who does. Maybe Billy knows someone. I'll let you know."

"I don't know how I'm going to pay you for all of this. I hope you take credit cards."

He doesn't answer. He just grins and his eyes drift out the window again. His grip on my inner thigh flexes gently. My hand is still over his, and I slide our fingers together.

"Remember when you saved me from the snake?" He seemed larger than life to me then. He still does now.

"Vividly." He chuckles. "You were so little. You were so loud."

"Hey!" I push his hand off me, and he laughs, putting it right back. "I was scared."

"You were only eight, but you picked me up and carried me to my mom."

"Right. You were heavy, too." He gives me a side-eye, but I only shake my head, holding my hair out of my face with the arm that's rested on my open window.

"Then you sat with me after Mamma died." The air in the truck feels quieter, more solemn. "You were so good to me."

His fingers move, stroking my skin tenderly, carefully. "I knew how it would be for you. How much it would hurt and for how long."

My hand moves to his arm, up his shoulder. "It's my turn to sit with you. I want to be there for you."

His smile tightens, and he looks out the window again. His hand doesn't move off my thigh. I feel like we're so close. Still,

it's not complete.

We pull into the neighborhood, and I know he'll retreat like before. Still, I've made good progress. I can get us back to here. Then it's a matter of moving forward.

He stops on the street at the end of my driveway. I grab my bag and my now-dry clothes. I'm not sure what he'll do sitting here in front of my house, with neighbors all around. Our eyes meet, and he reaches for me.

A surge of joy pushes me into his arms. His kisses are sweet, not devouring or passionate. A peck on my nose, on my lips.

"I'm heading back over to check out the Jag. I'll have it home for you tonight."

"I trust you." No truer words.

Another squeeze, and he lets me go. I hate climbing out of the cab, but I know I must. "I really enjoyed last night." I say through the open window when I close the door.

"Me too." His smile is touched with sadness. I hate it.

"Want to go out again next Friday?" I don't mind making the first move. I want him to know my arms are wide open.

"Let's see how the week goes."

"Okay."

He waits, watching as I slowly walk up the driveway, feeling like a girl, feeling like a woman. Knowing I'm so deep in love. I turn to walk backward, watching him as I get closer to the house.

I blow him a kiss, and this time his smile is a little less sad. He catches it and drives away.

Inside, my dad surprises me in the kitchen. "You're up!" I try not to sound too stunned. I don't want to embarrass him. "Did you sleep well last night? Everything okay by yourself here?"

"The house was quiet." He's holding a container of orange juice, which I take as a good sign. "How was your date?"

"It started kind of terrible, but then it got better."

He nods as if this is the usual course of events. "How is the

lake house?"

"Needs some work, but otherwise, same as always." I switch on the coffee pot, and sneak another glance.

My father's eyes have deep lines in the corners and dark circles underneath. His skin is the sickly sallow of a person who doesn't get in the sun much.

"I'd be happy to drive you out to check on the place if you want." My optimism knows no bounds, I guess.

"Sure." He does a little cough-throat clearing. "We'll go next weekend."

It's the same answer every time. He says he'll go then he backs out at the last minute.

"How's the Jag?"

"Oh." I almost drop my mug at that question. "It's ahh… well…"

That gets his attention. He squares off, facing me with one hand on his hip. "Andrea. What happened?"

I feel sick to my stomach. "Well, you know how it was raining last night? A stupid dog or raccoon or something ran out in front of me, and I sort of went off the road." Angry eyes flash at me, and I charge forward. "It's okay! I'm getting it fixed. Gray is picking it up, and he thinks he can probably repair the damage. The car needs new tires."

"Gray." He speaks the word like it tastes bad. "He finally dragged his sorry ass back to town? For how long?"

The sickness in my stomach is replaced with burning knots. I hate the way he talks about my love. "I don't know, Daddy, but Gray's a good guy. He's a hero."

"Ha." It's a bitter retort. "Some hero. He let half his unit get killed in a bomb explosion."

"Stop it! That is not fair. It wasn't his fault. The officers said it was an accident." My voice goes loud and high, defensive. "Listen to yourself. Are you suggesting Gray planted the bomb?"

"I did some research. His team was in charge of checking that road, making sure there were no explosives in their path before they left."

I've heard this story, too, and it still makes me nauseated. "That's completely unrealistic. They were being watched constantly. Some terrorist probably went right behind them planting more bombs."

My father makes a dismissive noise, and starts for the liquor cabinet. I follow him, beating him to it. "Wait. Please wait just a minute. I didn't mean to upset you."

He doesn't look at me. "You haven't done anything to upset me."

I catch his hand as he tries to reach around me. "Would you do something for me? Please?"

"Don't start with me today, Andrea. I'm not in the mood." He tries to move my body, but I put my hands behind my back and hold the edge of the cabinet. "Do you mind?"

"Please just listen to me a minute. I've been thinking about what you said about nothing being anonymous in this town." Like everyone doesn't already know my dad is a notorious alcoholic.

"What about it?" He's growing impatient, the withdrawals grinding his teeth.

"What if there was a pill you could take to help you quit drinking. Would you be willing to try it?"

"No." He tries to move past me again, but I slide to the left.

"You wouldn't even try it?"

"I like drinking, Andrea. I have no intention of stopping."

I'm breathing harder, anger coursing in my veins, from the way he talks about Gray to the way he insists on destroying his body. Still, I know from past experience of having this conversation with him, shouting and crying will only shut him down even more.

"You're all I've got now, Dad. It's just you and me."

He stiffens, and I know I caught him off guard with this approach. "That's not true, you have Ruby."

*And Gray*, which I don't add.

"She's not my family. You're my only family." Reaching out, I hold his hand. "Would you just try the pills and see if they help you? You don't have to stop drinking entirely. Just cut down some?" By like ninety-five percent.

He stands back, studying me closely with those judgmental eyes, those eyes so full of hate and hurt and defensiveness. "I'll think about it."

A smile breaks across my lips. I can barely believe he softened this much. "I'll get some samples from the clinic for you to try."

"Don't go talking about me up there at that clinic."

Again, I have to roll my eyes at his cluelessness. Does he really believe nobody knows what he does?

"I will not be talking about you at the clinic."

He continues past me now, taking out the whiskey as he grumbles under his breath. I sigh, trying to reassure myself I've made an important first step as I watch him pour a double into the thick crystal tumbler.

"I'll make us something hearty for dinner tonight. Beef stew sound good?"

"Eh." He does a dismissive shrug as he greedily takes a long sip of the amber liquid.

He tops off the glass again and leaves the room. I collapse onto the bar wondering if I'll even see him again today.

# CHAPTER *Twenty*

*Gray*

**B**ILLY IS HANGING AROUND THE GARAGE WHEN I GET THERE. "HEY, man, got time to come with me and fish that Jag out of a ditch?"

"What the fuu…" A worried look crosses his dark eyes, but I wave a hand.

"It's okay. You can say what the fuck around me. It's very much a what the fuck situation." I wave for him to climb inside the cab, and we start back out of town toward Lake Mary.

"We should have replaced those tires." Billy has another stick in his hand, and I figure I caught him mid-whittling. "The rain makes these roads extra slick."

We get closer, and I see the site that nearly destroyed me last night. Those red taillights sticking up from the gully.

"Ah, shit," I grumble. "I hope we can get it out without needing a tow."

Both of us walk over to the deep trench. "We can get it out." Billy jumps down, going under the vehicle. "It's not too bad from

under here, he calls. This tree limb kept it from hitting the rocks."

Damn, I can't express how happy I am at that news. I saw the worry on Drew's face when I dropped her off. I know her dad loves this car, and I don't want him having a setback or giving her shit. It was just as much my fault she was driving too fast on this road in the rain. I shouldn't have pushed her.

"I'll come down there and lift it. Help me attach it to the truck."

It takes us less than a half hour to get the car out of the ditch and back to the garage. Billy hangs around a bit longer, helping me check the axel and the oil pan, any parts that could have been damaged.

"The tires will be in tomorrow." Billy has an app on his phone that syncs with our shipping information.

"You'll have to show me how to do that." I look over his shoulder at all the useful information he's carrying around.

"Dude, you're so old." He starts to laugh and I punch him on the shoulder. "Ow! Don't hurt me old man!"

We both laugh, and I like the easy camaraderie we're developing. "Show me what you're working on now."

"Ahh," he grins. "Something inspired by our breakfast bunny."

I frown, but when he pulls out the cylinder of wood, I see it's carved in the shape of a woman's torso, shoulders to knees. The breasts are round and pointy, but he's only made a curved line in the lower area.

"Looks like the bow of a ship. You're really into this Moby Dick stuff." I give him a prod with my elbow, and he pushes back.

"I don't know what a moby is, but I don't want it on my dick."

I'm heading back to the office so I can send Drew a text. "Actually, *Moby* means something big or important."

"Shit. In that case, my dick is Moby. Magnum Moby."

"All right, get out of here with that."

He shuts the hood and takes off, waving back and calling something about Moby Monster. I've already picked up my phone, getting a little charge at the prospect of making contact with her again.

My drug of choice is back, and I smile thinking of reading her words, touching her through the ether.

***Me: Jag is out and at the garage. No damage to the body or paint. Looks like you got lucky, kid. I'll drop it off later, but no road trips before new tires. I'll do it Monday.***

I wait a few minutes, watching the little dots indicating she's typing. It's so easy to fall back into this with her. To fall back into these feelings.

***Drew: You are a lifesaver. Can't wait to tell Dad.***

***Me: Was he pissed at you?***

I don't like the idea of her dad talking to her the way he used to talk to Danny, especially if he's drinking. Danny was a shitty drunk.

***Drew: He wasn't happy, but I distracted him by talking about you.***

That actually makes me laugh.

***Me: I'm sure that went really well.***

***Drew: It went okay. Sometimes he's more open than others.***

***Me: I've never known your dad to be open when it came to me.***

***Drew: I'm open when it comes to you.***

For a moment, I only look at the words. I know what she's saying. Drew's a smart girl, and even though we've been close, she knows I haven't told her everything.

***Drew: Gray?***

***Me: Sleep well, Drew-baby.***

***Drew: I'd sleep better if you were here.***

I confess, that puts a little rise in my pants. I shake my head, grinning.

***Me: I'm certain your dad would not be open to me in your bed.***

***Drew: We can discuss it over breakfast.***

I'm full-on grinning now.

***Me: Let's build to that, okay?***

***Drew: Oooh kay.***

***Me: Goodnight. Bring the car Monday.***

***Drew: I will. (kiss emoji)***

I need a drink.

It's still early, so I walk up to the Red Cat pub, and push through the ancient glass door. Mack used to come to this place after work when he was having trouble sleeping. I had to come here and wake him up once, walk him home. I was only about sixteen, but even Mack had dark days.

It's dusty and old inside, and I know this place's reputation. The drinks are stiff and cheap, and the company is decent. A jukebox with actual vinyl records is placed against the back wall. It's usually spinning Frank Sinatra or Tony Bennett, but tonight it's Elton John's, "Mamma Can't Buy You Love."

I look around, and sure enough, Steve "Dagwood" Magee is at the bar, one of the biggest Elton John fans I know. We weren't as close as I was with Danny in high school, but we were good enough friends. Hell, I wasn't as close to anyone as I was with Danny. The thought is a kick to the gut.

The minute Steve sees me, he straightens up, smiling broadly. "I'll be damned, it's our hero. Mose, I'm buying Gray here a drink. Anything he wants. Have a seat, friend."

I wince at him calling me *hero*. "Hey man, you don't have to buy me a drink—"

"Stop!" He holds up a hand. "It's my first chance to welcome you home properly. That dinner was nice, but I was all the way at the other end of the fucking table."

It's possible my friend is a little buzzed.

Mose stops in front of me. He's been the bartender at the

Red Cat since the stone ages, and he looks as old and dusty as everything in here.

"Okay, hero. Pick your poison."

"Whisky up." I give him a thumbs up.

"A man's drink." Steve slaps my back. "You're a good man, Gray. I'm damn proud I know you. Have I told you that?"

Mose slides a tumbler of whiskey in front of me, and I lift it, taking a sip. "Why are you telling me now?"

"Look at all you've done." Steve waves his arm around. "First, you went to college and kicked textbook ass. Then you went to Africa and kicked terrorist ass. Then you came home and opened the garage. You hired that little Mexican kid—"

"You're proud of that?" I cut him off before he has a chance to get offensive. He's a good guy. "Some people might say opening a garage is wasting my education."

"Bastard people, Gray. Assholes." He leans forward. "We need a good garage in this town. Mack had vision."

"It's honest work." I look at my stained hands. "I don't know that I'll do it forever."

"Did that fucker Ralph Stern say something to you? I swear to shit I'm going to shove a bag of almonds up his ass next time I see him."

That makes me chuckle. "It's okay. He actually offered me a job."

"Don't do it, bro. That guy's a weirdo. He's obsessed if you ask me."

I can't argue with him, so I don't. I don't get a chance.

"Say, you any good at fixing up old cars?" He grips my shoulder.

"I don't do body work, but I helped Mack restore a few engines, mechanical shit. Why?"

"My friend Taylor Dawes has an old Chevy Bel Air he wants to restore. I could send him your way if you're interested. Make

you a little bank."

"Tell him to stop by." I don't need the money, but I want to work.

When I was in Dover, my therapist said working with my hands or creative work would distract my mind from the thoughts, from spiraling into depression. So far, it seems to be working.

Drew helps.

I take another pull off my whiskey as "Flyin High" by Marvin Gaye comes on.

Steve leans back, nodding. "This is your kind of music. Right?"

"Mack liked to play it in the shop." I look at the whiskey, tilting it side to side.

I liked to sing it when I was holding Drew. I can still see her with that shirt around her shoulders, her perfect little tits pointed up at me, peeking out of the top of that lace bra. We have to talk. I have to get this shit off my chest. Resting on my elbow, I wipe my hand across my eyes, fatigue hitting me now.

"What's on your mind, brother?" Steve's voice lowers. He's less bravado, and more legit concern.

I look to him, giving him a tight smile. "Sometimes the past doesn't want to stay past."

Mose is with us now. He's holding a white bar towel, drying a beer mug. "My old man was in WW two." He actually pronounces the letters. "He never could shake the memories."

My jaw clenches. I'm not looking to be the topic of conversation with these guys. Or their wives.

"I'm okay." I blink up and force a smile. "It just still feels close sometimes."

"You got a friend here, man." Steve's getting a little choked up. "I know you and Danny were tight. At least you were with him in the end."

"Thanks, Steve."

"Dagwood, man. Call me Dag."

"Thanks, Dag." I look at the whiskey. It's almost done. "I should probably head on home."

"It's a Saturday night, bro. You can sit with us a bit. Get some of that shit off your chest."

Mose drifts to the other end of the bar where a couple has come in. I look up at the clock. It's just after ten. "What's Dotty doing tonight?"

"Oh, you know. She's got a baby shower or some such shit. Woman stuff."

Again, I find myself chuckling. I'm wondering why Dagwood and I weren't closer friends in high school. It's possible I'm feeling a little buzzed myself.

"Anything else on your mind? I mean, besides the shit." He leans closer, giving me a knowing nod. "Dotty said Drew Harris has been waiting for you to come back for years."

Despite the numb of alcohol, my stomach twists at this information. Dagwood doesn't miss a thing.

"Yeah." He leans back like he won a bet. "I knew there was something there. Look, I get it, dude. Danny was a shithead when he drank. He'd probably have tried to kick your ass if he knew you were into Drew."

My forehead tightens. "He wasn't too thrilled."

He slaps me on the arm. "If that's what's bugging you, I say let that shit go. Danny's in a better place, and you gotta do what's right for you right here. Get that girl."

Dagwood makes it all seem so easy. I'm not even thinking when I pick up the second whiskey Mose put in front of me several seconds ago.

"Still, it stung," I mutter into the glass, as I take another sip. "He said I wasn't good enough… He was supposed to be my friend."

"I get it man. I really do. If you're good enough to be his friend, what the fuck is wrong with you dating his sister?"

"That's what I wanted to know." My voice is quiet, not animated like my drinking buddy's, but he's saying everything that's been eating at me for two years.

"Like I said, he's gone. You're here. Drew's here, and she is… so fine."

"Watch it." An unexpected flash of anger moves across my chest.

It's unnecessary, and I'm definitely buzzing to be pissed at him. Dagwood is no threat to me. He doesn't even want to be.

My response makes him laugh. "Easy, man, easy! I'm not after your girl."

"She's not my girl."

"Sure looks that way to me."

*Does it?* I feel like Drew and I have been an unspoken matter of fact for so long, but we've never come out with our feelings. We've only ever felt them.

He laughs more. "If Andrea Harris is not your girl, you need to do a little reflecting on what just happened right here. What's been happening a long time."

"You know?"

"Dude. Everybody knows."

I stand out of the stool, and pause a moment, putting my hand on Steve's shoulder. "Thanks, D. I have an errand to run."

"Any time, man. Any time."

# CHAPTER Twenty-One

## Drew

"WHEN WE HOLD ONTO GRUDGES, IT'S THE SAME AS HOLDING onto sin." My eyes drift around the small sanctuary as Pastor Hibbert talks. Since he took over after Pastor Stemple retired, the sermons have become less specific and more general.

I wonder if it'll change once he gets to know us better.

Sometime in the night, Gray returned the Jag. I was disappointed he left it in the driveway with no note or anything. He didn't even text or try to come inside. As I think back to our text exchange, I didn't specifically ask him to come inside. It was more playful teasing. Maybe he didn't realize I was serious… All I want now is him.

In front of me, Dagwood has his head bowed, and from this angle, I'm pretty sure he's sleeping. It's confirmed when a soft snore escapes his nose and Dotty elbows him hard.

He jumps and sits up. I pull my lips between my teeth and look away, across the aisle to where Ruby sits with her mother. She raises one eyebrow slowly, and I bite the inside of my cheek,

looking away again. I'm so happy after being with Gray, I'm ready to laugh at everything.

I should probably look at our new pastor and see what he's talking about. "Holding onto wrongs done to you is like cancer. It eats you from the inside out."

I think about his words. They're actually good. Roy Hibbert is about fifteen years younger than Paul Stemple. His wife is on the front row, looking at him as if he's Jesus Christ Superstar. Two young kids sit beside her, and I think he might be a nice addition to our small town.

He might want to start a series on gossiping and being judgmental wanks.

"It's an eternal truth: Forgiveness benefits the forgiver more than the one being forgiven." He holds out his hands. "Let us bow and pray God helps us with this difficult act. Learning to forgive."

I suppose I should learn to forgive the judgy church ladies. I might need help with that one, Lord. It's hard to forgive them after the way they treated Gray and his uncle.

Friday night floats into my brain again, and I shift in my seat. I might have to add *avoiding impure thoughts in church* to the list of things God has to help me do.

A tickle is in my stomach. It makes me want to squirm, but the prayer is over. The organ launches into our usual exit music, and everyone stands.

Ruby is across the aisle to me at once. "Why are you sitting by yourself?"

"I got here late, and I didn't want to make a big deal." I wave to the pew behind me. "I don't really mind. I'm used to it."

Dad stopped attending church regularly after Mamma died, and my brother's attendance was always spotty, depending on how much he'd had to drink the night before. I don't blame Gray for not wanting to come. If these good Christian people acted a little more Christ-like, maybe I could convince him, but for now,

I have one issue on my mind, and it's definitely not religious. Although, didn't God create the woman for the man?

She makes a sad face, but I wave it away. "Stop."

Her arm goes through mine. "You know you can always sit with us. We'll make room." She waits with me as we work our way around a cluster of old people waiting to shake the pastor's hand. "Speaking of room, Mom said for you to come over for lunch. She made extra dumplings."

My eyes move to the door, and I think about my dad. "I guess it'll be okay. Dad's probably still in bed anyway."

We finally make it onto the bright lawn, and she exhales heavily. "I'm sorry about your dad."

"He had a little breakthrough actually." I nod at Mrs. Stern, walking across the path to the fellowship hall.

I'm sure those Sunday school ladies have some luncheon or other planned. They're always trying to get me to join their volunteer ranks. No, thank you.

"I don't believe it." Ruby doesn't wave at Ralph's mother.

"We did. He agreed to give Naltrexone a try."

"Naltrexone… that's a drug for alcohol use disorder." Her tiny nose wrinkles. "Doctors rarely prescribe those. They're super controversial."

"Rarely is a far cry from never. I'm taking what I can get here."

She doesn't argue with me. If anyone knows how hard I've tried to help my dad—apart from Gray—it's Ruby.

We're just about to leave when I see Remington Key struggling across the lawn with his four-year-old daughter Lillie.

"Hi, Remi!" I give him a wave, and his face only partially relaxes.

Remington's really handsome for a single dad, light brown hair and warm hazel eyes, athletic physique. He moved to Oakville from Seattle when he married Sandy Burnside. Or Sandy

Key. Her name always made me think she should be a mermaid.

Anyway, I'd heard he'd made a mint in the tech industry. I'm not sure if it's true, but when he came to me for grief counseling and advice for talking to Lillie about her mom's death, he never had a problem paying his bills.

"Hi, Drew." He manages to get Lillie onto his hip, but she's twisting, trying to get down. "How's your family?"

"Oh, you know." I don't want to talk about it. "Have you met my friend Ruby? She works with me now at the clinic."

He gives her a short glance, adjusting Lillie on his hip, then I notice he does another, longer look.

My eyebrows rise, but my bestie is looking away, scanning the church lawn for God knows what. "Ruby." I elbow her in the side, and she jumps back to the present.

"Sorry. Hi... Remington." She is clearly not impressed.

I want to give her a good shaking. After all the drips she's dated, here's a possibly rich and stable hottie standing right in front of her. Granted, he has an insanely wiggly preschooler on his hip.

"Nice to meet you, Ruby. Is your family Korean?"

Even better... he knows his Asians! I try to give her an encouraging smile, but she could not be less engaged. "Yeah, my great grandpa moved here in the fifties."

"When I was in Seattle..." His voice trails off as Lillie manages to break free. "Sorry. It was nice meeting you."

He takes off after his escaped child, and I cross my arms, doing a little huff. There went a definite possibility, and he looked really hot in that expensive suit.

"Are you ready?" Ruby is impatient.

"Sure. Let's go."

We make the short drive to her house, and when we step inside, the delicious aroma of Asian cuisine touches my nose.

I get excited. "Did she make the broccoli I love?"

"She always does." Ruby pretends to be disgusted. "You'd

think she was your mother making all your favorite dishes."

"Your mother's food is like art. It's almost too pretty to eat."

Ruby's nose curls. "So it's like that. Kissing up to my mom?"

Mrs. Banks steps out of the kitchen. "Drew! I'm so happy you came for lunch. Come help me."

Ruby's mom never changes. She might spoil us, but she also makes us work for it. I'm happy to comply. It makes me feel like I'm part of a family again, even if it's only Ruby and her mom.

Twenty minutes later, we're sitting around the table passing dishes of kimche, a bowl of soup, and my favorite, a platter of round sticky dumplings nestled beside tart pickles and zesty fish sauce.

I spoon three onto my plate, but I hate to eat them. The bite-sized nuggets have smooth coverings and bright orange sprinkles of toasted shrimp flakes on top.

"They're almost too pretty to eat."

"Said nobody ever," Ruby shoves one in her mouth and moans loudly. "Better than sex."

"Ruby! And after church." Mrs. B shakes her head. "I taught you good Asian manners. You don't even use chopsticks."

"We're south Korean." Ruby shoves another dumpling into her mouth. "Much more relaxed."

The last time I tried to use chopsticks, I ended up with a dumpling in my lap. Still, I feel bad using my fork. "Sorry, Mrs. B."

"You enjoy your lunch, Andrea. You have every excuse. Unlike my ungrateful daughter."

"Oh, boy." Ruby groans. "Here we go again."

"You should be married and have three babies." Her mother easily uses her chopsticks to lift a dumpling to her stern mouth. "Not working all day with those crazy people, making no money."

"I'm building my practice!" She cries, biting into another dumpling she holds with two fingers. "And we don't call them crazy. I've told you this!"

"Ruby is really doing great building her practice. You should be proud." I try to defend my wacky friend. "Her clients love her, and she'll make more money eventually."

"She needs to help herself." Her mother shakes her head. "Not use her phone to find men. What kind of men, I ask? Men who forget their wallets and make her pay."

Years of practice as a therapist helps me keep my face neutral… instead of busting out laughing. "Bumble?" I look at her.

"I'm losing faith." Ruby sighs. "Still, I'm not dating any of the guys in this town. How else am I going to meet somebody?"

"If your father were alive, he would fix you up with a nice doctor from his work."

Mr. Banks had been a surgeon in Charleston. "It's kind of true, Mrs. B. Oakville is such a small town. We don't have a lot of options."

She pats my hand. "Now Grayson Cole is back. You don't need options." My jaw drops, but she continues. "I should have invited him to lunch. Ruby, why didn't you remind me?"

I'm sputtering, trying to cover, and my best friend doesn't even pause.

"I'll invite him next time." Ruby shoves another dumpling into her mouth. "In the meantime, more for me."

"Maybe it's good you have a purpose in your life. If you're never going to be a wife." Mrs. Banks, shakes her head, delicately eating half her second dumpling.

I'm on my third as well. "She's kind of following in her father's footsteps, don't you think?"

Mrs. B charges on, ignoring me. "Still, I don't know how you're going to help Darlene Holt. She sleeps with every man she knows. And that Riley Sturgiss is the biggest liar in St. Stephen county. Possibly the whole state. Her family needs to go back to wherever they're from." She shakes her helmet of dark hair. "How do you help people like this?"

"It's called compulsive behavior, Ma. We teach them techniques to manage stressors and we talk them through their feelings. It does help." Ruby is unfazed, but I'm horrified her mother knows so much about our clients.

Damn small-town gossip.

"And that Hunter McFee has been afraid of Richard Nixon since he was a little boy. He thought the Watergate burglars were behind September 11. As if Nixon could order it from his grave."

"I have an idea…" My brain is racing, and I can't eat another dumpling.

I don't really have an idea, but I've got to get us off this topic. Ruby and her mother look at me expectantly.

"Yes?" Mrs. Banks nods.

"Remember that time you showed me your fortune sticks and predicted our future? I'd love to do it again."

"No." Mrs. Banks looks down, her cheeks bloom pink. "I cannot do that again. Pastor Stemple said astrology and fortune-telling are *divination*. The work of the devil."

"Oh."

"Pastor Stemple is a party-pooping old windbag." Ruby jumps in. "What was all that garbage about the cow? I never could understand that story."

"The cow was God's will." Her mother starts, but Ruby cuts her off.

"I've been studying Chinese zodiac. Want to try it?"

"Sure!" I'll do anything to get out of discussing my clients over lunch with Ruby's mother. "How does it work?"

"Not at my table, Ru."

"Come on." Ruby gets up, and I start to follow, but Mrs. B stops me.

"You are just like your mother." She puts her hand lightly on my cheek. "Always trying to help others, defend others, even if it's misunderstood."

"I don't understand..."

Her hand goes to my shoulder, and she gives me a squeeze. "No worries. Now clean up!"

I follow my bestie to the kitchen, to deposit our plates in the dishwasher, then to her bedroom.

She still has a huge poster of the Backstreet Boys on her wall, and I flop on her purple-covered double bed.

For a second, I look around at her young-girl décor. "What would you do if you wanted to take a guy home after a date?"

"Are you kidding? I'd never bring a guy here." She flops on the bed in front of me. "Unless he was the first Korean president of the United States."

I start to laugh, but she quickly adds. "Maybe not even then. He'd be old. And probably not very good in bed. You know, powerful men and all. Let's see..."

She turns the pages of the glossy booklet covered in Chinese characters. "You're not Chinese..."

"Neither are you, but it's still fun." Finally she gets to a page with a sliding wheel on it. It's broken into three parts, so she can line it up over a pie chart of different animals.

"Okay, so your birthday is June..." She makes a note on one of our pads from the clinic. "Gray is August, four years later..."

Another note, then she flips a few pages. "You know, those notepads aren't cheap. You should use one of the legal pads instead."

"Oh! Look!" She turns the book towards me. "It says you're a perfect match! He's a horse and you're a dog."

My face pulls back. "Are you calling me a bitch?"

"Horses are clever, sensitive, and insightful..." She looks up and nods. "Totally Gray. And dogs are... honest, kind, frank, and tolerant! Totally you! Isn't it amazing?"

Leaning forward, I examine the book with her. "That's pretty... right on the money."

"It says horse males are very attractive to female dogs..."

"You're calling me a bitch."

"You were being kind of bitchy about the notepad."

My eyes narrow. "Those white pads are specially designed for the clinic. The legal pads are cheap. Anyway, who was your mom talking about on your date? When did that happen?"

She flops on her back on the bed. "I have to stop answering her when she asks how my date went."

"I can't believe you ever started. Some of them are pretty raunchy. Remember the guy who asked if you'd consider getting a boob job?"

"God, don't remind me!" She wails. "He was almost as bad as the guy who called me Ruthie the whole night."

"Did you ask him if he'd ever suffered head trauma?"

She starts laughing. "No! If I tell them I'm a therapist, they start trying to get me to diagnose their exes."

"What do you say is your occupation?"

"I say I'm a life coach. It's easier that way."

"Show me your profile. Maybe if we put our collective heads together, we can get you better results."

I scoot around in the bed so we're head to head, lying on our backs, looking at her phone. It's a comforting feeling, like we were when we were teens, laughing and talking about boys. My life was never the same after my mom died and my dad dropped out of society. Still, Ruby was always by my side, and Mrs. Banks was right there with the maternal input, making us eat, and giving us unsolicited advice.

It's late in the afternoon when I finally say goodbye, headed back to the dark and deteriorating mansion my dad never leaves. Mrs. Banks loaded me up with a container of dumplings and a big thermos of her warm soup for him. I wonder if he'll even eat it.

My mind has been on Gray all day. It was hard to resist checking my phone every two minutes for a text from him. None ever

came. I considered sneaking away to the restroom and texting him, but it made me feel too clingy.

He's still holding back, and I have to do the same. I have to let him come to me now… like he did at the lake house. *The lake house. Mmm…*

I'm in the garage now, and I close my eyes remembering him standing outside my door in the rain, fire burning in his eyes, his chest heaving. I could see the lines of his muscles through the transparent, wet shirt he wore. He grabbed me in his arms, and he held me so tight. He was desperate, hungry, so sexy…

The memory gives me a shiver, and I can't wait until tomorrow to make contact.

Walking quickly through the house, I check the kitchen before jogging up to the study where my dad always sits. I'm a little deflated to find him there, looking out the window. This time, at least, the empty tumbler is on the side table and not in his hand. Is it possible he drank a little less today?

"Hey, Dad. Mrs. Banks sent over some food for you. Hungry?"

He slowly turns to look at me, and when he sees the bag, he gives me the smallest smile. "Linda is one of the best cooks in town."

My heart releases a little at his words. "She really is. You should try these sticky dumplings."

I pull out the small container of the warm little morsels. He looks inside and takes one. It's so good to see him eating. After my happy afternoon, thinking of him locked away in this moldering mansion makes me sad.

The only thing sadder is the thought of me trapped in here with him forever. We are like Estella and Miss Havisham. *Dammit, Ralph Stern.* I can't let that happen.

"I drove the Jag to church this morning. It seems to be running fine. Just needs new tires, Gray said."

His expression darkens a bit, but I quickly hand him a large

soup spoon. "Try the soup. It's so delicious. A little like egg drop. Yes?"

He allows me to race past the mention of Gray. I don't know if it's because he's softening toward him or he's just too tired to get all worked up. I suspect it's the latter, but I'm not giving up hope.

As my father eats, I tell him about the sermon, how the new pastor seems a lot better to me than Pastor Stemple.

"Paul is an idiot. His sermons never made any damn sense," my dad growls, which I take as a good sign, even if he's talking about the preacher.

"I didn't really get his analogies half the time myself." I carefully take the container of soup he hands to me, replacing the lid and returning everything to the bag.

Dad exhales heavily, and his eyes go to the window. "Nothing anyone can say will bring back the dead. Nothing anyone can say will make it right. God's plan..."

His voice is bitter, and I think about the sermon today on forgiveness. I think sometimes the person God needs to help us forgive is God.

I'm not sure how that works.

He pushes out of his chair, and I sit back on the footstool where I was serving him. "Can I get you anything else?"

I reach out to take his hand, but he moves it away. "I'm going to bed. I've had enough of this day."

He slowly exits the room, and I look out the window again. At least I got him to eat something. Tomorrow, I'll get him that prescription. Then I can only hope for the best.

In the meantime, I scoop up the leftover Korean food and make my way downstairs. My phone is hot in my hand, and my heart beats faster when I think of messaging Gray.

I'm not trapped in this mansion. I'll do my best to save my dad, but either way, I'm getting out of this place.

# CHAPTER Twenty-Two

## Gray

*NOTE TO SELF: NEXT TIME YOU CAN'T SLEEP, DON'T GO BACK TO THE RED Cat and let Dagwood buy you whiskey all night.*

My head is pounding like an anvil when I finally open my eyes. My tongue sticks to the roof of my mouth, and the sun streaming through the blinds is like a laser cutting my brain in half.

"Jesus," I groan, moving slowly to the kitchen.

I pop a few ibuprofen pills and grab the orange juice out of the fridge. Sipping slowly, I wait as the coffee drips. My phone sits on the counter silent, taunting me with thoughts of Drew.

I left the Red Cat with good intentions of dropping off the Jag then coming back here and going to sleep. I didn't expect to stand in the driveway, looking up at that house, and wanting to text her. Knowing she was so close, my fingers curled with the need to touch her. I wanted to hear her voice.

I told myself it was too late, but by the time I walked back to my place, I was too keyed up to sleep. So I went back and had

more whiskey.

Like I could ever drink her away.

Dagwood spoke out loud all the thoughts I'd been holding inside. The only thing we didn't say, the question bothering my mind since the accident, is *why*?

Why would Danny say he was my friend and react the way he did?

It made me feel like a tool in his revenge against his dad. Like our friendship had been a lie, and all he'd ever wanted was to piss his dad off… by being friends with me.

It's a cynical view of the situation, and I know it's wrong. I remember how close we were through the years. Still, it tormented me in a way nothing else could.

The coffee pot bubbles and groans, and I have to break this line of thinking. I remember the therapy. It only takes thirty seconds to change a thought pattern. I have to focus on something else.

Anyway, like Dag said, Danny is dead. Nothing's going to change what he said to me, and holding onto it is just bringing me down. I have to let it go.

A fresh envelope is in the box. Inside are a set of car keys, ancient and easy to copy, and a torn-off sheet from a spiral-bound notebook. I peek out the window and see a shiny yellow land-barge in one of the spaces. A quick glance at the note tells me Taylor's number and a list of what he's done so far.

In a few minutes, I have it up on the lift, inspecting the insides, the lines and power train. These old cars are pretty basic, not like the hyper-technological insides you get in modern vehicles. It makes them easier to restore—if I can find the parts.

After an hour-long phone call, discussing what he wants, I spend most of the day making lists and fixing what I can on the old heap. Mack had a few telephone numbers and websites that helped me track down oil filters, hoses, and belts.

The timing belt is in decent condition. Must've been changed in the last hundred thousand miles. The radiator hose is also in pretty decent condition, which is a plus. Billy stops by for a few hours, and when he sees the old heap, he gets right under the hood with me. He tops off all the fluids, inspects the clutch, and checks the tires. They look fairly new.

Time passes quickly, and like the doc said, it distracts my mind from thinking too much about the past, things I can't change. Blaming myself.

What never goes away is Drew.

I haven't been thinking about bad things, but every time I slide my palm along the fender, I think of working on the Jag, which makes me think of Friday night, being alone with her in the lake house. Her body was so beautiful. We came together like nothing had changed. The truth hit me like a sledgehammer. I love her. I never stopped. But have I fallen in love with someone who can never be mine?

I'm hungry and tired when Billy leaves. My head stopped aching, but I'm sure I'll crash before long. I dig around in the refrigerator and settle on some leftovers from the dinner Mrs. Banks sent last week.

I wonder what Drew did today. I'm sure she went to church. She was always good like that because of her grandmother and her mother. She said they would have wanted her to keep going. I thought she might have texted about the Jag.

My phone buzzes in that moment, as if by force of will. I guess it's Taylor wanting to know when he can stop by tomorrow. I'm wrong.

***Drew: Spent the afternoon with Ruby and her mom. Learned you're a horse, I'm a dog, and we're a match made in heaven.***

The surge in my chest travels all the way to my lips, and without even thinking, I'm smiling like an idiot.

***Me: I'm pretty sure I haven't smiled all day today.***

I wait as the little gray dots float, thinking about her pretty fingers touching the screen.

***Drew: Rough day?***

***Me: Not so bad. Spent it working on an old car. Fix up for one of Dag's friends.***

***Drew: Dagwood smelled like a distillery in church.***

***Me: He was throwing them back last night.***

Another pause of dots.

***Drew: You went out last night? I'm not going to lie and say I'm not hurt.***

***Me: Don't be. I wanted to be with you.***

***Drew: You missed my butt?***

My breath is shallow. How can a simple question make me feel so good?

***Me: I'm more of a breast man.***

***Drew: Oh. My breasts aren't very big. (sad emoji)***

***Me: Your breasts are perfect handfuls.***

***Drew: Perfect for you?***

***Me: Yes.***

She has no idea.

***Drew: Can you still feel them?***

***Me: Yes.***

***Drew: I can still feel your hands on them. I can still feel your tongue touching me.***

The fly of my pants tightens. I can still taste her on my tongue. Shit, I'm getting a semi just texting with her.

***Me: Are you getting ready for bed?***

***Drew: Yes, but I need some help. I'm lying on my stomach with my back arched. My ass is bare and lifted, and I need you behind me… pushing inside, deep.***

My mouth goes dry. I can see what she's describing in my mind, and it focuses my brain. I want her.

Now.

A quick glance out the window tells me the sun has set. It's dark. Quiet.

***Drew: Gray?***

***Me: I'll help you with that. I'm trying to figure out how.***

***Drew: Come over. I'm waiting for you.***

***Me: But your dad.***

***Drew: Please come. I need you.***

*Shit*. I'm doing this.

***Me: Five minutes.***

***Drew: I'm in the pool house.***

Five minutes. What was I thinking? What the fuck am I going to do with my truck? With all the energy surging in my veins, I could run to her house, but the semi in my pants makes it difficult. Instead, I drive quickly and park around the corner in what I hope is a discreet location.

Dagwood made me pretty sure the entire town will be whispering about us tomorrow, but it won't stop me. I'm too focused to worry about small minds.

The back door to the cottage behind the pool is unlocked. It's dim-lit as I pick my way through it. It's not a big place, and a small lamp sitting on an end table seems bright in the darkness.

"Drew?" My voice is quiet. My eyes strain for her.

Her soft voice tightens my stomach. "I think that was more than five minutes."

"Where are you?"

"Behind the sofa."

I walk around to where the shadows are longer. The light doesn't quite reach this part of the room. There, in front of the windows facing the pool, I see her in silhouette. It stops me in my tracks.

The ripples on the water create wavy lights in the blackness, but I can see her, sitting in profile on what looks like a fluffy white palette on the floor. Her back is arched and the lace bra she's

wearing pushes her perfect breasts into swells that catch the light.

I can just see the tops of her dark areolas teasing me from inside the cups, and my dick hardens to a steel rod in my pants.

"You're beautiful," I whisper.

"You like what you see?" It's a sexy purr.

"Very much."

She pushes a lock of her long hair over her shoulder. She lifts her chin, and traces a finger down to her bra strap helping it to fall off her smooth shoulder.

"Will you help me?" With a sigh, she dives forward on the blankets, arching her back, so the light from outside casts her round ass in silver.

My shirt is over my head in a blink, and I'm unfastening my jeans, heeling off my boots, and shoving them down fast. Her eyes are fixed on my cock, and when it springs free, they widen. Her lips curl into a hungry smile. *Fuck me.*

I reach down and grasp my shaft, giving it a stroke. It's already weeping for her, but I give it a little wag. I can tease, too.

"What do you want, princess?"

She pulls her full bottom lip between her teeth and pushes up on her elbows. "I want you to take me hard."

"You want it hard?" I walk slowly to where she's lying, back arched, her beautiful breasts in full view.

My cock aches. I can't get any harder until she blows my mind.

Her voice is a velvet whisper. "I want your thick, fat, cock slamming into my soft, warm cunt over and over until I beg for more."

With that, I kneel behind her, catching her by the hips. "Get ready."

I slide my tip along the seam of her pussy, and she whimpers a *yes*.

"You're dripping." My voice is strained. I can't wait another breath.

She pushes up to meet me, and with one hard thrust, I sink, balls deep into her core.

"Fuck…" I groan, my voice broken.

My mind blanks. She is so hot and wet and tight. I'm trying to catch my bearings when she starts rocking her hips against my pelvis, pulling me in and out on her own.

"Shit, Drew, you feel so damn good."

She makes a little noise of pleasure, and it registers straight to my dick. My hands fumble around her waist, and I slide my fingers along her spread pussy. I'm stretching her good, hitting her hard, but I manage to find that rigid bud. When I touch it, she shudders.

"Yes, Gray… That's it."

I circle fast, doing my best to get her coming, while she bucks against me. I thrust right back, going so deep… impossibly deep.

"Yes… yes…" Her elbows bend, and my chest is to her back.

I can feel her breathing fast, feel the shuddering in her shoulders. I keep pumping, right there on that razor's edge of orgasm. All the energy surges below my navel. My ass tightens, and my balls constrict. This one's going to blow my mind I can feel it.

"Gray…" She moans my name.

*Shit.* It's like a stroke of lightning. I slide my hand over her creamy, round skin, tapping my thumb on that pink pucker arching up at me. Maybe one of these times I'll use more than a finger. For now… I sink the tip of my thumb inside, and it's so tight. She moans loudly, and her elbows collapse. I pump it gently, feeling the pull of her body on me.

My cock can't hold out much more. One more stroke, and she breaks into a cascade of orgasm. She comes so hard, she pulls me right along with her. I pulse deep into her swollen pussy while her cute little ass sucks my thumb.

Holding on, I close my eyes as her body blooms for me. I pulse, filling her, and she draws me in completely. For a minute, I

leave this planet, my only anchor is her gorgeous body.

I want nothing but her.

As long as I live.

We slowly come down, and I slip my thumb out, moving my palm to her flat stomach. I gently hold her to me, and we roll to the side on the soft blankets. Her head rests on my bicep, and I hold her beautiful shoulders. My other arm is secure around her waist, holding her to me. Our cheeks touch. Her body fits so perfectly against mine.

I give her another little thrust, and she exhales a soft noise. She does another buck against my pelvis, and it's another little charge.

"You feel like heaven," I murmur, kissing the side of her jaw, moving up behind her ear. She makes a little squeal and shivers in my arms. It makes me laugh.

"I never want to let you go." I take a slow inhale of her scent, warmth, flowers, soap.

Her hand slides over mine on her stomach. "Then don't."

*I won't…* She might ultimately tell me to go, but I'll never willingly leave Drew Harris.

Her fingers trace lightly along the lines of my forearm, and I pull a crochet blanket off the back of the couch over our bodies. She snuggles deeper into my arms when I do.

"What's this business about horses and dogs?" I ask, kissing the top of her shoulder.

She exhales a happy hum. "Chinese astrology. We're a wonderful pair. Our score was ninety percent compatible."

"I didn't need Ruby to tell me that."

Her body moves with a soft laugh. "It's not Ruby. It's Chinese."

"So I'm a horse and you're a dog? How does that work? Those animals don't go together."

"Horses are clever and sensitive. Ruby said it's very attractive

to the female dog." Sleep enters her tone, and I don't make the joke on the tip of my tongue.

I feel her relaxing, and I want her to sleep. I want to hold her in my arms all night like before.

"Again, I don't need Ruby to tell me that."

Her last words are carried on a whisper. "It's in the stars."

Sometime in the night, we've moved out of each other's arms. Cold creeps across the floor, and I try to find the blanket. I try to get closer to Drew, but I can't move. It feels like I'm being held down against my will. I try to fight it off and fail. Panic seizes my chest. I can't get whatever this is off me.

A loud popping noise, like the sound of gunfire is in my ears. In that instant, I'm plunged into chaos just like before. The bomb explodes under the truck. Everything goes from peaceful and calm, to flying in the air, crashing to the ground. My head slams against glass, and our whole world is blown apart.

"Danny..." I struggle against the paralysis in my limbs.

My body won't move. I'm having trouble breathing, and I'm covered in sweat. God, I can't breathe. I gasp, trying to breathe through the smoke, the sand.

My ears are muffled. That shrill hiss is back. *What the fuck?* Finally, I get the fucking seatbelt off me, and I can move. I try to climb across the cab, across the dead body of my passenger.

This scene is different. It's worse.

The man in the *shemagh* walking along the road is now walking toward me. In his hand is a machine gun. His brown eyes gleam with hatred, and I know he won't stop until we're all dead.

I have to stop him. I have to protect my men.

As soon as I have the thought, he starts to run toward me. I push out of the window and fall to the ground. The pain is indescribable, and I shout, holding my temples. When I look up he's closer. He's on me, lifting the gun straight in my face.

Somehow, through the confusion, I remember Drew sleeping on the floor behind me. She has no idea what's about to happen. She has no idea she's about be shot dead… Like Danny.

A fist of rage tightens in my chest. An explosion of fight mixed with fear. I can't lose her. He lifts the gun to level of his eyes, and I shout.

"NO!" Hands are on me, and I reach out to push them away.

I reach out to stop the man, but the gun explodes in my face. The force of the blast shakes me to my core. I fall to my hands and knees, my face in my hands.

I'm shaking, covered in sweat. My muscles are buzzing with adrenaline, and I'm gasping for breath.

Blinking hard, I come back to myself. I'm in the pool house, but I'm in the back of the house. I'm still frantic from the rage and the fighting and the fear of Drew being killed.

It's not real. I do my best to center my thoughts and breathe. I look around the room to center myself. I'm not in the desert. I'm in Drew's house. It's quiet, no chaos. I do my best to focus on the quiet. A panic hits my chest, and I hold the wall as I walk with trembling legs to the room where we were sleeping.

I stop at the corner and see her beautiful body. She's lying on the palette covered in the woven blanket. Her soft breath swirls in and out, and for a few moments I focus on the sound, the sweet sound of my Drew alive and breathing there on her makeshift bed. The one she made to share with me.

Watching her sleeping so peacefully, breaks me. Tonight, when I got free of the grip of this fucking madness, I was in another room, across the house. What happens when I wake up, and I'm hurting her?

I've heard the horror stories, night terrors that turn into real-life terror.

Shoving my hands in my hair, I take another deep breath, doing my best to calm the fuck down. My clothes are in a pile where

I left them, and I scoop them up, dressing quickly.

My eyes never leave Drew the entire time I pull on my clothes. Her face is so relaxed, so trusting. I call her a princess, a baby, but the truth is, she's like an angel. Dropping to one knee, I lightly move a strand of hair off her cheek. I don't want to wake her, but what I wouldn't give for one more kiss.

In the past, I protected her. I kept her safe and comforted in my arms. What I wouldn't give to find that comfort in her arms.

Instead I let her sleep. I slip out into the night alone.

# CHAPTER Twenty-Three

## Drew

"When Richard Nixon was defeated in the California governor's race in 1962, he famously said 'You won't have Dick Nixon to kick around anymore.'" Hunter is lying on his back on my couch today.

He's rubbing his eyes with his fingertips, and I'm doing my best to stay focused on my work.

In the night I'd been disturbed, and I woke to find Gray gone. It left me unsettled. I couldn't shake the feeling something bad had happened, and as soon as the sun finally rose, I sent him a quick text.

***Me: Hate waking up to an empty bed.***

My chest was tight, but I didn't want to come across as clingy.

***Gray: Sorry. Had to go. Don't want your neighbors talking.***

***Me: I'm sure it was too late for that.***

***Gray: I needed to get an early start.***

***Me: I'll bring the Jag over at lunch.***

***Gray: See you then.***

Our text exchange didn't go very far to ease my anxiety. I'd

hoped for a little something more, even just a *Drew-baby*. He's so hard to read now. When I got to work this morning, Dotty wanted to talk about how Dag and Gray hung out at the Red Cat. I didn't have time to gossip with Hunter coming, but I made a mental note to catch up with her later.

"After being a senator for three years then serving as vice president under Dwight D. Eisenhower, he still felt like a Washington outsider. Only, in his eyes, that was a bad thing. He wanted to be in the group." Hunter blinks at the ceiling a moment then turns to look at me.

It all clicks into place.

Nodding slowly, I give him a kind smile. "Is that how you feel? Like an outsider?"

He turns his head, facing the ceiling again. It's several seconds before he answers me. "I did what you asked me to do."

"You talked to Mrs. Green?"

He nods, again waiting several seconds before continuing. "She's got a little business. She calls it Extreme Gnome Makeovers." He looks down at his hands. "It's really a clever name for a business. It made me laugh."

I make a note on my legal pad. *Wants to be an insider.*

"I wonder if you and Mrs. Green might be friends."

His brow furrows, and he sits all the way up. "She's eighty seven… but I guess she's my neighbor. Jesus said to love your neighbor."

"Okay, new assignment." He nods slowly. "See if you can find one thing you have in common with Mrs. Green."

"One thing…" He looks around the room as if the answer might be here.

"It can be more than one thing, but I'm only asking for one."

Slowly he stands, his face contorted as if I've given him a massive challenge. "Thank you, Miss Harris."

"See you next week."

He's gone, and I lean back in my chair, thinking. What would it take for an outsider to finally feel welcome in the group? Who would he need to let him in? Who holds the key?

"I have six new possible matches on Bumble!" Ruby bounces into my office waving her phone at me. "One is even Korean!"

"You're kidding." I toss my pen on the legal pad and go around to look.

On the screen is a slim guy with short hair and a thoughtful smile. "Wow. He looks like that guy from the movies!"

"He just might be my insanely rich Asian husband!"

"It's crazy rich."

"Shh!" She puts a finger on my lips. "We don't say that word here."

Shaking my head, I scoop up my keys. "I've got to run the Jag over to have the tires replaced. Keep an eye on things, will ya?"

"How'd it go with my favorite boy?"

Pausing at the door, I put my hand on my hip, still puzzling over last night. "It started out great, but somewhere in the night it got sort of strange… Only I'm not sure if I was fully awake or dreaming."

"What the hell?" Ruby walks over and closes the door. "I was talking about Hunter. What the heck are you talking about?"

"Oh!" I step back, trying to recover. "I… um… I think Hunter might be on the road to a breakthrough. He seems to be circling the reason he can't trust people. He feels like an outsider. Like Richard Nixon."

"That's great. I'll add it to my files. Now let's get back to the strange night and possibly dreaming."

My arms are crossed, and I rub my palms up and down to ward off the sudden chill. "Gray spent the night with me last night."

Her eyes go wide. "At your house? Was your dad there?"

"We were in the pool house."

She nods, grinning. "Yeah, you were. It's about time you got some action." Her demeanor changes when I don't smile. "Why are you upset?"

"He left in the night without a word."

"So? I mean, he probably had to get to work or something. And you know how your neighbors are. It's probably all over town by now."

"Maybe…" Shaking my head, I try to push away my fears. "I'm probably just getting used to him being back is all. Every time he goes away, I feel like I might not see him again."

She walks over and puts her arms around me, and for a moment, we stand in the center of the room sharing a hug. "Totally understandable, my friend. But he's your white stallion. You're his little Pekingese."

My eyes narrow, and I push out of her arms. "Thanks."

"What? Those are the cutest little dogs ever!"

"They look like walking mops." I go to the door. "I've got to take the Jag in now."

"See? He's being so dependable, working toward a goal."

"That makes two of us." I'm out the door to her cat calling behind me.

# CHAPTER Twenty-Four

## Gray

THE RUSTED SPARK PLUG WON'T MOVE. I ROCK IT BACK AND FORTH gently, letting the penetrating oil Billy poured yesterday seep into the grooves. I'm focused, doing my best not to break them, doing my best not to let my thoughts go in a loop.

My dream from last night keeps resurfacing in my mind. I keep seeing the eyes of that guy, the hate sparkling in them. I see that gun pointing right in my face, and I feel the terror of knowing Drew is asleep behind me, vulnerable, next.

*Jesus*. I focus on my task.

The dream wasn't real.

"Yeah, I couldn't get it off last night either."

"Shit!" I toss the wrench at the sound of Billy's voice. My heart is racing, and a bead of sweat rolls down my cheek. It's not even hot in here.

"Hey, sorry!" He holds both hands up like I pulled a gun. "I thought you heard me come in."

"Don't sneak up on me like that." I step back, using the shop

towel to dry the sweat off my neck. Then I walk over to pick up the socket wrench.

Billy slides his current whittling project in the pocket of his blue jeans and pulls the heavy work shirt over his shoulders. It still has my name on the pocket.

"I should update that for you." I point to the patch. "If you're planning to stick around a while."

"No way, man. It's my good luck charm." He reaches up and twisting the spark plug I'd been working on. "It's like I'm here at the bottom now, but one day I could own the place."

The white socket drops into his palm, and he holds it up to me, grinning.

"I loosened it for you."

"Muscles of steel." He tosses it up and catches it again. "Like buns of steel, but the ladies can see it all. No imagination required."

"Try working the muscle between your ears." I look at the work order hanging on the wall. "I've found ladies like it more."

"Say, you went to college, right?" He picks up one of the tires and rolls it inside the garage.

"Four years. Graduated with honors."

He goes back for the next one. "Should I go to college?"

It's a good question. I walk over and to help him. "It's a big expense. If you're planning to be a mechanic forever, then probably not. Trade school is enough."

"So what are you doing here?" He's following me with the last new tire for the Jag.

"It's a long story." One I don't feel like discussing with Billy. Hell, I didn't feel like discussing it with Dag. "We'll put these on after lunch."

"She bringing the car by again?" I nod, and he watches me a beat.

Finally, I look up. "What?"

"Drew Harris is the prettiest girl in town."

"What about it?"

He shrugs, going to the box of new spark plugs and taking out four. "Back when my dad was fighting the dreams, the flashbacks, he told my mamma to leave. Told her to get out."

"Why'd he do that?"

Billy takes out his latest whittling creation. "He figured it'd just get worse, he'd end up hitting her or something."

"What happened?" I wince at the tone in my voice. I sound fucking desperate.

"She wouldn't leave. My mamma's stubborn as shit." He returns to the Chevy and puts the carving in his pocket. "Dad started doing transcendental meditation. All kinds of crazy assed shit. He said the chanting pulled him out of the… ah…" he looks around as if for a translation book. "The loop."

He circles his finger around his ear, and I start for the office. I don't like the implication his dad's crazy… or I might be.

Billy doesn't quit talking as he installs the final spark plug. "He finally got through the worst of it."

I pause before entering the small room. "Did he…" No. It's not a question I can ask. It's too personal.

My assistant seems to understand. "He never hit her. Never hit any of us. It wasn't in him to hurt us."

"Good morning, guys!" We both look up quick, and Billy lets out a low whistle.

Leslie is back, and this time she's wearing a green wrap dress that plunges low at the neckline. Her breasts rise out of it, and I remember I was headed to the office. I'm sure my expression is as strung out as I feel, and I don't need her getting any ideas.

"Hey, Leslie. Be right back."

"Can I help you?" Billy walks over to her, holding the wrench in his hands and smiling.

In the office, I take a minute to collect myself. I want to

believe the happy ending Billy's dad got could happen for me. Still, I know how PTSD usually goes, the violence and the depression, the increased risk of suicidal thoughts. I know when I'm having a dream or a flashback, I'm not completely in control.

*If I ever hurt Drew…*

The image of me hitting her, or worse, while in that state tries to form in my mind, and I shut it down. I'd never hurt Drew. Not intentionally.

That's the problem.

"Hey, sorry." Billy is at the door. "She needs an oil change, but I'm not sure we have the right filter for her car…"

Clearing my throat, I return to where Leslie is waiting by her yellow Mazda Miata. "I can order it."

She blinks up at me, smiling. "If you need me to come back next week—"

"It's okay." I walk up to look in the open hood. "The guys are pretty quick with supplies. We should be able to do it tomorrow."

Billy hands me the part, and I walk to the computer. I feel Leslie following, and when I stop she's right beside me.

"How's it going, Gray? Any trouble getting back into the swing of things?" She puts her hand on my arm.

"I'm doing okay." I continue entering the part number.

"Dag said you were at the Red Cat Saturday? He said you were feeling pretty down about Danny. It's completely understandable."

My throat tightens, but I hold steady. "I guess it's normal."

"Of course it is!" Her voice goes high, breathy. "You and Danny were inseparable. I remember." She exhales a laugh. "Remember that weekend at the lake? Did you get those photos developed?"

"You know, I forgot." The oil filter appears on the screen. "Here it is. If you think you'll be coming here pretty regularly, I'll order extras."

Just like Mack. I remember my first day and all the filters for Mrs. Green's station wagon.

"Definitely order extra." Our eyes meet, and she gives me a sly grin. "I'm sure I'll come very regularly with you here."

"Sorry to barge in like this." Drew's voice, causes me to take two steps back.

*Shit*. What's with everybody sneaking around these days?

"I'm just dropping off the Jag like you asked."

"Drew… hey." I go to where she's waiting, her eyes throwing flames. "You look really pretty today."

She's wearing navy slacks and a pink top that buttons up the front and has a little belt at the high waist. She looks like the gorgeous, professional nerd she is, and I want to unwrap her like a present.

I want to tell her she has nothing to worry about with Leslie. I've been dodging that girl for years.

"I don't really have time to stay." She gives me a pointed look. "Unless…"

Leslie walks out to the garage, and I wince when she stops to bend over, digging in the glove box of her small car. Her ass is right in the air, pointing at me.

"I could walk you back?"

Drew's pretty lips are pressed in a thin line. "It's just across the street. I think I'll make it. Will you?"

"You have nothing to worry about." My eyes hold hers. She can't think I'd prefer Leslie over her.

"Sometimes I' not sure." She leaves her keys and starts for the door.

Leslie walks around to the back of the Miata. "Gray? I could really use some body work. Are you up for that?"

My jaw clenches, and Drew's eyes narrow. "I don't do body work." I say the words clear and definite. "Not here."

"Really?" Leslie's voice is fake innocence. "It seems like you're

missing an opportunity."

"I do body work." Billy jumps in, and I follow Drew out to the parking lot where the Jag waits, shining in the sun.

Just when I think she's leaving without a word, she turns on her heel and steps toward me fast.

"What happened last night?" Her tone is sharp.

It causes me to take a step back.

I catch the finger she has on my chest. "I told you. I couldn't sleep."

She pulls her hand from mine, putting both on her hips. "Really. That's it?"

I don't like her being angry, but I want to have this conversation in a different place, a different way.

"You can talk to her about it, though? Be yourself around her?"

"No." Anger squeezes my lungs.

"Well, it sure looks that way to me."

"Well, you're wrong. I don't care about her." I catch Drew's arms. My voice cracks. "If it looks different, it's because I don't have to worry about hurting her. I never hurt her."

*Shit*. I've said too much.

Confusion lines Drew's face. "What does that mean?"

"Look." I release her and turn away, rubbing the back of my neck, trying to get the tension out of my shoulders. "I want to talk to you about this. We need to talk."

"We could talk on our date. Friday?"

Friday. Looking up at the sky, I wonder if I can wait that long. "Okay." It's a definite. "We'll talk Friday."

She steps forward and touches my arm. "I'm ready to listen."

With a gentle kiss, she says goodbye. I can't help wondering if she has any idea what I'm going to say. How could she possibly be ready?

# CHAPTER Twenty-Five

## Drew

THE JAG IS AS GOOD AS NEW. THE ENGINE IS RESTORED, AND WHEN I pick it up after getting new tires, Gray stands back looking at it with pride.

"One childhood dream come true."

"One?"

He gives me a wink. "I have a few more I'm still working on."

Happiness sparkles in my stomach. I can't wait until Friday.

"Maybe you can drive it on our date." When I take the car keys, I lean in a little too close.

He takes advantage and gives me a brief kiss on the lips. Too brief for me.

"Delivery guy just left those oil filters." Billy passes us, holding a black contraption with white accordion folds all around it over his head. "I'll call your friend and tell her to come back tomorrow."

I exhale a quiet little growl.

Gray grins down at me and shakes his head. "I'm letting Billy take care of that one."

"He seems to be very excited about the job."

With the tip of his finger, he touches the side of my nose. "Ned says for you not to let it bother you."

I reach up and slide my finger over my temple. "Tanya says you'd better watch your back."

He kisses my lips, and I take the keys. "I was thinking about Friday. It feels so far away."

"Yeah?" He follows me slowly to where my dad's old car is parked.

"Maybe you could come over for dinner one night this week… Maybe Wednesday?"

His brow furrows, and he drops his chin. When he looks up at me, his blue eyes are so round, so sexy. "With your dad?"

Reaching out, I slide the hair off his forehead with my finger. I just had to touch him. "If he makes it downstairs, which I'm hoping he does."

I've got the prescription bag in my car. Fingers crossed.

"I think I need to talk to you first." He looks so pained. I remember how he said he'd hurt me earlier, and my heartbeat picks up.

"Okay…" I think about it more. "Maybe we can have our date on Wednesday, then."

He shrugs. "Don't you go to prayer meeting?"

"I can skip a week."

"Always a bad influence." The anxiety in his eyes softens, and a little bubble of happiness pops in my stomach.

"The worst." I step forward and hold his cheek, kissing him out in the parking lot where everyone can see. I really don't care.

Warm hands cover my waist, but he only holds me a moment before pulling back. "Wednesday."

"What about Wednesday?" That familiar old voice causes me to spin around. "Grayson? Are you planning to attend prayer meeting?"

Ralph's mother is standing in front of us, frowning down like the witch from *The Wizard of Oz*. Miss Gulch.

"No!" I answer too fast.

It's ridiculous. I'm not a child. This woman doesn't scare me anymore. Her black eyes narrow like a crow, and a trickle of doubt moves through me.

"No? Is there something more important than learning to be the best version of yourself? Sacrificing your time to the lord?"

"Gray and I have other plans." I straighten my back, defiant. If anyone made him feel like an outsider, it was this woman. I'm proud to be seen with him.

"Hi, Mrs. Stern. I haven't seen you since I got back in town." Gray's manner is so cool, it bolsters my confidence.

"I need an oil change." She almost seems sorry to admit it. "Ralph told me you'd reopened the garage."

"Isn't it interesting how we actually need certain businesses?" I don't even try to hide the tone in my voice.

"Ralph also said you asked him out last Friday." She turns those beady eyes on me. "Back in my day, women didn't ask men on dates, but I guess that's neither here nor there."

"I didn't want to eat alone." I sense Gray listening to my reply. "Ralph wanted to tell me about his almonds."

The old woman squares her shoulders. "He planted ten acres of trees last month. It's a bold move. Very entrepreneurial. I'm glad to see people in this town being more appreciative."

"He's very enthusiastic. I hope it works out for him."

"It's very kind of you to say that." Her smile is as off-putting as her frown. "I'll be sure and tell him."

I remember Ralph's comments about starting a new dynasty, and now I'm sure I know who gave him that idea. I make a point of turning to Gray again and speaking clearly.

"I'll see you Wednesday, then. You can drive the Jag."

He shakes his head, warmth in his eyes, before turning to

Mrs. Stern. "You can just drive right in that first bay."

Wednesday feels like it will never arrive. I manage to get Dad to take the pills, and I do my best to keep from dancing a jig in the kitchen as he reads the instructions, the side effects, then nods and puts one of the white capsules on his tongue.

The next day, Darlene makes progress. "My mom asked why I haven't worn skirts in so long." She looks at her black fingernails then glances up at me. "I told her because the last time I wore a skirt, Mr. Johnson reached under it and touched me."

Holding my expression neutral, I nod slowly. "How did telling her make you feel?"

She shrugs. "I don't know. Like I'd gotten something off my chest finally."

"That's really good." I smile warmly. "What did your mother say?"

Her brow furrows. "She said she didn't like my outfit."

Anger tightens my stomach. I glance at the black skirt she's paired with knee-high pantyhose, but I don't make a judgment. "She didn't acknowledge what you said about the neighbor?"

"No. She made me feel like a loser." Her finger is in her mouth, and she chews on the cuticle a minute. "I told her I was experimenting with new trends."

"I like how you stood up for yourself." I can't fake a smile now, though. "Why do you think your mother would ignore what you said?"

She shrugs again, looking out the window. "She doesn't want to think about it? She feels guilty? She doesn't care."

Darlene speaks the words so fast, it's like she's solving a math problem. "Sometimes people pretend not to care to hide their fear. Or how much they're hurting."

She doesn't respond to this. I glance at the clock. "I have one more assignment. I'd like you to try and say one empowering

thing to your mother every day this week. Do you think you can do that?"

Her nose wrinkles, and she stands. "Why?"

"I think it would benefit both of you. Make you feel stronger and make her feel stronger as well. Can you do that?"

"What if I don't know anything empowering to say?"

It's a legit question. "Visit this website." I hand her a card.

She takes it, blinking a few times while reading. Then she smiles. "Okay."

"Okay." My chest is so full. It's the first time I've ever seen her smile.

After entering my notes, I hop up and rush out of my office. Dotty is behind the desk drinking a coffee and eating a muffin. It gives me an idea.

I give her a wave. "I just have to run out for ten minutes. I've got my cell."

She gives me a confused nod, but I don't wait around to explain. I know exactly what's happening right now. Billy's words are burning in my ears, and I have a plan. I trot down to the corner bakery and snag a box of muffins before heading to the garage.

Sure enough, when I get there, Leslie is sitting in a chair by the back wall. She's wearing black pants and a red sweater, and her arms are crossed so her breasts are pushed together and higher.

She doesn't see me enter, and I scan the room quickly, looking for Gray. I don't see him, and Billy emerges from under Leslie's tiny car.

"Oh, hey, Miss Drew." He pulls a towel out of his back pocket and walks over to me.

I notice for the first time he's wearing Gray's old work shirt. "Hey… I just brought you guys a little thank you gift." I look around again. "For working so hard on the Jag. Where's Gray?"

"Oh, he had to go get a part. We've been working on that old Chevy, you know? The exhaust system is shot. He found a replacement muffler for cheap at a junkyard and figured he'd take the truck and get it himself."

"Just like that?"

"He was worried it might not last long. Some of these parts go fast."

I shouldn't feel miffed. It's silly. He doesn't have to check in with me every time he runs an errand.

I look down at the box of chocolate chip muffins. "He can have one when he gets back, I guess. They'll still be good in a few hours, right?"

"Oh, he had to go to Bixby. I expect he'll spend the night."

My mouth falls open, but I quickly close it. I don't want sneaky Leslie to think anything is going on.

Too late.

She puts her magazine down and walks over to where we're talking. "What's that, Drew Poo? Muffins?" She sneers down at the box. "You know some people pay for their car repairs with money."

That does it. "And some people know when they've worn out their welcome."

Leslie looks me up and down and laughs. "I know you're not talking to me." She waves her hand in an arc. "It's called a place of business. Look it up."

"A place of business, as in car repairs. Not the kind of business you're after."

"What kind of business is that, princess?" She steps closer.

"Don't call me princess." My voice is low, just above a growl, and I notice Billy take a step back.

Part of me is embarrassed to be having this out in front of him. The other part of me is sick of Leslie's shit and ready to call her on it.

The other part is winning today.

Something in my eyes must warn her, because Leslie crosses her arms over her chest. "What are you worried about? Afraid your boyfriend's going to see something he likes better?"

"Gray is a man, and as long as I've known him, he's never been interested in you." I'm fighting hard to keep my voice calm, steady. "It's really pathetic the way you keep coming around here. Have some self-respect, please."

"What's pathetic is you trying to hold onto something that's over." She goes and sits in the chair again. "Gray has changed. He's not the same person who left here. You don't understand him anymore."

I walk straight to where she's sitting and look down at her. "Stay away from Gray."

She slaps her hands on her thighs and stands again, putting us practically nose to nose. "Don't tell me what to do, Drew *baby*."

"I'm also not a baby."

"You're also not going to call dibs on Gray." Her hands are on her hips. "He came back, and I waited to see if he'd pick up with you. He didn't. He's here."

"He's mine."

"It doesn't look that way to me."

"Look again."

We're both breathing hard, nostrils flared, and in each other's faces when Billy decides to risk his life. "Want me to take those muffins?"

My eyes drop to the box, which I'm gripping so hard, it's almost bent in half. I loosen my fingers and hand it to him. "Thanks, Billy."

"I'll tell Gray you brought these, but I'm sure he'll call or text you. He talks about you all the time." I meet his dark gaze, and he smiles.

Leslie shoves her hands on her hips with a huff. "Whose side

are you on?"

"I'd like to be on yours." He turns to her with a wink. "Gray's not available, but I am."

Adrenaline is surging in my veins, and Billy's overt flirting after what just happened pulls me out of the moment. A laugh starts at the top of my stomach, and hiccups out on a breath, but I quickly shove it down. I don't want to lose any ground here.

"Thanks, Billy. I'll see you later."

"See you around."

With great care, I turn on my heel and walk out the door. I continue walking boldly, fearlessly away from the garage, all the way back to my office. I think that was a win, but only time will tell.

# CHAPTER Twenty-Six

## Gray

"You got here just in time." Chuck Hopper steps across a pile of junk to the old rusted-out Chevy Bel Air. "Fella down in Atlanta just called. Said he needed it for a movie. Offered three times what you're paying."

I'm not sure what to say to that. I have no idea if Taylor's prepared to pay more for the part. "Thanks for holding it for me."

"I'm a man of my word." He stretches, scratching his oversized belly through the yellowed-white tank stretched over it.

"I can bring my truck around and load up what I need."

"Just let me know when you're done, and we can price it per part."

I spend the next several hours with my tools gutting the old heap. From what Billy and I can tell, Taylor's kept his car somewhat up to date. Still, we haven't looked at everything.

It's late in the afternoon when I'm done. Chuck has a stump of a cigar in the corner of his mouth, and his red face is sweaty.

"Let's see." He looks over in the bed of my truck.

I'm standing beside him looking as well.

"Muffler, radiator... what's that?"

"Clutch." I shrug. "You never know."

He does a nod and tallies it up, giving me the total, which comes in right at the amount Taylor authorized. I toss a canvass tarp over the parts and head to the Plucky Duck motel on the highway. It doesn't look like anyone's stayed here in fifty years, but the owner shows me to a clean room.

"Just staying one night?" The proprietor Elmer Pepper squints at me like I'm a bank robber.

"Just need a place to crash on the way home." I do my best to give him a reassuring smile.

"Where's home?"

The question gives me an unexpected pause. "Oakville."

His ancient eyes narrow. "You sure?"

The image of Drew waiting for me, sitting on that palette solidifies my answer. "You bet. I wouldn't be anywhere else."

"Welp," he shrugs. "The pool's clean if you feel like swimming. Otherwise, if you want to pay up front you can take off in the morning when you're ready."

"Sure." I walk with him to the small office and hand over seventy-five dollars.

"Got a card I can scan for damages?" I give him the plastic, and he scans it. "I won't charge it unless you break something."

"Sure." I start for the door, then I hesitate. "I'll take a picture of the room before I leave in the morning."

Elmer only shrugs. "Suit yourself."

I'm dead on my feet when I crash on the scratchy bedspread. I am not thinking about the horror stories I've heard about places like this and semen stains everywhere.

Okay, I am now.

I stand and rip the scratchy bedspread off, tossing it on the matching double bed across from me. I collapse again, now on

the bare sheets and pull out my phone.

One person has been on my mind all day. I send her a quick text.

***Me: Thinking about you, Drew-baby.***

Truth be told, when I found this car online, the idea of getting out, driving for thrcc hours to Bixby felt like a godsend. I needed to clear my head. Everything with Drew was building up, and I was fucking sharing my feelings with people like Dagwood Magee. *Shit*. Great way to have it all over town.

I'm saved from my cringe-fest by a reply from Drew.

***Drew: It's about time. I've had a miserable day.***

I'm immediately concerned.

***Me: What's wrong? What happened?***

Could it be her dad? Did somebody tell him my truck had been parked outside her house overnight? *Shit*. The little dots are torturous. Why the fuck did I leave?

***Drew: You didn't tell me you were going to Bixby. I was so confused.***

My exhale of relief turns into a chuckle.

***Me: Sorry, baby. This rehab got me distracted. I found a prized part. Had to beat the competition for it.***

***Drew: If that's all it was. You could have called.***

***Me: I will next time. I wasn't thinking.***

***Drew: I like when you call me baby. I like that you said next time.***

The surge of warmth moving through my stomach is like a drug. I love her words. Without hesitation, I hit the call button. I need to hear her voice. It only rings once.

"Hey." Her voice is like a soothing balm to my tired insides.

"Hey." I wonder if she can hear my smile. "You'll never guess where I'm staying?"

She exhales a light laugh. "Tell me."

"The Plucky Duck motel."

That makes her laugh for real, and I smile. I love the way she sounds.

"Where the heck is the Plucky Duck motel?"

"It's between Bixby and home. It's on the highway near Oceanside Village. Remember that place?"

"No." Her voice is soft, warm.

"Ah, I don't know. I guess I kept up with stuff like this. It's just a little bedroom community that was popular along the coast."

"How far are you from home?"

I look at my phone and do some quick mental math. "About one hundred and twenty miles."

She exhales in my ear. "How long is that?"

"About two hours, depending on traffic and road construction and—"

"You don't have to go off on male directions versus female."

I laugh again. She knows me so well. "I'm just saying. Distance is more reliable than time."

"I'm just making sure we're still on for our date tomorrow night."

"I wouldn't miss it for anything." I think about a place I haven't seen in a long time. "Is it okay if I hijack where we go?"

She makes a little frustrated groan, and I grin. Everything she says and does makes me smile or grin. Nothing has changed.

"I guess," she finally says in a pretend annoyed voice.

"I have a surprise for you. I think you're going to like it."

Billy's like a kid in a candy store when he sees the haul in the bed of my truck.

"Man, this is some serious shit." He picks up the clutch I swiped. "Taylor's clutch is in good condition."

"Chuck said some asshole in Atlanta was sniffing around. I figured I'd take what we might need for future jobs."

He smiles and nods. "Good thinking. Man, I wish I'd gone with you."

"We'd have bought the whole car." I laugh, feeling lighter than I have in two days. "Anything happen while I was gone?"

His face turns red, and I grab his shoulder. "What?"

"You're going out with Drew tonight?" I nod, and he gives me a tight smile. "You'd better ask her about it."

I have no idea what to expect when I pick up Drew. All I know is I've planned an evening for us where I hope all the things hanging over our heads will be forgotten. I tossed a blanket in the bed of the truck in case we want to go somewhere to look at the stars later. In the meantime, I pull up to her house and get out, ready to walk up and knock on the door.

Ready for her father to answer.

I'm lifting my hand when it opens on its own, and Drew swirls out in a chambray dress that hangs mid-thigh with a little belt around the waist. She's wearing short, brown cowboy boots, and her long hair is in a thick braid over one shoulder with little strands hang around her face.

Her lips are so full and pink. "Hey, beautiful." I lean down to capture them in a kiss.

She pulls the door closed behind her. "Where are you taking me?"

I glance up at the closed door of the huge mansion. It's stately red brick with an enormous white front porch and wide white stairs leading down to a circular drive. This fortress was never open to me. I let it go for now. It's not where I want my head to be tonight.

"I was going to say close your eyes." Our hands are clasped as I lead her to the truck.

She grins, letting me help her into the passenger's side. "How long do I have to keep them closed?"

"I changed my mind on that." I climb in the driver's side and

stretch my arm across the top.

She scoots over to the middle, buckling the lap belt and laying her head on my shoulder. "I don't mind closing my eyes from here."

I plant a kiss on the top of her sweet-smelling head. "Your call."

We cruise through her neighborhood out to the main drag through town, following the road that leads to the Interstate. We go a little farther until the lights of the park brighten the sky.

She sits up suddenly, bouncing around to face me. "Gray!"

"What?" I know she knows where we're heading, but I'm having fun with her.

"Are we going to…" She looks down at her outfit. "I should have asked what to wear!"

"I think you look amazing." Catching her neck with my hand I pull her in for another kiss on those pink lips.

"But you're taking me to The Fun Spot!"

"I sure am."

She claps and does a little squeal for the ancient amusement park. "I haven't been there since… hell, I think the last time I was there was with you."

"I was there with Danny. You were there with the youth group from church."

"Still, it was our first date."

We paired up the minute I saw her walking around with Ruby and another girl from her Sunday school class. It wasn't hard to ride every ride with her, and when we went into the tunnel of love…

"You French kissed me for the first time that night."

We're walking fast toward the gate, my arm looped over her shoulders, and I pull her head to my lips. "I almost came in my pants."

"Probably because I was rubbing you through your jeans so hard."

It's been a while since I've felt this relaxed. The memory of our first night here is one of my favorites from growing up in this town.

We wait in line for tickets, and once we're inside, I catch her hand. "First we have to eat something."

"But not too much. I don't want to barf on any of the rides."

I can't help a laugh. It feels so good. We're holding hands as we step up to the hot dog stand. I order us two Coney dogs with mustard and onions, and we take them to sit over on a bench in front of the Ferris wheel.

"Still the best hot dog I've ever had." She takes a big bite, and some of the meat relish falls into the paper cup.

A squeal, and I'm touching her chin with a napkin. I take a big bite, and it's pretty much the same.

"Carnival food is such a mess." She complains, stuffing the final bits in her mouth.

Her cheeks poke out, and I shake my head. "What would your grandmother say?"

"She'd already be dead seeing me here in a skirt with you eating hot dogs."

"You're adorable eating hot dogs." I catch her chin and kiss her. "Want another one?"

"Not until after we ride some rides."

She jumps up, and we toss all our trash in the nearby bin before heading over to the roller coaster. The Fun Spot is at least fifty years old, and its one rickety wooden roller coaster looks even older.

"The Wild Mouse is my favorite roller coaster ever!" She drags me to the very back car, and we climb in, lowering the bar across our laps.

"It doesn't even have shoulder straps," I complain pushing the bar down as far as possible on our laps.

"Don't be a baby," she sasses as we jerk forward, going

straight into the ticking uphill climb.

"If this thing flies off the tracks, I'm blaming you."

We don't have a chance to say any more. Drew's hands are over her head, and her eyes are closed as we charge down the hill. She screams, and I'm grinning watching her. The wind catches her skirt and it blows up, and I slip my hand between her soft thighs.

She squeals more, putting one hand over mine while keeping the other in the air. As we jerk around curve after curve, I slide my finger up and down her damp slit through her panties until I feel her thighs tremble.

When we're done, she leans over to kiss me. "Best ride ever."

I have to adjust my fly.

Next comes the swings, spinning out and around. I can't touch her, but I can't stop looking at her smiling, carefree. I love seeing her so happy. She's a demon in the bumper cars, hitting me hard every chance she gets. The handful of other customers, a few couples, a few teenagers, stay out of our way.

We pass a family with small children as we walk to get cotton candy. I imagine Drew and me bringing our children here… then all at once the weight of our pending conversation hits me in the chest, killing my joy.

I can't make plans like that with these secrets hanging over my head. She has to know the truth.

We walk up to the hill at the top of the park, where *The Fun Spot* is spelled out in big white letters similar to the Hollywood sign. I lead her to sit on a bench overlooking the park. The attendant told us they'd be closing at ten, since it's a weeknight, so I'm worried we're running out of time.

"Before we go, we have to ride the tunnel of love." She scoots closer, crossing her legs so her knees touch mine. I see her skirt rising higher.

"I might do more than kiss you this time."

She leans in to kiss my cheek. "Can we go now?"

"Soon." I put a hand over the outside of her thigh, and she puts her head against my shoulder.

"You wanted to talk tonight." Her voice grows serious.

"Yes." I pause a moment, not wanting to rush this.

My stomach isn't in knots like I'd expected. I feel calm, ready to have this conversation. I'm putting my cards on the table.

Her finger draws a line up and down my forearm. "Were you lonely in the desert?" A touch of fear is in her tone, but I put that fear to rest.

"Sometimes." Turning my hand over, I lace our fingers. "It helped that we stayed in touch. We talked almost every night."

"I lived for those conversations."

I give her hand a squeeze. "I did too."

Her eyes are full of relief. "You kept telling me to date other people, but I didn't want to date anyone. I only wanted to wait for you."

I trace the top of her cheekbone with my thumb. "It was the one time I was glad you didn't listen to me."

"I'm listening now." Her chin lifts, and her blue eyes are so open, so beautiful.

Clearing my throat, I straighten in the seat, putting both hands over hers.

Time to rip it off, Band-Aid style.

"That last day, when we were ambushed… it was like the blast came out of nowhere." Taking a beat, I remember that man, his eyes. "Or I don't know… maybe I should have sensed it coming. One minute we were driving along, the next we were thrown in the air. Almost everyone in the back of the truck fell out. I was trapped in the cab. I'd hit my head on the window. The medics said I had a concussion."

Mist fills her eyes, and she lifts my hand to her face, clasping it in both of hers and kissing the back of it. "I'm so sorry."

"I managed to climb out, but it was chaos everywhere. I couldn't see for the dust and the smoke. People kept running past, pushing. Men were dying all around me... explosions kept going off like aftershocks."

She holds my hand tighter, her eyes tightening as tears streak her pretty cheeks. Tension squeezes my chest.

"I'm sorry." I reach out to place my hand on her skin. "I'm not trying to make you cry."

An inhale lifts her chest and shoulders, and she looks into my eyes. "I can't imagine you going through something like that. It must've been terrifying."

My eyebrows clutch. "I didn't feel afraid. I felt... focused, determined. I had to get our guys to safety. I was one of the few still on my feet, even if I couldn't catch my balance."

"Because of the concussion." She reaches out to stroke my cheek again.

I put my hand over hers and bring it to my lap. "My CO needed help accounting for all the men in our company. Many of them were dead when we found them."

Her shoulders tremble, and her chin drops. "Danny."

Pulling her to me, I hold her against my chest, kissing the top of her head. "I'm so sorry."

"It's not your fault." She pushes out of my arms, searching for my eyes.

I rise off the bench and step forward, looking down over the glittering lights of the park. "It feels like my fault. Every day."

She stands beside me, putting her hand in the crook of my arm. We're quiet, watching the couples below walking from booth to booth. I have to tell her everything.

"A few weeks after it happened, I had this... moment." Shaking my head, I correct myself. "I still have moments."

Concern lines her face when she meets my gaze. "What do you mean?"

Turning to face her, I just tell her. "Some nights I'm right back in it. If I'm sleeping, it's like the most vivid dream I've ever had. Running, shouting, violence… I'm fighting."

"Post-traumatic stress." Then she pauses. "Only if you're sleeping?"

"It can happen when I'm awake, if someone surprises me. It's only been a few times, but I've come close—"

"Have you hurt anyone?"

I shake my head no.

"Yourself?"

Again, no.

Her lips tighten and she nods. "I've studied PTSD. It will diminish over time."

My arms cross over my chest, and I walk slowly away from her. "Will it? And how much time? What happens until then?"

She closes the distance between us, putting her hands on my shoulders. "It doesn't matter. I'll help you."

"It happened Sunday night."

Her lips part, and she hesitates. "The night you were with me?"

"The night we were in the pool house."

"I didn't even know…" She steps away, confusion lining her brow. "Is that why you were gone when I woke up?"

"I was worried…" My throat tightens. "I always worry. What if I—"

I'm not sure I can say the words out loud. The shame of admitting what I might do shoots across my shoulders.

She puts a hand on my side. "What are you thinking?"

My eyes close, and I speak the words. "If I ever hurt you, Drew… if I ever hit you or injured you or put you in danger—"

"No!" She pulls me close again. "You never would. Don't even say it."

"I can't do this." Pain is in my chest as I confess. "I had to

come back, to say goodbye to Danny, but I shouldn't stay here. I didn't mean to get so close to you again—"

"Stop saying this. You had to come back." Her voice breaks. She's crying, and it's shredding my insides. "You promised me."

My arms go around her, and I hold her so close to my chest. "I can't protect you anymore, Drew. I can't keep you safe when I'm the one who might hurt you."

Her small body shivers, and her fingers tighten on my shirt. "You won't hurt me. You never would. The only way you could hurt me is by leaving again."

Bowing my head, I hold her as she cries. I breathe in her sweet perfume of flowers, the soft scent of her soap, the warm scent of her skin. It's a blend I used to dream about at night.

"I need to go back to Dover, see if I can get better, be the man you deserve—"

"No!" She pushes out of my arms, her voice rising. "I won't hear you say that! All my life I've listened to people saying what I deserve, first my father, then these… these women. I know what I deserve. I know what want. You're mine, Grayson Cole. From the first day when you saved me from that snake to the day you held me when Mamma died and every day after…"

Her eyes flash and tears stream down her cheeks, until her shoulders break. Her hands cover her face, and I scoop her into my arms again, holding her against me so tight.

"Shh." I kiss her head, sliding my hand up and down her back like I've always done. "Stop crying."

"You're not leaving me." She whimpers, her tears staining my shirt. "I waited for you so long. Don't ever say it again."

Pain is in my head, and my eyes squeeze shut. Drew holds my heart in her hand. As much as I fear hurting her physically, I can't stand here and make her cry.

I clear the thickness from my throat. "I'll do what I can."

# CHAPTER Twenty-Seven

## Drew

GRAY LEAVES ME AT THE DOOR WITH A KISS AND A LONG HUG. I TRY TO make him come inside, but he won't.

"I'll see you tomorrow, Drew-baby." He kisses me again, his tongue softly curling with mine, igniting my panties despite my heavy heart.

"Dinner Friday," I remind him.

He only nods, a slight wince, storm clouds filling his blue eyes.

Walking slowly to my bedroom, I sit on my bed, pulling my purse onto my lap. Opening it, I dig around until I find the old memento I'd wanted to show him tonight. I'd carried it the whole time, waiting for the right moment.

It's the coaster from our last night at the lake house.

The one he signed.

Age has yellowed the paper, and the edges are frayed, but the writing is dark and permanent. The words are an indelible vow I've never let go.

All through his years in the desert, all through the dark year,

when he disappeared, when I was afraid he'd never come back, I'd look at this aging piece of cardboard and read the words, letting them comfort my broken heart. No matter what, I had his promise.

I wanted to show him tonight.

Instead, I tuck it safely in my drawer again.

Before I close my eyes, I send one last text.

***Me: We can get through this.***

I don't know if he'll respond. I pull the blankets over my shoulder, and I'm just laying my head on the pillow when my phone buzzes.

***Gray: Sleep, Drew-baby.***

Sleep did not come easy, and I go straight to Dotty holding the coffee when I get to the clinic the next day.

"Oh, great goddess of all coffee goodness."

She hands me a tall cappuccino with my initial in black on the side. "I put a little cinnamon in it for you again."

"You're the queen." I hold the cup in both hands like it's my grip on the planet. "Remind me to give you a raise."

Her eyebrows shoot up. "Can you do that?"

"I wish." I sip slowly. "It has to be approved by the board."

She frowns. "What do I need to do to impress them?"

"When you find out, let me know."

I'm starting for my office when she stops me. "Hey, I never got to tell you. Gray said something to Dag Saturday night—"

"What time is Riley getting here?" I'm not sure I want to gossip with Dotty about Gray. After what happened last night, I'm feeling pretty fragile.

"She called and said she's running a few minutes late." We both check the clock.

"So twenty minutes?"

"Probably." Dotty enters my office behind me. "It really bothered Dag. He didn't know if he should tell you or not, but I said

yes, he definitely should."

A painful knot is in my throat, and I stand behind my desk, looking at my black computer screen as I take another sip of hot coffee.

"I don't know, Dot. I mean, if it's something Gray wants me to know—"

Her voice drops to just above a whisper. "I think it'll help you understand why he's being so distant."

Chewing on the inside of my cheek, I study her face. "We've been talking a lot about the accident… and the aftermath."

She nods. "So he probably already told you. He and Danny had this massive fight right before it happened… about you."

Shock flashes in my chest. "About me?"

"Gray said Danny had found out you two were… together, I guess, and he really flipped out about it. Told Gray he wasn't good enough for you… he didn't deserve you." She shrugs. "All that stuff people used to say about you two."

This is news to me. "People knew we were together?"

"Good lord, of course we did." She shakes her head like I'm so naive. "You were always sneaking off together at the lake house. Leslie said she took a picture of you together. She was going to use it as blackmail, but I don't know what happened to that."

Anger burns at the base of my throat. "Leslie is such a bitch."

Dotty nods. "She's always wanted to have her cake and eat it, too. Or blow it, too."

Taking a deep inhale, I nod, ready to end this conversation. "I guess that does explain some things. Thanks, Dot."

"It was their last conversation before Danny died." Her eyes are round, mournful. "I'm sure it's just eating away at him."

Dotty and her drama. I know she means well, or I'd tell her to mind her own business. As it is, I simply say, "I'll talk to him about it."

Her face instantly brightens with a smile. "I knew you would. You'll talk to him, and that'll take care of that ole pesky distance. You two can pick right up where you left off."

I'm starting to understand Hunter's paranoia. It's like everyone in town knows more about my business than I do.

Riley's appearance in the lobby saves me from any more of this conversation. Too bad it doesn't take away my heaviness. First the PTSD, now the fight with Danny… I feel like I'm getting a headache, and all I want to do is put my arms around Gray and tell him none of it matters.

Only I know it matters to him. Danny's words must have hurt him so much. They're the same words he said to me last night.

A soft knock on the door snaps me out of it. "Are you ready to start now?" Riley's eyes are round.

"Yes, please come in." I gesture to the chair in front of me. "Have a seat. Here or on the couch, whichever you prefer."

She takes the chair across from my desk. "I'm sorry I'm late."

Turning to my computer I quickly type in her name. "I got a late start today myself, so we're all good."

I scan her notes quickly then turn to give her a smile, picking up my pen and taking out my notepad.

"I did what you said… about the lies." Her voice goes quiet as she says the word.

"This isn't about judgment." I smile reassuringly. "Sometimes lies are a defense mechanism."

"Last year, I told my teacher I was allergic to perfume."

My head tilts to the side. "How did that help you?"

"She let me sit in the hall with the door open during class."

I nod, waiting. I make a note on the paper, giving her a chance to say more if she wants.

"You told me to put down why… It's Madelyn Frist."

Our eyes meet, and my expression softens. "Does she make you uncomfortable?"

"She says I'm stupid." Riley's voice gets louder. "She says I don't belong here. I'm white trash. I need to go back to hillbilly West Virginia where I came from. She calls me a loser..."

The rage simmering inside me over Gray sparks to life in my chest. My anger with people pushing others down, telling them they're not good enough tries to overflow. Just in time, I grab the reins, making a Note to Self on my notepad: *Calm down.*

"Your school should have a policy against bullying." I clear the thickness from my throat. "Have you tried talking to a teacher?"

"Then I'll have to confront her. They'll bring us all in a room together, and I'll have to look at her face..."

"How do you feel about telling your mother?"

"No." It's a little cry, and I exhale slowly.

"Okay. I'm not trying to make you uncomfortable." Putting my hand on my chest, I smile calmly. "Let's practice breathing. Inhale... Exhale."

Her face is fixed in anger, but I continue. "Inhale... exhale."

It's as much for me as it is for her, and after the third time, she relents, inhaling deeply and exhaling slowly.

"That's good." Lowering my hand, I look at the white pad in front of me. "You shouldn't feel afraid at school. Maybe we can work out some strategies for dealing with Madelyn and staying in the classroom."

The last portion of her hour, I let her lead the way on things she can do to work around Madelyn. After Riley leaves, I make a note in her file to work on empowering her to go to a teacher or a trusted adult for help.

Ruby hasn't been in, and I shoot her a text to be sure she's okay. She says she has a stomach bug, and I tell her to rest and keep me posted.

I spend a good portion of the afternoon researching PTSD, symptoms, treatments, duration of the illness. Gray was right

about one thing—the prognosis is scary.

People with PTSD are prone to substance abuse, they're more likely to suffer mental illness, they exhibit higher rates of abusive behaviors, and worst of all, they're more likely to commit suicide.

All of it twists my stomach in knots, and by the time I leave for the day, I'm angry, sad, and exhausted.

Driving the Jag past the garage, I slow down to look inside. My chest warms when I see Gray standing with Billy, looking at that Chevy. He's so brave in spite of everything that's happened. He came back here, he opened the garage, and no matter what he says, he's never shown any signs of rage or abusive behavior. He moves to the side, and I smile, letting my eyes drift from his square jaw to his broad shoulders, his strong hands…

The car behind me honks, and I jump, continuing on to my house and not flipping them off.

When I enter the house, my dad is in the kitchen standing over a platter of lasagna.

"Where did this come from?" I drop my purse on the counter, looking around. "Did you cook?"

"Florence Stern brought it over."

My throat goes dry. "What made her do that?"

"She said you didn't go to prayer meeting last night. She was worried you might be sick."

Meddling old cow. My teeth clench, but I force a happy face. "It's actually Ruby who's sick. She has a stomach bug. I should probably make some soup and take it to her."

Dad waves a hand. "Linda makes better soup than anybody. We can have some of this."

Crisis averted. Not that I'm ashamed to tell my father about Gray and me. I just want to do it in my own way, gently. Dad's recovery is a big part of my plan to move out, to get my own place. I can't stay here with him forever, and if I want to convince Gray

we can start a life together, I need to start by having my own life.

We stand at the bar to eat. Dad takes down a tumbler and pours himself a drink. Tonight, I can't be upset about it. It's been a hellish twenty-four hours, and I need a little strength for what I'm about to say.

"I invited a guest over for dinner tomorrow night." I tap my fingers on the granite countertop as I wait for his response.

"Why would you do that?" His voice is strained, but I can't let it stop me.

"Grayson Cole has ben back for a few weeks now… I think we should have him over for dinner." Dad starts to shake his head, but I cut him off. "I already invited him. He'll be here tomorrow at seven. I'm making Frogmore stew."

My father's head bows, and I watch as his hand forms a fist on the top of the bar. Without another word, he puts the fork on the plate and picks up the tumbler.

I step up and catch his arm. "I want you to give him a chance. He was Danny's best friend."

Our eyes clash, and I see turmoil swirling in his. I don't know why he responds this way, but I won't let him ruin my dinner plans.

"Please, Dad."

It's the last thing he hears from me before he turns and walks out of the kitchen.

# CHAPTER Twenty-Eight

## Gray

For the second time this week, I'm standing in front of the Harris mansion, looking up at the enormous white entrance.

It's not as late this time, and as I wait for someone to answer the door, my eyes land on dry rot taking over the top left corner. Tracing my gaze down to an enormous window, I see the wooden shutter is home to a bird's nest.

A crack is running in a zigzag line along the brick in the far exterior, and something about noticing these little cracks and imperfections sparks that protectiveness in me. I want to take Drew away from this place…

What right do I have to think this thought? I can't take care of her any better than her own father.

The door opens, and our eyes meet. The anxiety I've been fighting since our night at the amusement park melts, and I open my arms as she steps into my chest, placing her cheek right above my heart.

"I've missed you," she sighs. "I'm so glad you're here."

We texted briefly last night, but I know what I told her has been weighing on her. I see it in her eyes. They're not as bright as they always are. It makes me feel like a dog. I only want to make her happy.

She steps back, and I let my eyes run over the white dress she's wearing. It's high-necked and sleeveless, tight down to her waist, but the bottom flairs out. It stops at her thighs, giving me a nice view of her long, shapely legs.

"You look beautiful."

She smiles, and even though it doesn't quite reach her eyes, I pull her fingers to my lips. "You look handsome as always." She gives my hand a pull. "Dad's waiting in the kitchen. I made Frogmore stew!"

"It's my favorite."

"I know." She leads the way, and I watch her cute little ass sway beneath that skirt as I follow her across the threshold into this massive home where I was never welcome.

It's actually my first time inside the main house, and walking through it now, I take in the ancient furnishings, portraits, and mirrors that line the walls.

It has dark wood floors throughout, and a long staircase with a white banister is against the wall on one side of the hallway Drew leads me down.

As we pass through, I notice beige lace doilies on the tops of chairs and sofas. A large circular one is on top of a piano in the corner. It looks like they never changed anything after Drew's mother died.

The hall opens, and we enter a bright kitchen. This part of the house seems more lived in, and it smells delicious. The Frogmore stew sits steaming on a massive platter in the center of the bar.

Frogmore stew is actually what some people call a low country boil. It's boiled shrimp with red potatoes, sausage, and corn

on the cob. When Mack would make it, we'd sit outside and drink beer.

When I see Carl Harris standing on the opposite side of the room, I know it won't be that kind of an evening.

"Daddy, you remember Grayson." Drew has one hand on my arm. The other she holds out to her dad as if beckoning him to come closer.

The old man stands straight, not smiling, a crystal tumbler of whiskey clutched in his hand.

"Good to see you, sir." I give him a nod, since I don't think he's ready for me to rush forward and shake his hand.

"Andrea said you've been back a few weeks now." He takes a stiff step toward where we're standing. "I heard you re-opened your uncle's garage."

"For now." I'm not looking to spill my guts with this guy, but I'm not afraid to answer his questions.

Drew walks around to the cabinet and starts taking down plates, gathering utensils. Mack and I would eat straight out of the pile with only a roll of paper towels between us. Again, this isn't that kind of dinner.

"What is that supposed to mean?" He pulls up and squints an eye at me. "You're not planning to stay?"

"The fellow working with me now has a good head for the business." I've only just started working out this plan in my mind, but I'll be damned if I let Carl Harris think he intimidates me. "I'm thinking about letting him run the shop while I do other things."

Drew pauses, mid-preparation and blinks at me. "What other things?" Her voice is high, and her dad looks from me to her slowly.

"My degree is in civil engineering. I'm thinking about Ralph's offer. Maybe I'll help him run his orchard."

Drew shakes her head, and when she takes wine glasses from

the cabinet, I notice her hands trembling. It's a pretty tense evening, that's for sure.

"Ralph Stern has some wild ideas," Carl muses. "Still, he has an entrepreneurial spirit. He could make something of himself after all."

Clearing my throat, I swallow my reply to that statement. My uncle was a small business owner in this town. I've taken over his small business. Heaven forbid something as concrete and reliable as a garage fall under the heading of entrepreneurial.

"Ready to eat?" Drew smiles, and when I catch her eye, I don't really give a shit what this man thinks.

All I care about is being sure he's wrong about one thing—I want to be strong enough to deserve her.

The food is delicious, but I've never been so glad to get to the end of a meal. Drew brings out a key lime pie, but her father declines. I hold up a hand myself, even though it's my favorite dessert.

I've drunk one glass of white wine and a tumbler of whiskey. The wine was for Drew. The whiskey was for Carl. I wasn't about to say no when he offered me a drink.

Now I'm ready to stop before I have a fucking headache in the morning.

"Grayson, I appreciate your visit." Her father stands, and all three of us rise. He steps over toward me, and for the first time all evening, he extends his hand.

Stepping forward, I grasp it firmly. I'm about to let go, but he holds it a beat longer, his brown eyes boring into mine. "I hope we still understand each other."

I'm not sure how to respond to his statement. I'm sure he knows I remember what he told me all those years ago at the garage. *Don't you* ever *touch my daughter again.*

Something about the way he says *still* makes me want to step even closer and tell him how many times I've touched his

daughter and how many more times I intend to do it. It's a rebellious teenager response, I know. This guy has always brought out the worst in me.

"I'm not sure what you mean, but it was interesting seeing you again, sir." Take that, fucking Carl Harris. Two can play at this game.

"Okay, then!" Drew steps toward us, hands clasped in front of her. "If nobody wants dessert, I guess I'll walk Gray out. Maybe we can take a stroll around the neighborhood."

"It's late, Andrea." Her dad snaps at her, lingering in my personal space.

"It's only eight thirty." Her voice is calm, and for the first time, I detect an edge in her tone toward her father.

He must notice it as well, because his eyes move from me to her before dropping to his glass. With a resigned sigh, he straightens and walks out of the kitchen. I feel like I can breathe easily for the first time since I entered this room.

Drew crosses to me and puts her hand in my arm. "I've thought a lot about what you said Wednesday. We have counselors at the clinic who I know would be happy to talk to you if you're interested."

I let her lead me out the side door to the brick-lined patio. A fire pit is situated in the center of the open space, and wrought-iron loungers are arranged around it with thick canvass cushions.

"I'll think about it." I nod, watching the flames licking the coals. "Is it anybody I know?"

"Do you have a preference? I can find someone you don't know if it makes you more comfortable."

My hands are in my back pockets, and I shrug. "This whole situation is pretty uncomfortable." I try giving her a smile, but her expression breaks.

She rushes to me, putting her arms around my waist again. "I'll do anything to help you, Gray. Just tell me what I can do."

For a moment, I forget where we are. I put my arms around her and hold her close to me. My chest is tight, and I feel my heart struggling to beat. I kiss her sweet head, wishing with all my might I could change things.

"It might be easier if I went away again. Just for a little while."

She whimpers against my chest. "Why would that be easier than being here with me?"

Stepping back, I lift her chin, moving her hair off her cheeks. "Because of Danny." *Fuck*, it's like a knife saying his name.

She blinks quickly. "Dotty said you two had a fight…"

I don't bother asking how she knows. I knew when I said it Dag would repeat every word.

So I just tell her.

"Sometimes when I touch you…" I swallow the ache in my throat. "When I hold you, I remember his words, my anger."

"You never got closure." Her voice is pleading. "It's understandable."

The last thing, the last nail in my coffin—it's time to say it.

"I was driving the truck, Drew." My voice is so quiet, her head tilts to the side. It makes me think of a little bird, easily broken.

"What?"

Clearing my throat, I say it louder. "I was driving the truck. I was behind the wheel when it exploded."

Her head begins to shake. "I don't understand…"

"I was responsible." Reaching up, I slide my fingers roughly over my eyes. "Now when I remember what we said… I can't help wondering if I wanted him dead."

Silence surrounds us. It's so loud I can feel it on my skin. It's like the hissing in my ears after my concussion. It only lasts a moment.

"What did you say?" Carl's voice is a machete cutting the night air.

When I turn to face him, his eyes blaze hotter than the fire. "Mr. Harris."

He throws the tumbler against the brick wall, and Drew lets out a little yelp. "Tell me what you just said about my son."

"I said… I was—"

"No." Drew steps forward again, closer to me. "You loved Danny just as much as we all did. The men from Washington said it was an accident. You're not responsible."

She touches my hand, but my eyes never leave her father's. I've seen hate in peoples' eyes before. I saw it in the eyes of the man on the side of the road just before the explosion. I see it blazing at me from the depths of her father's soul.

"Get your hands off my daughter." It's a low growl, but it quickly grows louder. "Get your hands off my family."

"Daddy, stop!" Drew tries to come between us, but he grabs her arm and steps in front of her, blocking her from me with his body.

"Get out of this house." He's shouting now. "Get out of this town. You never belonged here. You never should have come here."

Every word is like a whip against my skin, ripping me open, and leaving me to bleed.

"You've taken everything from me. You're not taking my daughter."

"Daddy!" Drew struggles to get out of his grip.

I can't stand to see her this way. I know how much she wanted to help him, and my presence is tearing them apart.

I take a step back, but he's right on top of me screaming. "Danny was the hero, not you. You should have died in the desert. Not him."

My vision clouds like the smoke from the blast. Still, I'm not afraid. The emotions burning my chest are different from before. This time, I feel like he's right. He's repeating the words I've said

to myself so many times.

For all his faults, Danny was the star of this town. He was the heir to his family's good name. I'm guilty. I'm broken.

I make my way to the exit, Carl screaming behind me. "I never want to see your face in my house again! I never want to see you in my town. GET OUT!"

# CHAPTER Twenty-Nine

## Drew

SUNDAY COMES, AND I STILL CAN'T FIND GRAY.

My dad is locked in his bedroom, but it's difficult for me to care. I know I should try to care. I know he's sick and broken, but I can't forgive what he said to Gray. I can't let go of my anger.

After Gray left, I tried calling him, but my calls went to voicemail. I jumped in the Jag and drove to the garage, but he wasn't there. I drove all over town, but he wasn't anywhere in Oakville.

For two days I've been calling and sending texts. I only got one answer, late last night.

***Gray: I have to go away, Drew-baby. Take care of your dad. Help him like you always wanted to do.***

Of course, I texted back as soon as I saw it.

***Me: Please come back. Let me help you.***

He never replies.

By Monday morning, my heart is in my throat and guilt is heavy on my shoulders. I finally break into my dad's room, and whiskey bottles are strewn all over the floor.

"How did he even get these?" I step over the discarded bottles, racing to where he's laying against the wall. "Dad?" I shake his shoulder.

His head lolls to the side, and he slurs my mother's name. Even through my anger, my heart breaks a little seeing him this way. He's too heavy to lift, which means I have to call 911 to get him to the hospital.

He'll be humiliated and furious when he comes around, but I can't worry about that now. It's a matter of life or death.

Driving behind the ambulance, I call Ruby and ask her to cover my appointments for the next few days—or reschedule them if the clients don't feel comfortable talking to her.

Pacing the waiting room of the hospital, I've never felt so alone. Dad is the last family I have... apart from Gray. My phone is in my hand, and I send another text.

***Me: I need you here.***

It's like the lost year, that dark year, all over again. Wrapping my arms around my waist, I crouch in a corner in the far end of the waiting room, closing my eyes as the tears fall.

I'm afraid he won't come back. Everything my dad said to him beats in my brain like a cruel drummer.

*You never belonged here. You never should have come here. Danny was the hero, not you. You should have died in the desert.*

I squeeze my arms tighter, seeing Gray's face as my dad shouted these words at him. With every syllable, Gray's expression grew darker. It was as if my dad were pounding him with his fists instead of lashing him with his tongue.

I tried to make it stop, but my dad was stronger than I expected, or pure rage gave him power. Years of built-up frustrations.

I know how guilty Gray feels. I know how much he blames himself, and with the PTSD, it just makes it all worse. At the same time, my anger at my father is difficult to sustain.

How can I hate this miserable, broken man? His words were

cruel, but they came from his pit of a soul, worn thin by the alcohol he used to survive for so long.

I sit for hours in a mix of families at the hospital, waiting, desperate for different reasons. HGTV keeps us all from going crazy, as we watch people fighting over house flipping, crying over home makeovers, debating whether they want to convert a garage into a master suite.

After what seems like an eternity, a nurse calls my name through the waiting room. "Andrea Harris?"

I raise my hand and go to her.

"A doctor will meet with you now." She leads me to a small room.

I step inside and close the door for privacy. A woman with dark hair and kind black eyes gives me a sad smile. "Your father was extremely dehydrated. Based on his blood work… I'm afraid he might have liver damage. It's possible he even damaged his heart."

My chin drops, and I exhale deeply. "He's been abusing alcohol since I was a girl. Since my mother died."

She nods. "His body can't keep this up."

"I've tried everything to get him help. He only fights me."

She exhales, leaning back. "The good news is we have him here now. We can start him on diazepam. We can get his nutrients up. Some of the damage will be irreversible, but perhaps we can break the cycle. Prevent further damage."

By the time I get home, I'm not sure I can keep going. My head is spinning, and the one time I was able to see my dad, he wouldn't stop saying Danny's name. I don't even take off my clothes before collapsing on my bed.

"Drew… Drew? Anybody home?"

My bed bounces gently, forcing my eyes to open. Ruby hangs over me, her long black hair touching my cheeks.

"She's alive!" She flops beside me, resting her head against mine. "I was worried about you. You okay?"

I don't even answer. I roll onto my side with my back to her.

In one fluid movement, she rolls behind me, curling her body to mine, her chest to my back as I cry for I don't know how long. It seems like forever. She only waits until I'm quiet again.

"Ma said for you to come eat with us. She actually said for you to come live with us. You know she wishes you were her daughter. Interested?"

Reaching out, I pull a tissue from the box on my nightstand. I figured it was just easier to leave it there.

"Your mom is one of the few people he likes." My voice is a wreck.

"Dude. Everybody loves my mother. Can you imagine how hard it is for me trying to fill her shoes?"

She's doing her best to make me laugh. I wish it would work.

"He left me, Rubes." The crack in my voice almost starts my tears again.

"We're going to have to use names. These male pronouns…"

"Gray left me." God, the pain in my neck is so intense. I try swallowing it away, but it's no good.

A quick inhale. "I don't believe it."

"He did."

Pain radiates from the hole in my chest through my shoulders, down my arms, up to my head. My best friend's arms around my waist are the only thing holding me together.

"I'm sure there's a reason. I know he wouldn't…" Her voice trails off, and for a moment the only noise is my shaky breathing. Finally, she asks softly. "How's your dad?"

Several steadying breaths later, I manage to answer. "He's stable. His doctor is actually pretty amazing."

"That's good!" She gives me a squeeze, a little rock. "One mountain at a time."

"What happened today at the clinic?"

"Hunter is doing amazing." She gives me another rock. "I'm going to nominate you for therapist of the year for that one."

"That's not a thing." I loosen out of her hold and roll to face her. The pain in my chest is relentless, but my brain can at least be distracted. "Why?"

"I mean, he's still convinced Richard Nixon is coming to get him."

"How is this progress?"

"Well, I was looking at your notes." She's lying on her back now. "You're on the right track with helping him find ways to feel less like an outsider. He and old lady Green are getting to be friends."

I sit up slowly. "What did he say?"

"He's helping her with her yard ornament restorations." She pushes up beside me. "You know she does it for pay, but she also does it guerilla style. She fixed my Dachshund, and I never even knew."

Sniffing, I nod, inhaling deeply. "There's some really nice people in this town."

She smiles warmly… a smile I know I've used myself. "I think it's the people who hurt the most who inflict the most pain."

For a second, I think about what she's saying. "That's not bad, Rubes. Maybe you should do calendars."

"Are you being shitty again?"

"No!" I start to laugh, and more tears come. "I'm serious. You say really nice things sometimes."

"Sometimes." She's still being dismissive, and I curl into her.

Skinny arms go around me. It's not Gray's warm, muscular embrace, but you know what? It's still pretty damn good.

# CHAPTER *Thirty*

## *Gray*

"SHE'S PEACEFUL. THAT'S THE BEST WE CAN HOPE FOR AT THE end." Sister Constance is beside me, watching Aunt Genevieve slip in and out of consciousness.

I give her a tight smile, as the old woman wavers between this life and whatever comes next.

My chest is still open and bleeding from the verbal laceration at Drew's place. I left knowing every word Carl Harris said was true. Drew's tears ringing in my ears were like salt in my wounds. I wanted to hold her, comfort her, but I knew her father was right. I would only bring her pain.

Midway into my drive to the garage, the phone rang. Sister Constance said I should come back to Dover as soon as possible. My aunt was dying. Her health had deteriorated to the point where she was having difficulty breathing, and the Alzheimer's was complicating her symptoms. They didn't know if she might have a moment of lucidity, and they weren't sure if I might want to be here.

Considering all the people I've let down, I figured I should at least try and be here for my last remaining relative, my father's youngest sister. My father, who had died long before I even knew his name.

Mack was his baby brother. Genevieve was his sister. All that's left now is me.

"Your aunt left few personal possessions, but we kept everything in a safe deposit box. When you're ready, I can take you to see it."

I watch the pale, shrunken form of my aunt, seeming to sleep. "How far away is it?"

"It's down in the basement. I can ask Sister Ilona to sit with her. She can call us if anything changes."

As we make our way slowly down the wide oak stairway to the main floor of the hospital, I feel the old nun glancing my way. Even wrapped in my own guilt, I do my best to smile, be grateful for her care to my family.

We take the final steps in silence. She lifts a heavy key from inside her robe and unlocks the door. I follow her through an oak paneled foyer to a smaller room, a room that actually looks like the inside of a safe.

She pulls the box an inch out of the space where it's housed. "Take your time."

With that, she turns and leaves me alone in the quiet room. The floors, walls, and ceiling are all shining silver, almost like steel. A bare table is behind me, and metal folding chairs are arranged around it.

I take the narrow box out of the chute and set it carefully on the table, lifting the lid, not knowing what to expect.

Aunt Genevieve never regained consciousness. She slipped away without a sound as I sat beside her bed, looking out at the snow falling gently. It hardly ever snows in Oakville. I wonder if

Drew would like the snow.

I haven't turned my phone on since I arrived here. I hate doing this again, but I know if I see her words begging me to come back, I'll drop everything and go. I can't do that right now. She needs to make peace with her father, and I need to give her space, settle my family's business here.

"Her long-term health insurance covered most of her time with us." Sister Constance sits across from me, her hands in her lap. "You shouldn't have any trouble covering the balance when you're ready."

"Long-term health insurance." I'm holding my aunt's will.

"Even without it, you wouldn't have had any difficulties." Her tone is all business. "You're one of the wealthiest landowners on the East Coast."

When Mack died, he'd left me what I thought was a large inheritance. What I found in my aunt's safety deposit box has been difficult for me to comprehend. In addition to money and holdings, I found the title deed for what the nun described as an enormous estate in Chateau Country. I didn't even know there was such a thing.

"It's been ten years since anyone lived there." She gives me a gentle smile. "From what I've heard, the Cole family estate is the largest in Brandywine Valley. It includes a mansion with extensive gardens and grounds extending for several miles."

The documents in my hands feel strangely light to carry such weight. "Why didn't I know about this?"

"I can't answer that question for you." Our eyes meet, and she smiles. "When your uncle came here, he was very concerned with getting all of the documents legally transferred to your name as the sole heir." Her laugh is gentle. "He drove Sister Marie crazy asking about it every day."

"Is she a lawyer?"

"She coordinated between him and the lawyer for our

convent. We have a rather extensive estate ourselves."

"Right." I've heard stories. Still, I'm not sure what to make of this news. It changes everything. "My aunt wanted to be cremated."

"I believe your family has a mausoleum on the grounds near one of the waterfalls." Waterfalls... I can't even imagine. "I can help you make those arrangements."

"Mack didn't ask to be buried in a mausoleum."

My uncle was buried beside his first wife, who was killed in a car crash before I went to live with him. Sometimes, late at night if he'd been drinking, he'd say it was why he wanted to work on cars. He wanted to make sure the brakes worked, make sure nothing was broken that might cause an accident. I didn't understand at the time. Now it makes so much sense.

"How are you feeling these days?" My eyes flicker to hers, which are full of concern. "I didn't want to say anything when you arrived. You seem more sad than when you left us."

My lips tighten in a smile. "Being back home was harder than I expected."

"I prayed for you daily." Constance had been my first counselor when I returned, but she'd referred me to a doctor for medication. "Did you settle the matters that were troubling you?"

I study the papers in my hands as I consider how my homecoming played out. "I visited Danny's grave. Drew was there." My chest tightens when I remember that night. "I tried to give her space. I'm not sure I can ever do it again."

"Drew is the girl you loved?" I nod, and she leans back in her chair. "Why would you want to give her space?"

"Her family doesn't like me." It sounds like a weak excuse. "I'm worried about my illness, what I might do to her if I'm not in control."

The documents I'm holding take on a different meaning as I speak. Money gives me freedom. I could go to my large estate

and stay there. Billy could take over the garage. It's what he always wanted. Drew never has to be hurt.

"Holding yourself apart from the people who love you seems like a Cole family trait." We exchange a glance and she smiles. "I've known your family a long time. I've seen them do it again and again."

"I don't know how else to keep her safe."

She exhales and stands, walking around the desk to face me. "I've heard it theorized Alzheimer's might be the brain's way of forgetting memories too painful to recall."

"Are you saying I'm at risk for developing Alzheimer's?"

"I suppose if that theory is true, we're all in danger of developing it." Leaning against the desk, she crosses her arms. "What are you trying to forget, Grayson?"

I'm uncomfortable answering her, but she's not letting me off the hook. The clock on her desk ticks louder. I look over her shoulder at the window, where the snowflakes drift past. My chest is tight with the answer, and when I glance up, her dark eyes are placid as a lake.

"I don't know." Clearing my throat, I shift in my seat. "Guilt? Depression?"

She nods. "Depression is anger turned inward. Who are you angry at?"

"Danny… myself." *For being so selfish.*

She takes a small book from the pocket of her apron. It's a leather-bound journal. "Start writing good things about yourself, about Danny, even if it's only one thing. Try to do it every day."

"What about my problem? The PTSD?"

Her lips press together and she walks around the desk again, pausing in front of her large window. "You have to bend with the ups and downs in life. God gives us partners to help us carry our burdens." A few moments pass, and she returns to her chair. "If it were me, I would let Drew decide what she can and cannot

handle. Remember the words of the lord, 'Love covers a multitude of sins.'"

I've heard the words before, but I still have doubts. "And her father?"

"He has to conquer his own demons. You can't do it for him."

I open the cover of the journal and place the very important papers inside. "I should go and check on the estate."

"I'm sure you'll be very pleased." She gives me a nod. "Just remember what you learned here. You can't live without love."

# CHAPTER Thirty-One

## Drew

THEY MOVED MY FATHER TO A NURSING HOME. HIS DOCTOR SAID THE damage wasn't as extensive as she'd feared, but she hopes by keeping him in a controlled environment, they might be able to help him with his addiction.

Speaking of help, I had to return to work. After being out a week, I see that Ruby is right. While he's still sure the government is wiretapping all our phones and the current president is channeling Richard Nixon, his friendship with Sylvia Green seems to have given him a focus for his life.

I look down at my past notes on the computer screen as he tells me about their exploits around town, and I can't help a sad little smile. Lifting my pen, I write slowly. *No longer an outsider.*

While I wouldn't characterize their relationship as anything more than friendly, I know they've developed a fondness for each other. Love is healing my client.

During my lunch hour, I walk down to the garage. I've driven past it several times, straining my eyes for any sign of Gray. He hasn't come back since the night of our dinner.

Billy, however, has been keeping the place up and running, which gives me an idea. He's talking to Remington Key when I tap lightly on the open door.

"Miss Drew." Both men turn and walk to where I'm standing. Billy's face is lined with concern. "You're not having trouble with the Jag?"

"Oh, no." Shaking my head, I smile up at them. "I was just… I just was wondering…" Shit. I'm going to look like a crazy stalker.

Or a dumped girlfriend who can't take a hint.

Is that what I've become? My stomach cramps at the notion.

"Gray had to go back to Delaware." Billy doesn't need help reading my mind. "He said his aunt died."

"He called you?" The thought of him calling Billy and ignoring me is even worse than not knowing anything.

"Not since he left. He didn't even call really. He just sent me a text."

That bit of information eases my suffering a tiny bit. "I was just… worried about him." No point denying it.

"Yeah, me too." Billy nods, holding the clipboard to his chest. "He didn't say when he'd be back."

My shoulders droop, and I almost forget Remi standing right beside us. "Was he close to his aunt?" His low voice has a nice resonance.

I blink away the mist from my eyes and give him a sad smile. "I don't know. I don't think so."

Remi is thoughtful a moment. "When my wife died… you remember? I wasn't up for talking to anyone. I just wanted to be alone. Then after a little while, I couldn't stand being alone."

It's a nice sentiment. I wish it made me feel better. "Thanks, Remi. See you around, Billy."

"No problem." Billy actually looks sad for me. I reach out and give his arm a squeeze. "If I hear from him, I'll tell him to call you."

Even though it changes nothing, it's nice to know somebody's rooting for us. I mean, in addition to Ruby. Someone who Gray might listen to… although, I have no way of knowing if Gray listens to Billy.

More time passes. My texts to Gray have become a daily journal of my life. I send him a text letting him know what the weather is like. I send him a text telling him the Jag is running so smoothly. I send him a text saying I'm going to the lake house to clean out Danny's things…

Cleaning out my brother's old room is a task I put off for too long. My dad won't let us touch anything in the main house in town, but the items in his lake house room are simply gathering dust.

Empty boxes are arranged around the bedroom. When I open the closet door, his scent hits me right in the face, and I have to sit down. For a moment, I think this might be a terrible idea.

I walk downstairs and start opening and closing cabinets. When Gray and I were here, we drank the bottle of red wine I'd ordered from the grocery. The cabinets are bare except for a box of crackers and a can of soup left from that order.

The refrigerator only has the rest of that loaf of bread and cheese. A few cans of soda are in the drawer below. Opening the freezer, a sad smile curls my lips. An old bottle of Skyy vodka sits in the very back.

"Way to go, Danny," I mutter, pulling it out and turning it in my hands.

It's cheap and old, but does vodka go bad? I pull down a tumbler ready to find out. I pour it straight over ice before stepping to the radio and switching on the streaming service.

It picks up right where we left off last time. Sam Cooke singing on the radio about bringing your love home to me. Snatching up my phone, I type another text to Gray.

***Me: At the lake house cleaning. Wishing you'd show up at my door again.***

That night has a different meaning to me now that I know about his PTSD. I realize now the panic he was fighting, the flashbacks. At the time, I only saw the fire in his eyes, his desire when my robe opened and he saw my body for the first time in so long.

My nipples tighten at the memory. It was wild and fierce and demanding, and I needed him so much. I need him now.

With a sigh, I take a long drink of the clear liquor. It only burns a little going down, and I walk slowly up to my brother's room again.

I gather his clothes into bags for donation to the Goodwill. I keep a few items back for memory. The pictures I put in a box along with his football trophies.

Gazing at those old group photos, I smile at the guys scowling, doing their best to look tough. Gray's image makes my heart beat faster. His steely eyes burn at me from the past. I was so in love with him back then, but he didn't notice me until he went away to college.

Blinking fast, I hope history repeats itself.

Perhaps by going away, he'll remember me again?

Several hours pass. Marvin Gaye, Sam Cooke, Al Green, and more filter through the radio as I finish boxing up the past. The last thing I find on the very top shelf of Danny's closet takes me by surprise.

It's a black leather-bound journal, and it looks ancient. I never knew my brother to keep a journal, and I walk over to sit on his bed and look inside.

At first I hesitate. Is it violating his privacy to read it now? I decide it's not, since he's not here to care. Cracking open the cover, I trace my finger over the handwriting.

"Who writes anything down anymore?" I whisper to myself.

At the same time, I guess I make my therapy notes on paper

first. I think it helps to organize my thoughts.

The first entries are pretty basic stuff. He's pissed about football practice. He thinks he was on the bench too much.

It goes on about the same. He records his and Gray's antics sneaking into the swimming pool at the senior center after hours, sneaking into the high school to steal a test.

All of these stunts sound masterminded by Daniel Harris. Gray was never much of a troublemaker. It's not until I get to the end that I read a passage that stops me.

*Dad says to keep him away from Drew, but Gray is one of the best guys I know…*

My breath catches, and I flip back a page. Scanning quickly, the words make my heart beat faster as I read them.

*He believes she was in love with Mack Cole and planning to leave with him. He says Mack comes from money back East. I don't believe that. Why would he work in a filthy garage in this little town?*

My jaw drops, and my hands begin to tremble.

As I dig deeper, I learn my father suspected my mother of having an affair with Gray's uncle.

"Oh my God…" The words slip out on a hiss. "It's why he always hated him."

Taking a deep breath, I lean my head back against the side of the bed, doing my best to calm my racing pulse. I never knew about any of this. Did Gray know?

Flipping ahead, I see the letter M and stop.

*…Mack's garage today. He claims it's a lie. He shouted at me it was worthless gossip. He was so angry, I think I believe him. He said Mom only tried to comfort him when he wanted to give up. That sounds more like it. Dad's drunk. The Cole's don't have any money. And Gray is still my best friend. He's the best guy I know.*

"Gray…" I look up where my phone sits on my bed.

I want to show him this. I want him to know how my brother really felt. Maybe it would help him heal. I'd do anything to take

that dark look out of his eyes.

Pushing off the floor, I stuff the journal in my purse. Now I have two things to show Gray when he gets back. If he ever comes back.

Grabbing my phone I send one more text.

***Me: I'm still waiting. Please come home. Let's heal together.***

"Remember what happened the last time you went on a date?" Ruby is wrapping her hair around the barrel of a curling iron, creating huge curls.

"Oh, no. I'd rather die than call Ralph again. Not only did I have to put up with him, I had to put up with his mother."

"But the night turned out really hot…" She sing-songs.

*Only because Gray was in town*, I mentally add, thinking how that was almost six weeks ago, thinking about the date of my last period. This morning I looked at my calendar, and I've been chewing my lip ever since, debating whether I should stop by a drugstore, trying to figure out what to do if I'm right.

"What are you thinking?" Ruby is like a hawk watching me.

My eyes flicker down to the glossy pages of the *Teen Vogue* in front of me. "I'm wondering why the hell you're still getting *Teen Vogue*. Are you having a crisis I should know about?"

She turns to the mirror again, lifting another lock of glossy, raven hair around the straight curling iron. "I thought it might help me relate to my younger clients. You know. Knowing about what they're interested in? Plus I love those cute shoes. And look at that little dress!"

"You can't wear these clothes. You'll look ridiculous." Although, as I say it, with her petite figure, she could probably get away with all of these styles.

Turning to face me, she rakes her fingers through her new waves.

"That looks really good on you."

"Really?" Her head whips back to the mirror, and the way she starts swishing it back and forth, making faces, almost makes me laugh.

It's the oddest thing. Ever since I found Danny's journal, I've had this unexpected flood of hope. Gray still hasn't replied to my texts, but I feel like a cosmic shift has occurred. It's like for the first time in my life, the universe is conspiring to help me. Like it might be okay if…

"I was thinking maybe I'd get that surgery done on my eyes." She pulls the corners of her eyes wider. "You know, to make them rounder?"

"Don't you dare!" I sit up quick on her bed. "I love your eyes just the way they are."

"You have no idea what you're talking about, Round Eyes." She shakes her now-wavy head, and I frown.

"You are beautiful. Stop picking yourself apart."

"Aw!" She stands and walks over to kiss my forehead. "Thanks, sis. Now. Let's get you changed. You don't have to call a guy, but you're going out with me."

"Nothing in me feels like going out." I allow her to drag me off the bed.

Unlike the universe, my bestie is always willing to help me… in a very meddling and pushy way. A lot like her mother.

"Your hair looks good." Standing side by side in the mirror, our hair looks almost identical, except mine is light blonde. "Try this on."

She tosses me a super short, high-waisted mini with a long-sleeved cropped shirt. "This is kind of… revealing."

"Sexy." She says the word on top of my observation. "You'll look amazing in that."

"I don't really want to look amazing. I'm not trying to meet anybody."

"That's the worst attitude I've ever heard in my life." I watch

as she changes into a velvet sheath dress.

It slides down her petite frame, and I step over to pull on the skirt and long-sleeved top. She's right about it looking sexy. The top stretches over my breasts, and the skirt makes my legs look a mile long.

With a little sigh, I wish Gray were here. He loves my curves.

"Okay, so where are we going on this girlfriend date?" I walk to her makeup mirror and touch some powder on my nose. "You hate everywhere in Oakville."

"I do not hate everywhere in Oakville. I just know everyone in Oakville. There's a difference." She pauses to slide deep red lipstick over her rosebud lips. "The Red Cat is super funky and vintage. Have you ever been there?"

"It's really more of an old person's bar, isn't' it?" My nose curls as I touch up my bright pink lips. "We always went to places on the lake."

She squeezes my shoulder. "Tonight we're doing something new. And you're going to love it!"

With a sigh, I give myself a reassuring look. *Come on, universe. Don't let me down this time.*

# CHAPTER Thirty-Two

## Gray

IT'S A NINE-HOUR DRIVE FROM MY FAMILY'S PLACE IN DELAWARE SOUTH to Oakville. I'm going to make it in a day.

I've spent the last two weeks settling my aunt's affairs and acquainting myself with my newly acquired property. The house… strike that. The forty thousand square foot mansion is pretty ridiculous.

From what I've learned, my great grandfather was in the steel business… and a bootlegger on the side. That second bit of information I found while digging in one of the old studies on the third floor. The place has a hundred and fifty rooms.

Sister Constance didn't tell me it came with a butler, a cook, and a housekeeper on call. I did call them, but more to help me figure out where everything was than to act as my servants.

Walking the halls of the old mansion, looking at all the furniture draped in sheets, gave me an unfamiliar sense of family pride. It's something I've never experienced before, and for the first few days, I allowed it to sink into my brain, restore a sense of

belonging I'd lost after my uncle died.

Mack never told me about all of this… I'm not exactly sure why, since he went through so much trouble making sure I'd inherit it after Genevieve died. Maybe he thought I'd be reckless with it?

More than anything, I feel a quiet sense of awe. A growing sense of security. A need to find healing so I can bring Drew here. The idea I had in Constance's office faded the longer I walked the dark wood hallways, looking at portraits of familiar-looking people I don't know.

I don't want to be like them. I don't want to be a recluse, growing old in a castle no one knows about, completely alone. Plus, Drew would shit twice and die if she saw the library in this place.

My assignment to keep a journal has helped me more than I believed it would. In the evenings, I walk down a flagstone path, past concrete urns bigger than me overflowing with vines, into a thick, wisteria-lined garden. It's cold, but the snow has stopped, and I sit on a wooden bench looking out over the vast property down toward the large pond where a boat sits waiting to be used.

Then I write.

I force myself to go back and remember the good days when we were teens. I remember when Danny and I really became friends in middle school. A fancy name doesn't matter much in public school, and we had to be allies against the bigger boys.

I remember the nights we spent in the pool house talking about our plans. I remember silly things like practicing spitting and learning to yo-yo. Then we got older, and Danny swiped his dad's old Playboys. Then we discovered the wonders of the Internet.

Danny used to say I was his best friend. Hell, all the way up until he died, we were thick as thieves. I was good enough to be his friend. I am good enough for Drew. Even more so now.

Writing it all down helps me to ask the questions and explore the answers, even if I can never have the conversation with Danny in person. Even if I never know why he said what he did.

I also got that old roll of film Leslie gave me developed. More than anything, it was the final kick in the pants I needed to get in my truck and drive south.

Out of a roll of twenty-four, almost all of them were taken that summer at the lake house. Most were selfies of Leslie and Danny.

It hurt seeing him so young and happy at first, but after a while, it made me smile to remember him having fun, acting silly. Him with his arms around Leslie. Him with his hands under her bikini top. *Asshole*, I laugh to myself, setting them in a stack to the side.

The ones I cherish the most are of Drew and me. It's weird because Leslie took shots of us… I guess they're pretty intimate. Times when we didn't know she was watching.

My favorite is one taken from behind Drew. I don't know why I didn't see Leslie take it. I'm facing Drew and her back is to the camera. Her bikini top hangs off one finger, leaving her topless facing me.

I chuckle to myself when I look at it. My expression is complete infatuation. I'm smiling because my dog is climbing a hill like it did pretty much that entire summer looking at her pretty breasts, touching them, making her mine.

In another shot, Drew's lying on her stomach on a towel, and my arm is over her lower back. My face is right on her cute little round ass, and it looks like my teeth are against her skin. Yeah, I'd bite that ass.

In another, we're sitting side by side, and Drew's looking up at me. So much love is in my girl's eyes. She's so beautiful. It cements my resolve. I don't want to grow old and forget these things. I want to learn to forgive myself. I want to forgive Danny.

I don't know why Leslie took these photos or what she was planning to do with them, but I'm glad she gave them to me. I guess I understand now how everybody knew we were a couple. We didn't do a very good job hiding it.

I'll just go on and admit it, the other reason I'm ready to head back south is to show up those assholes who always treated me like dirt. It kicks ass that my family is so fucking rich. I'm not going to lie about it. I'm also not going to be a dick. I'm just going to take care of business.

I don't have to put up with bullies or their bullshit anymore, and I'm ready to own who I am and who I love.

When I turned on my phone before I left the house, it wouldn't stop buzzing with texts from Drew for what felt like two whole minutes. I sat down on the marble floor of my enormous foyer and read them all, laughing at the words, imagining her pretty face saying them.

Some twisted my guts. Several made me rub the pain away from my stomach. I never want to make Drew sad. I change my mind about calling her. I want it to be a surprise. I got the message loud and clear. ***Come home...***

I'm driving all day.

It's exactly what I intend to do.

# CHAPTER Thirty-Three

## Drew

"Where have I been hiding?" I shout in Ruby's ear as we make our way through The Red Cat.

The place is ancient, with red shag carpet, a jukebox that plays real records, and lava lamps in the corners. The bar is carpeted as well, and it's packed solid.

"I told you this place was making a comeback!" She shouts in my ear so loud it tickles.

I stick my finger there and mouth an *Ow!* to her. She only laughs. I follow her closer to the bar, doing my best to avoid the overt stares of a few male patrons I don't recognize.

"Ruby Roo!" A loud voice hollers over the crowd.

Ruby spins around frowning. "Dammit to hell! I hate when he does that Scooby-Doo shit." Dagwood Magee slides up beside us, pushing into the bodies to lean on the bar. "And Drew too!"

"Oh my God." I start to laugh.

Ruby is not smiling. "What the hell are you doing here? And stop yelling that in public. You're fucking with my hustle."

"Hey, Dag!" I'm glad to see a familiar face. Correction, a

familiar face on a great big guy. "Is Dotty here with you?"

"Nah, I just stopped by after work. She's waiting for me at home."

Ruby and I exchange a glance. "Uh, Einstein, you do realize it's after ten, right?"

"What?" He lifts his hand off the bar. "Oh, fuck! I'd better give her a call."

"Let me call her!" I hop up and down on my toes, not really wanting him to leave. "I'll see if she'll come meet us."

"She's going to be so mad at me." Dag looks at the whiskey. "I was planning my fantasy football team… time goes by so fast."

"You're lucky I'm not Dotty. I'd kick your butt." Ruby waves at an ancient bartender. He looks as old as the place. "Two tequila sunrises."

"Tequila." I think about my calendar and my mental math this morning, but it's too late to stop her.

Ruby puts the plastic cup in my hand, and I lean into her ear. "How is it possible I don't know everyone in here?"

"Word gets out." She shouts back. "Cheap drinks mixed strong. It draws folks from all over the place."

"Fly Me to the Moon" by Frank Sinatra blasts from the jukebox. I start to sway my hips, wondering how I'm going to get rid of this tequila, when she leans forward, her black eyes huge. "Who is that?"

I start to turn, and she grabs my shoulder, stopping me. "Don't look! He'll know we're talking about him."

"Maybe that's a good thing?" The song ends with a flourish of brass instruments, and we can actually hear each other for a minute. "You could try meeting someone the old-fashioned way. In a bar."

"The old-fashioned way, according to my mom, is in church." She leans back and makes a disgusted face. "Not doing that either."

I sneak a glance over my shoulder, and I catch a glimpse of… sexy single dad! "That's Remington Key! Remember when I tried to introduce you after church that day? This is a good sign! You met him at church and in a bar!"

"You never introduced me to him. I'd have remembered." She turns and excited black eyes meet mine. "I'm going to investigate."

"Go for it." I'm wondering where Lillie is tonight when a wash of whiskey breath hits my nose so hard, I'm sure I'm contact drunk. If that's a thing.

"Hey, sexy. I've never seen you around here."

"Sorry." I try to step back, only to bump into a person behind me. "I don't come here very often."

"I'd remember if you did." The guy isn't bad looking. He's just really drunk and not Gray. "You live around here?"

"I actually need to make a call." I hold up my phone. "So I'll have to take a rain check… Um…"

"Name's Blaire. And I'll take that rain check." He swipes my phone out of my hand, and my heart freezes. "Let's see here. Oops. I need your pretty face to unlock it."

The music starts up again, loud as ever. This time it's Dean Martin singing about how you're nobody til somebody loves you.

"Give me my phone." My voice is lost in the trumpets, and I'm wondering where Ruby went.

I look around, over my shoulder, and see she's at the bar still talking to Remi.

The guy grabs my wrist while I'm not looking and lifts it to the screen. "Do thumbs still work on these?"

I try to jerk my arm away, but the person behind me rams into me, shoving me forward into Blaire's arms.

"Hey, baby." He slides his hand around my lower back, his whiskey breath way too close to my nose. "This is more like it."

"Let me go!" I yell louder.

"You don't have to go so soon." His hands slide down, over my ass, and my heart beats frantically in my chest.

I think I might puke, until a low, rich voice cuts through the noise. It cuts through everything, the fear, the panic, the disgust.

"She said to let her go." It's Gray, standing right in the guy's face, staring him down.

"Gray…" It comes out as a little squeal.

My fear turns instantly to happiness. I'm blinking so hard, I can't take my eyes off him, even though he's leaning dangerously close to Whiskey Blaire, who's still clutching my arm.

"Who the fuck are you?" Blaire steps to Gray, and my happiness gets a little panicky.

"Please just let me go." It's like I'm caught in the middle of some ridiculous face-off where this idiot thinks he's tougher than my sexy, six-foot-two war vet.

I try jerking my arm again, but this guy has a grip.

"Hey! Look who's back!" Dag's loud voice rings from across the bar, and I hope this means Blaire's going to get a clue.

I'm wrong.

"Last warning, buddy." Gray speaks through clenched teeth. The muscle in Gray's jaw moves, and his nostrils flare. "Let her go."

"What the hell's going on here?" Dag slaps a hand roughly on Blaire's shoulder. "You hassling my man Gray's lady?"

Finally, the guy relents. His grip on my wrist loosens, and I snatch my hand away. "May I have my phone back, please?"

Gray hasn't backed down. His eyes are still locked on Blaire, who slowly hands my phone with a dramatic flair. He's so stupid, I take it and shake my head. Dag's hand slides off his shoulder, and I'm ready to rush into Gray's arms.

"What? No thank you?" Blaire shouts at me, and that's it.

Gray grabs him by the jaw, lifting him off his feet and ramming his back against the wall so hard the photos bounce. "You'd

better get the fuck out of here before I throw you out."

The guy claws at Gray's hand on his neck, his eyes squeezed shut. "Put me down, man." His voice is a strangled plea.

"You're going to leave here and never come back." Protective fury ripples off Gray in waves.

I want to try and stop him before he kills the guy, but I don't want to get in the way.

"Gray, man…" Dag, like me, is holding out his arms and trying to diffuse the situation.

"Okay, break it up!" The ancient bartender Mose comes from around the end of the bar, a Louisville slugger in his hand. "Let him go, Rambo, before I have to do something I don't want to."

Gray still doesn't move. He blinks a few times, then another second ticks past.

"Come on, Gray. Let him go." Dag carefully puts his hand on Gray's shoulder. "He's done here."

Another second ticks by, and I see his fingers relax. He releases the guy all at once, and Blaire falls in a heap on the floor.

"That's it now pay your bill and hit the road, Jack." Mose stands over the guy, tapping the bat against his palm.

Gray takes a step back, and I see he's breathing hard. His eyes are still trained on the crumpled heap on the floor, but I'm ready for him to look at me.

"Holy shit, mini-orgasm!" Ruby is beside me fanning her face. "Gray is a total badass!"

Finally, the guy starts to move. He slowly rises to his feet, and Mose takes him by the arm, leading him to the other side of the bar to settle his bill.

Gray turns to me, and everything seems to fade away. The music gets quieter, the people disappear. It's like we're in a special tunnel, just Gray and me. Our eyes meet, and his are so stormy and intense, so focused.

I remember how focused he can be, and the space between

my thighs heats.

As if waking from a trance, a smile lifts his cheeks. A dimple appears, and my stomach squeezes so hard. I clasp my hands together, bringing them to my lips, and we slowly start to move, closing the space between us.

"Are you okay?" The low vibration of his voice does funny things to my insides.

"I'm much better now." I lift my hand, placing my palm on the top of his chest. "You came back."

"I couldn't stay away." He puts a hand on my waist, drawing me closer to him. "I made a promise."

"You said you couldn't keep it." My other hand is on his chest now.

He puts both hands on my waist. "I decided I didn't want to be a man who doesn't keep his promises."

A surge of self-preservation rises out of nowhere. "I'm not sure I can keep doing this. I can't count on you being here for me, then you ghost me again."

His brow furrows, and he pulls me closer to his chest. "What are you saying? You want me to leave?"

"It depends on what you plan to do."

Our eyes lock, and heat races to my core. "I plan to take you back to my place and spend the night in your arms. Is that okay with you?"

"Then what?" It's a breathless whisper.

He leans closer, his lips grazing the shell of my ear as he speaks, sending chills skittering down my arms. "Then I have a lot to tell you. Then we'll do whatever you decide."

He lifts his head to find my eyes, and when they meet, I can't stop a smile. "I'm ready to go anywhere with you."

"Let's start at the house first."

# CHAPTER Thirty-Four

## Gray

**B**EING IN DREW'S ARMS AGAIN IS BETTER THAN FINDING OUT I HAVE more money than God. It's better than winning the fucking life lottery…

*It's like drawing a long breath after a deep dive. I hold her body against mine, and she smells like heaven. She feels like forever. My body relaxes, the tension leaves my muscles…*

It's the same feelings I've always had in her arms.

After dealing with that asshole at The Red Cat—I swear to Christ, I was ready to finish that guy—I had to get out of that place.

Drew seemed to understand. She put her hand in mine, and we walked the short distance to the garage. I took the lead, walking her into the cottage and closing the door before turning and pulling her to me.

"Drew-baby." I speak the words against the skin of her neck.

She shivers, lifting her arms around me. "You have some explaining to do."

"I have so much to tell you." My lips trace a line up into her hair, to her temple. "You are so sexy in this little outfit. That skirt makes me crazy."

"Does it?" She steps back, putting a finger in her mouth. "What if I did this?"

She turns her back and I watch as she lifts the front. It only takes a moment for her to slide the thin strings of her thong panties down her long legs. When she gets to her ankles, she bends all the way over, flashing her pussy at me, and I nearly come in my pants.

"Holy shit, Drew." I step back, sitting on the edge of the coffee table. "You're killing me."

"Am I?" She turns around making big eyes. "I'm just getting comfortable."

Her hands go behind her back, and she lifts that crop-top. I watch in awe as she slowly removes her lacy bra, leaving her breasts to bounce as she walks over and straddles my lap.

"What do you have to tell me?"

With a groan, I slide my hands under her shirt, cupping her breasts with my palms, rolling her tight nipples between my fingers. "I'm never leaving you again."

She starts to laugh. "Are you just saying that because I let you touch my boobs."

"Yes," I answer fast, and she pulls back as if she'll run away. I only laugh and pull her closer. ""Touching your beautiful body is a bonus. It's the icing on the cake."

She relaxes, cupping my face in her hands and leaning forward to kiss me. Our mouths open, and our tongues curl together, searching, exploring, reuniting.

My dick is an iron rod in my jeans, and my hands slide up her back, pulling her closer. She tugs at the hem of my shirt, and I take a moment to whip it over my head. I pull her shirt over her head, and our bodies slide together her breasts bouncing along

the ridges of my chest.

Our mouths reunite, and I stand, lifting her in one fluid movement to carry her to the bed. Tossing her back, I push her thighs apart and bring my face to her beautiful pussy.

"Gray!" She sighs, her hips rocking as I trace my tongue along the path that makes her come.

I find the tight little bud at the top and circle it, sucking gently, before tracing my tongue down and fucking her with it. She moans, and I return to her clit, teasing and tasting, loving her moans, the way she pulls my hair, until I feel her legs begin to quiver.

"Oh… oh…" The sound in her voice tells me she's right on the edge, and I stand, shoving my jeans down, not even hesitating before I drive my cock balls deep into her throbbing core.

We both cry out. Her hips buck wildly against my cock. "Yes… yes!" I feel her gripping and coming, and I close my eyes, thrusting hard and fast, chasing my own release.

It's been so long since we were together, it doesn't take much. I'm holding her body, closing my eyes as the orgasm rockets through my pelvis, pulsing into her. I groan so deeply it makes me cough.

She's in my arms, and I grip her tightly, wanting to make good on my promise. Never wanting to let her go. Her arms are around me just as tight as we drift down from the clouds.

I lift up, onto my elbow so I can gaze at her beautiful face. Her eyes reflect the same love back at me.

My expression changes, briefly. "I'm sorry about your dad." I need to say it so she'll know I'm not holding a grudge.

Her brow furrows, and she shakes her head. "The things he said to you…"

"He was all messed up. He's been all messed up a long time."

"I found something I need to show you. I have a couple things to show you, actually." Her frown melts, and a sly grin is on her

lips. "I only have one with me."

It makes me insanely curious. "What is it?

She struggles to get up, and I reluctantly let her. She hops off the bed, making a pit stop in the bathroom to clean up. Lying on the bed, I put my hands behind my head. I haven't been careful at all with her, and I confess, part of me dreams of seeing Drew Harris pregnant with my baby.

I can see her cute and round, wearing one of those little dresses she likes, her long blonde hair down her back. *Damn*, I want that so much.

"You sure are smiling." She hops on the bed, and I push up to sitting, putting my hand on top of hers and lifting it to my lips.

"Just thinking about the future."

She digs in her purse then freezes, lifting her gaze to mine. "Funny. That's related to what I have to show you."

I look down at her purse then up at her. "Don't keep me in suspense."

"You have always been my hero, Grayson Cole. From the time I was a little girl, when you saved me. You dried my tears. You looked out for me."

Warmth moves through my stomach remembering the times she's describing. I remember her as a little girl, innocent and playful. She was always a cute little kid.

Then one day, she became a sexy, beautiful woman.

"I only did what you asked me to." Reaching out, I smooth her long hair away from her cheek. "I could never say no to you."

"I'm going to ask you to do one more thing." I'm confused as I watch her pull what looks like a round piece of cardboard out of her bag. "Keep your promise."

She hands it to me, and I slowly turn it over, the memories of that night so long ago coming at me in a rush.

"I can't believe you still have this." My voice is a whisper as I read my old signature.

I remember it well. It's a promise I made to her with all my heart the day before we left for the desert.

*When I come back, I'm going to marry you. I promise, I will make you mine.*

"It's a legally binding contract." Drew gives me that sassy, bossy look I love.

It makes me grin. "Is that so?"

"You signed it."

Lifting it up, I pretend to inspect it. "Your name's not on here."

She takes it out of my hands. "It's in my possession. It belongs to me just like you belong to me. Ever since that first day when you carried me out of danger."

"You want to marry some guy who lives in a one-bedroom shack behind a garage? A guy everybody says isn't good enough for you? A guy fighting PTSD? What kind of life is that for you, Drew-baby? You're a princess."

Her cute jaw clenches and she pushes on my shoulders. "Is that guy's name Grayson Cole?"

Raising my eyebrows, I shrug. "Sure looks that way."

"Then yes." She gives me a quick kiss. "I'm not a princess. I'm a regular girl who can save herself. I'm ready to save you, too."

At that, I catch her around the waist, rolling her onto her back and kissing her good and hard. Her squeal is consumed by the strength of my love. Lifting my head, I grin down at her, loving this girl more than she could ever know.

"I've got great news for you then."

# CHAPTER Thirty-Five

## Drew

I'VE HEARD PEOPLE SAY YOUR LIFE CAN CHANGE IN THE BLINK OF AN EYE.

I never believed it until Grayson Cole came back into my life the second time.

We're sitting together in church listening to Pastor Hibbert talking about love. He's talking about how perfect love covers a multitude of sins, and Gray's hand tightens over mine.

I glance up at him, drop-dead gorgeous in a slate blue Armani suit with a light blue shirt and yellow tie underneath. My man sure cleans up well.

He's also a fucking gazillionaire! *Holy shit!* Sorry, God.

After Gray agreed to keep his promise to marry me, he hit me with an even bigger surprise. His family is really obnoxiously rich.

Well, he is now. Like me, he's all that's left of his troubled clan. Unlike me, he has more than just a broken-down house and a name. Gray is the real deal, and I lost no time making sure the whole town found out about it.

How?

I told Dotty Magee.

In two days' time, all the assholes who'd ever been mean to him were falling all over themselves trying to kiss his butt.

Pastor Hibbert ties his sermon on love into his sermon on forgiveness, which I'm starting to realize is one of his favorite topics. It makes me think of my last visit with my dad.

I went to tell him Gray and I are engaged. I wanted him to be a part of my wedding, but I didn't know if that would be asking too much.

I said the words, and he only leaned back in the chair and looked far away. "I told you you'd end up leaving me."

"I'm not leaving, Daddy. I'm here because I want to bring you in. I want you to be a part of our new family."

His brow furrows, and I don't try to deny it. I haven't even told Gray yet. "He did exactly what I said he would."

"No, he didn't!" My voice rises, but I can't help it. "He asked me to marry him. He's richer than Bill Gates, and he wants to take care of us. To take care of you… Even though you're not giving him much of a reason."

"I'm not taking anything from him. His family tried to destroy ours."

My chin drops, and I decide to tell him what Danny wrote. "It wasn't like that. Mom was only trying to comfort Mack. It's probably where I got my desire to be a therapist. She saw a sad person, and she wanted to make him happy."

His expression darkens. "Don't defend him. You didn't know him like I did."

"Maybe not, but I knew my mother. She was devoted to her family." I reach out and touch his arm. "Can't you at least have faith in her?"

"I won't discuss this with you." He rises from the chair, walking unsteadily toward the nursing home.

I jog to catch up with him, holding his arm. "It's okay, Dad.

You don't have to talk about it. Just listen and hear me. I love you. I want you to be in our wedding. Gray wants to put the past behind us. Can't you at least do that for me?"

His cold blue eyes slide down his nose at me, and I can't tell if it's agreement or dissent. I step forward and wrap my arms around him, hugging him with all the feelings I've held back for so long.

"I love you, Daddy. Please try to let go of that old bitterness. Please come back to your family…"

Pastor Hibbert finishes his sermon with a prayer for God to help us learn to heal and forgive, and when it's over, we all file out to the lawn.

"Grayson!" Florence Stern waves her handkerchief as she jogs across the grass to where we stand, my hand in the crook of his arm. "Grayson Cole!"

I feel him exhale deeply as he turns to face her. "Hi, Mrs. Stern."

"My goodness!" She puts her hand on her chest, smiling like he just paid her a compliment. "What good manners you have, Grayson. You always were such a good boy."

I swallow the puking noise I want to make, and she proceeds to go on about how she's organizing a big welcome home celebration for him. Naturally, she didn't do it six weeks ago because she wasn't sure he'd be staying, what with all his East Coast family connections and all…

"Sure." He doesn't hesitate, but my eyebrows quirk up.

We're back at my family house eating my signature dish, shrimp and grits, before he even brings it up. "I guess it's okay for her to do what she does. It serves a purpose."

I'm indignant. "She's a two-faced bitch, and you don't have to go to her stupid party. In fact, I'd be happy to skip it."

He gives me a little smile. "We'll go. And we'll have a fun time with the good people in this town."

A few days ago, I gave him Danny's journal. He kissed me and

took it down to the grave to read it. When he came back, he was so changed. I could tell he'd been moved by what he read, but he didn't want to talk about it.

He didn't need to. I understood.

Looking around the kitchen, he nods before meeting my eyes again. "We can get some contractors in to do repairs on this place. We can stay down at the lake house while they work here. Then I'll have them fix up that place, too."

"Gray, you don't have to—"

His expression is stern. "It's going to be our place when we're married, right?"

"Yes, it is."

He nods. "And I want to move your dad to a better place. Do you think he'd agree to go to Betty Ford?"

I can't take it anymore. I go to him and put my arms around his waist, resting my cheek against his chest as the tears fill my eyes.

"Hey..." He puts his arms around me. "I'm sorry. I wasn't raising my voice at you. I really want to do these things." His words turn my tears of gratitude to tears of joy. He lifts my chin. "What's going on with you?"

"I guess I'm more emotional lately." Lifting my hand, I place my palm against his cheek. "I have another surprise for you."

His brow furrows, and our eyes meet. My stomach tickles, and I'm not sure I can say the words. I don't know why I'm suddenly so shy.

"What is it, baby?"

Swallowing fast, I just say it. "We'll need baby-proofing, too, since I'm... well, I'm pregnant."

For a brief moment, everything goes quiet. My heart beats so hard, I think I might be sick. I'm blinking fast, not sure what to do, if I should say something more, until at last his expression breaks.

He takes a step back, his eyes moving from my face to my

torso and back again, as the smile I love slowly curls his lips. "You're… pregnant?"

"I'm pregnant." I nod as we both say the word at the same time.

All at once, I'm off my feet. His face is in my chest, and I hug him to me as we turn around once.

"Drew." He lowers me to my feet, his voice full of wonder.

He places his hands on the sides of my head like I love, and I'm not sure I've ever seen him look this way as long as I've known him.

"How long have you known?"

"I started suspecting about a week ago, but I only took the test this morning."

"And you're sure?"

"Those tests are pretty accurate."

Once again, I'm pulled to his chest. His strong arms surround me, and we breathe together as I listen to his heart beating fast.

Then he starts to laugh. He holds me out again, pure joy radiating in his eyes. "We're going to have a baby."

A smile breaks across my face, and I'm laughing, too. "We are."

Next thing I know, I'm naked in my bed, thoroughly fucked with Gray's face right above my navel.

"Hello, in there," he calls softly, and I start to laugh again.

"You're acting like the baby's down a well."

He cuts mischievous eyes up at me. "We'll have to get her a dog."

"It could be a boy." Reaching down, I thread my fingers through his dark hair.

"Boys like dogs, too." I laugh and my stomach moves. His eyes widen, and he smooths his palm over my still-flat stomach. "We'll have to move up the timeline on that marriage thing. How does next weekend sound to you?"

I shake my head, reaching for his face, and he scoots up to capture my lips in another long kiss. I'm happy to marry him tomorrow if it's what he wants.

Our life is everything I dreamed it would be that night I asked him for a promise on a coaster.

Nope, it's better.

It's a life that started out heartbreakingly sad. It's a life where two orphans were saved by love. It's a life where Grayson Cole took a hero's journey through the darkness and the hatred, but he never lost his noble heart.

Now he's here with me promising never to leave. I promise him the same in response. It's the dream I've been waiting for all my life. It's the promise he made one night in a dark room.

*When I come back, I will make you mine.*

And I'll be forever his.

# Epilogue

I THOUGHT THE DAY I MARRIED DREW HARRIS WAS THE GREATEST DAY OF my life.

We fast-tracked the planning, with the help of Ruby and her mother, and I flew all of us up to Delaware to do the whole thing on my family's estate. What would become our family estate.

The thought of what's mine being Drew's made me happier than I realized it would. I was happier than a tornado in a trailer park.

Clearly, I'm still learning to be a rich asshole.

The housekeeping staff really showed their worth in getting everybody set up in rooms and helping arrange the gardens for a wedding. I know it all belongs to me, so maybe I shouldn't say this, but the place was pretty damn impressive.

Drew was a goddess. She walked down the aisle in a strapless ivory dress that hugged her curves all the way to her ankles. Over it all was this sheer lace veil with these branch-like patterns stitched into it.

I don't know a lot about fashion, but Ruby said it was the latest thing, very expensive. Drew said it would be an heirloom. I didn't care. I gave Ruby my credit card and told her to get Drew everything she wanted.

I had to give it to Ruby because my bride got some weird notion in her head that she didn't want to use my money for her wedding gown. Luckily her best friend said I'm the answer to her insanely rich fiancé prayers.

I have no idea what that means, and I don't really give a shit about being insanely rich—other than it lets me give my Drew-baby everything she deserves.

Needless to say, the wedding was fantastic, I married the girl of my dreams, the mother of my child… but the best part of it all was when Carl Harris stood and walked her down the aisle.

Before he left, he handed me a note, and once all the dances, toasts, cake cutting, and throwing of things was over, I slipped out of the party to read it.

*Grayson,*

*I cannot take back the years that have gone before, and I won't try to explain the reasons behind my actions. Some old ghosts are better left buried. Still, my anger was real. My hurt was real.*

*My daughter says I was wrong, and in her way, she forced me to look at the past through a different lens. Maybe I knew the truth all along. Either way, I couldn't let go of the shame, my wounded pride.*

*You don't have to accept my apology. You don't have to take my advice, but here it is. Don't let pride ruin your life like I let it ruin mine.*

*I don't blame you for what happened to my son. I don't blame you for what happened in the past. I'm sorry for the way I've treated you. I was wrong. You are a good man.*

*You make my Andrea very happy. Take care of my daughter.*

*With my blessing,*
*Carl Harris*

The words hit me harder than I expected, and I needed a minute before I could return to the reception. It seemed to come out of nowhere, but I later learned my bride had talked to her dad the week before.

I guess for once, he listened.

The highlight of the night came much later, when Drew met me in the bedroom wearing nothing but that expensive veil. It was sexy as shit seeing her beautiful breasts, her flat stomach, and round hips shrouded in sheer lace.

We made love so many different ways that night. She rode me like a champ, and when it was all over, the bed was nearly in the middle of the room.

In the meantime, we've restored the Harris home. We've updated and improved the lake house. It's better than it ever was.

I agreed to join the board of directors for Ralph Stern's almond business, and I have to agree with his mom, Ralph's pretty obsessive, but he could be onto something.

I even turned the garage over to Billy.

He claims he's never changing his work shirt again. He's convinced he'll wind up as Lee Iacocca one of these days. Hell, I told him if I'm any indicator, it could happen.

It just so happened, Leslie Grant was hanging around the garage that day. I told her to wait as I dashed into the cottage and found the stack of photos I'd set aside of her and Danny.

"I'm not sure why you gave me these." I held them out, and she gave them a quick glance.

"Thought you might see something you liked." Green eyes cut up to mine. "Something you might've wished you could have."

"I saw a lot of shots of Drew and me. Is that what you meant?"

Her expression sort of twisted, as if she just remembered something. Then she just shook her head and laughed.

"Misguided attempt at blackmail." Taking the small stack of prints from my hand, she slipped them into her purse. "You always

really loved her, didn't you?"

"Always."

And that was the end of that.

It's been nine months since my last vivid dream. I don't know if I can say I'm cured, but what I do know is I'm meeting with a counselor at Drew's clinic on a regular basis. I'm keeping a journal, and we're keeping on top of it. I'm not going to let the bad guys win.

So all of that has been amazing, but nothing… *nothing*… compares to today.

Drew started the morning feeling strange. She's so adorable, just as I imagined she would be with her pregnant belly under one of those cute little dresses. Her skin just glows, and I only want to feed her and rub her feet and treat her like a princess.

She won't let me do any of that shit. She says I'm trying to make her fat. You've heard of those ladies who love being pregnant? That is *not* Drew.

After waking up feeling strange, she decided to go for a long walk, to hopefully "get this thing out of me." I'm sure she'll feel a lot differently once our little girl is born.

It worked, because as soon as she got home, her water broke. It was all hands on deck after that.

I carried Drew in my arms to the truck along with her little overnight bag and called Ruby, who met us at the hospital. Ruby's mom kept going on about how long it takes for first babies to be born, but I guess Drew was really ready to give birth.

Our little angel made the scene screaming her head off in less than thirty minutes. Drew's doctor clocked her in, weighed her, and did all that technical stuff.

Now we're here, my little angel happily nestled on her mother's breast eating.

"Good call, little Dani," I tease, smoothing my palm over her halo of white-blonde hair.

Yeah, we decided to name her Danielle, in honor of her late uncle.

"She has your eyes." Drew's voice is soft. "She's really beautiful."

I tighten my arm around her shoulder, giving her a nudge. "Kiss me."

Her head drops back, and I cover her mouth with mine. All the times I wondered where I belonged, the answer was always right here. I don't know what brought us together or what kept her believing in me, all I know is I'll be forever grateful.

Our lips part, and she looks down at our little girl, who has finished eating and is now nestled on her mother's chest.

"Are you happy?" Drew looks up at me again, and I can't even put into words…

"I never knew this kind of happiness existed." Leaning down, I kiss her nose.

"You knew." She kisses my lips in response. "It's why you signed that coaster."

"It's why you kept it."

The world is cruel and hard. People put you in a box and try to keep you there. What I've learned is when you find the person who believes in you, hold on to him or her and never let go.

Drew's that person for me, and as hard as it got, our promise was irrevocable.

Dani makes a noise, and my chest squeezes with love. I touch her mother's cheek, and when our eyes meet, I mouth *I love you*.

I don't have to say it, but I make her a sacred vow, through good times and bad, no matter what I have to face, I'd do it all again.

She is forevermore mine.

*Thank you so much for reading Gray and Drew's second-chance love story, and be watching for MAKE ME YOURS, Ruby and Remi's sexy, single dad-nanny romantic comedy, coming March 2019!*

*While you wait…*

*When We Touch is my STAND-ALONE, second-chance romance set in Oceanside Village, a small-town on the Carolina coast.*

*It's swoony and sexy and hilarious, and it has all the FEELS.*

*Keep clicking for a special Sneak Peek…*

*(*Never miss a new release—text TIALOUISE to 64600 for an alert whenever I release a new book!)*

# WHEN WE *Touch*

By Tia Louise

**A USA Today *bestseller.***

Jackson Cane is ***red-hot cinnamon, salt water, and sin...***

He's the kind of trouble I don't need.
He's the kind of trouble that waltzes into my dreams
***Every. Single. Night.***

Emberly Warren is spicy-sweet seduction.
My biggest temptation.
My biggest regret.

I thought she'd always be waiting for me.
***I was wrong.***

Now I'm back in Oceanside searching for peace, hoping to escape what my life has become.

She isn't supposed to be here,
Dark hair blowing in the ocean breeze,
Luscious curves barely hidden by thin cotton.
Memories so hot they burn my mind...

I didn't come back for her.
But ***when we touch***, I know I'll do whatever it takes to ***make her mine...***

# Prologue

## Ember

WHERE IT BEGINS…

Jackson Cane tastes like red-hot cinnamon, salt water, and sin.

When he concentrates, his long fingers twist in the back of his dark hair, right at the base of his neck, and he tugs.

*Tugs…*

*Tugs…*

I like to weave my fingers between his and pull.

Then ocean-blue eyes blink up to mine, sending electricity humming in my veins. He smiles. I smile, and it isn't long before our lips touch. I straddle his lap as I open my mouth, and his delicious tongue finds mine, heating every part of my body.

Our kisses are languid and deep, chasing and tasting.

We sizzle like fireworks on a hot summer night.

Eventually, with a heavy sigh, I pull away, but hours later my mouth is still burning. I taste him everywhere I go.

Lying in my bed in the dark room, my heart aches, heavy and painful in my chest. Every breath is a burden. I blink slowly at the ceiling and slide my tongue against the backs of my teeth thinking about hot cinnamon, tangy salt, caramel and sugar, sunshine, and the best summer of my life.

The instant I hear it, I'm on my feet, tiptoeing to my open window. The low growl of an engine tells me he's there in the darkness, out on the street in the shadows just past the streetlight.

The late summer humidity hangs heavy in the air. Cicadas *scree* from the limbs of the mighty oak tree beside the house. Their damp wings make them too heavy to fly, and the sadness in my chest is replaced with breathless anticipation.

I'm panting. I've never felt this way for anyone, and I'm desperate to hold onto it. Somehow I know I'll never feel this way for anyone ever again.

Quiet as a mouse I scamper to my door and listen. The only sound is the hum of Momma's oscillating fan pushing the warm air around her room. I can't hear her breathing. I can't hear anything… except the noise of Jackson's engine on the street below, waiting.

*Red-hot cinnamon.*

*Salt water.*

*Sin.*

Pressure tingles around the edges of my skull, and a bead of sweat tickles down the side of my neck, dropping past my shoulder, slipping between my breasts.

I'm at the window slowly lifting the glass, and I don't care if she hears me. I dive through the space, out onto the cedar shake roof in my bare feet. I'll get a splinter if I'm not careful…

So many reasons to be careful…

I ignore them all.

I'm going to him like a siren's call in the ocean, like the mermaid story in reverse. I'm the hypnotized sailor. He's the promise of so many wicked pleasures.

Reaching for the tree limb, I swing my body across the narrow gap two stories high, gliding down the trunk as the skirt of my dress rises to my hips. My bike sits where I left it at the side of the house, and I carefully pull it away, holding it as I tiptoe down

the gravel driveway to the street.

I can't take a chance on anyone seeing us together and telling my mother. Instead, I dash across the street between the thick beams of his headlights. He flickers them to let me know he sees me, and I plunge into the dark woods, pedaling fast.

Tires crunch on gravel, and I shoot down the pine needle path leading away from this place, through the tall, skinny trees, all the way out to the barren jetty of sand stretching under the moonlit sky filled with stars, surrounded by the clear blue waters of the ocean.

It's our place.

The place where we're the only two people on Earth.

In the summertime, the visitors to our sleepy little town use it to spend the day sunbathing and playing on the wide stretch of undeveloped sand. Now, on the edge of fall, with all the children back in school and Jackson leaving for college tomorrow, we have it to ourselves.

His engine roars on the road above, and I stand in the pedals to push harder, fueled by the burning desire twisting in my lower pelvis. I want to be with him now. I don't want to waste a moment.

I go even faster as the trail slopes downhill. A narrow wooden bridge *thump… thump… thumps* with the pressure of my tires distressing the aging slats.

The instant the trees part, I toss my bike aside and run out of the darkness onto the glowing white sand. The sizzle of waves crashing on the shore fills the night, and the black ripples are tipped with silver light.

Jackson stands in his canvas shorts, his hands in his pockets, and a thin white tee rippling across his back in the slight breeze.

I'm breathing hard when I finally reach him, and he turns. White teeth in a full-moon night, deep dimples in both cheeks, he smiles down at me, and I feel so small. A lock of too-long dark

hair falls over his blue eyes, and my breath catches. He's so beautiful.

I swallow the knot in my throat as I gaze at him. What star crossed what planet in what solar system and said I could have him, even if it's only for a little while?

"You made good time tonight." His voice vibrates the warm air between us.

I force a laugh, moving to him until my hands are around his waist. My forehead rests on his chest, and I inhale deeply. He's leather and soap and a deeper, spicier scent that's pure Jackson Cane.

He feels so good in my arms.

His mouth presses against my head, and I lift my chin, reaching for his face. He leans down and claims my mouth, warm lips pushing mine open. I kiss him eagerly, curling my tongue with his, threading my fingers into the soft, dark hair falling around his cheeks, tugging.

An aching moan rises in my chest as he lifts me off my feet. Chasing his kisses, my mouth burns with cinnamon, my core tingles with need. He carries me to our place, a little shelter near the water's edge where an enormous log is slowly turning to driftwood. We lower to the sand, me on my back, him on his knees looking down at me.

My dark hair is all around us, my skirt is up around my waist. My panties are far away on my bedroom floor. A soft hiss comes from his lips, and he slides a finger down my center. My eyes flutter shut.

"Jackson…" I whisper. *I love you I love you I love you…*

He leans down to taste me, his tongue lightly tracing the line between my thighs, and my back arches off the soft sand. My body takes flight on the motion of his mouth, kissing me so deeply, tracing a pattern over my most sensitive parts.

The first time he did this to me, I didn't understand. I'd been

embarrassed by how fast my body responded, the way I shook, how wet it was between my legs when the shudders subsided.

Then I was afraid of how I tasted. I was afraid it was dirty and wrong like my momma would say. *Sin…*

Then he kissed me, and my mouth filled with a delicate, clean ocean flavor, like the air after a storm. It was our first time, and when he pushed inside me, my mind came apart. My soul shifted, and I was forever changed.

I was forever his.

The flutters begin in the arches of my feet, and he kisses his way up my stomach.

"Jackson… Jackson…" I can't stop chanting his name as I thread my fingers in his soft hair.

At last his mouth covers mine. At last we're one.

"Ember…" His mouth breaks away with a groan, and I lean up to run my tongue along the ridges of his neck. *Salt water…*

I lick his Adam's apple up to his square jaw.

Rough stubble scratches my tongue.

My legs are around his waist and we're working together, chasing that glorious release. He stretches me and fills me, massages me so deeply, I feel it the moment I start to break apart.

"Oh!" My fingers tighten on his back as every muscle in my body clenches…

Tighter…

Tighter…

Then *Yes!*

Glitter gun showers of pleasure flooding my insides.

"Yes," he groans, and I feel him finish deep inside of me.

Our bodies unite, but at the same time we're flying apart as waves of ecstasy fill our veins. It's magical like the ocean, silvery water tipped in moonlight.

We kiss softly now, rich and gentle, over and over. His tongue touches my upper lip, and he pulls the bottom one between his

teeth. *Red-hot cinnamon…*

We're breathing hard, and he slides a hand under my ass, turning us without ever losing contact, so I'm sitting in a straddle across his lap.

My dress is around my waist, and moonlight touches the tips of my breasts. We hold each other, skin against skin.

A hot tear spills down my cheek.

I'm not full-on crying. I'll save the ugly tears for tomorrow when he's gone. Instead, I find his blue eyes.

Dark brows quirk together, and he kisses my nose. "You're crying?"

My voice cracks with a whisper. "Aren't you sad?"

"I'm only going to college, Em. I'm not going to war."

"But we won't see each other for months."

I don't say what's truly scaring me. I don't voice the fear that I, a mere high schooler, couldn't possibly hold onto him.

He's traveling far away to where the girls are more mature, more experienced, more sophisticated.

"You're right," he nods. "It's going to suck. Especially when I want to kiss you."

He pulls me flush against his chest and groans deeply. Strong arms circle my shoulders, and I cling to him.

"But it's not something to cry about," he argues. "You're my girl, Em. That's never going to change."

My eyes squeeze shut, and I inhale his scent, doing my best to hold it in my memory, trying to absorb every part of him.

There's no way in hell I could even begin to argue. I am his, and he's… my everything. Jackson Cane is every first I've ever had. My first real kiss, my first real boyfriend, the first time I had sex… made love…

"Hey." He pulls back, blue eyes full of concern. "I'm right, aren't I?"

Blinking quickly, I try to find my bearings. "What?" I don't

know why he looks so worried.

"You are my girl, right?"

My chin jerks forward, and I have to cover my mouth. "You have to ask?"

Warm hands cup my cheeks, and he trails his thumbs lightly along my cheekbones. "So beautiful," he murmurs. "My Ember Rose."

His eyes move around my face, along my hair, down the side of my jaw like a caress.

"I'll never forget this." I'm ashamed at how desperate my voice sounds. "I mean… I just…" I'm such a baby.

He blinks a few times, and a smile curls his lips. With a nod, he pulls me against his chest, strong arms surrounding me. We stay that way a long time, listening to the crashing of the surf, the beat of our hearts. The seagulls cry, and the moon climbs higher. It's all so perfect, but it's all at an end.

Finally, with a sigh, he lifts me, helping me stand. We hold hands as he takes me into the gentle waves to clean up. I slowly restore my dress.

I feel so stupid. College girls don't need to be cared for like babies. They don't whine and cry about being left behind. They blow kisses and wink over their sunglasses. They sway their hips and turn the tables on saying goodbye.

My best friend Tabby is already one of those girls, and she's my age.

I'll never be one of those girls.

"Don't cry, Ember Rose," he says in a low whisper. "I never want to see you cry."

I hold him a while longer, listening to the steady rhythm of his heart. His hands slide up and down my back in a soothing motion.

After a while, they slide down my forearms to lace with my fingers. He steps back and leads me the way we came, stopping at

the edge of the woods where I left my bike.

"Get on home before your momma wakes up."

That sexy smile curls his lips. He shoves his hair behind his ears, and I step forward again, clutching the front of his shirt before I press my lips one last time to his.

*Red-hot cinnamon.*

*Sparkling blue sin.*

*Salt rocks breaking my heart.*

# CHAPTER *One*

## *Jack*

*Ten years and eleven months later...*

"LAST ONE IN HAS TO RIDE HOME NAKED!" TIFFANY HURLS HER SILKY red dress over her head and runs through the trees headed for the lake.

The wheels on my black Audi R8 have barely stopped moving. I haven't even killed the engine. An empty wine bottle clatters against an empty tequila bottle rolling around on the floorboards, and I briefly think I should toss them in a nearby trashcan.

Propping my elbow on the steering wheel, I scrub the back of my neck with my fingers. My hair is so short now, it's the best I can do.

I haven't had a drink in almost an hour. I'd finished a bottle of scotch in my office, standing in front of my floor to ceiling glass windows looking down on the city, disbelief vibrating in my chest.

My career...

My reputation...

It's over.

All of it.

File after file, telling me my win, my multi-million dollar defense... all of it is based on lies.

"Fuck!" I shout, slamming my palm against the wheel.

The buzzing in my head is gone along with the numbness in my chest, and all the shock and pain and pure, unadulterated outrage rush back like a wall of water before a hurricane.

A hurricane that will send everything I've worked for these last ten years crashing down around me.

Pulling the handle on the door, I push it open and step out into the darkness. The ground is covered in moldering leaves, and it smells like faintly mildewed canvas, damp lichens, and dirt.

"Jackson! What are you doing?" Tiffany shrieks between splashes out in the black water of the lake.

*Exactly*. "What the fuck am I doing here?"

My chest is tight, and each inhale is like claws ripping my lungs from the inside.

It took an hour to drive from my Eighth Avenue high-rise corner office building to this lonely, two-lane highway leading to the lake. Somewhere along the way, I realized I didn't know what the fuck Tiffany was talking about or why she was even in my car. She followed me down the elevator, into the parking garage, laughing and pouring another shot of tequila on the way.

I've got the fucking receptionist with me.

I need to get her back to the city.

Digging in the pocket of my blazer, I pull out my phone and stare at the face. My lock screen is a photo of crystal blue waters, and for a moment, my thoughts blur. I left my home near the ocean with big dreams.

Half of them came true.

I finished undergrad at the top of my class, went to law school on a free-ride, headed straight into a Top Five firm when I graduated, and now I'm one of the highest-paid litigators handling mostly corporate corruption with the occasional car crash thrown in for variety.

My face is in every "Top Thirty under Thirty" feature in the

city and online. My phone never stops ringing.

My fucking dad is so fucking proud.

I've done it all.

And I'm all alone.

"I've got to get out of here." Dropping my chin, I rub my eyes.

The *shush* of feet running through the leaves is punctuated with high giggles breaking the silence. My eyes have adjusted to the semi-darkness, and I see Tiffany coming back, completely naked, blonde hair glistening with water, tits bouncing with every step.

"What are you doing back here?" Her voice is thick, and she curves into my chest, holding my neck and trying to kiss me.

She's slippery and loose. Her kiss is easy to dodge, but not her wet body pressing against my dress shirt.

"I was just thinking the same thing," My jaw tightens, and I lift my chin away from her face.

"God, you're so hard," she giggles. My brow furrows. I'm not the least bit aroused. "Like a wall of granite."

"Look, Tiff, I'm calling you a Lyft." I'm back to tapping my phone. "What's your address?"

"What?" she whisper-shrieks. "Wait a second—"

"Never mind." I bring up the firm directory, and she's gone from my chest. It takes me a second to realize she's dropped to her knees in front of me and her hands are on my belt.

"Stop..." I tap the buttons on the app faster, using my free hand to sweep her away from my fly.

"Stop, stop..." She laughs, her voice high and teasing. "What guy doesn't want a blow job?"

"Stop!" I've managed to book her a ride, but she's got my pants open and is handling my dick.

"Fuck me," she moans. I look down, and she looks up. The whites of her eyes are visible, and her mouth is a delighted O. "The rumors are true!"

"Get up." Shoving my phone in my pocket, I grasp under her arms, pulling her to her feet.

"Oh, Jackson!" She pokes her lips out, face pouty. "Let me ride your big… huge… cock!"

"Where's your dress?"

Moving fast, I refasten my pants with one hand. I'm still holding her by the upper arm, keeping her with me as I circle, looking for where I saw red silk fly over her head.

"There it is." I take her to where the dress is laying discarded on the path.

"You're always alone," she sulks, stomping beside me as I lead her to the car and hold her against it. I brace her with one leg so she can't wiggle away, while I fumble with the fabric, searching for the neck hole.

"Are you gay?" Her voice sounds like every drunk college girl I ever turned away.

"No," I answer flatly.

"When's the last time you got laid?"

Her blonde hair catches in the fabric, and I untwist it, pulling the material down her sticky body as best as I can.

"I get laid," I growl, considering it has been a while.

I've been so focused on my work, this case… Now the last thing on my mind is fucking some drunk girl. First, her consent is dubious. Second, she's our receptionist and could yell sexual harassment or worse.

"I'm not dipping my pen in the company ink."

"I'll quit my job!" she cries, still holding onto me. "Just kiss me once."

"Where is that fucking Lyft?" I reach into my jacket again. "He's here!"

Sure enough, high beams cut through the woods, curving around the black trees. I start up the lane in the direction of the road.

"My shoes!" she shrieks, trying to run back the way she came. "They're Louboutins!"

My grip tightens on her arm, until I'm practically carrying her to the waiting car. "I'll ship them to you at the office."

"You're not coming back to work? What are you going to do?"

Hesitating a moment, I realize it's a good question. I know what I want to do—what's nudging at my brain. What I've wanted to do for so long…

I'm tired and my thoughts are twisted and cloudy, but I know what I want more than anything. "I have a meeting to attend."

"Now?"

"Right now."

The Lyft pulls away, taking Tiffany back home. I head straight to my car, pulling out my phone as I walk. My disbelief is gone, my head is clear, and I have to face this.

"Jackson." Brice Wagner's low voice is laced with condescension as he ushers me into his enormous wood-paneled study. "What brings you all the way out here at this hour?"

It took me two hours to drive to my elder partner's ocean front estate north of the city. From the smell of his breath, he's been working on his own scotch, luxuriating in the close of our case, no doubt.

Thinking how much we could have lost…

How much I saved.

How much he covered up.

"I was doing some housekeeping before I shut down tonight."

"You young bucks." He slaps my back, barking out a laugh as he rounds his desk. "After today's win, at your age, I'd be out on the town, a bottle in each hand and a blonde on each arm."

"No doubt," I say, placing a hand on the stiff leather wingback across the massive mahogany desk from my partner. "I had something like that in mind."

It's true. I'd been finishing up, pulling all the files together ahead of what I hoped would be a long weekend.

Until I opened the office intranet we shared on the case.

Until I discovered the hidden folder labeled "Disposed documents."

The folder password protected with a dead child's name.

"Well?" He pours a crystal tumbler of amber liquid and holds it out to me. "What stopped you?"

I take the crystal and tilt it side to side, studying the trail of the liquid as it moves. The room smells of antique furniture and oiled leather. It's moneyed and ancient, and knowing what I know now, it's all the rotten stench of corruption.

A strange calm filters through my chest as I say my next words. "I had in mind a long weekend, possibly a week off. We put in a lot of hours on this one."

"You're right." He rocks back in his desk chair and props a foot on the corner. I watch as he pulls out a fat cigar and clips the end. He doesn't offer me one, not that I'd take it.

Eventually, the pungent scent of cigar smoke drifts across to me as I continue. "But the settlement agreement and release need to go out. I had to be sure Lori could find what she needed to get it done…"

"Okay."

I've reached the end of my patience, so I say what I came here to say. I speak the heart of the prosecution's case. "Johnny Mauck had been driving for thirty hours straight when he lost control of his rig and skidded across that median."

Brice lowers his foot and turns slowly to face me. Anger fires red in his watery eyes, but it's nothing compared to the fucking inferno in my chest.

"Stop right there." His voice is a calm warning.

"Big Traxx paid for the amphetamines that kept him driving. You were at the scene. You knew it all along." Every breath is hot. "I found the documents, the logs, the prescription… everything that should have been provided during litigation."

"You found nothing." He speaks the words slowly, ominously, dark eyes like stone.

My eyes are flint. "I found it all."

We're silent, sizing each other up. The brass clock on the mantle above the fireplace is the only noise, ticking louder than the beating of a drum. If I had any lingering doubts, any question of what I had to do on the long drive out here, his response put the final nail in that coffin.

Finally, he leans forward. His leather chair creaks under his weight. "So you've made your decision?"

The fist in my chest still hasn't unclenched. Perhaps it never will. Either way, the answer is yes. "I'm not doing this anymore."

He has the nerve to look smug. "Where will you go?"

"Back to the beginning."

If I've lost everything, I might as well. I'll walk away. All the way to the only place I've ever known happiness.

I'll pick up the pieces and start over.

# CHAPTER *Two*

## *Ember*

IT'S A PENIS.

I stand in front of the table looking down, and there is no mistaking what it is.

Hours of online courses, too many YouTube videos to count (so many YouTube videos), correspondence courses at the community college, and this is what it comes down to…

Penis cakes for money.

Tabby rocks forward on her stool, leaning on her elbows watching me carve the corners off the beige sheet cake. Her jet-black hair is smoothed into thick curls, and a red handkerchief is wrapped around her head. Severe bangs, arched brows, and velvet-red lips. My best friend is punk rock Bettie Page.

"How can you make these and be so unaffected?"

I continue carving two round balls at the bottom of the long, almond-colored shaft. "It's cake."

"Still… you haven't been with a guy in what? Five years?"

"Don't go there."

"I'm just saying. That's one well-constructed penis."

"Again, it's cake."

"I wish Liam was black." Instantly her green eyes go round, and she leans closer, whispering, "Is that racist?"

"Depends on what you say next. Why?"

She falls back on the stool, her eyes fluttering shut. "Because your Devil's food cake with the coconut pecan buttercream icing and dark chocolate ganache is better than sex."

"Then you're not doing it right."

"You're not doing it at all!"

Cutting my eyes at her, I set the sharp knife aside.

She sniffs. "Well, you're not."

Choosing to ignore her jab, I return to her original statement, reaching for the bowl of vanilla pastry cream. "Liam is white. His penis has to match him." Pausing in my filling, I study the bisected cake in front of me. "I was planning to use all this cream for the inside, but maybe I should save some for the tip…"

"Oh my god," Tabby snorts. "Mousey little Donna White has totally knocked my socks off. This is the tackiest order in the history of Ember Rose Cakes!"

I arch an eyebrow at her. "Donna didn't order it."

Red-velvet lips part, and Tabby's eyes sparkle with mischief. "Who did?"

"Help me."

She lifts the opposite end of the top layer, and together we slowly place it over the cream-filled bottom.

The little bell over the door rings, and I step back, crossing my arms, admiring the lifelike almond-sponge penis cake with vanilla cream filling. "She doesn't like fondant, so I'm thinking I'll cover it in beige marzipan—"

"You're working late tonight, Ember." My mother's stern voice echoes through the large, empty store (a.k.a., my future bakery-slash-home).

With a hiss, Tabby spins beside me, blocking the cake with her body. I freeze, my heart thudding frantically in my chest. *Oh, shit.*

"Uh…" Tabby walks fast to meet my mother halfway

between the front door and the large table at the back wall where I do my decorating. "We got a last-minute cake order for Donna's shower."

I frantically look for anything to cover the oversized male member—as if that could possibly save us from the shit-storm about to erupt.

"That's nice." Condescension is thick in her voice. "Donna's mother has been a faithful member of the church since you were little girls. I'm sure she'll appreciate your talent…"

My mother stops, and a knot lodges in my throat. Seconds like hours tick past as she steps around my best friend, arms crossed, frowning down at the phallus. Thank God I haven't added the extra cream to the tip yet.

"What is this?" Her voice is hard, disgusted.

"Just what the doctor ordered!" Tabby calls out. "A little taste of what's to come!"

It's no use. My mother is impervious to humor.

"God gives you a talent, Emberly Rose, and this is how you thank him? By making *porn*?"

My mind drifts to a list of questions, the way it always does when her lectures start: *Would God really be angry about a cake shaped like Donna's future husband's penis? Doesn't God have bigger fish to fry? Does God even fry fish? Jesus ate fish…*

"Are you listening to me, Emberly Rose?"

I blink back to attention. "It seemed like an interesting challenge."

The sweetest little voice cuts through the tension in the air. "Mommy's cake! Mommy's cake!" Everything is forgotten as I dash forward, scooping my little girl into my arms.

"Coco bean!" I spin her around and kiss her velvety cheek. The entire world is suddenly brighter.

"The purple monster says *tres*!" she chants.

"*Tres*?" I pretend to be confused. "What is *tres*?"

"Three!" she cries holding up three small fingers.

"That's right!" I hug her body snug against mine.

All the shame and fear are gone when I hold Coco, but she starts to wiggle. She wants to get down.

"I want cake! Mommy cake!"

My mother is quick to interrupt. "Colette, come to Grandmother."

"Cake! Cake! Cake!" Her little eyes sparkle and two dimples punctuate her cheeks as she cheers for cake.

Happiness rises in my chest with every pump of her cute little fist over her head.

"How about this..." I go to her and kneel, putting my hands on her tiny waist. She puts her hands on the tops of my shoulders, her dark eyes suddenly serious. "I'll make you a special cupcake with a purple monster and a big three on it."

"I'm four now."

"This isn't a birthday cake." I smooth my fingers in her hair, moving a cluster of silky brunette curls behind her ear. "It's a special cake, and I'll give it to you tomorrow."

"You won't spend the night?"

My heart sinks with her question, but I can't spend another night in my mother's house. I just can't.

"I have to fix this house for us. Remember? We're going to live upstairs. And I'll be over first thing tomorrow with your cupcake."

I carry her to the door where my mother waits, disapproval lining her thin lips. "Church tomorrow. I expect you to be there."

"I will." I give Coco another hug, taking a deep inhale of her sweet little girl scent. "Go with Granny now."

"Grandmother." My mother corrects me. "Come, Colette."

"Let's go, Granny!" Coco wiggles out of my arms to the floor then hops out like a kangaroo.

Tabby snorts behind me, and my mother's eyes narrow.

"We'll finish this tomorrow."

With that she strides out, and I push the door closed behind them, resting my forehead against the glass.

"I swear, if that little girl were any less stubborn, I'd be worried about her," Tabby says from behind me.

I watch them a few seconds longer—my mother trying unsuccessfully to hold Coco's hand while they walk the four blocks to her house, the old house where I grew up.

"She'll be okay a little while longer," I say, feeling like my heart is hopping away from me, batting at her grandmother's hand with every bounce.

"Old battle axe. I guess you survived living with her."

"She wasn't like this before Minnie died." My voice is quiet, repeating a memory.

"Says who." It's not a question. It's a skeptical retort from my bestie.

"Aunt Agnes. She said my mother used to know how to have fun."

"I don't believe it."

"To be honest, I've never believed it either." I don't even remember my older sister.

"You're too independent for her. She can't handle it. She almost lost her mind when you took up with Jackson Cane so young—"

Cutting my eyes, I stop that line of conversation. "We don't talk about him."

"We should." Tabby studies my face. "He's the only guy you were ever serious about."

*He said he'd come back, and he never did…*

Exhaling deeply, I return to my phallic creation. "Ancient history. Now let's finish this thing before it's too late…"

Get *When We Touch* today, and fall in love with Emberly and Jackson's second-chance love story.

Available for FREE in Kindle Unlimited, and in print format!

Never miss a new release!

Sign up for my New Release newsletter and get a FREE Tia Louise Story Bundle!

Sign up now!
http://smarturl.it/TLMnews

# ACKNOWLEDGMENTS

I have so many amazing people in my life supporting and helping me. How can I begin to thank you all?

Let me try…

For starters, thanks to my precious family, Mr. TL and my two daughters, for being so patient and sometimes not so patient. I love you guys!

HUGE THANKS to Candi Kane, Dani Sanchez, and Lulu Dumonceaux for all the incredible marketing and logistical support. You help me think, you listen when I'm exhausted, and you're just the best.

Even MORE Huge Thanks to Ilona Townsel for always being there, for dropping everything to help, and just for being the absolute best. You're my rock.

HUGE THANKS to my incredible beta squad… Tijuana Turner, Rebecca Barney, and Sarah Sentz—you ladies give amazing notes.

To my rocking Mermaids admins, Tammi Hart, Tina Morgan, Helene Cuji, Lisa Kuhne, and Ellie King. You ladies have no idea how much I need and appreciate your help!

Harloe Rae (those teasers!), Jenika Snow, Carly Phillips, Saffron Kent, Kathy Coopmans, AL Jackson… you were my early encouragers, and I thank you from the bottom of my heart. I'm blessed to know you.

To ALL the FABULOUS author-friends who made room for me in your crammed schedules, I appreciate YOU so much more than I